Dear Reader,

A Wanted Man is the story of two passionate people with secrets to keep. Rowdy Rhodes appeared very briefly in *The Man from Stone Creek,* and the first time he walked onto the stage of my mind, I knew he would have his own story. Rowdy is a fascinating enigma, an outlaw with honor, a fugitive with courage, a teller of truth whose whole life is basically a lie. Lark Morgan, the woman he didn't plan on meeting, let alone loving, is guarding dangerous secrets of her own. So come along with Rowdy, Lark and me on a journey to Stone Creek as it was in the turbulent early years of the last century.

I also wanted to write today to tell you about a special group of people with whom I've recently become involved. It is The Humane Society of the United States (HSUS), specifically their Pets for Life program.

The Pets for Life program is one of the best ways to help your local shelter—that is to help keep animals out of shelters in the first place. Something as basic as keeping a collar and tag on your pet all the time, so if he gets out and gets lost, he can be returned home. Being a responsible pet owner. Spaying or neutering your pet. And not giving up when things don't go perfectly. If your dog digs in the yard, or your cat scratches the furniture, know that these are problems that can be addressed. You can find all the information about these and many other common problems at www.petsforlife.org. This campaign is focused on keeping pets and their people together for a lifetime.

As many of you know, my own household includes two dogs, two cats and four horses, so this is a cause that is near and dear to my heart. I hope you'll get involved along with me.

May you be blessed.

With love,

Linda Lael Miller

Praise for the novels of LINDA LAEL MILLER

"Loaded with hot lead,
steamy sex and surprising plot twists."
—*Publishers Weekly* on *A Wanted Man*

"This spin-off of *The Man from Stone Creek* will more than satisfy Miller's fans and draw in new readers seeking a realistic, powerful western."
—*Romantic Times BOOKreviews* on *A Wanted Man*

"Miller's prose is smart, and her tough Eastwoodian cowboy cuts a sharp, unexpectedly funny figure in a classroom full of rambunctious frontier kids."
—*Publishers Weekly* on *The Man from Stone Creek*

"[Miller] paints a brilliant portrait of the good, the bad and the ugly, the lost and the lonely, and the power of love to bring light into the darkest of souls. This is western romance at its finest."
—*Romantic Times BOOKreviews* on *The Man from Stone Creek*

"Intrigue, danger and greed are up against integrity, kindness, and love in this engrossing western romance. Miller has created unforgettable characters and woven a many-faceted yet coherent and lovingly told tale."
—*Booklist* on *McKettrick's Choice* (starred review)

"An engrossing, contemporary western romance… Miller's masterful ability to create living, breathing characters never flags…combined with a taut story line and vivid prose, Miller's romance won't disappoint."
—*Publishers Weekly* on *McKettrick's Pride* (starred review)

"Linda Lael Miller creates vibrant characters and stories I defy you to forget."
—*New York Times* bestselling author Debbie Macomber

LINDA LAEL MILLER

ISBN-13: 978-0-373-77296-4
ISBN-10: 0-373-77296-3

A WANTED MAN: A STONE CREEK NOVEL

This edition published by arrangement with Harlequin Books S.A.

www.HQNBooks.com

Printed in U.S.A.

For Shaun Bleecker,
who identifies so strongly with Rowdy—
perhaps because he's a hero, too.

Also available from

LINDA LAEL MILLER

and HQN Books

The Stone Creek series

The Man from Stone Creek

A Wanted Man

The McKettricks series

McKettrick's Choice

McKettrick's Luck

McKettrick's Pride

McKettrick's Heart

The Mojo Sheepshanks series

Deadly Gamble

Deadly Deceptions

In October 2008 return to Stone Creek in

The Rustler

And in November 2008 celebrate the holidays McKettrick-style with

A McKettrick Christmas

A Wanted Man
A Stone Creek Novel

1

Stone Creek, Arizona Territory
January, 1905

ROWDY RHODES LEANED BACK in the whorehouse bathtub, a cheroot jutting from between his teeth, and sighed as he waited for the chill of a high-country winter to seep out of his bones.

Jolene, an aging madam with pockmarked skin, three visible teeth and a bustle the size of the Sonoran Desert, sloshed another bucketful of steaming water at his feet. "I done seen everything now," she told him, her eyes narrowed in lascivious speculation as she studied Rowdy's submerged frame. "Ain't nobody never brought a *dog* to my bathhouse before."

Pardner, the old yellow hound, sat soaked and bewildered in the tub next to Rowdy's. He'd gotten pretty scruffy on the long ride up from Haven, the dog had, and Rowdy meant to take him for barbering next. They could both do with a haircut, and Rowdy was itching for a shave.

Pardner was just plain itching.

"Always a first time," Rowdy said, drawing on the cheroot and then blowing a smoke ring.

Jolene lingered, probably hoping to do less-hygienic business, but willing to settle for whatever conversation might come her way. "It's one thing, you payin' for clean water for yourself, but I don't see how as it makes a difference to the dog."

Rowdy grinned and blew another smoke ring. "We'll be wanting steaks, soon as we're dried off and decent, if you can scare them up," he told Jolene. "Pardner likes his rare."

"If that don't beat all," Jolene said, pondering the hound. "I can get steaks, all right, but they'll cost you a pretty penny. And if you've a mind to pass the time upstairs with any of my girls, cowboy, your *partner* here will have to wait in the hall."

Given that he was naked, and in a prone position, Rowdy didn't see any profit in pointing out that he didn't have truck with whores. His .44 was within easy reach, as always, but shooting a woman, saint or sinner, was outside the boundaries of his personal code. Unless, of course, she drew first.

"No time for idling with the ladies," he said, feigning regret. He idled with plenty of ladies, whenever he got the chance, but he favored fine, upstanding widows.

"You lookin' for ranch work?" Jolene asked, in no apparent hurry to rustle up the steaks.

"Maybe," Rowdy answered. The truth was, he'd been summoned to Stone Creek by none other than Major John Blackstone and Sam O'Ballivan, an Arizona Ranger he'd chanced to encounter down south, a little over a year before, in the border town of Haven. He'd come partly because he and Pardner hadn't had anything better to do, and because he was curious. And there were a few other reasons, too.

He suspected his pa was somewhere in these parts, up to his old tricks, for one.

"Try Sam O'Ballivan's place," Jolene said helpfully. "Sam's a fair man, and he's always hirin' on hands to feed them cattle of his."

Rowdy nodded. "Obliged," he said.

"Not that you're hurtin' for money, if you can afford clean bathwater and a steak for a dog," Jolene added.

"A man can always use money," Rowdy allowed, wishing Jolene would order up the steaks, go back to riding herd over the drunks he'd seen out front in the saloon swilling whiskey, and leave him to bathe in peace.

Pardner gave a despairing whimper.

"Just bide there for a while," Rowdy told him quietly.

Pardner huffed out a sigh and hunkered down to endure. He was a faithful old fella, Pardner was. He'd trotted alongside Rowdy's horse for the first few miles out of Haven, but then he'd gotten footsore and come the rest of the way in the saddle. As they traveled north, the weather got colder, and they'd shared Rowdy's dusty old canvas coat.

Remembering the looks they'd gotten from the townsfolk, him and Pardner, riding into town barely an hour before, Rowdy smiled. Even with a new and modern century underway, the Arizona Territory was still wild and woolly, and odd sights were plentiful. He wouldn't have thought a man and a dog on the back of the same horse would attract so much notice.

"You run along and see to those steaks," Rowdy told Jolene. Even with the bucketful of hot water she'd just poured into his tub, the bath was lukewarm, and there was cold air coming up through the cracks between the ancient, warped floorboards. He wanted to scrub himself down with the harsh yellow soap provided, dry off, and get into the clean duds he'd saved for the purpose.

Of course, Pardner needed sudsing, too, and Rowdy didn't reckon even Jolene's services extended quite that far.

Jolene hadn't had her fill of visiting, that much was clear by her disgruntled aspect, but she lit out for the kitchen, just the same.

Rowdy finished his bath, dressed himself, then laundered Pardner as best he could. He was toweling the poor critter off with a burlap feed sack when he heard the sound of spurs chinking just outside the door.

Rowdy didn't hold with the use of spurs, branding irons or barbed wire. Whenever he encountered any one of those three things, he bristled on the inside.

Out of habit he touched the handle of his .44, just to make sure it was on his left hip, where it ought to be.

Pardner bared his teeth and snarled when two drifters strolled in.

"Easy," Rowdy told the animal, rising from a crouch to stand facing the strangers. One was short, and the other tall. Both were in sore need of a bath, not to mention the services of a dentist.

The short one looked Pardner over, scowling. His right hand eased toward the .45 in his holster.

Rowdy's own .44 was in his hand so fast he might

have willed it there, instead of drawing. "I wouldn't," he said affably.

"It's a hell of a thing when a man's expected to bathe himself in a dog's water," the taller one observed. He had a long, narrow face, full of sorrow, and thin brown hair that clung to the shape of his head, as if afraid of blowing away in a high wind.

"For an extra nickel," Rowdy said, "you can have your own."

The short man took a step toward Rowdy, and it was the tall one who reached out an arm and stopped him. "Me and Willie, here, we don't want no trouble. We're just lookin' for hot water and women."

Willie subsided, but he didn't look too happy about it. Rowdy reckoned he'd have shot Pardner just for being there, if he'd had his druthers. Fortunately for him, his sidekick had interceded before it would have been necessary to put a bullet through his heart.

Pardner, who looked a sight with his fur all ruffled up and standing upright on his hide like quills on a porcupine, from the rubdown with a burlap sack, growled low and in earnest.

Yes, sir, Rowdy thought, looking down at him, he did want barbering.

"That dog bite?" Willie asked. A muscle twitched in the beard stubble along his right cheek. He carried himself like a man of little consequence determined to give another kind of impression.

"Only if provoked," Rowdy answered mildly, slipping the .44 back into its holster. He was hungry, but he tarried, for it was his habit to take careful note of everyone he encountered, be they friend or foe.

Pappy had taught him that, and it had proved a useful skill.

Just then Jolene trundled in with the littlest Chinaman Rowdy had ever seen trotting behind her. The sight put him in mind of a loaded barge cutting through the muddy Mississippi with a rowboat bobbing in its wake.

"Ten cents if you want clean water," Jolene told the new arrivals, clearly relishing the prospect of ready commerce. "A nickel if you don't mind secondhand."

Willie and the sidekick didn't look as though they were in a position to be too picky.

"A dime for a tub of hot water?" Willie demanded, aggrieved. "It's plain robbery."

The tall man took a tobacco sack from the inside pocket of his coat and dumped a pile of change into a palm. After counting out the coins carefully, he handed them over to Jolene.

"We'll have the best of your services," he said formally.

The Chinaman, strong for his size, nodded at a go-ahead from Jolene and turned Pardner's tub over onto its side, so the water poured down through the gaps between the floorboards.

"I ain't bathin' in the same tub as no dog, Harlan," Willie told his friend stoutly.

Harlan sighed. "Willie, sometimes you are a trial to my spirit," he said. "That mutt was probably cleaner than you are before he even set foot in this place."

"Them steaks are about ready," Jolene informed Rowdy, giving Pardner a dark assessment. "I don't reckon the dog could eat out back, instead of in my dining room?"

"You 'don't reckon' right," Rowdy said pleasantly. With cordial nods to Harlan and Willie, he made for the bathhouse door, Pardner right on his heels.

LARK MORGAN WATCHED slantwise from an upstairs window of Mrs. Porter's Rooming House as the stranger strode across the road from Jolene Bell's establishment to the barbershop, the dog walking close by his side.

The man wore a trail coat that could have used a good shaking out, and his hair, long enough to curl at the back of his collar, gleamed pale gold in the afternoon sunlight. His hat was battered, but of good quality, and the same could be said of his boots. While not necessarily a person of means, he was no ordinary saddle bum, either.

And that worried Lark more than anything else—except maybe the bulge low on his left hip, indicating that he was wearing a sidearm.

She frowned. Drew back from the window when the stranger suddenly turned, his gaze slicing to the very window she was peering out of, as surely as if he'd felt her watching him. Her heart rose into her throat and fluttered there.

A hand coming to rest on her arm made her start.

Ellie Lou Porter, her landlady, stepped back, her eyes wide. Mrs. Porter was a doelike creature, tiny and frail and painfully plain. Behind that unremarkable face, however, lurked a shrewd and very busy brain.

"I'm so sorry, Lark," Mrs. Porter said, watching through the window as the stranger finally turned away and stepped into the barbershop, taking the dog with him. "I didn't mean to frighten you."

Lark willed her heart to settle back into its ordinary place and beat properly. "You didn't," she lied. "I was just—distracted, and you caught me off guard."

Mrs. Porter smiled knowingly. There wasn't much that went on in or around Stone Creek, Lark had quickly learned, that escaped the woman's scrutiny. "His name is Rowdy Rhodes," she said, evidently speaking of the stranger who had just entered the barbershop. "As you may know, my cook, Mai Lee, is married to Jolene's houseboy, and she carries a tale readily enough." She paused, shuddering, though whether over Jolene or the houseboy, Lark had no way of knowing. "It's got to be an alias, of course," Mrs. Porter finished.

Lark was not reassured. If it hadn't been against her better judgment, she'd have gone right down to the barbershop, a place where women were no more welcome than in her former husband's gentlemen's club in Denver, and demanded that the stranger explain himself *and* his presence in her hiding place.

"Do you think he's a gunslinger?" she asked, trying to sound merely interested. In her mind she was already packing her things, preparing to catch the first stagecoach out of Stone Creek, heading anywhere. Fast.

"Could be," Mrs. Porter said thoughtfully. "Or he might be a lawman."

"He's probably just passing through."

"I don't think so," Mrs. Porter replied, her face draped in the patterned shadow of the lace curtains covering the hallway window.

"What makes you say that?" Lark wanted to know.

Mrs. Porter smiled. "It's just a feeling I have," she said. "Whoever he is, he's got business around here. He moves like a man with a purpose he means to accomplish."

Lark was further discomforted. She barely knew her landlady, but she'd ascertained at their first meeting that Mrs. Porter was alarmingly perceptive. Although the other woman hadn't actually contradicted Lark's well-rehearsed story that she was a maiden schoolteacher, she'd taken pointed notice of her new boarder's velvet traveling suit, Parisian hat, costly trunk and matching reticules.

Stupid, Lark thought, remembering the day, a little over three months before, when she'd presented herself at Mrs. Porter's door and inquired after a room. *I should have worn calico, or bombazine.*

Now, in light of the stranger's arrival, she had more to worry about than her wardrobe, plainly more suited to the wife of a rich and powerful man than an underpaid schoolmarm. What if Autry had found her, at long last? What if he'd sent Rowdy Rhodes, or whoever he was, to drag her back to Denver or, worse yet, simply kill her?

Lark suppressed a shudder. Autry's reach was long, and so was his memory. He was a man of savage pride, and he wouldn't soon forget the humiliation she'd dealt him by the almost-unheard-of act of filing for a divorce. Denver society was probably still twittering over the scandal.

"Come downstairs, dear," Mrs. Porter said, with unexpected gentleness. "I'll brew us a nice pot of tea, and we'll chat."

Lark wanted to refuse the invitation—wished she'd said right away that she needed to work out lesson plans for the coming week, or shop for toiletries at the mercantile, or run some other Saturday errand, but she hadn't. And she'd surely aroused Mrs. Porter's assiduous curiosity by jumping at the touch of her hand.

"Thank you," she said, smiling determinedly and under no illusion that Mrs. Porter wanted to "chat." Lark knew she was a puzzle to her landlady, one the woman meant to solve. "That would be very nice. If I could just freshen up a little—"

Mrs. Porter nodded her acquiescence, returned Lark's smile and descended the back stairway, into the kitchen.

Lark hurried into her room, shut the door and leaned against it, staring at her own reflection in the bureau mirror directly opposite. She'd dyed her fair hair a dark shade of chestnut, in an effort to disguise herself, but her brown eyes, once her greatest vanity, were her most distinguishing feature, and there had, of course, been nothing she could do about them. She supposed she might have purchased dark glasses and pretended to be blind, but her funds had been nearly exhausted by the time she reached Stone Creek, and she'd needed immediate employment. Even in an isolated place like that one, where teachers were hard to come by, nobody would have hired someone with such a hindrance and, besides, the illusion of blindness would have been almost impossible to sustain.

Keeping her hair dyed was hard enough.

She laid a hand to her bosom and forced herself to breathe slowly and deeply. She mustn't panic. Most likely Mr. Rhodes was merely passing through, whatever Mrs. Porter's speculations to the contrary.

Lark smoothed her crisp black skirt, straightened

the cameo at the throat of her white shirtwaist, patted her hair. She'd been reckless, keeping the clothes from her old life, and she should have changed her first name, too, as well as her last. Autry had taken everything else from her—her pride, her self-respect, her dignity. She'd fled with her favorite gowns, two weeks' allowance, and the money he kept hidden in the humidor in his study.

A few garments and the name her mother had given her at birth seemed little enough to claim as her own.

After steadying herself as best she could, Lark walked decorously to the top of the stairs, glided down them and swept into Mrs. Porter's spacious, homey kitchen. The huge black cookstove, with its shining chrome trim, radiated warmth, and the delicious scent of brewing tea filled the room.

"I've set out a plate of my lemon tarts," Mrs. Porter said, with a nod to the offering in the center of the round oak table. "Mr. Porter loved them, you know." She paused, sighed sadly. "Dear Mr. Porter."

Lark assumed Mr. Porter was deceased, since Mrs. Porter always referred to him in the past tense, but there were signs of his presence all over the house. His hat still hung on a brass hook in the front entry way, for instance, and books with his name inscribed on the flyleaf lay open, here and there, as though he'd just been perusing them. A half-smoked cigar lay in the ashtray on his desk in the study, and his birthday—January 28—was noted on the wall calendar next to the pantry door.

Not quite daring to inquire after him, Lark simply nodded and helped herself to one of the tarts.

"Sit down and make yourself comfortable, dear,"

Mrs. Porter urged. "One shouldn't eat standing up. It's bad for the digestion."

Circumspectly Lark took a chair, careful to avoid Mr. Porter's. Roomers came and went, but, as if by tacit agreement, no one ever sat in Mr. Porter's place. At present, Lark was the only permanent boarder, although a traveling dry goods salesman occasionally took the large room adjoining the kitchen.

Secretly Lark coveted that room, because it had its own entrance, a brick fireplace, a desk and a small sitting area, but the price of it was beyond her means. Ironic, she reflected, since her weekly budget for freshly cut flowers to grace her dining room table back in Denver would have covered a month's rent, with money to spare.

"Maybe he's come to work on the railroad," Mrs. Porter speculated suddenly.

Lark hoped the look on her face would pass for puzzlement, though it was actually apprehension. Had she realized the railroad was coming to Stone Creek, she wouldn't even have gotten off the stagecoach at all, let alone taken a room and applied for the recently vacated teaching position at the town's primitive little school. Indeed, she'd been settled in before she'd known, with the last of her funds spent to secure living quarters.

Mrs. Porter smiled brightly, setting two bone china teacups on the table with a merry little clatter. "I'm referring to Rowdy Rhodes, of course," she explained, her tone cheerful, her eyes alert. "Mr. Porter always complained that I just say things, out of the clear blue sky, with no sort of preamble whatsoever." She paused, frowning a little. "Yes, I'm sure he's here to help build the railroad."

"It's quite all right," Lark said. Everyone else in Stone Creek was excited at the prospect of train tracks and a depot linking them to such far-flung places as Flagstaff and Phoenix; the economic benefits were considerable. To Lark, however, the coming of the railroad meant disaster, because Autry *owned* it. By spring, the countryside would be crawling with his minions and henchmen—he might even show up himself.

Just the thought of that made her shiver.

Mrs. Porter sat down, then poured tea from the lovely pot, which matched the cups and saucers. Looking at the delicate objects, Lark was seized by a sudden and poignant yearning for the life she'd left behind. Unfortunately, that life had included Autry Whitman, and therefore been untenable.

"How are things going at school?" Mrs. Porter asked companionably, but the questions she really wanted to ask were visible in her eyes.

Who are you, really?

Where did you come from?

And why are you so frightened all the time?

A part of Lark would have loved to answer those questions with stark honesty. Her secrets were a very heavy burden indeed, and Mrs. Porter, while an obvious gossip, was a friendly woman with motherly ways.

"Little Lydia Fairmont is finally learning to write her letters properly," Lark said, glad of the change of subject. "She's a bright child, but she has a great deal of trouble with penmanship."

Mrs. Porter sighed and stared into her teacup. "Mr. Porter loved to read," she said. "And he wrote a very fine hand. Copperplate, you know. Quite elegant."

"I'm sure he did," Lark replied, saddened. Then, tentatively, she ventured, "You must miss him very much."

Mrs. Porter's spine straightened. "He's gone," she said, almost tersely, "and that's the end of it."

Feeling put in her place, Lark busied herself stirring more milk into her tea. "I'm sorry," she said. "I didn't mean to pry."

Mrs. Porter patted her hand, her touch light and cool. The house was large, and it was cold, except for the kitchen, since the fireplaces in the parlor and dining room were never lit. When she wasn't at school, where there was a potbellied stove and plenty of wood, Lark either shivered in her room, bundled in a quilt or read at the table where she was sitting now.

There had been no snow since before Christmas, but the weather was bitter, just the same. Would the winter never end? Though spring would surely bring trouble, Lark longed for it with helpless desperation.

"No need to apologize, dear," Mrs. Porter said graciously. "Have another lemon tart."

Lark, who had been hungry ever since she'd fled Denver, did not hesitate to accept the offered refreshment.

The back door opened, and Mai Lee, Mrs. Porter's cook, dashed in, a shawl pulled tightly around her head and shoulders. She carried a grocery basket over one arm, with a plucked chicken inside, its head lolling over one side.

"Make supper, chop-chop," Mai Lee said.

"Have some tea first," Mrs. Porter told the woman kindly. "You look chilled to the bone."

"No, no," Mai Lee answered, hanging up her shawl

and setting the basket decisively on the worktable next to the stove. "Stand here. Be warm. Cook chicken."

Mrs. Porter rose from her chair, fetched another china cup and saucer from the breakfront, with its curvy glass doors, and poured tea, adding generous portions of sugar and milk. "Drink this," she told Mai Lee, "or you'll catch your death."

Dutifully Mai Lee accepted the tea, only to set it aside and grab the dead chicken by its neck. "I tell man at mercantile, chop off head," she announced. "But he no do." Her eyes glowed with excitement. "On way there, I see Rowdy Rhodes in barbershop. He getting haircut. *Dog* getting haircut, too. Horse at livery stable, plenty of grain."

Mrs. Porter sat down again, poured herself more tea and took a tart, nibbling delicately at the edge. "Mai Lee," she said appreciatively, "it will be the Lord's own wonder if I don't lose you to the newspaper one of these days. You'd be a very good reporter."

"I no read or write," Mai Lee lamented good-naturedly, spreading her hands wide for emphasis before slamming the chicken down on the chopping board to whack off its head with one sure stroke of the butcher knife. "Cannot be reporter."

"How did you know Mr. Rhodes's horse was at the livery stable, let alone how much grain it receives?" Mrs. Porter asked, both amused and avidly curious.

Mai Lee frowned as she worked her way through the intricacies of the question, put to her in a language that was not her own. "I hear man talking outside barbershop," she said finally. "He work at stable."

"Ah," Mrs. Porter said. "What else did you learn about Mr. Rhodes?"

Mai Lee giggled. She might have been sixteen—or sixty. Lark couldn't tell by her appearance, and it was the same with her husband, who joined her each night, late, to share a narrow bed in the nook beneath the main staircase, and was invariably gone by daylight. Both of them were ageless.

From the limited amount of information she'd been able to gather, Lark surmised that the couple was saving practically every cent they earned to buy a little plot of land and raise vegetables for sale to the growing community.

"He *handsome,*" Mai Lee confided, when she'd recovered from her girlish mirth. "Eyes blue, like sky. Hair golden. Smile—" here, she laid a hand to her flat little chest "—make knees bend."

"He smiled at you?" Lark asked, and could have chewed up her tongue and swallowed it for revealing any interest at all.

Mrs. Porter looked at her, clearly intrigued.

Mai Lee began hacking the chicken into pieces and nodded. "Through window of barbershop. I look. He wink at me." She giggled again. "Not tell husband."

The pit of Lark's stomach did a peculiar little flip. She'd seen Mr. Rhodes only from a distance; he might have been handsome, as Mai Lee claimed, or ugly as the floor of a henhouse. And what did she care, either way, if he winked at women?

It only went to prove he was a rounder and a rascal.

With luck, he'd move on, and she'd never have to make his acquaintance at all.

Unless, of course, Autry had paid him to track her down.

Suddenly Lark was as cold as if she'd been sitting outside, under a bare-limbed oak tree, instead of smack in the middle of Mrs. Porter's cozy kitchen.

Mai Lee proceeded to build up the fire in the cookstove, then placed a skillet on top and lobbed in a spoonful of lard. She peeled potatoes while the pan heated, a model of brisk efficiency, and politely spurned Lark's offer to help.

Mrs. Porter sat in companionable silence, sipping her tea and flipping through that week's copy of the *Stone Creek Courier*. Lark set the table for three, while the aroma of frying chicken filled the kitchen. Steam veiled the windows.

Lark picked up a book, a favorite she'd owned since childhood, and buried herself in the story. She'd read it countless times, but she never tired of the tale, in which a young woman, fallen upon hard and grievous times, offered herself up as a mail-order bride, married a taciturn farmer, slowly won his heart and bore his children.

The knock at the back door brought her sharply back to ordinary reality.

"Now who could that be?" Mrs. Porter mused, moving to answer.

A blast of frigid air rushed into the room.

And there in the open doorway stood Rowdy Rhodes, in his long, black coat, freshly shaven and barbered, holding his hat in one hand. Mai Lee had been right about his blue eyes and his smile.

Lark was glad she was sitting down.

"I heard you might have rooms to let," he said, and though he was addressing Mrs. Porter, his gaze strayed immediately to Lark. A slight frown creased the space between his brows. "Of course, you'd have to let my dog stay, too."

The yellow hound ambled past him as if it had lived in that house forever, sniffed the air, which was redolent with frying chicken, and marched himself over to the stove, where he lay down with a weary, grateful sigh.

Mrs. Porter, Lark thought, with frantic relief, was a fastidious housekeeper, and she would never allow a dog. She would surely turn Mr. Rhodes away.

"It's two dollars a week," Mrs. Porter said instead, casting a glance back at Lark. "Normal price is $1.50, but, with the dog—"

Rhodes smiled again, once he'd shifted his attention back to the landlady. "Sounds fair," he said. "Mr. Sam O'Ballivan will vouch for me, if there's any question of my character."

"Come in," Mrs. Porter fussed, fond as a mother welcoming home a prodigal son, heretofore despaired of. "Supper's just about ready."

No, Lark thought desperately.

The dog sighed again, very contentedly, and closed its eyes.

Mai Lee stepped over the animal to turn the chicken with a meat fork and then poke at the potatoes boiling in a kettle. She kept stealing glances at Rhodes.

"I'll show you your room and get a fire going in there," Mrs. Porter said, only then closing the door against the bite of a winter evening. "Land sakes, it's been cold lately. I do hope you haven't traveled far in this weather."

Lark stood up, meaning to express vigorous dissent, and sat down again when words failed her.

Mr. Rhodes, who had yet to extend the courtesy of offering his name, noted the standing and sitting, and responded with a slight and crooked grin.

The pit of Lark's stomach fluttered.

Mrs. Porter led the new boarder straight to the room at the back, with its fireplace and outside door and lovely writing desk. The dog got up and lumbered after them.

For a moment, Lark was so stricken by jealousy that she forgot she might be in grave peril. Then, her native practicality emerged. Even presuming Mr. Rhodes was not in Autry's employ, he was a stranger, and he carried a gun. He could murder them all in their beds.

Mai Lee set another place at the table.

Voices sounded from the next room. Lark discerned that Mrs. Porter had undertaken to lay a fire, and Mr. Rhodes had promptly assumed the task.

Lark stood up, intending to dash upstairs and lock herself in her room until she had a chance to speak privately with Mrs. Porter, but Rhodes reappeared before she could make another move. She dropped back into her chair and was treated to second look of amusement from the lodger.

Indignant color surged into Lark's face.

Mrs. Porter prattled like a smitten schoolgirl, offering Mr. Rhodes a tart and running on about how it was good to have a man in the house again, what with poor, dear Mr. Porter gone and all. Why, the world was going straight to Hades, if he'd pardon her language, and on a greased track, too.

Rhodes crossed to the table, took one of the tarts and bit into it, studying Lark with his summer-blue eyes as he chewed. He'd left his coat behind in his room, and the gun belt with it, but Lark was scarcely comforted.

He could be a paid assassin.

He could be an outlaw, or a bank robber.

And whatever his name was, Lark would have bet a year's salary it *wasn't* Rowdy Rhodes.

2

PAYTON YARBRO—Jack Payton to anybody who asked—sat with one booted foot braced against a windowsill, in the apartment back of Ruby's Saloon and Poker House in Flagstaff, smoking a cheroot and pondering the sorry state of the train robbing business in general and his feckless sons in particular.

He had six of them, at least that he knew of. Wyatt was the eldest—he'd be thirty-five on his next birthday, sometime in April, though Payton was damned if he could recall the exact date. Then came Nicholas, followed in short order by Ethan and Levi, who were twins, then Robert and, like a caboose, young Gideon, who'd just turned sixteen. He'd come along late, like an afterthought, and Miranda had died giving him life.

Payton tried not to hold it against boy—it purely wasn't his fault—but sometimes, when a melancholy mood struck, he couldn't help it.

She'd driven her ducks to a poor pond marrying up with Payton Yarbro, Miranda had. Five of her sons were wanted by the law, and the sixth, Gideon, was likely to get himself into trouble first chance he got. Like as not, that opportunity wouldn't be long in coming, for Gideon, like his brothers, was a spirited lad, half again too smart for his own good, hotheaded and reckless. By necessity the boy already lived, without knowing, under a partial alias—went by the surname of Payton.

Robert—he'd been Miranda's favorite, and she'd called him Rob, after some swashbuckling fellow in a book—used his nickname and a moniker meant to stick in Payton's craw.

There was no telling what the others had come to by now.

Maybe Miranda's prayers had been answered, and they'd all married and settled down to live upstanding, law-abiding lives.

Of course, the odds were better that they'd been hanged or gotten themselves killed in a gunfight over a woman or a game of cards, out behind some whiskey palace.

Payton sighed. At least he knew where Gideon was—sulking in the saloon, where Ruby had set him the task of raking the sawdust clean of cigar butts, peanut shells and spittle. Wyatt and the others, well, if they were alive at all, could be just about anyplace. Scattered to the winds, his boys.

Miranda, God rest her valiant soul, was probably rolling over in her grave. She'd been a good, church-going woman, hardworking and faithful—at least, so far as Payton knew—with a Bible verse at the ready to suit just about any situation. She'd never given up hope that her sons would find the straight-and-narrow path and follow it, despite all contradictory evidence.

She'd called it faith.

Payton called it foolish sentiment.

How she'd ever fallen in love with and married the likes of him—and borne him six sons into the bargain—was a mystery to be solved by better minds than his.

She'd stayed with him, too, Miranda had, even with another man ready to offer for her, if she'd been free. She'd died wearing his narrow gold wedding band and honoring the vows they'd made in front of a circuit preacher nine months and five minutes before Wyatt had come along.

Pity he hadn't lived up to her example.

He shifted in his chair, wished he could shut the window against the bitter chill of that Sunday afternoon, shut his mind against his thoughts, too, but Ruby was a stickler for fresh air, and the memories clung to him like stall muck to a boot heel.

Ruby didn't countenance pipes, cigars or cheroots in her private quarters, for all that the saloon and card room were always roiling with a blue-gray cloud of tobacco smoke. She was a complex woman, Ruby—she'd joined a brothel when she was Gideon's age, and now she was a former madam, retaining an interest in the sinful enterprises of gambling and the purveyance of strong spirits.

For all her hard history, she was still beautiful and, ironic as it seemed, as fine a woman, in her own way, as Miranda Wyatt Yarbro had ever been.

Both of them had had the remarkable misfortune of crossing paths with him. He and Ruby had never married, but she'd given him a child, too. Ten years back, she'd been delivered of a daughter. Little Rose.

Payton's throat tightened at the recollection of the child. Redheaded, like her mother, she'd been smart and energetic and sweet, too, for all her bent to mischief. She'd been run down by a wagon when she was just four, chasing a kitten into the street out in front of the saloon, and they'd had to bury her outside the churchyard fence, in unsanctified ground.

Innocent as the flower she was named for, Rose had, after all, been a whore's daughter.

Behind him the door creaked open. Instinctively Payton stiffened and went for his gun, though a part of him knew who was there. In the end, he didn't draw.

"I told you not to smoke in here, Jack Payton," Ruby said. "It makes the place smell like—"

He flipped the cheroot out through the window, stood and shoved down the sash. Turned, grinning, to face the second of the two women he'd loved in his fifty-seven years of life. "Like a saloon?" he finished for her.

She pulled a face. "Don't go wasting your charming smiles on me," she warned. "I see right through them. And besides, I know full well you'll light up again, as soon as I turn my back."

Come evening, Ruby would be resplendent in one of her trademark silk gowns, all of them some shade of crimson or scarlet. She'd paint up her face and deck herself out in jewels she'd earned the hard way. For now, though, she wore practical calico, and around her scrubbed face her dark-auburn hair billowed, soft and fragrant with the lilac water she always brushed through it before pinning it up in the morning.

Looking at her, Payton felt a familiar pinch in some

deep, unexplored region of his heart. She deserved a better man than he was, just as Miranda had.

"There's a young fella out front, asking after you," Ruby said.

Payton raised an eyebrow, instantly wary. "He didn't offer his name?"

"Didn't have to," Ruby answered, with a slight sigh. "He's one of your boys. I knew that by looking at him."

Something quickened inside Payton, a combination of hope and alarm. "I reckon you'd better send him in," he said.

Ruby nodded, but she looked thoughtful. "How do you suppose he knew where to find you, Jack?"

Payton spread his hands. "No idea," he answered, wondering which one of his elder sons was about to walk through that doorway. "Did Gideon see him?"

"No," Ruby replied, still frowning. "I sent him to fetch the mail a little while ago. I could say you're not here—"

Payton shook his head. "No," he said.

Ruby took a last long, worried look at him, then opened the door and went out, closing it crisply behind her.

Payton drew a deep breath, let it out slow and easy, and straightened his string tie. Tugged at the bottom of his gray silk vest, too.

There was a light rap at the door, and then it swung inward on its hinges.

Payton squared his shoulders, regretted that he hadn't taken the time to throw back a slug of whiskey, just to steady himself.

"Well, Rob," he said, when his next-youngest son stood on the threshold, "it's good to see you again."

"I'LL JUST BET IT IS," Rowdy replied dryly, setting his hat aside on a table just inside the room. "It's been a few years." He'd left Pardner back in Stone Creek, in Mrs. Porter's care, and bought new clothes for the occasion.

Fact was, though, he'd looked forward to several funerals more than he had to this meeting.

"Come in and sit down," Payton Yarbro said, as if he meant it. But his ice-blue eyes were shrewd and watchful, and a muscle ticked in his jaw, under the stubble of a new beard. He still cut a fine figure, Pa did. He must have been pushing sixty, but he looked younger, despite the gray in his hair and the meager promise of an expanding middle.

And he still wore a .45 on his right hip.

Rowdy hesitated a moment, then steeled himself and walked full into the room, waited until his pa sat down in one of the chairs facing the cold brick fireplace before taking the other.

"What are you doing in this part of the country?" Payton asked, settling back and resting the side of one foot on the opposite knee. "Last I knew, there was a price on your head. You still wanted?"

"Still wanted," Rowdy said. "Thanks to you."

"I didn't force you to help rob those trains," the old man argued, taking a cheroot from a silver box on a side table, clamping it between his teeth and striking a match on the sole of his boot to light it. "You were hell-bent to join up, as I recall."

Rowdy didn't reply.

"How'd you find me?" Payton wanted to know, and though he put the question casually, the look in his eyes belied his easy tone. Shaking out the match, he leaned forward to toss it into the grate.

"I had a letter from Wyatt while I was still down in Haven. That's—"

"I know where Haven is," Payton said, sounding exasperated. "Little shit hole of a place just this side of the Mexican border. And what the hell was Wyatt thinking, to put news like that down on paper for anybody to see?"

"He didn't use your real name, nor his. And he wrote to say he was in prison. He mentioned that someone he knew had seen you in Flagstaff, running a faro table at Ruby's Saloon." Rowdy paused, solemn at the mention of Wyatt. He'd been the brother Rowdy'd looked up to, the one he'd wanted to be like. "The letter must have been forwarded four or five times before it caught up to me."

"What were you doing in Haven?"

"Passing through," Rowdy said, reining in his temper. Whenever he got within shouting distance of his pa, he always wanted to fight.

"Wyatt's in prison?"

"Last I heard," Rowdy replied. "The letter was dated two years back, so he might be out by now."

"Or dead," Payton mused, and he had the decency to look troubled by the possibility, though he probably didn't give a rat's ass what happened to Wyatt or any of the rest of them. He'd never cared much about anybody but himself.

"If Wyatt was dead," Rowdy said evenly, "I'd know it."

"How?"

Rowdy's jaw was clenched. He released it by conscious effort. "I just would."

"You ever hear from Nick or Levi or Ethan?"

"No," Rowdy said. "I guess Gideon's still at home." He looked around. "If you can call the back end of a brothel home," he added.

"Don't you get smart with me, boy," Payton warned. "I can still whup you and three others like you without breaking a sweat. Anyhow, this ain't a brothel. Ruby and me, we're honest saloonkeepers."

An involuntary grin tilted one side of Rowdy's mouth. "Whatever you say, old man."

"You look fit," Payton allowed, though grudgingly. He was a stubborn old rooster, and sparing with his approval. "You ever get hitched? Sire me a grandbaby or two?"

Rowdy wanted to avert his eyes, but he didn't. He waited a moment or two, letting his silence serve as all the answer he was willing to give, then countered with a question of his own. "You still robbing trains, Pappy?"

Payton hated to be called Pappy, which was why Rowdy had addressed him that way, but he had to give the old bastard credit for self-control. The only reaction was a reddening above the collar of his tidy white shirt. "Now why would you make a rude inquiry like that?"

Rowdy thought before he spoke, even though he'd planned what he would say all during the two-hour ride over from Stone Creek. He'd left Haven, where he'd drifted into a job as town marshal, for two main reasons—first, because he'd gotten that cryptic telegram from Sam O'Ballivan and Major Blackstone, summoning him north for a meeting in the lobby of the Territorial Hotel, and second, because a Wanted poster had landed on his desk with his real name and description printed on it.

He was taking a chance, continuing his acquaintance with O'Ballivan. Rowdy believed in hiding in plain sight, moving on when his feet itched, with most folks none the wiser for knowing him.

Sam O'Ballivan wasn't most folks.

"I need to know if you're still robbing trains, Pa," Rowdy reiterated. "The railroad's laying tracks from here to Stone Creek, and then all the way down to Phoenix. I'm hoping it's a coincidence that you're here in Flagstaff and two trains have been boarded and looted, not ten miles from here, in the past six months."

Payton drew on his cheroot and blew a smoke ring. "You find religion or something?" he hedged. "Or maybe you're just looking to make an extra dollar or two by riding my coattails."

Rowdy leaned forward in his chair, lowered his voice. "Listen to me, Pa," he said. "I came to Stone Creek because I was asked to, by two Arizona Rangers. I don't know for sure what they want with me, but I've got a hunch it has to do with the railroad coming in. Most likely the territorial governor is putting some pressure on them to put an end to the robberies. If folks don't feel it's safe to settle and do business here, the men back in Washington might not be willing to grant statehood."

Payton's eyes widened slightly, then narrowed. "What the hell do you care if Arizona ever becomes a state? You're an outlaw. There's *a price on your head,* Rob. You can't *afford* to cozy up with rangers!"

"If Sam O'Ballivan had me figured for an outlaw, he'd have tried to arrest me by now."

Payton went pale as limestone in a creek-bed. *"Sam O'Ballivan?"*

"I see you know him," Rowdy observed.

"Hell, everybody in the territory knows him!"

"He's a good man," Rowdy said.

"He's a *ranger,*" Payton returned. His hands tightened like talons on the arms of his chair, and he looked as though he might bolt out of it, crash through the window and hit the ground running. "First, last and always, Sam O'Ballivan is an Arizona Ranger. You have truck with him, and you're likely to find yourself dangling at the end of a rope!"

Rowdy looked around, spotted a decanter half-filled with liquor, and got up to pour a dose for the old man.

"Drink this," he ordered, holding out the squat glass. "And calm down. Otherwise, you're likely to bust a blood vessel or something."

Payton clutched the glass, and his hand shook a little as he raised it to his lips, closing his eyes almost reverently, like a man taking a sacrament. He swallowed, shuddered, opened his eyes again.

"You bring the rangers down on me, boy," Payton said, when he'd recovered enough to speak, "and I'll die in a jail cell. It'll be on your head."

"I came here to warn you," Rowdy replied, hooking his thumbs under his gun belt. "That's more than you would have done for me. From here on out, you're on your own—Pappy."

With that, Rowdy figured his business was concluded. He turned and made for the door. Took his hat from the fancy three-legged table, held it in one hand.

Payton hoisted himself out of his chair and turned to face Rowdy. "You don't owe me any favors, boy. I won't argue that you do. But if you have an honorable bone in your body, you'll ride out of here and keep on going, without a parting word to Sam O'Ballivan or anybody else."

Rowdy put his hat on, laid a hand on the fancy glass doorknob. "You're right, Pa. I *don't* owe you any favors. And I'm not going anyplace until I've heard Sam out. If you don't want him coming after you, don't rob any more trains."

"I gave that up a long time ago."

All of a sudden, the backs of Rowdy's eyes burned, and his throat drew in tight. He didn't know what he'd expected—it had been five years since he'd ridden with his pa's gang—but it wasn't this, whatever this was. "For your sake, I hope that's the gospel truth. At the same time, your word and two cents would buy me a cheap cigar."

"I guess we understand each other then."

Rowdy nodded glumly. "One more thing," he said, his voice coming out hoarse. He oughtn't to linger, he knew that, but he did it just the same. "Is Gideon all right?"

"He's fine."

"You haven't brought him into the family business, then?"

"He's only sixteen, Rob."

"I was fourteen, the first time I rode with you."

"I'm a different man than I was then," Paytor

Now that the whiskey had hit his bloodstream, he was his familiar, cocky self. "Older. Wiser. And one hell of a lot sadder."

Rowdy didn't reply to that. He simply nodded, opened the door and went out. He looked neither to the right nor the left as he strode through the saloon beyond. The swinging doors crashed against the outside walls when he struck them hard with the palms of both hands.

GIDEON PAYTON CROUCHED beside the small grave outside the picket fence surrounding the churchyard. The monument was white marble, the finest to be had, and there were no dates, no Bible verses or lines of mournful poetry—only two plain words, chiseled into Gideon's heart as well as the stone.

"Our Rose."

In the ten years since his sister had died, Gideon had visited this spot under the spreading limbs of an oak tree on all but a handful of days. He'd been a child himself when Rose was killed, only six, but the memory was as vivid as the town surrounding him now, the people coming and going in wagons and on horseback out there in the street, the bell tolling in the little steeple of yonder church.

In spring and summer he brought her flowers, usually stolen from someone's garden. In the fall the leaves of the great oak blanketed the long-since-sunken mound in glorious shades of crimson and russet and yellow and gold. In winter he offered trinkets—a bright bottle cap, a woman's ear bob found on a sidewalk, a colorful stone from the banks of Oak Creek. Sometimes he read to her out loud from a story book.

Rose had loved stories, but he hadn't known how to read yet when she was living.

He supposed he ought to have gotten over the loss of her by now, since he was sixteen and almost a man, but some wounds never heal, no matter what the preachers said.

Today Gideon laid a letter at the base of Rose's headstone.

"It's from a college back east," he told her quietly. "Pa went and signed me up for it." He paused, frowned. "I don't even like school that much, but I guess I'm good at it. Pa and Ruby say nothing worthwhile can come of my staying here, once I finish up my lesson-work this spring."

A flicker of motion at the edge of Gideon's vision interrupted his speech before he could get to the part that sorrowed him most—he knew he'd have to go, and that would mean he couldn't pay Rose any visits for a long time.

A rider sat watching him from the road. His horse was a gelded pinto, and his boots were good, probably handmade in Mexico. He wore a hat pulled down low over his brow, and a pistol, butt forward, showed where he'd pushed back one side of his long black coat, so it caught behind the holster.

Gideon took in all those things in the space of an instant, but they weren't what caught his attention. Something in the stranger's countenance sent a thrill through Gideon, made him rise slowly to his fu' height.

The man resettled his hat, briefly revealing ; of straw-colored hair. Then he nudged the hr motion with the heels of his boots and rode along the length of the picket fence.

"Strange place for a grave," he said, drawing up close to where Gideon stood. His eyes were almost the same shade of blue as Pa's were, Gideon noted, and his mouth was like his ma's had been—still, but ready to smile. Not that Gideon rightly recollected his mother; she'd died when he was born, and he'd only seen one likeness of her, a faded old picture tucked between the pages of a Bible.

Gideon stiffened, gestured toward the cemetery flanking the small church. "Nobody in there's got a better marker than my sister, Rose," he told the rider. His heart was beating fast and, cold as it was, sweat tickled the skin between his shoulder blades.

"I didn't know you had a sister," the stranger said quietly.

Gideon straightened his spine. He wasn't afraid of the man. Standing on the ground, not sitting a horse, he'd be no taller than Gideon, but he was older, and seasoned, if the easy way he wore his gun was any indication. "I reckon there's a lot you don't know about me, mister," he said, intrigued.

The rider grinned. "I know a little more than you probably think I do," he said, shifting in the saddle, standing briefly in the stirrups as if to stretch his legs. "Your name is Gideon…Payton. You're sixteen years old. Ponder it a bit, and you'll realize that you've seen me before."

That little hesitation before he said "Payton"—what did that mean?

And Gideon *did* recall a previous encounter, a

shadowy glimpse that teased at the edges of his memory but wouldn't show itself.

"Who are you?" he asked bluntly.

"I call myself Rowdy Rhodes," the man answered. "And I'm your brother."

Gideon had known he had brothers, but he hadn't been able to get much more than that out of his pa. They were all older than he was, but he couldn't have said how many of them there were, or recited their names with any certainty. Now one of them was sitting right in front of him.

"You *call* yourself Rowdy Rhodes? If you're my brother, you ought to be a Payton, not a Rhodes. And what the hell kind of name is Rowdy, anyhow?"

Rhodes chuckled and leaned forward in the saddle, resting one forearm on the pommel. "One that suits me just fine," he said. "Are you still in school, Gideon?"

Gideon glanced at the letter lying in front of Rose's gravestone, and wished he hadn't. Rhodes made him uneasy, with his watchful, knowing eyes, and yet Gideon wanted to know all about him. "I'll be going away to college, come autumn." He swallowed. "I mean to be an engineer. Maybe work for the railroad."

"Now, that's ironic," Rhodes said wryly.

Gideon was affronted, though he didn't know why. Felt like a rooster with its feathers ruffled. "I'm smart," he said.

"I don't doubt it," Rhodes replied. He looked down at Rose's grave, maybe noticed the letter, and the bottle caps, some of them rusting now, and the ear bobs and bits of frayed ribbon, with all the color weathered out of them. "How come they buried your sister out here, instead of in the churchyard, with the others?"

An old rage, all the worse for being helpless, surged up inside Gideon, stung the back of his throat like gall. "Because Ruby Hollister is her mother," he said.

Again, Rhodes adjusted his hat. "But not yours."

Gideon shook his head. "No, sir," he said. And he waited. If Rhodes was his brother, like he claimed, let him prove it. Let him say Ma's name.

He did, just as surely as if Gideon had demanded it of him aloud. "Your mother was Miranda Wyatt… Payton."

There it was again, that little hitch between words, subtle but sharp as a tug on reins already drawn tight.

Gideon wanted to ask about it, but his audacity didn't stretch quite that far. Rhodes's manner was kindly enough, yet there was an invisible fence line behind it, enclosing places where it wouldn't be wise to tread.

"You ever need any help," Rhodes went on, when Gideon didn't speak, "you'll find me boarding at Mrs. Porter's, over in Stone Creek."

Gideon nodded. Stone Creek was a fair distance from Flagstaff, and he didn't own a horse. Still, it was good knowing he could go there and expect some kind of welcome when he arrived.

Rhodes moved to rein his horse away, toward the road.

"Wait!" Gideon heard himself say.

The familiar stranger turned in the saddle, looked down at him.

"How many of you are there? Brothers, I mean?" Gideon blurted.

Rhodes smiled. "Five," he answered. "Wyatt, Nick, Ethan, Levi and me."

Gideon drew a step closer. "Are they Paytons?"

The answer was slow in coming. "No," Rhodes said.

Gideon frowned. It was bad enough that he hadn't known his own brothers' Christian names. Now he wasn't sure he knew who *he* was, either.

With a nod for a goodbye, Rhodes took to the road headed in the direction of Stone Creek.

Gideon watched him out of sight, half-sick with wondering. Then he bent, picked up the letter from the college in Pennsylvania, the only mail to come that day, and tucked it into his shirt pocket.

Without a fare-thee-well for Rose, he headed for Ruby's place.

THE YELLOW DOG LAY in the doorway to Mr. Rhodes's quarters as though guarding them, looking utterly bereft.

Lark, alone in the house because Mrs. Porter had gone to an all-day meeting at church and Mai Lee was off somewhere with her husband, Hon Sing, set aside the lesson plans she'd been drawing up, in preparation for the week to come, and regarded the animal with compassionate concern.

"He hasn't left you—your master, I mean," she told the dog.

Pardner, muzzle resting on his forepaws, gave a tiny whimper.

"Perhaps you're hungry," Lark said, getting up from her chair. Mr. Rhodes had given the creature table scraps the night before, with Mrs. Porter's blessings, and he'd had leftover pancakes and a scrambled egg for breakfast.

While she certainly didn't have the run of her landlady's well-stocked larder, Lark had seen the heel of a ham in the pantry earlier, while seeking the tea canister.

But perhaps Mai Lee was saving the bit of ham for her hardworking husband. For all Lark knew, it might be the only thing Hon Sing had to eat.

No, she couldn't give such a morsel to a dog.

In the end, she cut a slice of bread and buttered it generously, then tore it into smaller pieces. She was approaching Pardner with this sustenance when the kitchen door suddenly swung open and Mr. Rhodes strode in.

Pardner gave an explosive bark of jubilance and nearly trampled Lark in his rush to greet his master.

Mr. Rhodes bent, ruffled the dog's ears, spoke gently to him and let him out the back door, following in his wake.

Lark, recognizing a prime opportunity to make herself scarce, stood frozen in the middle of Mrs. Porter's kitchen floor instead, one hand filled with chunks of buttered bread.

Mrs. Porter returned before Mr. Rhodes reappeared, her cheeks pink from the cold and religious conviction. Beaming, she untied the wide black ribbons of her Sunday bonnet. "You missed an excellent sermon," she told Lark. "All about the tortures of eternal damnation."

"Sounds delightful," Lark said mildly and with no trace of sarcasm, depositing Pardner's refreshments on a chipped saucer and setting it on the floor. Having lived two years under Autry's roof, she knew the highways and byways of hell, and had no desire to revisit the subject.

Mrs. Porter removed her woolen cloak and hung it on one of several pegs beside the door. "You really should consider the fate of your immortal soul," she said.

The door opened again, and Pardner bounded in, his master behind him.

"Wouldn't you say we should all consider the fate of our immortal souls, Mr. Rhodes?" Mrs. Porter inquired, looking for support.

"Rowdy," Mr. Rhodes said. He watched Lark as he took off his hat and coat and hung them next to Mrs. Porter's bonnet and cloak, probably noting the high color that burned in Lark's cheeks.

His perusal made her uncomfortable, and yet she could not look away.

"Yes, indeed," he told Mrs. Porter, in belated answer to her question. "I've run afoul of the devil myself, a time or two."

If Lark had said such an outrageous thing, Mrs. Porter would have taken her to task for flippancy. Because Mr. Rhodes—*Rowdy*—had been the one to say it, she simply twittered.

It was galling, Lark thought, the way some women pandered to men—especially attractive ones, like the new boarder.

"You're personally acquainted with the devil, Mr. Rhodes?" Lark asked archly, when Mrs. Porter went into the pantry for the makings of supper.

"He's my pa," Rowdy answered.

3

ROWDY RARELY LOOKED at Lark Morgan during the Sunday supper of hash, deftly made by Mrs. Porter since it was Mai Lee's night off, but that didn't mean he wasn't aware of her.

He should have been thinking about his pa or about Gideon or about the meeting with Sam O'Ballivan and Major Blackstone coming up the next morning.

Instead the mysterious woman sitting directly across the table from him, intermittently pushing her food around on her plate with the tines of her fork and eating as though she was half-starved, filled his mind.

She hadn't told him anything about herself. What Rowdy knew, he'd gleaned from Mrs. Porter's eager chatter.

Lark was a schoolteacher, never married, popular with her students.

She'd been in Stone Creek for three months, during which time she'd never sent or received a letter or a telegram, as far as Mrs. Porter could determine. And Mrs. Porter, Rowdy reckoned, could determine plenty.

Lark Morgan's clothes gave the lie to a part of her story—they were costly, beyond the means of any schoolmarm Rowdy had ever heard of. He wasn't convinced, either, that she'd never been married; there was a worldliness about her, as though she'd seen the seamy side of life, but an innocence, too. She'd been a witness to sin, he would have bet, but somehow she'd managed to hold her expensive skirts aside to avoid stepping in it.

Mentally Rowdy cataloged his other observations.

She'd dyed her hair—there was a slight dusting of gold at the roots.

Her dark eyes were luminous with secrets.

She was unquestionably brave.

And she was just as surely afraid. Even terrified at times.

He'd joshed her a little earlier, claiming the devil was his pa, and she'd flinched before she caught herself.

Could be she was a preacher's daughter, and the devil was serious business to her. Some folks, Rowdy reckoned, paid so much mind to old Scratch and his doings that they never got past a nodding acquaintance with God.

Mrs. Porter finished her meal, setting her plate on the floor so Pardner could have at the leftovers, and set about brewing up a pot of coffee. A lot of people didn't drink the stuff at night—said it kept them awake—but Rowdy thrived on it. Could consume a pot on his own and sleep like a pure-hearted saint until the dawn light pried at his eyelids.

Lark hesitated, then took a second helping of hash. She was a small thing, with a womanly shape, but Rowdy had seen ranch hands with a lesser appetite. He wondered what kind of hole she was trying to fill up with all that food.

His own hunger appeased, he excused himself from the table, noting the look of relief that flickered briefly in Lark's eyes, and scraped what was left of his supper onto Pardner's plate. When he returned to his chair, the pretty schoolmarm was clearly startled, bristling a little.

"I'll clear away the dishes," Rowdy said to Mrs. Porter, once she'd gotten the coffee started and showed signs of lingering to fuss and fiddle.

Mrs. Porter looked uncertain.

"It was a fine supper," Rowdy told her. "And I'm obliged for it."

The landlady's eyes shone with pleasure. "I *am* a little weary," she confessed girlishly, sparing nary a glance for Lark, who seemed torn between tarrying and rushing headlong for the back stairs. "Perhaps I shall retire a little early, leave you and Miss Morgan to get acquainted. Mai Lee and the mister ought to be home soon. I always leave the back door unlocked for them."

Lark rankled visibly at the prospect of being alone with him, but she didn't rise from the table. She'd put down her fork, and her hands were out of sight. Rowdy was pretty sure, from the tense set of her shoulders, that she was gripping the sides of her chair with all ten fingers.

Rowdy stood, out of deference to the older woman. "A good night to you, Mrs. Porter," he said, gravely polite. "I'll wait up for Mai Lee and her man and see that the door is locked before I turn in."

Mrs. Porter nodded, flustered, mumbled a good-evening to Lark, and departed, pausing once on the stairs to look back, naked curiosity glittering in her eyes. Like as not, she'd wait in the upper hallway for a spell, eavesdropping.

Rowdy smiled at the idea. Sat down again.

Lark stared into her plate.

"I guess I'll take Pardner out for a walk," Rowdy said. "Maybe you'd do me the kindness of keeping us company, Miss Morgan?"

Lark's gaze flew to his face. She bit her lower lip, then nodded reluctantly and got to her feet. He'd been right to suppose there was something she was itching to find out, but it was clearly a private matter, and she knew as well as he did that Mrs. Porter had an ear bent in their direction.

Together they cleared the table, setting the dishes and silverware in the cast-iron sink. Rowdy pushed the coffeepot to the back of the stove, so it wouldn't boil over while they were out, and watched out of the corner of his eye as Lark took a cloak from the peg by the door and draped it around her shoulders. Pardner, eager for an outing, dashed from Rowdy to Lark to the door, exuberant at his good fortune.

Lark smiled and leaned to give the dog's head a tentative pat.

Something stirred in Rowdy at the sight.

"Does he have a leash?" Lark asked, as Rowdy crossed the room to stand as close to her as convention allowed, donning his own hat and coat.

He smiled. A leash? She was from a city, then, and probably a large one, where respectable folks didn't allow their dogs to run loose. "No, ma'am," he said. "Pardner sticks pretty close to me, wherever we go.

Wouldn't even chase a rabbit unless I gave him leave, and I never have."

Rowdy opened the door, braced himself against the chill of the night air, and went out first, so if there was trouble, he'd be a barrier between it and Lark Morgan.

Pardner slipped past them both but waited in the yard, turning in a circle or two in his impatience to be gone, until they caught up.

"Your name isn't Rowdy Rhodes," Lark said, in a rush of whispered words, the moment they all reached the wooden sidewalk.

Pardner proceeded to lift his leg against a lamppost up ahead, while Rowdy adjusted his hat. "And yours isn't Lark Morgan," he replied easily.

Lark reddened slightly under her high cheekbones. Lord, she was a beauty. Wasted as a small-town schoolmarm. She ought to be the queen of some country, he reckoned, or appear on a stage. "Lark *is* my name," she argued.

"Maybe so," he answered. "But 'Morgan' isn't. You're running from something—or somebody—aren't you?"

She hesitated just long enough to convince Rowdy that his hunch was correct. "Why are you here, Mr. Rhodes?" she asked. "What brings you to a place like Stone Creek?"

"Business," he said.

She stopped, right in the middle of the sidewalk, forcing Rowdy to stop, too, and look back at her. "Am *I* that business, Mr. Rhodes? If…if someone hired you to find me—"

"Find you?" Rowdy asked, momentarily baffled. In

the next moment it all came clear. "You think I came here looking for you?"

She gazed at him, at once stricken and defiant. She had the look of a woman fixing to lift her skirts, spin on one dainty heel and run for her life. At the same time, her chin jutted out, bespeaking stubbornness and pride and a fierce desire to mark out some ground for herself and hold it against all comers. "Did you?"

Rowdy shook his head. "No, ma'am," he said quietly. "I did not."

Lark still didn't move. "How do I know you're telling the truth?"

"You don't," Rowdy answered, keeping a little distance between them, so she wouldn't spook. "But consider this. If I'd come to Stone Creek to fetch you away, Miss Morgan, you and me and Pardner, we'd be a ways down the trail by now, whether you wanted to go along or not."

Her eyes flashed with indignation, but the slackening in her shoulders and the slight lowering of her chin said she was relieved, too. "You are insufferably confident, Mr. Rhodes," she said.

He grinned, tugged at the brim of his hat. "Call me Rowdy," he said. "I don't commonly answer to 'Mr. Rhodes.'"

"I'd wager that you don't," Lark said. "Because it isn't your name. I'm sure of that much, at least."

"You're sure of a lot of things, I reckon," Rowdy countered. *"Miss Morgan."*

"Very well," she retorted. "I'll address you as Rowdy. It probably suits you. You've fooled Mrs. Porter with your fine manners and your flattery, that's obvious, but you do *not* fool me."

"You don't fool me, either—Lark." He waited for her to protest his use of her given name—it was a bold familiarity, according to convention—but she didn't.

She came to walk at his side, between him and Mrs. Porter's next-door neighbor's picket fence. The glow of the streetlamps fell softly over her, catching in her hair, resting in the graceful folds of her cloak, fading as they passed into the pools of darkness in between light posts.

"Did your mother call you Rowdy?" she asked casually, while Pardner sniffed at a spot on the sidewalk.

"Yes," Rowdy said, remembering. Miranda Yarbro had always used his nickname—except when she was angry. On those rare occasions, her lips would tighten, and she'd address him as Robert. When she was proud of him, she'd call him Rob.

"Bless my boy, Rob," she'd prayed, beside his bed, every night until he left home with his pa, at fourteen. "Make a godly man of him."

Guilt ambushed him. He reckoned the good Lord had attempted to answer that gentle woman's prayer, but he, Rowdy, hadn't cooperated.

"Where do you hail from, Mr.—Rowdy?"

Grateful for the reprieve from his regrets, Rowdy smiled. "A farm in Iowa," he said. "Where do you hail from, Lark?"

She didn't reply right away.

"Fair is fair," Rowdy prompted. "You asked me a question and I gave you an answer."

"St. Louis," she said. "I grew up in St. Louis."

And you've been a lot of places since, Rowdy thought, but he kept the observation to himself. After all, he'd covered considerable territory himself, in the years between here and that faraway farm.

Pardner trotted back to them. Nuzzled Rowdy's hand, then Lark's.

To his surprise she gave a soft laugh.

"You are a dear," she said fondly.

Rowdy was both amused and disturbed to realize he wished she'd been talking to him instead of the dog.

LARK WATCHED from the steps of the schoolhouse that Monday morning as Maddie O'Ballivan, carrying her infant son in one arm and steering his reluctant older brother, Terran, forward with the other, marched through the gate. Ben Blackstone, the major's adopted child, followed glumly, his blond hair shining in the morning sunlight.

Behind the little procession sat a wagon with two familiar horses tied behind. It had been the sound of its approach that had caused Lark to interrupt the second-grade reading lesson and come out to investigate.

Class had begun an hour earlier, promptly at eight o'clock.

Lark had missed Ben and Terran right away, when she'd taken the daily attendance, and hoped they were merely late. It was a long ride in from the large cattle ranch Sam and Major Blackstone ran in partnership, and for all that those worthy men must have deemed the journey safe, there were perils that could befall a pair of youths along the way.

Wolves, driven down out of the hills by hunger, for one.

Outlaws and drifters for another.

"Go inside, both of you," Maddie told the boys, when she reached the base of the steps. Samuel, the baby, had begun to fuss inside his thick blanket, and Maddie bounced him a little, smiling up at Lark when Terran and Ben had slipped past her, on either side, to take their seats in the schoolroom.

"Rascals," Maddie said, shaking her head and smiling a little. "They were planning to spend the day riding in the hills—I guess they didn't figure on Sam and the major heading into town for a meeting half an hour after they left, and me following behind in the buckboard, meaning to lay in supplies at the mercantile."

Maddie was a pretty woman, probably near to Lark's own age, with thick chestnut hair tending to unruliness and eyes almost exactly the same color as fine brandy. Until the winter before, according to Mrs. Porter, Maddie had run a general store and post office in a wild place down south called Haven. She'd married Sam O'Ballivan after the whole town burned to the ground, and borne him a son last summer. Lark's landlady claimed the ranger's bride could render notes from a spinet that would make an angel weep, but she'd politely refused to play on Sunday mornings at Stone Creek Congregational. Said it was too far to travel, and she had her own ways of honoring the Lord 's Day.

Lark liked Maddie O'Ballivan, though they were little more than acquaintances, but she also envied her—envied her home, her obviously happy marriage and her children. Once, she'd fully expected to have all those things, too.

What a naive little twit she'd been, with a head full of silly dreams and foolish hopes.

"No harm done," Lark said quietly, smiling back at Maddie. "I'll give them each an essay to write."

Maddie laughed, a rich, quiet sound born of some profound and private joy, patting the baby with a gloved hand as she looked up at Lark, her eyes kind but thoughtful. "You're cold, standing out here. I'll just untie Ben and Terran's horses, so they'll have a way home after school, and be on about my business."

"I'll send the boys out to do that," Lark said, hugging herself against the chill. She hated to see Maddie go—she'd been lonely with only Mrs. Porter and Mai Lee for friends—but she had work to do, and she was shivering.

"Miss Morgan?" Maddie said, when Lark turned to summon Terran and Ben to see to their horses.

"Please," Lark replied shyly, turning back. "Call me Lark."

"I will," Maddie said, pleased. "And of course you'll call me Maddie. I was wondering if you might like to join Sam and me for supper on Friday evening. You could ride out to the ranch with the boys, after school's out, or Sam could come and get you in the wagon."

Lark flushed with pleasure; in Denver, as the wife of a powerful and wealthy man, she'd enjoyed an active social life. In Stone Creek, she was a spinster schoolmarm, and she probably roused plenty of speculation behind closed doors. Since she was a stranger and had all the wrong clothes for her station in life, folks seemed reticent around her. No one invited her anywhere, and she hadn't thought it proper to attend community dances; she didn't want the parents of her students thinking she was forward or looking for a husband.

"I'd like that," she said. "But I don't ride."

Maddie smiled. "I'll send Sam, then. Go inside now, before you freeze."

Lark nodded and went back into the schoolhouse. She told Terran and Ben to go out and unhitch their horses, and they scrambled to obey.

"Miss Morgan?" A small hand tugged at the side of her skirt, and she looked down to see Lydia Fairmont holding up a page torn from her writing tablet. "I copied the words off the blackboard. Will you tell me if all my letters are headed whence they ought to go, please?"

AS AGREED, Rowdy met Sam and the major in the lobby of the small, rustic Territorial Hotel, the only such establishment in Stone Creek, just before nine o'clock that morning. He'd walked over with Pardner from Mrs. Porter's, having left his horse at the livery stable the night before after returning from Flagstaff.

Both men stood when he entered, Sam looking fit and a little grim, though he had the peaceful eyes of a happily married man. Rowdy had never met the major, only seen him briefly when he'd come to Haven on sad business over a year before.

"Thanks for making the ride up here," Sam said, sparing a slight smile for Pardner as he and Rowdy shook hands. "Good to know your sidekick is still with you."

Rowdy nodded, then turned to the major, a tall, broad-shouldered man with a full head of white hair and a face like a Scottish banker.

"Major Blackstone," Rowdy said respectfully.

"Call me John," the major said, his voice deep and gruff.

"That would be an honor, sir," Rowdy replied. Blackstone was a legend in the Arizona Territory and beyond—before signing on with the Rangers, he'd led cavalry troops at Fort Yuma. In his spare time, he'd founded one of the biggest spreads that side of Texas, fit to rival the McKettrick ranch over near Indian Rock, and served two terms in the United States Senate.

Sam had told Rowdy some of these things back in Haven. Rowdy had made a point of finding out more after receiving the telegram.

They all sat down in straight-backed leather chairs pulled up close to the crackling blaze on the hearth of a large natural rock fireplace. The lobby was otherwise empty and silent except for the ticking of a long-case clock. Pardner stuck close to Rowdy and lay down near his feet.

Rowdy saw Sam sit back, clearly taking his measure, and Pappy's anxious words came back to him with an unexpected wallop. *First, last and always, Sam O'Ballivan is an Arizona Ranger. You have truck with him, and you're likely to find yourself dangling at the end of a rope.*

"I guess you know the railroad is headed this way from Flagstaff," the major ventured, after clearing his throat like a man preparing to make a speech.

Rowdy felt a quiver in the pit of his stomach. It wasn't fear, just a common sense warning. "So I've heard," he said moderately.

Sam finally spoke. "Maybe you know there's been some trouble. A couple of train robberies out of Flagstaff."

With just about anyone else, Rowdy might have

feigned surprise. With Sam O'Ballivan the trick probably wouldn't work. "Heard that, too," he said.

"According to Sam here," the major went on, "you made a pretty fair lawman, down there in Haven. Stayed on after the fire, and all that trouble with that gang of outlaws. Shows you've got some gumption."

Rowdy did not respond. Blackstone and O'Ballivan had issued a summons, and he'd honored it. It was up to them to do the talking.

"We need your help," Sam said forthrightly. "The major's getting on in years, and I've got a wife and family to look after, along with a sizable herd of cattle."

"What kind of help?" Rowdy asked.

"Rangering," John Blackstone said.

Wait till Pappy hears this, Rowdy thought. Not that he'd get a chance to share the information in the immediate future. "Rangering," he repeated.

"I can swear you in right now," the major announced. "'Course, that part of things will have to be our secret. Pete Quincy, the town marshal, up and quit a month ago, and you'd be filling his job, far as the good people of Stone Creek are concerned. The job doesn't pay worth a hill of beans, but it comes with a decent house and a lean-to barn behind the jail, and you can take your meals at Mrs. Porter's if you aren't disposed to cook."

Rowdy swept the room with his gaze. The hotel seemed as empty as a carpetbagger's heart, but if they looked around a few corners or behind the curtains, they'd probably find Mrs. Porter, or someone of her ilk, with ears sticking out like the doors of a stagecoach fixing to take on passengers.

Sam interpreted the glance correctly. "There's nobody here," he said.

"You seem mighty sure of that," Rowdy replied easily.

"Cleared the place myself," Sam answered.

Rowdy tried to imagine anybody staying when Sam O'Ballivan said "go," and smiled. "All right, then," he said. "If I understand this correctly, I'm to pose as the marshal, but I'll really be working for the major, here."

"John," the major said firmly.

"John," Rowdy repeated.

"You've got the right of it," Sam said. "All the while, of course, you'll be keeping your ear to the ground, same as John and I will, for anything that might lead us to this train-robbing outfit."

Rowdy chose his words carefully. "Might not be an outfit," he offered. "Could be random—drifters, or drunked-up cowpokes looking to get a grub stake."

John and Sam exchanged glances, then Sam shook his head.

"No," he said. "It's not random. Both robberies were carefully planned, and carried out with an expertise that can only come with long experience. These men aren't drifters—they're too sophisticated for that. The first robbery was peaceable. They felled a couple of trees across the track, in a place where the engineer would be sure to see the obstruction soon enough to put the brakes on. But there was a railroad agent aboard the second train, and the robbers seemed to know him. Singled him out right away, and relieved him of his weapons. A passenger tried to intercede, and he was shot for his trouble. Might never regain the use of his right arm."

"You suspect anybody in particular?" Rowdy asked lightly.

"All we've got is a hunch," John said. "My gut tells me, this is Payton Yarbro and his boys."

Rowdy did not react visibly to the name—he'd had too much practice at hiding his identity for that—but on the inside, things commenced to churning. "I haven't heard anything about the Yarbros in a long time," he said. "I guess I figured they'd scattered by now. Even gone out of business. The old man's got to be getting pretty long in the tooth—might even be dead."

Both Sam and John were silent, and the speculation in their eyes unnerved Rowdy. He realized that if he'd followed his first impulse, which was to pretend he'd never heard of the Yarbros, they'd have been suspicious. Not to know of the Yarbros would have been the same as not knowing who the James brothers were, or the Earps.

"It's only fair to tell you," Rowdy went on, "that I've got no experience tracking train robbers. I sort of stumbled into that marshaling job down in Haven, and just did what was there to do. I've been a ranch hand, mostly."

Sam watched him for a long moment, and with an intensity that would have made anybody *but* a Yarbro squirm in his chair. On the off chance Sam knew that, Rowdy shifted slightly.

"Sam tells me you're a good hand in a gunfight," John said. "You could have lit out when things got rough in Haven, but you stayed on. Even helped with some of the rebuilding, along with wearing a badge. You've got the kind of grit we're looking for."

Rowdy's hat rested in his lap. He turned it idly by the crown. "I'm not inclined to settle down permanently," he said.

The major nodded once, decisively. "That's your prerogative. Run the Yarbros to ground and ride out, if that's what you want to do. We'd be glad to have you stay on in Stone Creek, though."

Rowdy studied John Blackstone. "You sure do seem to think highly of me," he remarked, "given that I'm a stranger to you, and all you've got to go on is my reputation."

For the first time since the palaver had begun, Blackstone smiled. "I'd stake my life and everything I own on Sam O'Ballivan's assessment of *anybody's* character. I might not know you from Adam, but I sure as hell know Sam."

Rowdy knew Sam, too, and that was what made him wary. He was a fast gun, maybe as fast as Rowdy was, and he had a fortitude rarely seen, even in the wild Arizona Territory. Of course, it was possible, too, that Sam had already pegged Rowdy for a Yarbro, and meant for him to lead them right to Pappy's den.

A more prudent man would have taken his pa's advice and ridden out, put as much distance between himself and Stone Creek as he could, pronto. Rowdy was a gambler at heart; he wanted to stay and see how the cards would fall, but that wasn't his main reason for sitting in on this particular game.

He had another, even more intriguing puzzle to solve, and that was Lark Morgan, though there was no telling when she'd strike out for parts unknown.

Sam and the major sat waiting for him to announce

his decision, though they probably already knew what it would be.

"I'll see what I can do," he said.

"Good," John replied, with the air of a man completing important business. "I'll swear you in as marshal, and Sam's got a badge in his pocket. You just remember, the rangering part is between us."

"I might need a posse, if I'm going after a bunch of train robbers," Rowdy said. Whatever his private differences with his pa, he had no intention of rounding the old man up for a stretch in the prison down in Yuma, or even a hangman's noose, but he'd put on a show until he knew what was what.

There was an off chance, of course, that Payton had been telling the truth when he claimed he'd had no part in robbing those trains. Should time and some investigation bear him out, Rowdy would find the real culprits and bring them in.

"If a posse is called for," Sam said, handing Rowdy a star-shaped badge, "we'll get one up."

When the major produced a battered copy of the New Testament, Rowdy didn't hesitate to lay a hand on it. He wasn't a believer—at least, not the usual kind—but his mother had been, and that made the oath a solemn matter.

Fortunately, there was nothing in it about handcuffing his own pa, or any of his brothers, not specifically, anyhow. He swore to uphold the law, and he'd do that—up to a certain point.

After the swearing in, the major went off on some errand over at the Stone Creek Bank, while Sam, Rowdy and Pardner headed for the jailhouse, down at the far end of the street.

Would have made more sense to put the marshal's office in the center of town, where the saloons were and trouble was most likely to break out. Rowdy figured folks wanted a lawman around, but at a little distance, too.

The jailhouse was about like the old one in Haven, before it burned. One cell, a potbelly stove with a coffeepot on top, somebody's old table to serve as a desk.

It was the cabin out back that surprised Rowdy a little. It had three rooms, a good fireplace and a cookstove to rival the one in Mrs. Porter's kitchen. The floors were hardwood and the windows were sound, with no cracks around them to let in the winter wind. The bed had a good feather mattress and plenty of blankets, and there was a sink with a working pump. An indoor toilet and a stationary bathtub with a copper hot water tank and a wood-burning boiler under it raised the place to an unexpected level of luxury.

"The last marshal had a wife," Sam explained simply. "Come on. I'll show you the barn."

Rowdy grinned. "I'd probably feel more at home out there," he said. Back in Haven he'd slept on a cell cot, when there were no prisoners, and with a certain accommodating widow when there were.

"Maybe you'll take a wife," Sam said, making for the back door.

"Not likely," Rowdy replied.

Sam chuckled. "I thought the same way once," he said. "Then I met up with Maddie Chancelor."

LARK AWAKENED with a start, heart pounding, afraid to open her eyes. She was certain she would see Autry Whitman looming over her bed if she did.

The room was frigid, and the fine sweat that had broken out all over her body in the midst of her nightmare exacerbated the chill stinging the marrow of her bones. She forced herself to breathe slowly and deeply, and raised one eyelid, every muscle in her body tensed to roll off the side of the mattress and grab for something, anything, to use as a weapon.

Autry wasn't there.

Tears of relief clogged her throat and burned on her cheeks.

Autry wasn't there.

She sat up, fumbled with the globe of the painted glass lamp on her bedside table, struck a match to the wick. Shadows rimmed in faint moonlight receded and then dissolved. According to the little porcelain clock she'd brought with her from St. Louis, it was after three in the morning.

Inwardly Lark groaned. She wasn't going back to sleep.

After summoning all her inner fortitude, she swung her legs over the side of the bed and stood. The wooden floor felt frosty under her bare feet, and, shivering, she thought with longing of the wood cookstove downstairs.

She would go down there, build up the fire, if it hadn't gone out after Rowdy banked it for the night. Light another lamp and wait, as stalwartly as she could, for morning to come.

Lark grabbed up her wrapper—it was a thin silk, and therefore useless against the cold—and went out into the corridor, feeling her way along it in the gloom. She would have brought the lamp from her room, but it was heavy, and an heirloom Mrs. Porter prized. Breaking it might even be grounds for eviction, and Lark had nowhere to go.

She descended the back stairs as quietly as she could and gasped when she saw a man-shaped shadow over by the cookstove.

Autry?

Rowdy Rhodes stepped out of the darkness, moonlight from the window over the sink catching in his fair hair. He moved to the center of the room and lit the simple kerosene lantern on the table.

Lark laid a hand to her heart, which had seized like a broken gear in some machine, and silently commanded it to beat again.

"I've put some wood on the fire," Rowdy said quietly, offering no apology for startling her. "Go on over and stand next to the stove."

Lark dashed past him, huddled in the first reaching fingers of warmth, dancing a little, because the kitchen floor, like the one above stairs, was coated with a fine layer of frost.

Rowdy was fully clothed, right down to his boots.

"I th-thought you'd moved out," Lark said. "Gone to live in the cottage behind the marshal's office." He'd told them about his new job at supper that evening, said he'd still be taking his evening meals at Mrs. Porter's most nights.

He didn't answer right away, but instead ducked into his quarters behind the kitchen and came out with a woolen blanket, which he draped around Lark's shoulders. "I paid Mrs. Porter for a week's lodging," he said. "Since it wouldn't be gentlemanly to ask for my two dollars back, I decided to stay on till I'd used it up."

Pardner came, stretching and yawning, out of the back room. Nuzzled Lark's right thigh with his nose and lay down close to the stove.

Rowdy dragged a chair over and eased Lark into it. Crouched to take her bare feet in his hands and chafe some warmth into them.

Lark knew she ought to pull away—it was unseemly to let a man touch her that way—but she couldn't. It felt too good, and Rowdy's callused fingers kindled a scary, blessed heat inside her, one she wouldn't have wanted to explain to the school board.

"What are you doing up in the middle of the night?" Rowdy asked, leaving off the rubbing to tuck the blanket snugly beneath her feet. While he waited for Lark's reply, he took a chunk of wood from the box, opened the stove door, and fed the growing blaze. Then he pulled the coffeepot over the heat.

"I sometimes have trouble sleeping," Lark admitted, sounding a little choked. Her throat felt raw, and she wanted, for some unaccountable reason, to break down and weep. The man had done her a simple kindness, that was all. She was making far too much of it.

"Me, too," Rowdy confessed, with good-natured resignation.

Heat began to surge audibly through the coffeepot. The stuff would be stout since the grounds had been steeping for hours, ever since supper.

Taking care not to make too much noise, Rowdy drew up another chair, placed it next to Lark's.

"Makes a man wish for the south country," he said. "It never gets this cold down around Phoenix and Tucson."

Lark swallowed, nodded. The scent of very strong coffee laced the chilly air. "I ought to be used to it, after Denver," she said, and then drew in a quick breath, as if to pull the words back into her mouth, hold them prisoner there, so they could never be said.

"Denver," Rowdy mused, smiling a little. "I thought you said you came from St. Louis."

"I did," Lark said, her cheeks burning. What was the matter with her? She'd allowed this man to caress her bare feet. Then she'd slipped and mentioned Denver, a potentially disastrous revelation. "I was born there. In St. Louis, I mean."

"Tell me about your folks," Rowdy said. He left his chair, went to fetch two cups, and poured coffee for them both. Handed a cup to Lark.

She had all that time to plan her answer, but it still came out bristly. "My mother was widowed when I was seven. She and I moved in with my grandfather." Lark locked her hands around her cup of coffee, savoring the warmth and the pungent aroma.

"Were you happy?"

Lark blinked. "Happy?"

Rowdy grinned. Took a sip of his coffee. Waited.

"I guess so," Lark said, suddenly and profoundly aware that no one had ever asked her that question before. She hadn't even asked it of herself, as far as she recollected. "We had a roof over our heads, and plenty to eat. Mama had a lot to do, running Grandfather's house—he was a doctor and saw patients in a back room—but she loved me."

"She never remarried?" Rowdy asked easily. At Lark's puzzled expression, he prompted, "Your mother?"

Lark shook her head, telling herself to be wary but wanting to let words spill out of her, topsy-turvy, at the same time. "She was too busy to look for another husband. Men came courting at first, but I don't think Mama ever encouraged any of them."

"Is she still living?"

Lark swallowed again, even though she'd yet to drink any of her coffee. "No," she said sadly. "She took a fever—probably caught it from one of Grandfather's patients—and died when I was fourteen."

"Did you stay on with your grandfather after that?"

Lark resented Rowdy's questions and whatever it was inside her that seemed to compel her to answer them. "No. He sent me away to boarding school."

"That sounds lonesome."

Emotion welled up inside Lark unbidden. Made her sinuses ache and her voice come out sounding scraped and bruised. "It wasn't," she lied.

Rowdy sighed, spent some time meandering through his own thoughts.

Lark snuggled deeper into her blanket and tried not to remember boarding school. She'd loved the lessons and the plenitude of books and hated everything else about the place.

Pardner, slumbering at their feet, snored contentedly.

Rowdy chuckled at the sound. "At least *he* has a clear conscience," he said easily.

"Don't you?" Lark asked, feeling prickly again now that she was warming up a little. If Rowdy Rhodes was impugning her conscience, he had even more nerve than she'd already credited him with.

Rowdy leaned and added more wood to the fire. "I've done some things in my life that I wish I hadn't," he said.

Lark sighed. Why did he have to be so darn *likable?* She'd been a lot more comfortable around Rowdy Rhodes before he'd warmed her feet with his hands. "So have I," she heard herself say.

They sat for a long time in a companionable, if slightly uncomfortable, silence.

"Maybe I'll go someplace warm when I leave here," Rowdy said presently.

So he *was* just passing through, as she'd suspected. And devoutly hoped.

Why, then, did the news fill her with sudden, poignant sorrow?

"Mrs. Porter will certainly be disappointed when you leave," Lark said.

"But you'll be relieved, won't you, Lark?"

"Yes," she replied quickly but without enough conviction.

Rowdy smiled to himself. "Why don't you tell me what—or who—you're so afraid of? Maybe I could help."

"Why should you?"

"Because I'm the marshal, for one thing. And because I'm a human being, for another."

Lark swallowed. "I don't trust you," she said.

"Well," Rowdy sighed, taking up the poker, opening the stove door and stirring the fire inside, "that much is true, anyway."

"Are you calling me a liar?"

"In a word, yes."

Lark felt an inexplicable need to convince him. "I *did* grow up in St. Louis, in my grandfather's home. I went to boarding school, too."

"And you lived in Denver. Beyond those things, though, you've been lying through your pretty teeth."

Lark was indignant, and she forcibly suppressed the little thrill that rose inside her at the compliment couched in his accusation, as she had the delicious, strangely urgent languor she'd felt when he touched her feet. "I cannot think why you're interested in my personal affairs," she said, as haughtily as she could.

"You'd have been better off not to be so secretive," Rowdy observed. "When somebody presents a puzzle, I have to figure it out. It's part of my nature, I guess."

"Maybe you're just nosy."

He laughed, low and soft. Something quivered in resonance, low in Lark's belly, like a piano string vibrating because the one next to it had been struck. "Maybe I am," he agreed. "Nevertheless, there will come a day—or perhaps a night—when I know everything there is to know about you, Lark Morgan, and a few things you don't even know about yourself."

The implication, though subtle, was unmistakable. Lark was suddenly too warm, and would have thrown off the blanket if it hadn't meant sitting in close proximity to Rowdy in a gossamer nightgown and a woefully inadequate matching wrapper.

An achy heat suffused her as she imagined herself—the images flooded her mind and body, quite against her will—naked beneath Rowdy Rhodes's strong, agile frame.

Worse, he knew what she was thinking. She could tell by the look in his eyes and the amused way he quirked up one side of his mouth, not quite but almost grinning.

"You are the most audacious man I have ever encountered," she said.

"I'm a few other things you've never encountered, too," he drawled.

She stood up, swayed, flinched when Rowdy steadied her with one hand.

"Sit down," he said, "before you trip over that blanket and take a header into the stove."

"I don't have to listen to—"

He tugged on the blanket, and she landed, not in her own chair, but square on his lap. For a moment she was too stunned to struggle. She simply stared at him.

"Just let me hold you," he said.

If he'd made a move to kiss her, or touched her in any inappropriate place, she'd have had some way of defending herself. As it was, he simply wrapped his arms loosely around her and pressed her head to his shoulder with one gentle hand.

She was helpless against him.

He propped his chin on top of her head. "There, now," he said soothingly.

Lark closed her eyes, bit her lower lip and fought back tears. Other men had held her, particularly Autry, but never in that undemanding way. No, never once in all her twenty-seven years.

Perhaps Rowdy knew that had he risen to his feet, carried her to his bed and made love to her, she wouldn't have resisted him. Perhaps he didn't.

Lark finally stopped shivering, relaxed against his hard chest, cosseted inside the blanket, and promptly fell asleep.

HE WOKE HER AT DAWN, figuring Mai Lee would be up and around soon, or Mrs. Porter.

It wouldn't do for either of them to come upon such a scene.

Lark yawned and stretched, wreaking havoc with Rowdy's senses—he hadn't so much as closed his eyes since she'd landed on his lap, all soft and warm and woman scented.

He'd felt acquiescence in her, and been sorely tempted to bed her.

He knew she'd be responsive, give herself up to him with shy fervor. He knew precisely where to touch her, where to kiss her, how to set her ablaze with need.

He'd been a fool not to, and he'd suffered for his restraint.

She'd surely been with a man before.

And yet there was that troublesome, contradictory innocence about her.

With an inward sigh, he set her on her feet, held her firmly by the waist until, blinking and sleepy, she found her balance.

"Go," he said hoarsely. "They'll be awake soon, Mrs. Porter and the others."

Lark bit her lower lip, hesitated, then hiked up the blanket and hot-footed it for the back stairs.

Rowdy stood up, groaned. He was hard as tamarack, and it would be a while before the raw wanting slackened.

Pardner got to his feet, went to the door and whimpered to be let out.

Rowdy didn't bother to put on his coat and hat. He just worked the latch and opened the door, welcoming a rush of wind so cold that it made his eyes water.

Yes, sir.

A little fresh air was just what he needed.

UPSTAIRS, IN THE SAFETY of her room, Lark washed hastily and donned her primmest dress, the modest, high-collared black wool she'd been wearing when she'd fled Denver during a funeral. She'd feigned a headache, knowing Autry wouldn't flaut convention by leaving the huge, stuffy church before the service was over, and asked his carriage driver to take her home.

Once there, she'd packed in a desperate rush and prevailed upon that same driver to deliver her to the railroad depot, claiming she'd just gotten word, by telegram, that her sister had taken gravely ill.

She'd been anxious all the way to the station. She knew the train schedules by heart, and if she missed the two-o'clock, she'd never escape. Moreover, Autry would realize she'd deceived him, and the consequences of *that* didn't bear considering.

The carriage driver, the oldest retainer on Autry's large household staff, might have been suspicious, but he hadn't questioned her orders. He'd simply taken the most direct route to the depot, unloaded her belongings onto a porter's cart, tipped his hat to her, and wished her Godspeed.

Now, standing in a boardinghouse room, trembling with cold and the fear stirred up by remembering, Lark considered filling a single reticule and running away again.

There wouldn't be a stagecoach through town until Thursday morning, and she didn't have the fare, but perhaps she could prevail upon someone, a freight driver or a peddler, for instance, to give her a ride to—where?

Flagstaff?

She sat down heavily on the edge of her bed. What would she do when she got to Flagstaff?

Perhaps she could pawn her cameo brooch there and buy passage on a train—

No, *not* a train.

Autry might have agents aboard, because of the recent robberies, to protect his financial interests. And any one of them might recognize her as the upstart wife who'd dared to fly the coop and add insult to injury by having divorce papers served upon her outraged husband only ten days after her departure.

Tears filled Lark's eyes. She pinned the cherished cameo brooch, her mother's most precious treasure, to the bodice of her dress. How could she part with it?

Besides, she didn't want to run. She loved her pupils, loved seeing the light of understanding in their eyes when they suddenly grasped some new concept or idea, mastered some elusive skill. She loved Stone Creek, damnably cold though it was in winter and, anyway, she'd been invited to the O'Ballivans' home for supper on Friday night.

She bit down hard on her lower lip. She'd behaved like a hussy, down there in the kitchen. Sat in Rowdy's lap, like some…dancehall girl. And, dear God, at the slightest encouragement from him, she'd have gone willingly, even eagerly, to his bed.

He'd been so tender.

He'd been so strong.

And he'd as much as said, outright, that he'd have her.

Nevertheless, there will come a day—or perhaps a night—when I know everything there is to know about you, Lark Morgan, and a few things you don't even know about yourself.

She blushed at the memory of his words and the way he'd said them.

He meant to seduce her, sooner or later, and he'd taken the first step in the process the night before, in Mrs. Porter's kitchen.

What would be next?

A kiss? A caress?

Rowdy Rhodes was a patient man, that much was obvious. One by one, he would strip away her defenses, like garments.

If she stayed in Stone Creek, her downfall was inevitable.

She'd barely resisted him the night before, barely kept herself from lifting her head from his shoulder, finding his mouth with her own, *kissing* him, like some brazen trollop, some tramp—

Some saloon singer.

Lark gave an involuntary whimper.

Even now, at what should have been a safe distance, with Mrs. Porter and Mai Lee up and about, she *wanted* him.

Wanted his hands on her breasts, her hips, her thighs.

"Stop it!" she said aloud, squeezing her eyes shut.

After several minutes of deep, slow breathing, Lark regained some semblance of self-control.

A light rap sounded at her door. "Mai Lee has breakfast ready, dear," Mrs. Porter called cheerfully. "And if you don't hurry, you'll be late for school."

"Coming," Lark called back, with an effort at equal good cheer. But her voice quavered a little.

The creaking of the front gate sent her scurrying to her window. She tugged aside the curtain and looked out.

Rowdy was just stepping onto the sidewalk, Pardner cavorting at his side.

She let out a long breath. At least she wouldn't have to sit across the table from him, choking down her breakfast, pretending she hadn't let him rub her feet the night before, hadn't sat in his lap and felt so foolishly safe that she'd fallen asleep.

She watched from the window until she was sure Rowdy wouldn't double back, then hurried downstairs with as much dignity as she could manage. Their two chairs, she was glad to see, were back in their usual places at the table, and there was no indication that either of them had been in the kitchen at all during the wee, scandalous hours of the morning.

Except for the two coffeecups sitting beside the sink.

Mai Lee looked at them curiously, then glanced at Lark, frowning a little.

Thankfully, Mrs. Porter didn't seem to notice the stray cups. She took Lark's cloak from the peg by the door, carried it over to the stove and draped it over a wooden rack alongside, so it would be warm when she wore it to the schoolhouse.

Lark's eyes burned again.

"Rowdy suggested it," Mrs. Porter explained brightly, smiling at Lark. "He said you're uncommonly sensitive to the cold. He even said you might want to move into his room—once he's gone to live in the new place, of course." Here, she paused to blush girlishly. "I don't know why I didn't think of that before. There's no reason you couldn't use the best quarters when they're not rented."

Lark straightened her spine. "Th-thank you," she said.

"No reason at all," Mrs. Porter prattled on, still caught up in her musings. Then, with a pointed glance at the clock, she added, "Hurry up, now. You'll have to gobble your food and practically run to the schoolhouse as it is, if you're going to ring the bell at eight o'clock."

Lark nodded gratefully. She consumed a fried egg

and a slice of toasted bread and drank her coffee so quickly that she burned her tongue. Mai Lee had packed her lunch in a lard tin, as she did every weekday morning, and set it on the counter nearest the back door. Mrs. Porter had made special arrangements with the school board, soon after Lark's arrival in Stone Creek, when she realized her boarder was going without food between breakfast and the evening meal.

"I'll be having supper with Maddie and Sam O'Ballivan this Friday night," Lark said, out of courtesy and because she was a little proud of the invitation.

Mrs. Porter went still.

So did Mai Lee.

"Is something wrong?" Lark asked, carrying her plate and silverware to the sink, setting them on the drain board next to the cups she and Rowdy had used earlier. She was putting on her cloak before either of them answered.

"It's just that nobody's been invited out there since Sam brought Maddie home as his bride," Mrs. Porter said, trying to smile but not quite succeeding.

"I'm sure they mean to entertain more once they've settled in," Lark was quick to offer.

"It's been over a year since Maddie came," Mrs. Porter said uncertainly.

Lark assumed a confidential tone. "Terran and Ben tried to skip school yesterday," she said, as though imparting a secret that must be guarded at all costs. "Maddie probably wants to speak to me about—disciplinary measures."

Mrs. Porter brightened immediately. "I'm sure that's it," she said.

"Of course it is," Lark replied briskly, grabbing up her lunch pail and reaching for the doorknob. "Naturally, I'd like you to keep this in strictest confidence."

"Naturally," Mrs. Porter said eagerly.

By the time school let out for the day, Lark figured, the news would probably be all over town.

ROWDY STOPPED OFF at the mercantile to order supplies, like coffee and sugar, and then picked up the pinto, who'd come with the name Paint, and installed him in the barn behind the marshal's house. A supply of hay had already been laid in; probably Sam and the major's doing.

Polishing his badge with the sleeve of his trail coat, Rowdy surveyed the yard, enclosed by chicken-wire fencing, and the land beyond it. There was a house back there, if it could be called that, since it leaned to one side and probably didn't measure more than eight-by-eight. A cardboard sign, crudely lettered and attached to the door frame, proclaimed the place was for sale, with some scribbling underneath.

Rowdy decided to investigate, and Pardner went along, like he always did. If Rowdy'd gone through the gates of hell itself, he figured the dog probably would have followed.

The inside of that shack looked even worse than the outside. The stone fireplace was crumbling, and half the floorboards were missing. Those that remained were probably rotten.

He paused on the threshold, stopped Pardner with a movement of his knee when he would have ventured inside.

Rowdy stepped back, walked around the perimeter of the place, noted the overgrown vegetable garden, the teetering privy and the well. Returning to examine the cardboard For Sale sign, he noted from a scribbled addition that the whole place, a little under an acre, could be had for fifty dollars in back taxes.

He rubbed his chin, thinking about becoming a landowner.

He'd saved most of his pay while he was in Haven, so he was flush, and he'd developed a penchant for carpentry, helping to rebuild the burned-out town. He liked the smell of freshly planed lumber and the release of swinging a hammer or wielding a saw.

It was a fool's notion, of course.

What could he do with an acre of ground?

And, anyhow, he planned to move on, once he'd gotten the truth of the train-robbing situation and unraveled the secrets behind Lark Morgan's brown eyes.

Still, with the railroad headed in that direction, the land might make a good investment. He'd need something to fill his free time, since Stone Creek didn't appear to be a hotbed of crime or social activity, and putting that shack to rights seemed like a sensible occupation.

Resolved, he went back to the jailhouse and built a fire in the potbelly stove. By the time he'd adjusted the damper and shifted the chimney pipe to close the gaps issuing little scallops of dusty smoke, the supplies had arrived from the general store.

He put a pot of coffee on to brew.

Pardner, meanwhile, padded into the single jail cell, jumped up on the cot inside and settled himself for a snooze.

Jolene Bell showed up before the coffee was through perking.

"I hope you'll be a better lawman than old Pete Quincy was," she said.

"I guess that remains to be seen," Rowdy replied. He'd have offered her some of the coffee, but it was still raw and he only had one cup.

"I run a clean place," Jolene told him, after working up her mettle for a few seconds. "My girls are all of legal age, and my whiskey ain't watered down, neither."

Rowdy bit the inside of his lip, so he wouldn't grin. Obviously, Jolene was there on serious business. He'd learned a long time ago that if a woman had something to say, it was best to listen, whether she was the preacher's wife or the local madam.

"Am I gonna have trouble with you?" she asked, frowning.

Rowdy hooked his thumbs in his gun belt. "Not unless any of your 'girls' are there against their will," he said. "And I'll be by to collect pistols, if I see more than a dozen horses tied up at your hitching rail."

Jolene's gaze slipped to the .44 on his left hip. "Might be some as protest a rule like that one," she asserted.

"I don't give a damn whether they protest or not," Rowdy replied.

"Since when is there a law on the books that says cowboys got to surrender their sidearms afore they can do any drinkin'?"

"Since now," Rowdy said. "They'll get the guns back when they're ready to ride out, sober."

"I'd be interested to see how you plan to make that

stick," Jolene told him. "There's a lot of big spreads around here. The cowboys work long, hard hours, and when they get paid, they like to come into town and have themselves a good time. They get pretty lively, sometimes—especially if there's a dance down at the Cattleman's Meeting Hall, like there is next Saturday night."

"All the more reason," Rowdy said, "to enforce the Rhodes Ordinance."

"The Rhodes Ordinance? I ain't never heard of it." Her tiny eyes widened as revelation struck. "Say—that's your name, ain't it? Rhodes?"

"Yep," Rowdy said.

"You can't just go around makin' laws and expectin' the rest of us to abide by 'em," Jolene protested, drawing herself up in righteous indignation.

"I imagine the town council will support it," Rowdy replied.

"If that don't beat all," Jolene marveled. "Ol' Quincy was a piece of work—I had to pay him fifty cents a week just to stay clear of my place—but I figure you just might be worse."

Rowdy smiled. "I won't be staying clear of your place," he said. "I might even sit in on a hand of poker now and then."

Jolene narrowed her eyes. "You gonna put any kind of nick in my pocketbook, Mr. Rowdy Rhodes-Ordinance?"

"Nope," Rowdy said.

A slow grin spread across Jolene's pockmarked, sallow face. "Well, now," she said. "Looks like we're all in for a time of it."

"Looks that way," Rowdy agreed affably. He cocked a thumb over his right shoulder. "Who do I talk to about buying the place on the other side of the back fence?"

Jolene told him, and half an hour later, he was a man of property.

PA'D SADDLED UP and gone off someplace, in the middle of the night. Bent over a book at his desk in the back of the big schoolroom, Gideon couldn't take in the words he was supposed to be reading. He just kept remembering.

He'd awakened out of a sound sleep, hearing noises he thought were coming from the shed out behind the saloon, gotten up out of his bed, pulled on his clothes and boots, and headed out there to investigate.

And there was Pa, dressed to ride a distance, fastening his rifle scabbard to the saddle. His gelding, Samson, snorted and tossed his big head, eager to be away.

"You go on back inside, Gideon," Pa'd said. He wore his round-brimmed hat, and there was a bandana tied loosely around his neck. Under his long coat, he wore a gun belt, with a holster on either side. The pearl handle of one of his .45s flashed in the gloom as he swung up onto the horse.

"Let me go along, Pa," Gideon had said, at the edge

of pleading. "I can get a horse over at the livery stable—"

"You stay here and look after Ruby," Pa replied. He'd clamped an unlit cheroot between his strong, white teeth, and he shifted it from one side of his mouth to the other, looking as though he might ride Gideon down if he didn't get out of the way.

If there'd ever been a woman who didn't need looking after, it was Ruby Hollister. She kept a loaded shotgun behind the bar, and everybody in Flagstaff knew she wouldn't hesitate to use it. No, sir. She would not be requiring Gideon's protection.

"At least tell me where you're off to, Pa," Gideon had argued.

"That's none of your never-mind," Pa had answered, narrowing his chilly blue eyes with impatience. "Now, step aside."

Gideon stood his ground for a long moment, but in the end, he couldn't prevail against his pa's hard stare. "When'll you be back?" he'd asked.

Pa hadn't said anything in response. He'd just nudged the gelding into motion with the heels of his boots—not the fancy ones he usually wore, Gideon noticed, but the light, supple kind, made for moving fast, but soled for hard going.

Gideon had moved out of the shed doorway, lest he be trampled, and Pa had bent low over the saddle to avoid knocking his head as he passed through.

He'd vanished into the darkness, the hooves of his horse beating on the hard dirt, the sound growing fainter as he gained the road.

When the cold of that winter night finally penetrated

Gideon's awareness, he'd gone inside. Shed his boots and lay down on top of his bed in his clothes, staring up at the ceiling, knowing he wasn't going to sleep.

At breakfast, Ruby had been pale and unusually fidgety.

Gideon had been bursting with questions, but he hadn't dared put a one of them to her. When Ruby didn't want to talk, the devil and ten red-hot pitchforks couldn't make her do it.

Now, sitting in the schoolroom, he felt restless, as though there were something else he ought to be doing, and wasn't.

He thought about Rowdy, the brother he barely knew.

You ever need any help, you'll find me boarding at Mrs. Porter's, over in Stone Creek.

A hand came to rest on Gideon's shoulder just as he was recalling that conversation for the hundredth time, nearly scaring him right out of his hide. He wasn't commonly the jumpy sort, and it embarrassed him mightily, the way he'd started. He felt his neck and face go warm.

"You're not concentrating, Gideon," Miss Langston said good-naturedly, smiling down at him. She was about a thousand years old, short and square of build, a phenomenon that had confounded him until Ruby had explained the mysteries of a lady's corset. "It's too early for spring fever, but I'll vow, you're already afflicted."

Gideon tried to smile, because he liked Miss Langston. She was briskly cordial, and never made sly remarks about Ruby or his pa, like a lot of folks did. And she'd attended Rose's funeral, too, he remembered.

Cried into a starched hanky with lace trim around the edges.

"I've got some trouble at home," he confided, keeping his voice down so he wouldn't have to fight later, out in the schoolyard. He'd never lost a one of those battles, but, as his pa liked to say, there was no shortage of idiots in the world. There was always somebody ready to take him on.

Pa'd had things to say about that, too.

Pa.

"You'd best go and see to things there, then," Miss Langston said, kindly and quietly. When he hesitated, she prodded him with, "You're excused, Gideon."

He fairly knocked his chair over backwards, getting to his feet.

You ever need help—

Did he need help? He didn't know.

He couldn't have explained why he felt so nervous and scared. Something was bad wrong, though. He was sure of it. The knowledge stung in his blood and buzzed in his brain.

He ignored the quizzical stares of the other pupils—they ranged from tiny girls in pigtails to farm boys strong as the mules they rode to town—and shot out of the schoolhouse, down the steps, across the yard. He vaulted over the picket fence and sprinted for the livery stable four streets over.

ROWDY PLACED AN ORDER down at the sawmill, bought a hammer, a keg of nails, and some other tools at the mercantile, paid extra to have them delivered, Pardner tagging along behind him. Then, figuring he ought to do some marshaling, since he was getting paid for it, he walked the length of Center Street, speaking quietly to folks as he passed, touching the brim of his hat to the ladies.

He looked in at the bank and the telegraph office, introduced himself and Pardner.

He counted the horses in front of the town's three saloons, and went inside the last one, which happened to be Jolene Bell's place.

"That your deputy?" a grizzled old-timer asked, leaning against the bar and grinning sparse-toothed down at Pardner, who was sniffing at the spittoon.

"Leave it," Rowdy told the dog.

Pardner sighed and sat down in the filthy sawdust.

"Don't see no badge on him," quipped another of the local wits.

Rowdy smiled. "This is Pardner," he said. "Guess he is my deputy."

"He bite?" asked the skinny piano player, looking worried.

"Not unless he has just cause," Rowdy answered.

The old-timer's gaze went to Rowdy's badge, then shifted to his .44. "You a southpaw, Marshal?"

"Nope," Rowdy said, looking straight at the old man, but noticing everything and everybody at the far edges of his vision, too.

Always know what's going on around you, boy. Ignorance ain't bliss. It can be fatal. He'd been raised on those words of Pappy's, drilled on them, the way some kids were made to learn verses from the Good Book.

"Gun's backward in the holster," the piano player pointed out helpfully.

Rowdy glanced down at it, as if surprised to find it such. In the same moment, he drew.

The old-timer whistled.

The piano player spun around on his seat and pounded out the first bars of a funeral march.

Rowdy shoved his .44 back in the holster.

"Come, dog," he told Pardner, and they went back out, into the bright, silvery cold of the morning.

From there, Rowdy and Pardner proceeded to the Stone Creek schoolhouse. He didn't have any official business there, but he thought he ought to familiarize himself with the place, just the same.

And he wouldn't be averse to a glimpse of Lark, either.

The kids were out for recess, running in every direction and screaming their heads off in a frenzy of brief freedom, while Lark watched from the step, wrapped tightly in her cloak, her cheeks and the end of her nose red in the bitter weather.

She didn't see Rowdy right away, so he took his time sizing things up.

The building itself was painted bright red, and it had a belfry with a heavy bronze bell inside, sending out the occasional faint metallic vibration as it contracted in the cold. There was a well near the front door, and an outhouse off to one side. A few horses and mules foraged at what was left of last summer's grass—come the end of the school day, they'd be carrying Lark's students back home to farms and ranches scattered hither and yon.

Pardner lifted himself onto his hind legs and put his forepaws against the whitewashed fence, probably wishing he could join in a running game or two.

"Sit," Rowdy told him quietly.

He sat.

The dog's movement must have caught Lark's attention, because she spotted them then. Made an awning of one hand to shade her eyes from the bright, cool sun.

Rowdy grinned, waited there, on the outside of the fence, while she hesitated, made up her mind and swept toward him, her heavy black skirts trailing over the winter-bitten grass.

"Good morning, Marshal Rhodes," she said formally.

Marshal Rhodes? The woman had sat in his lap the night before, wrapped in a blanket and not much else, and settled herself against him with a little sigh of resigned surrender that still echoed in his bloodstream.

Rowdy remembered their present whereabouts—a schoolyard, in the bright light of day—and touched the brim of his hat respectfully. "Miss Morgan," he said. He let the look in his eyes say the rest.

Lark blushed, so he figured she'd understood.

"Surely you don't have business here," she said, taking in the shiny star-shaped badge pinned to his coat.

"No, ma'am," he replied. "Pardner and I, we were just making our rounds. Keeping the peace, you might say."

Lark tried mightily to smile, but she didn't quite succeed.

He realized, with a start, that she'd expected him to deliver some kind of dire news or maybe even arrest her.

Damnation. He'd figured she was running from a man, but now it struck him that he might have been wrong. Could be she was wanted by the law.

The thought of that gave Rowdy serious pause.

He recalled the way she'd glanced at his badge, and he searched the recollection, as well as her face, for any sign of anxiety.

Meanwhile, a little girl with blond pigtails approached the fence, stuck a hand through to stroke Pardner's head.

"Lydia," Lark said immediately, "you should not touch strange dogs." Her gaze moved briefly to Rowdy's face. "Some of them bite."

Reluctantly Lydia withdrew her hand.

"Does he?" the child asked, looking solemnly up at Rowdy. "Bite, I mean?"

Pardner tried to force his head between the fence pickets, looking for another pat.

"Sit," Rowdy told him.

Pardner sat, but he looked as forlorn as a martyr in a piece of bad religious art.

"No," Rowdy said to Lydia. "Pardner doesn't bite. He's a good dog."

"I wish I had a dog," Lydia said. "If I did, he could walk me home, and Beaver Franks wouldn't chase after me and pull my hair."

Rowdy crouched, well aware that Lark was watching him, and looked through the fence at Lydia. "My name is Mr. Rhodes," he said. "I'm the new marshal. Which one of those yahoos is Beaver Franks?"

"That's him over there, in the overalls and the plaid shirt," Lydia answered, in a whisper, not willing to risk pointing. "With the freckles and the red hair and the big front teeth."

Hence the nickname, Rowdy thought. He spotted

Franks and narrowed his gaze on him before shifting his gaze back to Lydia. "You want me to talk to him?"

Lydia shook her head. "I only live just a little ways from here," she said, pointing out the general direction of home. "And, anyhow, I can outrun Beaver Franks."

"Lydia," Lark said mildly, "go and tell the others recess is over. It's time for arithmetic."

Rowdy raised himself off his haunches.

Lydia stood still for a moment, then reached through the fence again to give Pardner a parting pat on the noggin before turning to scamper away.

Rowdy watched the child join the others, gesturing importantly as she explained, no doubt, that the fun was over and arithmetic was about to descend on them all like a plague. Beaver Franks, meanwhile, watched Rowdy, his broad face reddening a little, his fists tightening at his sides.

Rowdy felt his hackles rise.

Franks might be a schoolboy, but he had the body of a man.

"I can manage *Roland* Franks," Lark said, apparently reading Rowdy's thoughts as clearly as if they'd been written on her blackboard in big letters.

"Can you?" Rowdy asked. "How old is he, anyway?"

"Twenty-two," Lark answered crisply. "He might not be so troublesome of the children wouldn't call him 'Beaver.'"

"Twenty-two?" Rowdy echoed.

"He's in third grade," Lark said, with a strange combination of pride and defensive conviction.

Rowdy stared at her, at a loss for words.

"He's been working on his father's ranch since he was a little boy," Lark explained. "He didn't get a chance to attend school until this year."

Rowdy opened his mouth, then closed it.

Lark smiled, plainly enjoying his consternation. "Roland's best subject is reading, believe it or not. He's really quite intelligent."

"Twenty-two?" Rowdy repeated.

Lark folded her arms, tapped one foot on the frozen ground. Waited for Rowdy to take the hint and leave.

Pardner gave a sad moan as all the kids trooped back inside the schoolhouse, with Roland "Beaver" Franks bringing up the rear and casting sour looks back at Rowdy over one meaty shoulder.

"It doesn't bother you that he chases Lydia home and pulls her hair?" Rowdy asked, shoving his hat to the back of his head, peeved.

"I spoke to him about it," Lark said. "And he stopped immediately."

"Not according to Lydia, he didn't," Rowdy said. He took his grandfather Wyatt's watch out of his inside coat pocket, popped the lid with a practiced motion of one thumb and checked the hour. Ten forty-five. "What time does school let out?"

"Three o'clock," Lark answered, already turning to go. "Why?"

Rowdy didn't answer. He just looked down at Pardner and said, "Three o'clock."

Lark sighed and walked swiftly away.

When she got inside, she shut the door hard behind her.

Rowdy stayed where he was for a minute or so, pondering the presence of a twenty-two-year-old man in a schoolhouse.

Mentally he added one more item to the list of things he knew about Lark Morgan.

She was dangerously naive.

PROMPTLY AT THREE, Lark opened the schoolhouse door to dismiss her students, and was taken aback to see Rowdy's dog sitting patiently outside the gate.

Baffled, she descended the three narrow steps to the ground and looked down the road, first toward town, then, seeing no sign of the marshal, she scanned the countryside.

Apparently, Pardner had come alone.

Children streamed past Lark.

Terran O'Ballivan and Ben Blackstone mounted their horses, bareback, and made for the ranch. Roland lumbered by, muttering a goodbye to Lark as he went, a *McGuffy's Reader* clasped in one big hand. The others left, too, the older girls, slates and tablets and schoolbooks clutched to their chests, prattling and giggling about the dance to be held at the Cattleman's Meeting Hall on Saturday night.

Pardner watched the human parade go by, panting now.

Lydia, as usual, was the last to file out of the schoolhouse.

Pardner gave a welcoming yelp when he saw her, and rose to all four feet.

"He came to see me home, Miss Morgan!" Lydia marveled, in a whisper of high excitement, when she caught sight of the dog.

Troubled, Lark hastily banked the fire in the potbelly

stove, gathered up her cloak, lunch pail and lesson books. By the time she'd locked the schoolhouse door, Pardner and Lydia were already well on their way.

In the brief time Lark had known Rowdy Rhodes, she'd seldom seen him parted from that dog, but he was nowhere around now.

Was he sick?

Injured perhaps?

Lark hurried to catch up with Lydia and her canine escort.

"Maybe Mabel will let me give him a bone," the little girl told Lark eagerly, as she joined the procession. "We had one in our soup last night, at supper."

Mabel, Lydia's very young stepmother, was "no better than she should be," by Mrs. Porter's assessment. Lydia's father, the only doctor in Stone Creek, was a lithe, delicately built man with almost womanly features and—also according to Mrs. Porter—did not wear the pants in his family. Lark had observed, upon making the doctor's acquaintance, that he seemed dreamy, and somehow detached from the world around him. She'd wondered if he took a tipple now and then, or had a habit of dosing himself with laudanum.

Still a little breathless from hurrying and at once worried about Rowdy and feeling eminently silly for doing so, Lark summoned up a smile.

They crossed the road, woman, child and dog, headed for the row of tiny clapboard houses lining Second Street. The homes were set at some distance from each other, and several had small barns. Milk cows watched their passage, from barren, postage-stamp pastures, with interest.

"You don't have to walk me home, Miss Morgan," Lydia said. "I've got this dog for company." She frowned. "Do you know his name?"

"Pardner," Lark said, feeling ridiculously proud to be the possessor of this information. "Like *partner,* only with a *d.* The way cowboys pronounce it."

"Oh," Lydia said. "I think Rover would suit him better."

"I don't think he's much of a rover," Lark answered, still glancing anxiously this way and that, expecting, even hoping, to see Rowdy somewhere close by. "Marshal Rhodes says he doesn't wander."

Pardner sticks pretty close to me, wherever we go. Wouldn't even chase a rabbit, unless I gave him leave....

"Are you worried about something, Miss Morgan?" Lydia asked, looking up at her in concern.

"No," Lark lied. "I was just thinking about tomorrow's spelling bee."

"I guess you don't have to know which way letters are supposed to face to say what words they make," Lydia mused. She was such a serious child, desperate to do everything right.

Lark smiled and touched the little girl's shoulder gently. "You're making very good progress with your letters, Lydia," she said quietly. "You got most of them right today."

Lydia patted Pardner's back thoughtfully as they walked.

Soon they reached the Fairmont house, a modest place built close to the road. The yard was rocky dirt, and there were no trees close by. There was no barn, either—no fence and no milk cow.

It made, Lark thought, a bleak visage.

Pardner stopped when Lydia started up the foot-hardened path leading to her front door.

"I'm going to ask Mabel for that soup bone," the child called from the threshold.

Pardner and Lark waited.

"Where's Rowdy?" Lark whispered to Pardner.

Of course he didn't answer, he just looked up at her with warm, trusting brown eyes.

A moment later Lydia reappeared, her small face creased with disappointment. "Mabel won't give me the soup bone," she reported.

Lark smiled, anxious to reassure the child. "I don't think Pardner is disposed to eat right now," she said, before turning to go. "I'll see you at school tomorrow, Lydia."

She felt Lydia watching her and Pardner with a sort of clutching hunger as they walked away.

Lark fretted over Lydia, but her attention soon turned to Rowdy. It was silly to be concerned about him, she scolded herself silently, as she and the dog made their way toward the marshal's office. He was a grown man—a marshal, for heaven's sake.

He could take care of himself.

Nevertheless, Lark followed Pardner, who seemed to know precisely where he was going. Mrs. Porter would be waiting at home, with tea and gossip, and Lark knew she shouldn't be tardy.

Still, she stuck right with Pardner, instead of turning toward the boardinghouse. Her shoes pinched and she was cold and she wanted that tea with a powerful yen. What in the world was she doing, tramping through town behind a dog?

Pardner bypassed the jailhouse, trotting around back.

Lark trekked on.

They passed the little lean-to barn, and Rowdy's horse was inside.

The sound of a hammer cracked in the brittle air.

Pardner woofed once, happily, and broke into a run.

Lark hurried along behind, hoping no one had noticed her.

Rowdy appeared in the doorway of the tumbledown house on the property behind the jail, grinning. A stack of lumber stood on the ground nearby, and Pardner streaked past it to hurl himself at Rowdy, who laughed and crouched to greet the dog with an ear-ruffling and a few words of welcome.

Lark stopped, dizzy with an incomprehensible degree of relief at the sight of him.

"Afternoon, Miss Morgan," Rowdy said, standing again. He'd set the hammer down on the threshold to pet Pardner, and now he braced one shoulder against the framework of the shack's doorway.

"Good afternoon, Mr. Rhodes," Lark replied, feeling all the more foolish for the blush that burned in her cheeks. She wanted to walk away, but something held her rooted to the spot, like some venerable old tree.

"Anything wrong?" Rowdy asked, still leaning against the doorjamb, though his arms were folded now.

"I was just—I was worried when—"

He waited, damn him, enjoying her misery.

Lark tried again. She must complete her errand here, such as it was, and leave. Just leave. "It's only that Pardner came to the schoolhouse alone, and—"

"You were worried about me?"

"I didn't say that."

"Yes, you did. And why else would you follow Pardner all the way back here?"

Lark sighed. "All right. I *was* worried. Are you satisfied now?"

"Yes," Rowdy said, with a sudden and dazzling grin. "Flattered, too."

Lark finally worked up the will to turn away, only to turn back again. "What are you doing with all this lumber?" she asked.

"Replacing the floor in this old house," Rowdy said. "I'd invite you in, but you'd probably fall through and break a leg."

Lark instantly bristled. "If *you* didn't fall through, I probably won't, either," she argued, even though she had no desire whatsoever to set foot inside that tilting hovel. There were probably rats and insects in there. Cobwebs, too.

Rowdy's grin flashed again. He straightened, made a be-my-guest gesture with one hand. His blue eyes twinkled with challenge.

"I don't have time to dally," Lark replied, tacitly refusing. Why wasn't she moving? Heading home to Mrs. Porter's, for tea and news and a seat near the fire?

"Let me see if I understand this correctly," Rowdy said. "You were insulted when I said you oughtn't to come in. Then I invited you, and you balked." He paused for a long, strangely charged moment. "And when we 'dally,' Miss Morgan," he went on at last, "it won't be in a cold, dirty shack with the wind blowing through cracks in the walls."

Lark took three furious steps toward him. "We are not going to *dally!*" she replied, in a bursting whisper.

He threw back his head and laughed. When he looked at her again, though, the twinkle was gone from his eyes. They smoldered like the banked embers of a blue fire.

She waited for him to speak, which was her second mistake. Coming here at all had been her first, and she had only herself to blame for the consequences.

He was standing in front of her before she actually saw him move.

He rested his hands on her shoulders, searched her wind-chapped face and kissed her.

Lark made a startled "mmmm" sound, when their mouths collided, and then he was really kissing her. His tongue moved against hers, and his lips—well, *his lips*—

Drunken heat flashed through Lark. She trembled, and stood on tiptoe, and kissed Rowdy Rhodes right back.

When they finally broke apart, Rowdy looked stunned.

"Oh, *shit,*" he muttered. Hatless, he shoved a hand through his hair.

"Well, *that* was a gallant thing to say," Lark retorted.

He laughed again, quietly this time, but the baffled expression lingered in his eyes. "Go home, Lark," he said. "Go back to Mrs. Porter's place, right now. If you don't, I can't promise I won't take you inside my nice, warm marshal's house, kiss you until your clothes melt, and have you like you've never been had before."

Lark started to speak, then stopped herself, because she had no idea what she'd say. Her cheeks ached, and so did every inch of flesh beneath her somber black woolen frock, her camisole and petticoats, and her bloomers.

Mortification gave her the impetus to turn on one heel and start to walk away. Fury made her turn back again, though, with a hand shooting up to slap Mr. Rowdy Rhodes for his outrageous impudence.

Kiss-you-until-your-clothes-melt, *indeed.*

He caught her by the wrist, easily stayed the blow she'd fully intended to deliver, and with all her might, too.

"Go *home,*" he said.

"Let go of my hand," Lark replied tartly, breathless.

Slowly, staring into her eyes, Rowdy opened his fingers and released her.

Lark's hand fell to her side.

There was nothing to do *but* go home.

Feet as heavy as if they'd suddenly turned to bedrock, Lark straightened her cloak, patted her hair, pivoted smartly on one heel and walked away with all the dignity she could muster.

She'd only covered a few yards when he halted her with a single hoarse word.

"Lark?"

She stiffened her spine. Did not turn around.

He chuckled, and she actually *felt* the sound, ruffling the fine hairs at her nape. "I'll see you at supper," he said.

She made a strangled sound of pure fury and left.

Pardner followed her as far as the street, gazing up at her in piteous concern.

She paused, sighed and patted the dog's head. "Thank you for walking Lydia home," she told him. "Unlike your master, you are a gentleman."

ONCE LARK WAS OUT OF SIGHT, Rowdy let out his breath and muttered a curse. He shouldn't have kissed her like that. Shouldn't have said the things he'd said.

Oh, he'd meant them, all right.

Meant the kiss, too.

But now, because he'd said what he had, it was all going to happen. He *would* make love to Lark Morgan. And then his pa would rob a train, or a Wanted poster would come in the mail, with a sketch of his own face on it, and he'd have to hit the trail.

It had happened before.

It would happen again.

Rowdy thrust a hand through his hair. He was fed up with running, and in that moment, if Sam O'Ballivan had been standing in front of him, he probably would have turned himself in, just to be done with it.

But what would happen to Pardner if he did that?

What would happen to Lark?

He was asking himself those things when an old white horse trotted around the side of the jailhouse with Gideon on its back.

Seeing Rowdy, Gideon visibly gathered his resolve, reined in the horse and swung down out of the saddle. There was some gear tied on behind, wrapped in an ungainly bundle, and the boy wore an old wool coat and a brown hat pulled low over his face.

Pardner approached to sniff at his hand, and Gideon grinned at the dog and mussed Pardner's ears, but when he turned to Rowdy again, his expression was serious as an undertaker's.

"This where you live?" he asked.

"This is where I live," Rowdy confirmed. "I guess somebody at Mrs. Porter's must have told you where to find me."

Gideon nodded. Swallowed once. "You said to come if I had trouble."

Rowdy approached his younger brother, laid a hand on his shoulder. "What happened, Gideon?" he asked.

Gideon flushed. Chewed a while on what he wanted to say, maybe figuring how to put it. Finally, he said, "Pa took off last night, in a big hurry. Wouldn't say where he was going, and wouldn't let me go with him."

Rowdy closed his eyes. *No,* he thought fiercely.

I'm not ready to run again.

I'm not ready to leave Lark.

Damn you, Pappy.

Damn you.

"Did I do right to come?" Gideon asked warily.

Rowdy nodded. Smiled. "Come on along with me," he said. "I reckon you could do with some supper."

6

Mai Lee was alone in the kitchen when Lark arrived at Mrs. Porter's and divested herself of the lunch pail and lesson books, which she'd nearly dropped when Rowdy'd kissed her—in front of God and everybody. Hanging up her cloak, she frowned, immediately sensing something out of the ordinary, an uncomfortable shift in the atmosphere.

The Chinese woman stood at the sink, peeling potatoes, her back to Lark. Her child-size shoulders were stooped, and she didn't say a word, or turn to offer her usual smile of welcome.

Lark put aside disturbing thoughts of Rowdy Rhodes and her concern for Lydia Fairmont, renewed when she'd walked the little girl home from school, a nameless fretting that came and went.

"Mai Lee?" Lark ventured, looking toward the stairs and the inside doorways, expecting Mrs. Porter to appear. "Is something the matter?"

Mai Lee did not respond. Usually she chattered, in her oddly cobbled English, full of news.

Still frowning, Lark took the teakettle, which would already have been singing on the stove on any other afternoon, and stood beside Mai Lee to pump cold water into it. Once again she repeated the woman's name.

A tear slipped down Mai Lee's cheek. "He buy house," she lamented. "He buy *garden*."

"What house?" Lark asked, setting the kettle back on the stove to heat, her voice gentle. "What garden? And who is 'he'?"

Mai Lee sniffled, but she still wouldn't look at Lark. "I save for house," she said. "Save for garden." A shiver went through her. "Now, is gone."

Tentatively Lark touched her friend's shoulder. Mai Lee and her husband had undergone staggering hardship and privation before leaving China, by Mrs. Porter's account. Even now, they slept under a staircase, in a bed hardly big enough for one person, let alone two. They both worked long hours, never shirking, and while they seemed to consider themselves fortunate, given their cheerful spirits and quick smiles, glad of having ample food to eat and shelter, they nevertheless lived with a bare-bones simplicity that would have been difficult for other people—Lark included—to endure.

Lark was singularly alarmed by Mai Lee's obvious upset, and still confused by her attempt at an explanation.

"Mai Lee," she said quietly, "please, help me to understand. What house? What garden?"

"House behind jail," Mai Lee said, her face a mask of wretched sorrow, even in profile. "Me save to buy. Have almost enough. Now *gone*."

Suddenly it was all clear to Lark. Her heart sank.

Mai Lee and her husband had hoped to purchase the tiny place where she had seen Rowdy last, replacing floorboards. The homestead, one of the first in the area, had been abandoned years ago, and stood empty since then. The town of Stone Creek had held title to it, offering it for sale to anyone who would pay the back taxes.

And Rowdy had bought it. That answered a question she'd hadn't thought to ask. She'd been too flustered to ask what he was doing there, pulling up floorboards and driving nails.

Lark stiffened. She couldn't assume he'd known he was destroying a dream—he hadn't been in town long enough to be privy to things she was still garnering after three months' residence—but he was the source of Mai Lee's despair, nevertheless.

"Oh, Mai Lee," she said, "I'm so sorry." Sympathy seemed a poor offering, in the face of the other woman's sorrow.

Mai Lee nodded once, tersely, and went on peeling potatoes, rubbery from their long tenure in a wooden barrel in Mrs. Porter's root cellar.

Knowing nothing else to do, and certainly nothing helpful to say, Lark went about brewing her tea. Presently, a noise at the door and a sweep of chilly air brought Mrs. Porter bustling in, carrying a shopping basket.

"I saw Mr. Rhodes on my way here," she announced. "He's got a young man with him, too—came by here earlier, while you were at school. The boy had a horse when he came, but they're both on foot now."

Mai Lee promptly flung down her paring knife. The potato she'd been skinning landed in the kettle with a splashy *plunk*. She turned and scurried from the room, and the door to the little nook under the main stairs closed audibly.

"Merciful heavens," Mrs. Porter marveled. "What's gotten into Mai Lee?"

Before Lark could reply, the door swung open again, and Pardner pranced in, closely followed by Rowdy and a handsome lad of sixteen or seventeen years. The resemblance between man and boy was so strong that Lark blinked once, certain she was seeing things.

Rowdy was taller than the youth, more muscled, graceful where his companion was awkward. The newcomer had yet to grow into his strength, and his hair was a few shades darker than Rowdy's, a butternut color, but Lark knew that in high summer, it would be fair as corn silk.

Despite these differences, they had the same blue eyes. The same expressive mouths, on the verge of a wicked grin, though the boy's was set in a wary line at the moment.

The youth stood shyly just inside the door. At a nudge from Rowdy, he removed his ancient brown hat, held it with a diffidence that was not reflected in his taut jaw or watchful eyes.

Pardner lay down heavily, to one side of the cookstove.

Rowdy, meanwhile, made the introductions. "Mrs. Porter," he said, "Miss Morgan, this is my brother Gideon."

Gideon nodded politely, first to Mrs. Porter, then to Lark, though he didn't smile. "Pleased," he said, and blushed crimson.

Mrs. Porter, evidently over that morning's chagrin

at not being included in Maddie O'Ballivan's invitation to Friday-night supper, fussed happily. "Come on in, Gideon," she said. "Let me take your hat and coat. I'm sure Mai Lee—" She paused, realizing her cook was not present. "Where is Mai Lee?"

Lark pinned Rowdy with a brief but sharp glance. "Mai Lee," she replied, "has retired to her quarters. She's suffered a keen blow to her hopes."

Rowdy frowned as he took off his coat and hat and hung them in their places.

In the interim, Mrs. Porter fairly tore the hat from Gideon's hand. "I can't imagine what would be troubling Mai Lee," she chattered giddily. "The girl is the very soul of good cheer most of the time."

Lark fixed her gaze on Rowdy. "It seems," she said carefully, "that Mai Lee and her husband were hoping to purchase the property behind the jailhouse."

Rowdy sighed, clearly registering the gravity of the situation.

Mrs. Porter, however, made to peel Gideon's short wool coat off his shoulders, and he shrugged out of the garment with some haste, probably to avoid her fussing. "What a ridiculous idea," the landlady prattled, with a wave of one hand. "Why, that house is barely fit to serve as a woodshed, and the well's fallen in, too. There isn't enough land there to do anything with, either. Mr. Porter always favored burning it clear and letting the weeds take it." She tugged at Gideon's arm. "Do sit down, Mr. Rhodes," she urged.

"Payton," Gideon said, casting a glance at his brother that was both beleaguered and stubbornly defiant. "My name is Payton, not Rhodes."

Lark's attention quickened at this. She watched Rowdy even more closely than before.

"Sit down, Gideon," Rowdy told his brother.

Gideon sat, somewhat grudgingly.

"I'd like to speak with Mai Lee," Rowdy said, neatly sidestepping Mrs. Porter, who appeared ready to herd him toward the table where young Gideon waited, looking uneasy, as though he might spring up and dash for the back door at any moment, not even stopping to retrieve his hat and coat from the pegs.

"I'm afraid that's impossible," Lark told him, and her stiff countenance had more to do with the kiss they'd exchanged earlier than any personal judgments regarding his buying the property Mai Lee had wanted so much. "She has taken refuge in her private quarters."

Rowdy leaned in, spoke gruffly, as though they were alone in the room, he and Lark. "Then perhaps you will be so kind, Miss Morgan," he said, "as to roust her?"

"I'll do it," Mrs. Porter chimed, ever-helpful. Her lack of sympathy for Mai Lee's position chafed at something in Lark, like sandpaper against raw flesh.

She glared at Rowdy as Mrs. Porter rushed out of the kitchen, so anxious to do the man's bidding that she was breathless just calling Mai Lee's name. "You might have given the poor woman a little time to get over the shock," she said coolly.

His blue gaze moved over her face, came to rest, with exquisite focus, on her mouth. Her flesh tingled; she relived the kiss as surely as if he'd hauled off and done it again, right there in Mrs. Porter's kitchen.

"I like to deal with situations directly," Rowdy told her. He seemed to be implying that seducing her was one of those "situations," but of course Lark couldn't be certain. When she was around Rowdy, she seemed incapable of rational thought.

She colored up, incensed that it should be so.

He merely grinned.

Mai Lee appeared in the kitchen, following puffy-eyed and sullen in the wide, invisible path Mrs. Porter cut for her.

Rowdy studied Mai Lee, his gaze pensive, and then dismissed Mrs. Porter, Gideon and Lark from the room as grandly as if he were the owner of that house, and not merely a temporary boarder.

They all adjourned, at Mrs. Porter's behest, to Mr. Porter's study.

There, Gideon stood in the center of the room, looking as uncomfortable and anxious as he had in the kitchen.

Mrs. Porter straightened Mr. Porter's desk, but did not, of course, throw away the cigar stub resting in the ashtray.

Lark paced, wondering what Rowdy was saying to Mai Lee.

She had her answer when Mai Lee suddenly sprang up in the study doorway, beaming.

"I quitting cook!" she cried triumphantly.

IN HIS THOUGHTS Rowdy reviewed the events leading up to the present prickly situation.

He'd offered to rent the ramshackle place behind his own temporary residence to Mai Lee and her husband, and she'd accepted immediately.

In her enthusiasm she'd flown the coop, dashed right

out of the house, no doubt to find her husband and bend his ear with the news.

Mrs. Porter had promptly developed a sick headache and repaired to her bed.

He and Gideon and Lark had eaten, after Rowdy patched together a half-made supper from Mai Lee's beginnings.

"What is Mrs. Porter supposed to do without a housekeeper and cook?" Lark demanded the moment Gideon had finished his meal, dutifully carried his plate and utensils to the sink and taken Pardner outside so he could attend to the customary dog business.

Rowdy sighed. Lark was clearing the table, doing a lot of bustling as she went about the task, while he ladled hot water from the stove reservoir into a pair of dented dishpans. "I don't think Mai Lee meant she was quitting tonight," he said, hoping he was right. "She and her man can't plant anything for a couple of months, anyway, and the shack isn't fit to live in. She just got a little excited when I told her I'd rent her the property for a dollar down and a dollar a month, that's all."

Out of the corner of his eye, Rowdy noted with some satisfaction that Lark had softened a mite. She'd been huffy before. Had about glared a hole through him when Mrs. Porter practically swooned at the news of her servant's imminent departure and had to be escorted upstairs to her room.

Lark had undertaken that duty, because the situation was delicately female, and when she returned, she'd been narrow-eyed and tight around the mouth.

She sank into a chair at the table, evidently accustomed to letting other people do the dishes without offering to help.

Rowdy added the observation to the list he kept in his head.

It didn't mean she was selfish or lazy, he reflected. Lark was neither of those things. She simply wasn't used to housework, a fact that tallied with her too-fine clothes and a certain elegance in her manners.

She could kiss, though.

Damnation, she could kiss.

"Some people," he said easily, "would think it was a kindly gesture, my offering the use of that place to Mai Lee on terms I knew she could manage."

Looking back at Lark, he saw that she'd propped an elbow on the tabletop and rested her chin in her palm. "Why is Gideon's last name Payton, when yours is Rhodes?" she asked. That was another thing he'd noticed about her—that she had a way of switching horses in the middle of the stream, conversationally speaking. "Did you have different fathers?"

It was a tricky question.

The honest answer was no—Payton Yarbro had sired both Gideon and him. Still, with the fourteen-year gap between their ages, and the disparate ways they'd grown up—Rowdy on the home place in Iowa, Gideon in the back of Ruby's Saloon and Poker House in Flagstaff—it would be just as true to say they'd come from separate families.

He was about to say yes, even though it went sorely against his grain to mislead Lark—which was an odd thing in itself because she hadn't exactly been lavish with the truth herself—when she saved him the whole conundrum.

"I shouldn't have asked you that," she said, appearing at his elbow and taking up a dish towel. "It was far too personal an inquiry."

He grinned at her. "Do you always talk like that?"

She frowned, puzzled, and swabbed a plate dry after he set it in the second basin, full of clear water. "Like what?"

"Like you're reading aloud from a page torn out of an etiquette book," he said.

"I don't!" she protested.

"Maybe it's because you're a schoolmarm," he teased.

"I'm not—"

"A schoolmarm?"

She turned pink. "I *am* a school*teacher*," she insisted.

"And what else?"

"*Nothing* else."

He let his gaze drift over her face, taking care not to venture further south than her chin. Even the hollow of her throat was dangerous territory, covered, though it was, by that high-collared dress of hers. "Well," he drawled, "there does seem to be every indication that you're a woman, as well as a schoolm—teacher."

Her blush deepened. "You are *deliberately* baiting me," she accused.

"If I gave you that impression," he said with exaggerated sincerity, "I certainly apologize."

"You're not one bit sorry!"

He chuckled. "Guess not," he said. "It's a pleasant thing, riling you."

She stopped all pretense of drying dishes and stared at him. "Why?"

"Your eyes flash, and you get all warm and pink. The way you would if I laid you down and proved to your complete…satisfaction that you surely are a woman before anything else."

She blinked. For a moment he thought she'd move to slap him, the way she'd tried to in the yard in front of the shack. This time, since he had a plate in one hand and a dishtowel in the other, she might succeed.

Fortunately—or unfortunately, given that he might have enjoyed even that kind of physical contact with Lark Morgan—Gideon chose then to open the door and come back into the house, Pardner with him.

"You can bed down in that room back there," Rowdy told his brother, with a nod toward the doorway nearby, after a brief interval spent adjusting to the intrusion. "I'll sleep over at the new place."

"I'd rather stay with you," Gideon said. "I've got a bedroll. I can bunk on the floor."

"Whatever suits you," Rowdy told him. Gideon was still a kid, for all that he probably believed himself to be a man, and he'd ridden some distance to get to Stone Creek. It wasn't surprising that he'd be a little skittish about staying at Mrs. Porter's and being fussed over by a pack of women.

Lark looked from Gideon to Rowdy and back again. "How old are you, Gideon?" she asked.

"Sixteen," Gideon said, as though that were an august age, worthy of some awe.

Lark smiled at him, laying aside the dish towel. "Well then, if you're staying in Stone Creek a while, you'd best come to school in the morning. We start at eight."

Gideon's blue eyes goggled, then narrowed a little. "I'm not going to school," he said flatly.

"Yes," Rowdy said, "you are."

A thick silence fell.

"Miss Morgan," Rowdy went on, after watching Gideon try to gulp down his Adam's apple three or four times, "is your teacher."

Gideon's eyes widened.

"I'll see you tomorrow, Gideon," Lark said pleasantly.

And then she left.

Nothing about seeing *him* tomorrow, Rowdy thought, with a private grin.

But she would. He'd make sure of that—put himself square in her path at least once.

"I don't want to go to school," Gideon said stoutly. "I thought maybe I could be your deputy or something. Both of us could go looking for Pa."

Rowdy dried his hands, the dishwashing job finished at last. "*I'm* going looking for Pa," he said. "*You're* going to school."

Gideon had the Yarbro temper, all right. It glittered in his eyes and bunched a certain muscle in his jaw. "Does it matter a whoop to you that I just said I didn't want to?" he snapped.

Rowdy grinned. "Not even that much," he said. Then he summoned Pardner, who was lounging by the stove again, and fetched down his hat and coat from the pegs by the door. They had a warm, comfortable place to sleep right there at Mrs. Porter's, but Gideon's horse was over behind the jailhouse, and so was his bedroll.

Might as well make the move, though the truth was, Rowdy didn't much like doing it. Lark was here, under this roof, after all, and he wasn't real keen on the idea of leaving her unprotected from whoever she was so scared of.

He wished he'd told her to wait up and lock the door behind them, but Mai Lee was still out, and she might not have a key.

Maybe he'd just come by later, in his capacity as the marshal of Stone Creek, and make sure the lock was turned.

Gideon plunked his hat on his head and jammed his arms into his coat sleeves as he came down the back steps behind Rowdy and Pardner.

"I think you're sweet on that schoolteacher woman," he said.

"Stop thinking," Rowdy replied. "You might hurt yourself."

"I reckon you meant that to be funny," Gideon scowled, clearly not amused. "It wasn't."

"Does Ruby know you're here, Gideon?" Rowdy asked, as they gained the sidewalk, "or is she out knocking on doors all over Flagstaff, looking for you?"

"I left her a note," Gideon said. "Anyhow, I didn't come here so I could go to *school*. I came because you said I ought to, if I needed help, and I need help to *find Pa*."

"I've been thinking I might require a deputy," Rowdy said.

Gideon looked at him with new, and slightly less hostile, interest. Rowdy wondered if the kid was always this testy, or if it was just because he was so worried about Pappy. "I could do it," the boy said, squaring his shoulders. "Be your deputy, I mean."

"You might want to hear me out before you agree," Rowdy told him. "It's night work, and it pays next to nothing. You'd have to sit in the jailhouse while I'm making my rounds. In case somebody came by, looking for help. That would leave you free to go to school in the daytime."

"When am I supposed to sleep?" Gideon demanded.

"You can rest in the cell, as long as there aren't any prisoners," Rowdy answered, holding back a grin.

"Do I get a gun?"

"No," Rowdy said. "You do not get a gun."

"Suppose there's trouble?"

"A gun would only complicate matters."

"*You* carry one," Gideon argued. He was Payton Yarbro's baby boy, all right. He'd probably stand flat-footed and argue with an angel sent from Almighty God, just for the sport of it.

"I'm the marshal," Rowdy reminded him.

"I've never heard of a deputy who didn't even have a *gun,*" Gideon said. "It's wrong. It's just wrong."

"That's my offer," Rowdy said. "Take it or leave it."

"Do I at least get a badge?"

Rowdy chuckled, raised the collar of his coat against a chilly wind. "I think I can scrounge up one of those," he said. He'd seen an old tin star, partially rusted and with the pin bent, under a stack of musty papers at the jailhouse. "It might need a little polishing and fixing, though."

They'd reached Center Street by then.

Rowdy counted the horses in front of all three saloons, found the number to his liking and headed for the jailhouse. Opened the door, went inside, lit a lamp on the table he'd be using as a desk.

"You go on around back and see to your horse," he told Gideon, after finding the badge and tossing it to him. "Then you'd better turn in for the night. You've got school in the morning and there'll be your deputy duties to see to tomorrow evening."

Gideon frowned, probably wondering if he was being hornswoggled, but when he looked down at the battered old badge in his palm, he finally smiled. It was the first time he'd shown the slightest inclination toward good humor.

"If you've got any ideas on where I might start looking for Pa," Rowdy said, "I would appreciate your sharing them."

Gideon's hand closed around the tarnished star, and he looked serious again. "You meaning to saddle up and ride out, once I'm asleep?" he asked suspiciously.

"No," Rowdy said. "Like I said before, I've got rounds to make."

He intended to visit all three saloons and make sure everybody was minding their manners, and he might walk the side streets, too. After all, there were only two of them—probably not more than twenty houses in the whole town.

Once he knew the place was buttoned down tight, he'd try Mrs. Porter's back door. If he found it locked, then he'd head on home and maybe try out that fancy copper bathtub.

Gideon tucked his badge into his coat pocket and left.

Pardner started to follow him, stopped, looked back at Rowdy.

"Go on," Rowdy said to the dog, feeling a strange tightening in his throat. "You go on with Gideon and rest up. You've already put in a good day's work."

Pardner stood stock-still for another few moments, then he turned and followed Gideon outside.

It was better this way, Rowdy told himself. Pardner was getting old, and though he'd been a stalwart traveler on the trip up from Haven, he wouldn't be able to keep up on the trail, especially if a fast pace was required.

Tracking Pappy down would take some doing as it was.

No, sir, he did not need a dog to make it harder.

Despite this conclusion, a somber mood settled over Rowdy as he walked the streets of Stone Creek. When he'd done that, he checked the saloons.

Business was slow and, while Jolene and the other owners might not have agreed, he saw that as a good thing.

He tried Mrs. Porter's kitchen door last.

It was locked, and all the lights were out.

Rowdy's melancholy deepened a little.

He secured the jailhouse last, laying kindling and newspaper for a morning fire, emptying the coffeepot and pumping water out in front, by the horse trough, to rinse out the grounds.

His horse and Gideon's were settled in the lean-to barn.

Rowdy went inside the house, wondering what it would be like to have a wife waiting for him. Not just any wife, either.

It was Lark Morgan he imagined greeting him with a warm smile.

He tried to shake off the images, but they stayed with him.

Gideon lay in front of the fireplace, where he'd built himself a blaze, asleep in his bedroll. Pardner had settled right up alongside him, and he lifted his head and looked closely at Rowdy, awaiting a command.

Rowdy sighed. "Good night, Pardner," he said.

Pardner rested his muzzle on his forepaws, let out a weary breath and closed his eyes.

Damnation, Rowdy thought glumly, it was purely a hard thing to give up a dog, even if the process was gradual.

The boiler in the bathtub room was fed by a pipe leading to a tank on the roof, and it was full of fresh water. Rowdy lit a fire under it, wiped the copper tub out, and got soap and a towel from the box of supplies he'd had sent over that morning from the mercantile.

The water was a long time getting hot, but he didn't mind that. He used the time to shake out the bedding and check the mattress for cooties.

The bath was worth waiting for.

Rowdy soaked for a while, then scrubbed. It sure beat using one of the public tubs over at Jolene's.

As soon as the sun came up, he decided, he'd saddle his horse and ride toward Flagstaff. Follow the railroad tracks for a while, and see if he came across his pa.

He leaned back in the tub and closed his eyes.

It wasn't much of a plan, he reckoned, but he had to start someplace. If Pappy had ridden out in the middle of the night, as Gideon said, and with some haste, he'd probably gone to meet up with his gang.

There were plenty of places in the rugged countryside for outlaws to roost.

The old man had asked about Wyatt and the others when Rowdy paid him a call in Flagstaff, acting like he didn't know where any of them were. That didn't mean, of course, that the Yarbro boys weren't around, waiting to rob a train.

Rowdy swore.

What if it wasn't just Pappy he had to find? What if Wyatt and Nick and Ethan and Levi were out there, too?

Pappy liked to conduct "peaceable" robberies, back in the old days, but he was nothing if not unpredictable. There'd been two holdups out of Flagstaff in the recent past, and one of them had ended in gunplay. A man had been shot in the arm and maimed.

There was a distinct possibility that Pappy had changed the way he did things. Age mellowed most folks, but it might not have had that effect on Payton Yarbro. The man was a law unto himself.

He had to find Pappy. That was all there was to it.

Rowdy closed his eyes, drifted off to sleep.

Woke to cold bathwater and what sounded like a hard kick to the side of the copper tub.

Cursing himself for not leaving the .44 within reach like he always did, Rowdy slammed into wakefulness, every muscle tense, ready to fight.

A pistol cocked, and the barrel pressed into the end of his nose.

"Stay right there in that water," Pappy warned. "Don't you move a muscle, you little badge-wearing bastard."

7

PAYTON SAT DOWN HEAVILY on the lid of the commode in Rowdy's bathing room. His hands, with one of his .45s clasped in them by its fancy butt, inlaid with mother-of-pearl, dangled between his knees.

"I'm not little," Rowdy said gravely, "and given my mama's reputation, with absolutely no credit to you, old man, I'm not a bastard, either." He grabbed the towel off the side of the tub, stood and wrapped it around his middle. As his head cleared, he realized he hadn't heard a sound out of Pardner. "You better not have done anything to my dog," he warned.

"Worthless mutt just lifted his head and looked at me as I went by him," Payton said. "He knows I ain't dangerous."

"Tell that to the man on that train, the one with half his right arm shot off," Rowdy said, keeping his voice down on the off chance that Gideon might wake up.

Payton's expression was pained. He needed a shave, not to mention a scrubdown with a wire-bristled brush, and his hair poked out wildly under the edges of his hat.

Given the state of his clothes, he might have been dragged five miles behind a manure wagon.

"I didn't shoot that damn fool," Pappy said, indignant at the suggestion.

Rowdy picked his pants up off the floor, pulled them on, fastened the buttons. "Who did, Pappy?"

"Don't call me 'Pappy.' Makes me sound like some old fart with a hitch in his get-along."

"You *are* an old fart," Rowdy maintained furiously, "and if you don't quit robbing trains, you're going to have more than a *hitch* in your get-along."

"How many times do I have to tell you I've given up robbing trains?"

"You rob trains?" Gideon asked, looming sleepily in the doorway, with a sight more admiration than Rowdy would have liked.

"Shit," Rowdy said.

Payton looked at his youngest son and sighed as he labored slowly up off the lid of the commode. "That was a long time ago, boy," he told Gideon. "I have changed my ways."

Gideon's eyes glowed. "You're an *outlaw?*"

"I *was* an outlaw," Pappy said, giving Rowdy a baleful glance as he spoke. "Though, sadly, there are those who won't let me live it down."

Rowdy snorted at that. Pushed his way past Gideon and almost fell ass-over-teakettle over Pardner, who'd stretched out crossways behind the boy.

"I never heard of any outlaw by the name of Jack Payton," Gideon mused. Evidently, he followed the doings of such men. Probably read dime novels and penny-dreadfuls. Maybe he even admired cold-blooded, pimply little killers like Billy the Kid.

"It's about time you knew the truth about me," Payton told his younger boy, as they all progressed to the center of the house.

"Hell," Rowdy mocked, grabbing the coffeepot off the stove to pump water into it at the sink, "you probably don't *know* the truth about yourself."

"He's got a self-righteous streak in him," Payton told Gideon, jabbing a thumb in Rowdy's direction. "Just like your mama did. Good woman. She could pray the angels right down out of heaven to fetch and carry for her, but she didn't have much patience with lesser folks like me."

Rowdy glared at the old man. "What are you doing here?"

"At least he saved us the trouble of turning the countryside over looking for him," Gideon said, determined, evidently, to fix his attention on the bright side of things.

Figuring there *wasn't* a bright side, Rowdy banged the pot down on top of the stove and scooped coffee into it. Remembered that the brew wasn't going to boil without a fire under it, cursed, and yanked open the door to jam in newspaper and kindling, then light a match to the works.

Pappy sank into one of the three chairs at the table, long-suffering. Yes, sir, he was misunderstood, mistreated and generally a pity to behold—to hear him tell it, anyhow.

A muscle twitched in Rowdy's jaw.

"If my own son won't grant me refuge in my time of trial and tribulation," Pappy murmured, every line of his face and body bemoaning his sorry lot and wrongly inflicted sorrows, "I don't know what I'm going to do."

He was a regular Job. All he lacked was the boils and a pile of dust to sit in.

"I'm your son, too, Pa," Gideon pointed out. "I'll help you."

"Shut up," Rowdy told him. "Go out and put Pappy's horse away, before somebody sees it."

Gideon's face went hard, but he did as he was told.

Pardner didn't make a move to follow him but stuck close to Rowdy, like a burr snagged on his pant leg. It lifted Rowdy's spirits a little, when the dog stayed.

"I asked you not to call me Pappy," Payton said.

"I asked you not to rob trains," Rowdy countered. "I reckon we're even."

"You're not the least bit glad to see me, are you?" Pappy asked, pulling a long face. Then, half under his breath, he scoffed, "Town *marshal*."

"If you're not going to tell me what the hell you're doing here in the middle of the night, then shut the hell up," Rowdy said, banging the stove door closed now that he knew the blaze had caught under the wood he'd added.

"I'm in trouble," Pappy said, all wheedling charm now. "Shovel another spoonful of grounds into that coffeepot. I like it strong."

"What kind of trouble?" Rowdy asked. As if he didn't know.

"There's been a train looted," Pappy said with a shake of his head, as if to marvel that the world had come to such a state. "Twenty miles or so the other side of Flagstaff. The law is sure to blame me for it."

"Pappy," Rowdy said, keeping his voice down in case Gideon came back before time, "I *am* the law—I'm the marshal of Stone Creek. Did it occur to you that I might just throw your worthless ass in the hoosegow and let things take their course from there?"

"No," Pappy said, with certainty. "Because if you did that, I'd naturally have to tell whoever might be inclined to listen that you're my own precious boy, Rob Yarbro, and you showed an early talent for getting in the way of the occasional train yourself."

Behind Rowdy's agitation, which was considerable, trembled a new and fragile hope that he'd be able to stay on in Stone Creek a little longer. All he had to do was get rid of Pappy.

"Don't say that name again," Rowdy ordered, hauling back a second chair and sitting down hard at the table, across from his pa.

"What name?" Pappy asked innocently. "Rob Yarbro?"

Rowdy set his back molars and glanced uneasily toward the door.

"You don't call me Pappy," Pappy bargained craftily, "and I won't call *you* Rob Yarbro."

Rowdy was silent.

Pappy grinned. "Deal?"

"Deal," Rowdy growled, after a long struggle to release his jaw.

"I came here because I didn't know where else to go," Pa said. "I guess I got spooked when I heard about that train."

"You just *heard* about it? Or you were there?"

"All right," Pa admitted. "I was there. Saw the whole

thing. Six riders, all carrying rifles, with their faces covered. They felled a tree across the tracks and piled some brush on it, then lit the whole shebang on fire." He paused and smiled in rueful reflection. "Works every time," he went on. "But, damn it, that's *my* trick. My trademark."

"When did this happen?"

"Today, a little before noon. I had to ride like the devil to get here, and my poor horse is all but done in."

"And there was shooting?"

"One of the riders was wounded." Payton's expression was bleak, recalling the scene. "The way the bullets flew, I'd say some of the passengers must have been hit, too. Nobody fought back, far as I could tell, when the bandits went in to get the strongbox, and they were in there a long time, too. Came out whooping like a bunch of cowpokes on a binge, and one of them was wearing the contents of some lady's jewelry box. Reminded me of some of the Indian raids, back in the old days."

Rowdy swore.

The coffeepot began to rattle on the stove.

"Did you recognize any of the outlaws?" Rowdy asked, and held his breath for the answer.

Not Wyatt, he prayed silently. *Not Nick or Ethan or Levi. Please, not them.*

"Not a Yarbro in the bunch," Pa said confidently. "Is that coffee about ready?"

"You said the robbers had their faces covered," Rowdy persisted. "How can you be sure it wasn't a family reunion?"

"I know my own boys when I see them," Pa insisted,

a little affronted. "Bare-faced or with a bandanna hiding their features. Anyhow, none of your brothers would shoot anybody."

"But they *would* build a fire to stop the train," Rowdy reminded him.

"I remember when that was your job," Pa said, smiling fondly. Some men recalled going fishing with their sons, or teaching them to ride or whittle. Payton Yarbro had taught *his* boys—except, mercifully, for Gideon—to carry out a holdup with finesse, and subsequently evade some of the best lawmen in the country.

The hinges of Rowdy's jaw ached. "Now what, Pa?"

"I need to rest. Lay low a few days. Then I'll require money and a fresh horse. You go to Ruby, after the dust of my hasty departure settles, and she'll make good on whatever you have to spend. Tell her I'll send for her when I get where I'm going."

"What makes you think I have money?"

Pa grinned. "You always had the damnedest knack for turning fifty cents into a five-dollar gold piece, even since you were that high." He raised his grimy hand, palm down, about level with the tabletop. "You've got money."

Just then Gideon banged in from outside.

"That horse," he said, "is fair run down to a nubbin. Somebody been chasing you, Pa? Due to your being an outlaw and all?"

"For the last time, Gideon," Payton said, drawing his trail-worn self up with a scruffy kind of dignity, "I am retired from that life. You think Ruby Hollister would take up with a common outlaw?"

"I think Ruby Hollister might *be* an outlaw," Gideon

speculated cheerfully, helping himself to the third chair at the table. "I reckon I might like to be one, too."

Rowdy hadn't had time to develop a particular attachment to the boy, but he knew what it meant to live outside the clear boundaries of the law, and he wasn't about to let Gideon take that path if he could help it. "Like hell you will—"

Pa's words ran right over the top of Rowdy's, like a bunch of thirsty cattle stampeding for a water hole. "You're staying right here with your brother!"

Both Gideon and Rowdy turned to stare at Payton.

"Staying here?" Gideon echoed.

"With me?" Rowdy asked.

"Safest place there is," Pa said, rocking a little in his chair and looking satisfied with his own brilliance.

"I don't see how you figure that," Rowdy said. When he'd told Gideon to come to Stone Creek if he ever needed help, he'd meant what he said, straight up and solid. He just hadn't expected it to be any kind of long-term deal, that was all.

"By now," Pa explained, with exaggerated patience, "the telegraph wires are buzzing with the news of that train robbery. Come tomorrow morning, Flagstaff will be crawling with railroad agents and rangers—" He halted, smiling, perhaps relishing the image of all that fuss being raised on his account. "And they're all going to think I'm behind it. Ruby and me, we've lived real quiet, on purpose, all these years, but somebody's bound to pick up the trail at least as far as her saloon." Again Pa stopped talking, and he had the good grace to frown at what came next. "I don't want Gideon dragged into this."

There was a flaw in Payton's logic—Rowdy was a Yarbro, and if anybody figured that out, like Sam O'Ballivan, for instance, the trail wouldn't end at Ruby's Saloon. It would lead right to the marshal's office at Stone Creek.

"Maybe you ought to go back east early," Rowdy said to Gideon.

"Doesn't anybody want me around?" Gideon demanded.

Pardner whimpered, raised himself onto his haunches and laid his muzzle on Gideon's thigh.

Gideon stroked the dog's head.

Rowdy felt another pang, one that had nothing to do with the topic under discussion.

"You'll stay right here," Pa said to Gideon, though his blue gaze drilled into Rowdy's as he spoke, "and that's the end of it."

WHEN LARK CAME DOWN for breakfast the next morning, Mai Lee was at the stove, as if nothing had happened, frying eggs and humming a tune. Mrs. Porter was there, too, looking much restored, and busily brushing copious dust from a gentleman's suit coat.

"Mr. Porter's birthday is coming up on Saturday," she said. "He always liked to make an occasion of it."

Lark glanced at Mai Lee, hoping for enlightenment, but the cook kept her small back to the room and hummed a little more loudly.

"And of course I'll have to bake a rum cake. Mr. Porter did favor my rum cake over anything else."

Don't ask, Lark instructed herself firmly, glancing at the calendar, with the red circle marking Saturday's date.

"Thank heaven Mai Lee will be here to help me with the preparations," Mrs. Porter rattled on. "She and Hon Sing won't be moving until the ground thaws out enough to plant vegetables."

Relieved, Lark smiled and helped herself to a cup of hot coffee. "I was wondering if I might put some of my things in Mr. Rhodes's room, after school lets out," she said. Then, at Mrs. Porter's quick glance, she blushed and added, "Since he's going to be occupying other quarters from now on."

"He's paid up to the first of the week," Mrs. Porter said.

Lark went to the doorway of the spacious room, looked with longing at the fireplace and the feather bed and the writing desk and the small table with two chairs. It would be almost like having her own home again, what with the separate entrance, and she'd be *warm.*

"I suppose it would be all right if you used the room," Mrs. Porter mused, sounding less uncertain than before. She was right at Lark's elbow, but for once, Lark had heard her approaching, so she wasn't startled. "Of course, if another renter comes along, you'll have to give it up. I can't have gentlemen sleeping *upstairs,* you know. It just wouldn't be proper."

Lark smiled down at Mrs. Porter. "I won't bring everything down," she promised. "Just my nightdress and my hairbrush."

Mrs. Porter patted her arm. "That's fine, dear," she said.

A loud knock at the kitchen door made both women turn.

Rowdy, Lark thought, with a little rise of her heart.

But it wasn't Rowdy, she discovered, when Mai Lee answered the door. Roland Franks stood on the step, looking earnest and shy.

"I come to drive you to school, Miss Morgan," he said, blushing. His ears were red with the cold, and with the embarrassment of presenting himself at a town woman's door. "Pa said it was all right, so I brung the buckboard."

Lark could think of no gracious way to refuse. She did not want to give Roland the wrong idea, but she didn't want to hurt his feelings, either. Lord only knew how long he'd been working up his courage to do her this kindness.

"That's very considerate of you, Roland," she said.

Mrs. Porter, meanwhile, stared at Roland in what might have been alarm. He made even her big kitchen seem small and cramped, and there was a sense that if he moved suddenly, he might send every dish in the room crashing to the floor.

Roland went even redder. Fidgeted with his worn hat, clasped tightly in both hands. "I'll just wait in the buckboard until you're ready," he said, and turned to go out.

Mrs. Porter looked as though she might rush over and lock the door behind him. "Merciful heavens, Lark," she whispered urgently, "that bear of a man is *courting* you!"

"He's only offering me a ride to school," Lark said.

"I kept my opinions to myself when Beaver Franks signed up for third grade," Mrs. Porter insisted, "but *this*—"

Lark reached for her cloak, the lunch Mai Lee had prepared for her, and her lesson and attendance books.

"In the unlikely event that *Roland* has…hopes where I'm concerned, I will tell him as gently as possible that I'm not interested," she assured her landlady.

"I tell you, he's looking to take himself a *wife,*" Mrs. Porter fretted. "And he's got you in mind for a bride!"

"Don't be silly," Lark said. "I'm his teacher."

"He's a grown man and you're an unmarried woman—"

"Please don't worry," Lark said.

"But you haven't even had breakfast!"

In point of fact, Lark was ravenously hungry, but she knew that the longer Roland's team and buckboard stood in front of the rooming house, the quicker word would spread. With luck she could persuade him to take the back way to school, along Second Street, and they would not be noticed.

"I'll be fine," Lark said.

Stepping outside, she saw that the sky was overcast, the clouds heavy with the possibility of snow. Roland sat rigidly upright in the box of his father's buckboard, his bare red hands clasping the reins.

Seeing Lark, he flushed again, jumped down from the wagon and waited to help her up into the seat.

She had, foolishly, not anticipated this part—the necessity of Roland touching her in the process of assisting her into the conveyance. The seat of the buckboard was on a level with her head, and there was no step or rung, as a carriage would have had.

She was still deliberating on the logistics of the problem when Roland suddenly grabbed her by the waist and swung her up. She landed on the hard seat with a thump that practically cracked her tailbone.

"Oh, my," she said.

Roland rounded the wagon and climbed up next to her, tilting the rig on its axles with his weight. The ancient team, a pair of shaggy gray farm horses, shifted within their worn harnesses, as if bracing themselves to pull again.

They lurched into motion with a great clattering of wheels and wagon fittings and hooves over rutted ground, and Lark might have been thrown clear if she hadn't gripped the edges of the seat in both hands.

Roland cleared his throat and then shouted over the din, "I reckon you know there's a dance at the Cattleman's Hall this Saturday night!"

Lark barely refrained from squeezing her eyes shut. *Oh, no,* she thought.

Instead of taking the wide path leading to the schoolhouse, Roland steered straight for the main street of town.

"I'm not much of a dancer," Roland yelled, making Lark want to cover her ears with both hands. She might have, too, if she hadn't needed to hold on so tightly to the wagon seat. "But I'd admire to escort you, Miss Morgan!"

They were almost to the jailhouse, and several people passing by on the sidewalks turned to stare at the spectacle of the schoolmarm and the twenty-two-year-old third-grader in the wagon seat beside her, booming out that he wanted to take her to the Saturday-night dance.

Desperate, Lark laid a hand on Roland's arm. "Roland," she called, "please stop this wagon."

Instantly abashed, he drew up directly in front of Rowdy's office.

"I didn't mean here," she said, flustered.

Rowdy should have been off marshaling, rounding up miscreants or something, but instead he came strolling out of the jailhouse, a little grin curving one side of his mouth. His gaze, resting briefly on Roland, was as icy as the creek the town was named for.

"I can't go to the dance with you, Roland," Lark said miserably, figuring she might as well get the refusal over with. After all, she'd *asked* him to stop the wagon.

"Why not?" Roland asked, his face darkening and his hands tightening on the reins.

"Because she's going with me," Rowdy said mildly, setting aside the coffeepot he was carrying and coming to stand next to the wagon, looking up at Lark.

He was the first man she'd ever encountered who could communicate with his eyes. They clearly asked, *Are you all right?*

She felt her face go warm. "Yes," she said, with a gulp. "That's right. I've already promised to go to the dance with Marshal Rhodes."

"And anyway," Rowdy put in helpfully, "it wouldn't do for a teacher to keep company with one of her students."

"It ain't against no laws!" Roland protested. All his shyness was gone, replaced by venomous ire. His small eyes bulged, and even his dull red hair seemed to stand a little on end.

"I'd like a word with you before school starts, Miss Morgan," Rowdy said pointedly, raising his hands to help her down. Waiting. "About my brother Gideon."

Lark leaned toward him, fretful and distracted. She should have listened to Mrs. Porter and made up some polite excuse for not riding in Roland's wagon. She had indeed given the poor man the wrong impression by agreeing in the first place, and now she was in an uncomfortable situation because of it.

Rowdy's hands felt blessedly strong as he set them on either side of her waist and lifted her easily down from the wagon box. It was odd, how different one man's touch could feel from another's; Roland's grip had an aspect of clutching to it, where Rowdy's was light and easy.

Despite that, Lark was shaken, placing herself in Rowdy's hands that way. They were making a scene folks would probably gossip about for weeks.

Did you see that schoolteacher, riding right through the middle of town with Beaver Franks, bold as you please?

She's from someplace else, you know. Just turned up here one day in her big-city clothes, and took over the schoolhouse like she owned it.

She's no better than she should be.

"This ain't right," Roland said, glowering, trembling all over like a mountain with a geyser about to shoot off its top from the inside.

"Move along," Rowdy told him quietly.

"I'll see you at school, Roland," Lark said warmly, trying to pretend she hadn't just made a complete and utter fool of herself in front of all of Stone Creek proper and half the countryside.

Pardner came out of the jailhouse and nudged at the back of her right hand with the cold, wet end of his nose.

Rowdy left Lark standing on the sidewalk with Pardner to round the team.

Roland lifted the reins slightly, as though tempted to run him down.

"I asked you to move along," Rowdy said from the other side of the wagon.

Roland hawked and spat, missing Rowdy by inches. "She's mine," he snarled. "I saw her first!"

Lark blinked. The whole wagon shook, and then Roland was toppling sideways out of the wagon. She rushed around the back only to see her student lying on his back in the road, with his arms and legs spread wide.

By now spectators had gathered.

Roland's face contorted with hatred, but he was a moment getting his breath—a moment Lark used to pray frantically, albeit silently, that he wouldn't get up and tear Rowdy limb from bloody limb.

"Roland Franks," she said, summoning all her authority as a schoolteacher, "you behave yourself!"

He eased himself up onto his elbows, dazed. "You had no call to drag me out of my own wagon that way," he said to Rowdy, wheezing a little. "I could have got hurt."

"You *will* get hurt," Rowdy said, "if you ever try to spit on me again."

"You think you can take me—Marshal?" Roland shook himself, but he didn't get up off the ground. He'd gone a muddy shade of crimson and, despite the cold, he was sweating.

"I know I can," Rowdy replied, with such cold certainty that a little chill ran down Lark's spine. He unbuckled his gun belt and handed it off to Gideon, who had been a mere flicker at the edge of Lark's vision a moment before but had now solidified at Rowdy's side. "If you'd like to settle the question once and for all, just get up."

Roland sat cross-legged in the dirt. "I could be

injured," he said. "It wouldn't be right to hit a man who's injured." His gaze swung, resentful, to Lark. "I ain't comin' to school no more," he added. "I got my pride."

Rowdy stepped back so Roland could stand.

Roland lumbered to his feet, swayed and then climbed up into his buckboard. He released the brake lever with a screech, slapped the reins down on the horses' backs, turned the wagon in a wide loop in the middle of the street and headed the other way.

Lark closed her eyes, mortified.

Now, thanks to her, Roland would never read beyond a third-grade level.

"It's over, folks," Rowdy told the gawking townspeople, startling Lark by taking hold of her arm and propelling her in the direction of his office. "Go on about your business."

He all but flung her over the threshold.

"Gideon," he told his brother, gesturing, "you go over to the schoolhouse—it's around the next bend and down the hill—and tell the kids today's a holiday."

Gideon scrambled to obey.

Lark sputtered. After several false starts, she said, "You have no right to cancel an entire day of school!"

"Miss Morgan," Rowdy said, grim-jawed, "I just did."

"By what authority?" How was she going to explain this to the parents? Some of those children traveled miles to attend class.

"By the authority of the Rhodes Ordinance," Rowdy replied.

"The Rhodes—"

"Ordinance," Rowdy finished for her. "When I need

a law, I usually just make one up." He gestured toward the open doorway of the jailhouse. "There's bad weather coming. Like as not, you'd have had an empty classroom anyhow."

Narrow-eyed, Lark looked past him and saw flat, lazy flakes of snow drifting down, thickening fast to fury.

8

PAYTON YARBRO SETTLED himself contentedly in Rowdy's fancy copper bathtub, up to his chin in water hot enough to scald the hide off a boar. He took a swig from his flask, then set it aside, clamped a cheroot between his teeth and lit it with a match, after making two tries because of the heavy steam.

There was a special softness to the air, a certain muffled purity like the silent chime of some celestial bell. Payton knew, even without a window to look through, that the snow had finally come.

He sighed, thankful he'd made it to Rowdy's before the ground was blanketed in white. He'd have left a clear trail then, and probably frozen his ass off into the bargain.

He wished he could send Ruby a telegram, since she'd surely have heard about the train robbery by now, and let her know he was all right. He didn't dare contact her so directly, of course, because the law would be keeping track of whatever came and went over the wire. He'd stay right where he was until he'd rested up a little. Once Rowdy got him a horse and staked him to some traveling money, he meant to head straight for the Mexican border.

A bang from the main part of the house made him stiffen, then reach over the side of the tub to grab one of his .45s off the floor. He cocked the pistol and waited.

The door of the bathing room swung open, and Payton nearly shot the damn dog.

"Dern fool critter, sneaking up on a man like that," he scolded. "I almost blew a hole right through you."

Pardner approached and stuck his nose over the side of the bathtub, shoved it right into the side of Payton's bare arm. It made for an unpleasant contrast to the luxurious heat of the bathwater, and he flinched.

"Get out of here," he grumbled, but not too forcefully. He wasn't much for keeping useless critters around a place, but this one made quiet and undemanding company.

The dog sat down on his hind end and panted, in no recognizable hurry to get lost.

"Pa?"

It was Gideon's voice, coming from outside the door.

Payton set the .45 down and reached for the flask again. "Can't a man bathe in peace around this place?" he grumbled. "What do you *want,* boy?"

"Rowdy's in the marshal's office, sparking the schoolmarm," Gideon answered. "I figured while he's busy, I'd come and talk to you about letting me ride out with you when you go."

"You'd slow me down," Payton answered. "You don't know shit about horses or shooting, and I'd have to wet-nurse you all the way to Juarez." He winced. He hadn't meant to give away his intended destination.

"Is that where you're going? Juarez?"

"No," Payton lied and, to his exasperating credit, Gideon did not believe him.

"You wouldn't have to worry about me at all, Pa. I could keep up. I swear I could. And I could help, too—"

"You'll stay right here in Stone Creek, like I told you," Payton answered sternly, though it bruised him a little, hearing the plea in Gideon's voice, having to refuse his companionship. Of all his sons, he was closest to this one, the youngest, the one he'd had a daily hand in raising. Unlike his brothers, Gideon wasn't an outlaw—yet—and Payton still had hopes for him. "You aren't wanted for anything," he said more gently. "And I'd like to keep it that way. You ride with me, the law will have business with you from that day forward."

Gideon's sigh was audible even through the half-closed door. "You want me to ride over to Flagstaff and see about Ruby? I've got to return that livery stable horse anyhow. And I have a little money stashed in the shed back home. I could buy myself another mount and get you one, too."

Payton pondered the offer, decided it had merit.

"You come back here with two horses, folks will be suspicious," he said. "Still, I am concerned about Ruby. You go there, boy, and you return that horse and tell her I said to get you another one and take a thousand dollars out of the safe. She's not to go near the bank to make a withdrawal—you make that real clear. And you don't say anything to anybody else. Ruby will give you some grief about the money. You just stand your ground until she gives over, though, because this could mean your old pa's life, boy. You understand that?"

"Yes, sir," Gideon said gravely. "I reckon I ought to go right now."

"No," Payton answered. "You do that, and Rowdy'll be right on you. Wait till tonight, after he's gone to sleep." He leaned forward and turned a spigot, so more hot water flowed into the tub. "Leave me to my bath, now, boy. And call this dog. He's staring at me like I just sprouted a pair of horns or something."

"Pardner," Gideon said, sounding glum, "come along."

The dog got up, turned a half circle, and left, slinking past the edge of the partially open door.

When the last of the hot water was gone, Payton got out of the tub, dried himself off, and donned the clean clothes he'd borrowed from the marshal of Stone Creek.

The marshal of Stone Creek. Payton smiled at that august title.

Miranda would have been real proud, sure that her darling boy had finally seen the light. Rowdy had been, for all practical intents and purposes, the baby of her brood, since she hadn't lived long enough even to hold Gideon in her arms, let alone get to know him. He'd been a particular favorite with her, Rowdy had.

Poor, naive Miranda. In that moment Payton missed her with a swift ferocity that fairly took his breath away. It came when he least expected it, this keen sense of loss, brutal and sharp-edged.

He leaned across the slowly emptying tub to retrieve the .45 and the flask.

Right then he couldn't have said which one he needed more.

LARK REFUSED Rowdy's offer to walk her home to Mrs. Porter's place, even though the snowstorm was already working itself up to a fine frenzy. If it kept this up, it would be a blizzard before nightfall.

"Some of the children may have come to school," she fretted.

Rowdy supposed there was some substance to her concern. He'd seen this storm coming before dawn, felt it in his bones as he sat up through the night. He'd had no place to sleep, with his pa sprawled facedown across his bed like he was gut-shot. It seemed unlikely that farm and ranch people wouldn't have seen the signs, and kept their kids home from school, but it was surely possible. The weather hadn't stopped Franks from driving to town, after all.

Rowdy had sent Gideon to the schoolhouse earlier, but he hadn't seen him since, so he didn't know whether any of the kids had showed up there or not. And there might have been a few stragglers, arriving after Gideon left.

"All right," Rowdy said, strapping on the gun belt he'd taken off earlier, thinking he might get the satisfaction of pounding the hell out of Franks, and reaching for his hat and coat. "We'll go down there and make sure."

"I can get to the schoolhouse on my own," Lark protested, but she didn't look as though she really wanted to try it.

"I reckon you can," Rowdy agreed, opening the door. "But I'm going with you, just the same." He was worried that Franks might still be around, waiting for a chance to press his case with Lark, and there was always the possibility that the storm would suddenly get a lot worse.

He'd known folks to freeze to death in this kind of weather, rounding up cows in their own pastures, and even in the short distance between the house and the woodshed.

Lark double-stepped to keep up when he took her arm and strode in the direction of the schoolhouse. Pardner joined them, snapping at the occasional snowflake like a pup, and his presence eased Rowdy's tension a little.

He'd been all wound up, ever since his pa had chosen his place as a rabbit hole.

"About the dance on Saturday night," Lark began, her breath huffing white in the snowy air as she hurried along at his side.

Rowdy gave her a sidelong glance, reluctantly let go of her once they'd crossed the road. "You're not about to back out on me, are you?"

She looked at him in quick surprise. "I assumed you were only trying to help me out of a—situation."

He smiled to himself, but he knew by the flare of color in her cheeks that she'd seen his amusement. "Roland Franks is a 'situation,' all right," he agreed. "If you care anything for his pride, you'll be at the dance, just like you said you would be. And you'll be with me."

"I can't see how that would appease his pride."

"You don't see a lot of things, Miss Morgan. What possessed you to let a full-grown man come to school?"

"He wanted to learn!"

"You can't possibly be that innocent."

She stared at him, angry, but worried, too. "He said—"

"He *said,* Miss Morgan, what he knew you wanted to hear."

"Stop calling me 'Miss Morgan.' I don't like the way you say it—like you're mocking me."

"I am mocking you—Lark. When are you going to tell me your real name?"

"When you tell me yours," Lark retorted. "Perhaps."

He was tired and, blizzard or none, he expected news of the train robbery his pa had told him about to arrive at any moment. Most likely there would be a telegram sent to Sam O'Ballivan or the major, and once it had been delivered to the ranch, they'd be riding in to demand some rangering of him.

In the meantime, he had to pretend he didn't know anything about it.

The combination of circumstances made him prickly.

"I do not have the time," he said, "to keep you out of trouble, *Lark,* so I would appreciate it if you would use your head for something other than a decoration. Franks didn't come to school so he could learn the three *R*s."

She blushed. "You have no responsibility to keep me out of trouble," she blustered. "And *I* would appreciate it if you didn't make disparaging remarks about my intelligence. I have read Shakespeare, *Mr.* Rhodes, and all the Greek and Roman myths—"

"So have I," he said, enjoying the look of surprise that sprang into her eyes. "And I've got to say, I haven't found that accomplishment real handy, out here at the tail end of noplace."

Lark bit her lower lip. "Knowledge," she said firmly,

blowing out the words because the wind was against her, "is valuable everywhere."

"Not if you don't use it," Rowdy argued.

She fell silent, and he hoped he hadn't hurt her feelings. Somebody else had done plenty of that, in some other time and place, and he didn't want to add to it.

"I'm sorry, Lark," he said, as they reached the hill above the schoolhouse. Even with its belfry and bright red walls, it barely showed through the swirling snow. "I've got some things on my mind, but I shouldn't have taken that out on you."

She blinked, then smiled. Snowflakes gathered on her thick lashes, and she raised the hood of her cloak in a graceful motion of both hands.

"That was a very nice apology," she said.

He grinned at her.

They descended the hill and rounded the edge of the schoolyard, the tops of the fence posts already mounded with snow, and there, on the front step, sure as death and taxes, huddled Pardner's little friend, shivering.

"Lydia!" Lark cried, horrified.

Rowdy barely managed to get the gate open before she would have vaulted over it in her haste to reach the child.

Lydia smiled at them through the tumbling, blowing snow.

Lark sat down beside the little girl, opened her cloak to enclose her inside it, then rummaged in her pocket for the key. Rowdy took that from her, stepped past them to unlock the door and open it.

Lark got to her feet and hurried Lydia into the schoolhouse.

Rowdy went straight to the stove and got a fire started,

"Lydia," Lark said, chafing the child's bare hands between her own, "why didn't you go home when you arrived and no one was here? And where are your mittens?"

"I lost one of them." Lydia batted her eyelashes, on the verge of tears. "Did I do wrong coming to school, Miss Morgan?"

Lark hugged her, and the sight made Rowdy's throat hurt, the same way it did when he thought of riding out and leaving Pardner behind with Gideon.

"No, sweetheart," she said quickly, glancing once at Rowdy, in a silent I-told-you-so kind of way. "No, you didn't do a single thing wrong."

Rowdy felt knee-high to a bedbug. Lydia probably would have sat there on that step until she iced up solid if Lark hadn't insisted on making sure none of her charges had come to school.

He got the fire going, then took off his coat and wrapped it gently around Lydia's tiny form. She looked lost in the dark folds, and smiled up out of the garment with beatific trust.

"Lydia," Lark repeated, sitting down beside the child on one of the long benches students normally occupied, "why did you stay?"

Lydia's lower lip wobbled. "Mabel's feeling poorly," she said, her voice very small, even for somebody the size of a newly hatched barn sparrow. "She told me not to come home until I could be quiet, and I don't reckon I'm *ever* going to be able to do that."

Lark raised her eyes to Rowdy's face, and something passed between them, though neither of them spoke right away.

"Lydia," Lark asked presently, "where is your father?"

"Papa's way out to the Bennington ranch," Lydia answered. "He went yesterday, in his buggy. They're having a baby out there." Her small face brightened. "It's the first one, so they wanted a doctor to come. Papa helped them pull a stuck calf out of a cow last spring, and they gave him a whole bag of sweet potatoes."

Lark blushed, probably because of the stuck-calf image. "Let's sit a little closer to the fire," she told Lydia, "now that Marshal Rhodes has been so kind as to start it."

Lydia allowed herself to be steered to another seat, but her eyes were wide and suddenly pensive as she looked up at Rowdy. "Marshal, do you suppose my papa will be able to get home, with all this snow?"

"Tell you what," Rowdy said. "If he's not back in the next little while, I'll go out looking for him."

Lark spared him a grateful look, unwrapped Lydia from his coat and replaced it with her cloak. "We'll stay here for a little while," she said. "But I think Marshal Rhodes has things to do."

Rowdy didn't want to leave them, but Lark was right. He *did* have things to do, and searching the road between Stone Creek and the Bennington ranch, wherever that was, would be one of them, if the doc didn't show up pretty soon.

"Lock the door when I'm gone," he said, resigned, as he put the coat back on. He checked the wood supply and found it adequate.

"We never lock the schoolhouse," Lydia said, earnestly helpful. "Not when there's somebody inside."

"Just this once," Lark told her softly. "Later, when you're warm, we'll go to Mrs. Porter's and sit in her kitchen by the stove and drink tea."

Lydia's small, thin face went luminous at the prospect.

Rowdy headed for the door, and Lark followed.

"Perhaps you ought to stay," she whispered. "I know I said you had work to do, but the weather—"

"I'll be fine," Rowdy answered, wanting to touch her. Maybe brush her cheek lightly with the backs of his fingers. He didn't, of course, because they were in a schoolhouse, and Lydia was there, and both those things made it more than improper. "You've got plenty of firewood, and I could send Gideon to get you in a wagon from the livery stable. I'll come myself, if I don't have to leave town to look for the doctor."

Lark moved a little closer to him, lowered her voice another notch, until it was barely more than a breath. "You might stop at Dr. Fairmont's house and see about Mabel," she suggested.

Rowdy's jaw tightened. "Oh, I'll speak to Mabel, all right," he promised.

Lark nodded. "If she answers the door, and she might not, tell her I will keep Lydia with me overnight."

"I'll tell her," Rowdy confirmed. Then he cleared his throat and said quietly, "Lock this door, Lark. Franks is probably home, sitting close by the fire, but if he's not—"

"I'll lock the door," Lark promised. She touched his face, her fingertips light and smooth and still cold from outside. Then she pulled them back, as though she'd done something inexcusably bold.

He wanted to kiss her. Wanted to but didn't, for the same reasons he hadn't caressed her cheek moments before.

"About Gideon and the wagon—"

"We'll be fine on our own, Rowdy. Really."

He nodded, opened the door, careful not to let the bitter wind sweep inside the schoolhouse, and went outside.

Waited until he heard her key turn in the lock.

Then, not wanting to leave, he did anyway.

LYDIA, STILL SNUGGLED in Lark's cloak, yawned, lay down on the long bench closest to the stove and went to sleep. Lark straightened all the books and dusted all the shelves and desks, and watched through the windows as the snow spun against the glass.

The big clock behind her desk ticked ponderously.

Lark checked the level of water in the drinking pail and found it nearly empty. She had tea leaves and a kettle on hand, but Lydia was swaddled in her cloak, and she knew the cold air would bite into her flesh if she went out without it to the well.

She was hungry, too, and she'd left her lunch in Roland's wagon, along with her lesson books. Remembering the morning's incident, she cringed.

Then she felt ashamed.

She was making too much of this.

Roland would probably show up for school tomorrow and bring back the things she'd left behind in his wagon. He would surely apologize, and Lark, keeping in mind that she had contributed to the misunderstanding by accepting a ride to school in his buckboard, would accept graciously.

Franks didn't come to school so he could learn the three R*s*, she heard Rowdy say.

A momentary disquiet rose up in Lark, and she frowned.

Rowdy didn't understand, that was all. He couldn't put himself in Roland's place, imagine what it would be like to be full grown and still unable to read. It was a dreadful hardship, and Roland, instead of pretending to be literate, as other people did, had had the courage to come to school and ask for help.

No, Rowdy simply didn't understand.

Feeling much better now that she'd reasoned things through, Lark decided to brew a pot of tea. There was still a little water in the pail, after all, and she could put on her cloak and go outside for more after Lydia woke up.

Lydia did not wake up when the tea was ready.

Lark added wood to the fire, sat down at her desk and sipped from the cup she'd found on a shelf in the storeroom the day she'd undertaken her duties as Stone Creek's one and only schoolteacher.

Darkness began to gather at the windows.

Lark bent over Lydia, frowning, and touched a hand to the child's forehead. Her flesh was so hot that Lark actually flinched.

"Lydia?" she said softly, not wanting to frighten the little girl.

Lydia moaned, opened her eyes halfway. The whites glittered eerily in the dimness.

Hastily Lark found the lanterns she kept on hand for dark winter afternoons and lit one.

"Lydia?" she repeated, drawing closer to the child. "Sweetheart, wake up. I've made you some tea."

Lydia's eyelids fluttered, and she made a slight whimpering sound, but she didn't respond in any other way.

Lark set the lantern aside and cupped Lydia's face in the palms of both hands. Dear God, the child was ablaze with fever.

Lark took her gently by the shoulders. "Lydia!" she whispered hoarsely, "Lydia, *please*—"

"Water," Lydia pleaded, her voice so small and raw and dry that Lark's panic deepened with a lurch.

She'd used the last of the water to prepare her tea.

"Just a minute," she told Lydia, as calmly as she could. "I'll get you some water right away."

Lydia began to shiver violently, even though her flesh was hot to the touch. Lark wrapped the cloak more closely around the child, who flailed weakly against it, then rushed to fetch the bucket. She'd never drawn water from a well—she'd always sent one of the bigger boys out to do that.

What if she couldn't make the mechanism work?

What if the well was already frozen over?

She paused on the schoolhouse threshold, braced by the rush of wind that slammed into her the instant she opened the door.

Rowdy. Where was Rowdy?

Why hadn't he come back, or sent Gideon?

Because she'd told him she and Lydia would be all right, and he'd believed her. By now he was probably out in this awful storm himself, looking for Dr. Fairmont.

Lark pulled the door closed against the heavy force of the wind, and dashed to the well. Dropped the bucket and grabbed the handle attached to the crank.

It wouldn't turn.

She struggled.

The handle wouldn't budge.

Panic seized her again—she wanted to scream, but who would hear her? The storm muffled all sound, and she could barely see the schoolhouse, near as it was. The town beyond was cloaked in darkness and snow.

Snow.

Desperately exultant, Lark began gathering up handfuls of the stuff, plopping them into the bucket she'd brought from inside. When she had it half-full, she hoisted it—it was heavy in her numb hands—and hurried back toward the door.

Collided with a huge form on the steps.

Roland.

For all her high-minded attitude earlier, when she'd decided to accept Roland's apology, should he offer one, and go on with his education as if nothing had happened, fear scalded through her like venom.

"Miss Morgan?"

But it *wasn't* Roland.

It was Gideon, looming there, barely discernible.

A sob escaped Lark, tore itself painfully from her throat. "Gideon," she wept. "Oh, Gideon—"

He took the bucket from her hand, opened the door and steered her inside, much as his older brother had done, when they'd come to the schoolhouse together and found Lydia sitting on the step.

"Lydia—she's one of my students. She's sick."

Gideon looked into the bucket. "What do you want snow for?"

"Water. Lydia needs water, and I couldn't make the well handle turn. When it melts…"

"I'll get the water," Gideon said. "You go stand by the stove. You shouldn't have been out there without a coat or anything."

Lark nodded. Sat down and gathered Lydia in her arms, cloak and all.

Gideon returned quickly with the water.

"There's a ladle on the bench," Lark told him, rocking the child. Lydia's clothes were drenched in perspiration. Even if Gideon had a wagon, they wouldn't be able to take her out in this cold.

He fetched the ladle.

Her hand shaking, Lark dunked it into the bucket, lifted it to Lydia's mouth so she could take a sip. She lay immobile in Lark's arms, though, her eyes still partially open, beyond the ability to drink.

Frantic, Lark dipped her index finger into the ladle, and placed it on Lydia's tongue. The child stirred. Lark dunked her finger again. If she had to give Lydia that whole bucket of water, drop by drop, she'd do it.

"I'd fetch Rowdy, but he's gone," Gideon said uncertainly. "I was just passing by, on my way to Flagstaff, and I saw the lantern light and wondered what you were doing here so late—"

"I'm thankful that you came, Gideon," Lark said, trying the ladle again, because Lydia seemed to be rallying, though only slightly. "Do you happen to know if Dr. Fairmont has returned to town?"

"I think that's who Rowdy went looking for," Gideon answered, after shaking his head once. His eyes widened as he watched Lydia struggle to take even a sip of the water she needed so desperately. "That's why I—"

"That's why you were traveling to Flagstaff in this terrible weather," Lark observed. "Gideon, I can't tell you how foolish I think that is. What if you got lost along the way, or your horse went lame? You would die of exposure, that's what."

"Tell me what I ought to do," he said, visibly shouldering her gentle rebuke. He was Rowdy's brother. Likely he was stubborn. He was also brave, and he'd stopped by the schoolhouse to look in on her when he might have gone on. "Snow's deep. I could get a wagon down the hill all right, but back up, that would be another matter."

Lark was trying hard not to imagine the very same perils she'd described to Gideon happening to Rowdy—perhaps at that moment he was lost, or simply so paralyzed by the cold that he couldn't sit his horse any longer. "Go to Mrs. Porter's, Gideon. Tell her what the situation is, and bring back as many blankets as she has to spare. We'll wrap Lydia up warm and you can take her back to the rooming house on your horse."

"What about you, Miss Morgan? You can't stay here by yourself."

"I'll be perfectly fine until you've gotten Lydia safely to Mrs. Porter's. You can come back for me then, if you're not too cold to ride." She paused, looking up at this sturdy young man, little more than a boy, really. "You can find your way to the rooming house, can't you, Gideon?"

He pushed back his shoulders. "Of course I can," he said.

"Go, then. And Gideon—be careful."

Gideon hesitated, touched Lydia's fevered head with a curiously gentle gesture. "Don't you die, little girl," he murmured, his eyes haunted. "Don't you die."

And then he was gone.

He returned twenty long minutes later, his arms full of folded quilts.

Lydia had taken more water during his absence, but she was half-delirious and followed his movements with large, frightened eyes. Lark stripped the child to the skin while Gideon stood with his back turned, then wrapped Lydia in several of Mrs. Porter's quilts, swaddling her like an infant.

"Gideon is Marshal Rhodes's brother," Lark explained, when Lydia shrank from him. "He's going to take you to Mrs. Porter's house."

"I'm Pardner's friend, too," Gideon said, taking Lydia from Lark's arms. "You know Pardner, don't you?"

9

ROWDY COULDN'T FEEL his feet—took it on trust that they were still at the end of his legs and in the stirrups where they belonged—and it was a fortunate thing he'd borrowed an old dray horse at the livery, instead of riding Paint. The nag was slower than cold honey in the bottom of a flat pan, but it plodded stolidly through the ever-deepening snow and seemed to know where the trail was, which was more than Rowdy could claim.

He kept his hat brim pulled down low over his face and wore a bandanna to keep from getting frostbite, but the truth was, his clothes were suited more to Haven's temperate climate than the high country.

And he kept riding.

Rounding a bend, he came on the buggy, little more than a distinctive shape in the stinging gloom, though the odd stray moonbeam got through somehow. The horse was still upright, and so was the rig, but that was about all Rowdy could discern, until he got closer.

The doctor sat upright in the buggy seat, the reins still in his hands.

And he was dead.

Rowdy's first thought was of the little girl back at the schoolhouse, though by now she was surely at Mrs. Porter's with Lark, trying to worry her papa home safe. His second was that he was likely to end up in the same fix as the doctor if he didn't find a way to keep warm till morning.

He swore, got stiffly down from the livery-stable horse, and stomped his feet in the vain hope of getting his circulation going again. Just to be sure his original assessment was correct, and the doc was indeed dead, he tugged off one glove, using his teeth because his other hand was too stiff, and pressed his fingers to a pulse point in the man's neck.

Cold as a graveyard statue.

Yep. Fairmont had gone to his Maker way too soon, and left his frozen carcass behind for good.

Rowdy swore again. There was a lantern fixed to the front of the buggy, though it had long since gone out. Praying it had guttered when the wind picked up, instead of burning the kerosene down to fumes, he fumbled to examine it, got a match from his coat pocket and struck it, shielding it with an unsteady hand as he held the flame to the wick. The mingled scents of oil and sulfur stung the insides of his nostrils.

The fire caught, and Rowdy was careful to shut the lantern again before letting out his breath in relief.

In the light of that lantern, the doctor looked even more bizarre than he had in the relative gloom. He'd turned blue-gray, and icicles dangled from the brim of his eastern hat, and from his chin and ears and eyebrows, too.

For the time being, Rowdy had no choice but to

leave the man right where he was. There was no saving the doc. Rowdy had his own survival to manage, and that of the two horses.

Recalling his pa's taunts that he'd had a talent for starting fires on the railroad tracks, Rowdy pulled his glove back on, took the lantern by its handle, and examined the horse hitched to the front of the rig.

It nickered at him, ice clinging to its shaggy hide.

Rowdy freed it from the harness and waded into the snow, now nearly to his knees, looking for dead branches. The work warmed him a little, and he was encouraged by the fierce ache in his feet. His blood was moving again, anyhow.

He laid the blaze right there in the road, and stood by it a while. The horses drew up close to each other, sharing their body heat.

When he'd thawed out a little, Rowdy gathered more deadwood and fed it to the fire, but he knew it wouldn't last. He'd been lucky up to now, but a good blast of wind would put out the flames, and he couldn't search for more wood without going too far off the trail.

He hadn't even considered bringing Pardner along on this jaunt, but he surely wouldn't have minded his company now—a good dog had kept more than one man alive in a blizzard.

He paced, clapping his gloved hands. Wished he could lie down and sleep, right there in the middle of that old trail. The temptation wooed him, sweet and warm as a willing woman, but he knew if he gave in to it, he'd never get up off the ground again.

So he kept pacing.

Kept the fire going as long as he could.

When it was finally quelled, there was no getting it going again.

Rowdy wedged himself between the two horses, leaning against one or the other of them when his legs needed a rest, and waited for morning.

GIDEON WAS GONE for such a long time that Lark began to despair of him. Mrs. Porter's house wasn't far away, maybe three-quarters of a mile, but in this storm, it might as well have been in Kansas.

Was he lost, with Lydia, blinded by the vicious fury of the snow?

And what was happening to Rowdy? Had he found Dr. Fairmont?

Or had they both perished?

Lark paced, sat down, got up again and paced some more.

And then Gideon returned, with a man's coat for Lark to wear in lieu of her cloak, which was still damp with Lydia's perspiration.

"Mrs. Porter and that Chinese woman are in a fair tizzy," Gideon reported, handing Lark the coat and opening the stove door to bank the fire. "Fixing to make soup from a bunch of dried weeds." He paused, watching as Lark buttoned up the coat. "I'll ride my horse up close to the steps, if you're ready to go, and you can get on behind me."

Just as Lark had never drawn water from a well, she had never ridden a horse, either. She felt suddenly and woefully inadequate for life in Stone Creek, or anywhere beyond her parlor in Autry's mansion, and even indulged in a brief, distracted regret that she'd ever left Denver.

She'd had plenty of comforts there, and people to do for her.

Water from a tap. Gas lights. A coal furnace. Hot drinks served to her by a maid whose name she couldn't remember.

And she'd taken it all for granted.

"Very well," she told Gideon staunchly. "I'll ride behind you."

The leap from the top of the steps onto the back of Gideon's horse proved awkward, because of her long skirts. The cold stung her legs, even through her thick woolen stockings, and she covered them as best she could, clutching at Gideon's coat with both hands when the horse moved forward with a sudden, slogging jolt.

Lark buried her face between Gideon's shoulder blades and prayed the ride to Mrs. Porter's could be accomplished quickly.

It wasn't.

The snow was so deep that the horse could only move through it by bunching its haunches and springing ahead in a crow-hopping motion that sent Lark's stomach surging up her windpipe. Once, she nearly bit off her tongue.

What seemed like an hour passed in this jostling fashion, before the lights of Mrs. Porter's house came into view, faintly golden and snow-muted, like the flames flickering in the streetlamps.

As he had done at the schoolhouse, Gideon rode up beside the back porch and waited while Lark dismounted. Her legs almost crumbled beneath her, and pain shot through the balls of her feet, but she managed to land without falling.

"Best rest this horse awhile," Gideon said, raising his voice to be heard over the low howl of the wind. Then he swung a leg over the animal's neck and joined Lark on the little porch.

The door opened behind Lark, and Mrs. Porter grabbed her by a handful of coat and hauled her over the threshold with surprising strength, considering her diminutive size.

Gideon followed, after politely stomping the snow off his boots first. "I need one of those quilts for the horse," he said. "A length of twine, too, if you have it."

Mrs. Porter gave him several quilts, plucked from the pile Lydia had been wrapped in, and Mai Lee provided the string. After adjusting his coat collar and pulling his hat down a little, he went out again, ostensibly to blanket the horse and secure the covering with twine.

Lark's attention was all for Lydia.

The child lay on a cot set up in the middle of the kitchen, within the radius of blessed warmth from the cookstove, but not too close. Hon Sing, Mai Lee's husband, sat beside her, straight-shouldered, unrolling a small length of embroidered silk on his lap.

Lark drew closer, divesting herself of the borrowed coat, which Mrs. Porter hastened to take from her.

"How is Lydia?" Lark asked, terrified of the answer.

Needles, long and very fine, glimmered in the piece of silk Hon Sing was holding. His hands were poised gracefully over the sewing kit, if that was what it was, fingers spread, like those of a pianist preparing to play a concerto.

"Bad sick," Hon Sing said.

Lark touched Lydia's forehead and found it only

slightly cooler than when they'd parted at the schoolhouse. The child's skin felt dry now, but it was still very warm, and her eyes, though open, seemed glazed, even sightless.

Lark glanced curiously at the needles.

Hon Sing and Mai Lee exchanged a few quiet words in their own language. Then Mai Lee brought a chair from the table and urged Lark to sit in it.

"Hon Sing doctor in China," she said. "Give girl medicine. She not better."

Gideon returned and noticed the needles immediately.

"What's he mean to do with those?" he asked.

"Some heathen thing," Mrs. Porter fretted, pressing a cup of hot tea into Lark's unfeeling hands and then hovering at a little distance, wringing her own.

If Hon Sing had heard Mrs. Porter's remark, he gave no sign of it. He took one of the needles carefully from the cloth case, examined it, looking pleased at the way it winked in the lamplight, and poked the sharp end into the top of his own wrist.

Lark flinched, and felt Gideon, now standing near her chair, do the same.

"Not hurt," Hon Sing assured them.

"Like hell," Gideon argued.

Hon Sing plucked the needle from his flesh and put it in another part of the case. Then he took Lydia's hand and inserted the needle with a deft, skilled motion of his fingers.

Lark gasped.

Gideon yelped in protest.

But Lydia didn't make a sound.

"Take that needle out of her right now," Gideon commanded, and moved to intercede.

Lark stopped him with a motion of her arm.

Hon Sing gave Gideon a placid, measuring look, then proceeded to place another needle in Lydia's opposite wrist. Soon, she was bristling with little silvery spines. After a few tense minutes had passed, she suddenly sighed, as though relieved of some burden that had been crushing her, and then her breathing, ragged and shallow before, began to deepen and slow.

"Yes," Hon Sing said quietly. "Breathe now."

Behind Lark, a little thump sounded. Mai Lee gasped, and Lark spun backward off her chair.

Mrs. Porter lay in a heap on the floor.

Before either Mai Lee or Lark could reach the poor woman, Gideon had hooked his hands under her arms from behind and hoisted her onto her feet.

Dazed, Mrs. Porter blinked and sagged into the chair Lark placed behind her.

"Needles," the landlady explained, fluttery.

No one spoke in response.

Hon Sing remained where he was, watching over Lydia, occasionally moving a needle from one part of her anatomy to another.

Lark was at once horrified and fascinated. She'd heard of strange Chinese healing practices, but she'd never actually witnessed anything like this.

When Hon Sing ceased rearranging the needles and simply sat silently, with his hands resting on his thighs, Lark approached him. Tentatively extended her hand.

Hon Sing looked at her face, smiled the barest semblance of a smile, and took another needle from the case.

Lark stiffened, biting her lower lip, but when the tip of the needle penetrated the skin on top of her wrist, there was no painful prick. She stared, amazed, and slowly became aware of a pooling sensation surrounding the needle, rapidly coalescing into a heavy ache.

Watching, Hon Sing nodded sagely, as though in response to some private question he'd seen no reason to voice aloud.

Lark's eyes widened with chagrin. To her, Hon Sing had always been Mai Lee's husband, an odd, foreign little man who swept and fetched and carried for Jolene Bell at her saloon and slept in the bed under the main staircase in Mrs. Porter's house.

She would never have credited him with the wisdom he exuded now. In fact, she hadn't seen him as anything more than a peripheral figure, moving like a shadow at the perimeters of her awareness.

Shame burned in her cheeks, and she swallowed hard. What an ignorant, complacent dolt she'd been.

Without speaking, Hon Sing removed the needle from Lark's hand, and instantly the ache began to fade.

And so did a lot of Lark's assumptions about what was true.

THE SNOW HAD STOPPED a little before dawn, and the sky was clear, though it was still cold enough to turn a man's breath solid in midair.

The doc looked worse in the daylight than he had in the spooky glow of his road-lantern the night before—and that, Rowdy thought, was saying something. There was no hope of moving the buggy, even with two horses to draw, since it was mired above the wheel hubs in ice-crusted snow. Anyhow, what passed as a road was under at least eighteen hard-crusted inches of yesterday's weather.

Rowdy pried the corpse out of the buggy seat and carried it, bent double over his right shoulder like a rolled rug. He laid Dr. Fairmont's remains over the back of his own borrowed horse, since he knew the animal to be of patient temperament, and secured the rigid body with rope.

That done, he mounted the doc's buggy horse and waited to see if the critter would buck. When it didn't, Rowdy urged it in the direction of Stone Creek.

With the snow so deep, it was slow traveling.

He had to stop and rest the horses every fifteen or twenty minutes, and he wished he had a blanket or something to cover the doc. It wasn't that he minded looking at him, but it was an undignified way for a man to make his last ride, and Rowdy would have spared him that, spared the little girl, too, but there was no means of doing so.

Having plenty of time to think, if not much else, Rowdy considered Mabel, the doctor's wife. He'd met her the night before, when he stopped by to ask if her husband had returned from the Bennington place and pass on Lark's message that she'd look after the child until morning. She was a piece of work, Mabel Fairmont was. She'd come to the door half-dressed and sloe-eyed and smelling of medicine—probably laudanum.

The doctor wasn't back, she'd said, with a whining note in her voice, and Lark could keep Lydia forever, as far as she was concerned. The kid was pesky, anyway.

She'd asked if Rowdy wanted to come in and visit for a spell.

He'd refused politely, said he had a long ride to make. Tipped his hat to her out of habit, not respect. It galled him to remember it, and he spat.

What would become of Lydia, with her pa gone, and only that woman to offer solace?

Rowdy's throat ached at the prospect. The child would probably wind up in an orphanage, if she was that lucky. From what he'd seen of her stepmama, it was more likely she'd simply be left behind.

He glanced back at the corpse, bouncing behind him on the second horse, for all that he'd tied the ropes down tight. "Not to speak ill of the dead," he said aloud, "but you ought to have looked after your daughter a little better than you did."

That said, Rowdy turned his attention to the hard trail ahead, and his thoughts strayed, as they liked to do, to Lark Morgan.

She would want to take the child in, he knew she would.

But she was a schoolmarm, and on the run from somebody mean enough to spark fear in her eyes whenever her past was mentioned. She wasn't in a position to raise a little girl, any more than he was.

Rowdy frowned and pulled his hat down lower over his eyes.

Thought about his own mother, and what she would have done in his place. She'd always wanted a girl-child, but rambunctious boys were all she got.

She'd been left on a hardscrabble farm, often and for long stretches, while Pappy was off robbing stagecoaches, then trains, though he always told her he had mining shares, someplace in Oklahoma. She'd had five boys to feed and clothe, and no help doing it—until John T. Rhodes bought the neighboring place, right around Rowdy's eighth birthday.

John T. was probably still a sore spot with Pappy, even after all these years. He'd been everything Pappy wasn't, a hardworking, respectable man, with a penchant for books and the fine thoughts they contained.

A book's like a chariot with wings, Rowdy. It can take you anyplace.

He'd loved Miranda Yarbro, John T. had. But he'd done it honorably. A widower himself, he'd never asked anything of Rowdy's mother except the pleasure of her company. He'd chopped wood and carried water. He'd shared his corn crops, since the ones Ma and the older boys planted always seemed to fail, and when he butchered a hog or a steer, there was meat in Miranda's larder, as well as his own.

Whenever Pappy came home from one of his sprees, his pockets heavy with money and his stories taller than the highest building in New York City, John T. stayed clear.

It wasn't that he was scared of Payton Yarbro, though. John T. was never scared of anybody—he just didn't like fighting, that was all. Once, Rowdy had seen the man lift a yearling calf clear off the ground.

When Pappy's money ran out, he got restless, and then he'd light out again. And John T. would quietly take up where he'd left off before the latest homecoming.

Since the nearest schoolhouse was thirty miles away and Ma needed help at home, Rowdy never had a day of formal learning. John T. had taught him to read and work sums, along with Levi and Ethan. Ma had schooled Wyatt and Nick herself, since they were older, coming along before despair and hard work had worn her down, using the Good Book and a pair of slates she ordered through Sears-Roebuck. Scant as their educations were, either Wyatt or Nick could have passed for a university professor by the time they were old enough to vote.

Remembering all this, Rowdy was almost glad to be alone in a barren place, with only two horses and a dead man for company. He could think about Ma without choking up, but recalling John T. was something else again.

In some ways, he'd never gotten past the spring of his thirteenth year.

He'd been helping John T. plow a cornfield one warm spring day, and they'd stopped, in the heat of the afternoon, to rest themselves and the team in the shade of the only tree on the Rhodes place—a single, towering maple, planted by some long-gone homesteader, probably yearning for New England.

They'd drunk from a water bucket brought along for the purpose, and John T. had grinned at Rowdy and said he ought to start going by Robert, now that he was almost a man.

Wyatt and Nick had taken to running with Pappy by then, despite all Ma had done to keep them home, and Ethan and Levi were getting restless, too.

Rowdy meant to stay right there on the farm, run

some cattle and raise a few hogs and chicken. Grow corn that didn't wither on the stalk. He wanted to be like John T., not like Pappy. He'd decided then and there to use his given name, and he'd said so.

John T. had slapped him on the shoulder and looked proud. He'd dipped the ladle into the drinking bucket, and poured the contents down the back of his neck.

Rowdy'd laughed, and reached for the ladle, meaning to do the same.

At first, seeing John T.'s face contort, Rowdy had drawn back, afraid he'd somehow offended the man whose respect he'd wanted above all things in life.

John T. had clasped a hand to his chest and pitched forward onto the ground. Rowdy stood still for a long moment, stricken. When he finally crouched and rolled John T. over onto his back, he knew he was gone.

He'd sat there, keeping a vigil, until after sunset, when his ma finally came looking for them with a lantern to say supper was getting cold.

Together, she and Rowdy had loaded John T.'s body onto the plow horse's back and made the slow trip home.

With the help of some neighbors, they'd buried John T. Rhodes two days later, under the lone maple tree out in his field.

The next time Pappy came home, he'd taunted Ma for crying. Said John T. had gotten his just due for coveting another man's wife, and didn't the Good Book say, "Let the dead bury their dead"?

Rowdy had expected his ma to finally lose her temper, or at least defend John T.'s honor, along with her own, but she hadn't. She'd dried her eyes and let Pa kiss her, and acted sweet and docile around him, even laughed at his stories, and Rowdy had hated her for it, with all the misguided passion of a thirteen-year-old boy.

Without John T. there to guide him, Rowdy knew he'd never grow into the name Robert. He'd never raise corn crops, either. John T.'s absence was like one giant toothache pulsing through his spirit, worse every day.

And he couldn't bear it.

When his pa rode out that time, Rowdy went with him.

He'd never intended to learn the train-robbing trade, he just fell into it, because he was young and because Pa said the railroad barons were the real thieves, driving good folks off their land and laying tracks across it.

After the first robbery, Rowdy had been too ashamed to go home, and when the Yarbro name gathered some notoriety and Pa went by Jack Payton, Rowdy had started calling himself Rhodes.

It had galled Pa plenty, that tribute to John T. Probably still did.

And that was fine with Rowdy, then and now.

GIDEON PRATTLED like a mouthy woman, that cold, still winter afternoon, and gave his old pa fits in the process.

"And then this Chinaman, he stuck *needles* into that little girl."

Payton was busy ransacking Rowdy's saddlebags. He could feel the law closing in on him, tightening like a noose. Snow or no snow, winded horse or none, he had to hightail it for Mexico.

Gideon babbled on. "And she got better, too, right away."

Payton upended the saddlebags, and a black leather pouch fell out with a solid, satisfying *thunk*. He grinned around the unlighted cheroot jutting out of the side of his mouth. Yes, indeed, Rowdy always had money.

"Pa," Gideon said, abruptly interrupting his discourse on Chinese medicine, "what are you doing?"

"Borrowing something from your brother."

"That's stealing!"

"No, it ain't," Payton said, impatient. If one of the other boys had talked to him like that, he'd have back-handed them for it. But Gideon was special, if sorely trying at times. "It's *borrowing*."

The dog, resting by the stove, sat up and whimpered. Payton had been shut up with that mutt ever since Gideon had gone arescuing the night before, and he'd had his fill of being followed around and stared at.

"Just because you decided to call it that?" Gideon challenged, reddening a little, in tiresome conviction. Damn, if he wasn't like Miranda, too, Payton thought. All his sons were, to one degree or another, but she hadn't had a hand in Gideon's raising and could not have imparted her influence. "You'd better put that money back, Pa. Right now."

"You going to make me?" Payton asked. He dropped the pouch back in the saddlebags, and Gideon looked relieved—until he realized the saddlebags were going, too.

"You said you weren't an outlaw anymore," Gideon said, moving into Payton's way when he made for the door.

"And *you* said you wanted to be one," Payton retorted. He didn't like speaking harshly to the boy, but maybe it was the best thing, considering present circumstances. Turn him sour on his old man, once and for all. The ire might carry him right into college and out the other side, with something more to trade on than a fast gun and an even faster temper. "You don't have the stomach for it."

He pushed past Gideon, blinked in the bright dazzle of sunlight on snow.

"What about Ruby?" Gideon asked. "What about the horses and that thousand dollars you wanted me to fetch back?"

"When the road thaws out between here and Flagstaff," Payton called, already halfway to the lean-to, where there was a perfectly good pinto gelding awaiting him, rested and ready to cover a lot of territory fast, "you go see Ruby, then turn in that livery-stable nag. She'll make it right with old Charlie, Ruby will, and you won't be hanged for a horse thief." He went into the lean-to. He'd have favored a less memorable mount than that splashy paint, but borrowers couldn't be choosers. He commenced to saddling the gelding, patted the horse he was leaving behind. Gideon had followed him all the way out there, and the dog was with him. "You can have old Samson here, for your very own."

"I don't want your stupid horse, and you can't just leave, Pa. You can't take Rowdy's money and his horse and even his goddamned *clothes* and act like there's nothing wrong with it!"

"You just watch me, boy," Payton answered, slipping the bridle over the pinto's head and adjusting the bit. That done, he threw on the saddle blanket, then the saddle. When he'd cinched it and fastened the buckle, he headed for the doorway of the lean-to.

Gideon didn't move out of his way. His face was rigid, and his eyes flashed. Steam snorted from his nostrils, he was breathing so hard. He might have been quite a hand at the train-robbing trade, given the training and experience.

Payton sighed. "Step aside, Gideon."

Gideon still didn't move.

Payton advanced.

And Gideon landed a haymaker in the middle of his face, knocked him flat on his backside, and spooked the pinto so that it nearly trampled him.

"Damn," Payton gurgled, trying to stanch the blood flowing down the front of his shirt. "You broke my nose!"

"Like I said," Gideon told him, flexing the fingers of his right hand and looking serious as all get-out, "you aren't stealing Rowdy's money *or* his horse. In fact, as a deputy marshal, I could arrest you. Throw you in that cell in there in the jailhouse."

Payton tried to smile, which wasn't easy, given that he felt as if a mule had just kicked in his face, and he was too woozy to get up out of the manure and sawdust covering the floor of that lean-to. "You wouldn't do a thing like that to your own pa," he said. "Would you?"

Gideon offered him a hand.

Payton hesitated, then took it.

Gideon jerked him to his feet, wrenched one of Payton's arms behind his back, and marched him straight for the jailhouse. When had the kid gotten to be so bull strong?

"Listen to me, Gideon," Jack reasoned, still bleeding

from the nose like the proverbial stuck pig. "This is a small town. If you put me in that jail, folks are going to notice, and that will cause Rowdy problems you can't even begin to imagine."

"There's a back door," Gideon said. He wrenched said back door open and hurled Payton through it. "Let folks talk all they want. And whatever these 'problems' are, I figure Rowdy can handle them."

Before Payton recovered his balance, Gideon was on him again, shuffling him into the cell, slamming the door, turning the key in the lock.

Stunned, Payton stared at his youngest son—his *favorite*—from between bars with rust spotting them wherever the grimy white paint was peeling off. He'd outrun U.S. Marshals and rangers, Pinkertons and railroad agents, and now he'd been thrown into the hoosegow by a sixteen-year-old boy.

If it hadn't been so damn tragic, Payton would have laughed out loud.

"You let me out of here, you ungrateful little whelp! I'm going to kick your ass from here to Sunday breakfast!"

Gideon found a rag and shoved it through the bars. "If you could," he said, "you'd have done it out there in the lean-to."

Pardner, who had witnessed the whole sorry episode, suddenly gave a little woof and dashed for the front door, jumping up and pawing at it.

"I guess Rowdy's back," Gideon said.

"Shit," Payton said. He jammed the rag against his bloody nose, winced at the pain and sank down onto the only piece of furniture in that cell. "That's all I need."

The door opened, and Rowdy came in. Stopped to make a fuss over the damn dog.

"I arrested Pa," Gideon said, taking a stubborn stance and folding his arms. Maybe he and Rowdy would get into it; the spectacle would be some consolation to Payton, if not much.

"I can see that," Rowdy replied evenly. He took off his hat, hung it on a peg, then shed his coat, too. He'd put in a hard night, from the looks of him, but Payton didn't much care. He had his own problems to worry about. "Make some coffee, will you, Deputy?" Rowdy added.

Gideon nodded, grabbed the coffeepot and hurried outside to get water.

"What happened to your face?" Rowdy asked idly. Gideon had left the cell key lying on Rowdy's desk, and Rowdy looked right at it. Made no move to use it, though.

Hope sprang up in Payton's heart, just the same. "Gideon sucker punched me," he said. "Let me out of here. I'll just leave, and there'll be no trouble. You have my word on that."

"You know how I value your word," Rowdy said dryly.

Gideon came back in with the coffeepot, his face as white as last night's snowfall. "There's a dead man tied to one of those horses out front," he said.

"Just make the coffee," Rowdy replied wearily.

10

It was along toward evening when Rowdy came.

Lark, sitting in the rocking chair close by the cookstove, with a quilt-bundled Lydia sleeping in her lap, knew it was him by the way he knocked.

Mrs. Porter had gone to bed, worn-out from the long night just past and the wearying day that followed. Mai Lee was off somewhere, probably helping Hon Sing with saloon duties neglected during the crisis with Lydia.

"Come in," Lark called.

Rowdy opened the door and stepped over the threshold, Pardner with him. And Lark saw the grim tidings in his face, even before he voiced them.

"How is she?" he asked, nodding to indicate Lydia, as he hung up his hat.

"Weak," Lark said, "but she'll recover, thanks to Hon Sing."

Rowdy took off his gloves, stuffed them into a pocket in his coat, shed the garment, and laid it over the back of one of the chairs at the kitchen table.

"What about you, Lark?" he asked, very quietly,

stopping at a little distance and watching her with eyes that would see right through any lie she told. "You look pretty done in yourself. Have you had anything to eat? Slept a little, maybe?"

She managed a thin smile, shook her head. Waited.

"Well," he said philosophically, "neither have I."

"Rowdy," Lark said.

"No," he sighed, gazing down at Lydia's still, sleeping form. "The doctor didn't make it home."

Lark closed her eyes, held Lydia a little more tightly. "Where is the—where is he now?"

"At the undertaker's," Rowdy answered. "I took him to his house first, but Mrs. Fairmont didn't want him laid out there." He sighed again. "I reckon I can't blame her."

"You've gathered, I suppose, that Mabel Fairmont isn't the most dedicated mother?" Lark's eyes burned. What was Lydia going to do? Was there a family somewhere—grandparents, perhaps, or aunts and uncles? Anyone who might take her in?

"I gathered that much, all right," Rowdy said.

Pardner, sitting as close to Lark's chair as he could without being in her lap, gazed mournfully at Lydia. Nuzzled her cheek with his snout.

Lydia stirred, smiled a little, tried to stroke the dog's head. Murmured a greeting.

Meanwhile, Rowdy went to the sink, rolled up his shirtsleeves and pumped water to wash his hands. That finished, he headed for the pantry and came out with a bowl of eggs and a loaf of bread.

"Supper," he explained.

Supper. Lark was reminded of the plans she'd made with Maddie, to visit the O'Ballivan ranch on Friday.

Though she had barely a hope of getting there, it made her feel a little better to imagine being a guest at Sam and Maddie's table, speaking of pleasant things. After the meal was over, Maddie might even be persuaded to play the spinet.

Lark ached for music.

Rowdy cracked four eggs into a bowl, whipped them to a froth with a fork and set a skillet on the stove to heat. The lard he added smelled good as it melted.

"Do you think there's more snow coming?" Lark asked with a note of dread in her voice, starting to come out of her stupor. For once she was too warm—the kitchen, kept hot because of Lydia, felt close and stuffy.

"I don't know," Rowdy said, slicing bread and then forking it into the bowl of beaten eggs. "The roads will be impassible for a while, though. No sign of a thaw, as far as I can tell."

Lark studied him, intrigued. Had there been a hint of relief in his voice, when he'd spoken of the roads?

"The ground will be too hard for a—" she paused, looked down at Lydia, who was nodding off again "—burial."

"Do you think she'd eat something?" Rowdy asked, again indicating the child.

Lark shook her head. "She can take broth, that's all."

Rowdy set the egg-coated slices of bread in the pan, one by one. They sizzled, and sent up an aroma that made Lark's empty stomach grumble.

"Gideon told me you put in a rough night," he said. "I'm sorry I wasn't around to help, Lark."

"You had your hands full," Lark replied. He'd never know, if she could help it, how desperately she'd longed for him, during those dark and endless hours of uncertainty.

He turned the frying bread—by then Lark's mouth was watering—and then pushed the skillet to the back of the stove.

When he approached Lark, stood in front of her chair, looking down into her eyes, her heart skittered. Gently he took Lydia from her arms and, his every step closely supervised by Pardner, carried her into the adjoining room.

All Lark's limbs had gone numb, sitting in the chair for so long, holding Lydia. She stood, and swayed slightly before regaining her equilibrium. Then she followed Rowdy.

He was tucking Lydia under the covers, quietly promising to build a fire on the nearby hearth right away.

The sight struck Lark to the heart.

One day Rowdy would make a fine father.

Lydia grabbed at his hand when he would have straightened and turned away.

"My papa?" she whispered. "Did he come home? You promised you'd find him if he didn't come home—"

Lark held her breath.

Rowdy hesitated, indecision visible in the line of his shoulders and the set of his head. "I found him, honey," he said sadly.

"He died, didn't he?" Lydia asked, brave and small and clinging to Rowdy's hand with both her own.

Rowdy didn't answer right away. He was probably weighing his words, trying to find ones that would soften the blow, realizing there *were* none.

"Your papa's gone," he said. "I'm sorry about that, Lydia—sorrier than I can ever say."

Lydia sighed, released his hands. "I need to sleep now," she told Rowdy, as Lark watched through tear-blurred eyes. "Can Pardner get up on the bed with me?"

Rowdy's voice was hoarse. "Sure he can," he told her.

Pardner looked questioningly up at Rowdy.

"Take care of your little friend, here, will you, boy?" Rowdy asked.

At a gesture from Rowdy, Pardner bounded onto the mattress, huddled close against Lydia's side, sighed contentedly and closed his eyes.

Lydia gave a little shudder, perhaps struggling to hold back tears of grief, flung a small arm across Pardner's furry side and slept.

Lark meant to step back out of the doorway before Rowdy saw her, but she didn't manage it. Her mind gave the order, but her befuddled body couldn't seem to translate it into action.

Rowdy's gaze collided with hers as he turned to start the fire he'd promised Lydia, and his blue eyes were bleak with sorrow.

"I'll set the table," she said.

"Thank you," he replied.

The fried bread was lukewarm when they sat down to eat, Rowdy and Lark, alone in Mrs. Porter's kitchen. Even so, with butter and a little raspberry jam, the stuff was delicious.

They said little, during the meal. Both of them were too tired to talk.

"Do you reckon I should have made something for

Mrs. Porter?" Rowdy asked, later, while he was making coffee and Lark was clearing the table.

Lark shook her head. "She specifically said she didn't want to be disturbed. Saturday is Mr. Porter's birthday, and she plans to bake a rum cake. Evidently, the process is quite involved."

Rowdy looked mystified. "Mr. Porter? I didn't know there *was* a Mr. Porter."

Lark stood very close to him and lowered her voice. "His things are all over the house, as though he'll be back at any moment, and there's the rum cake, but surely he must be, well, dead."

"Mysterious," Rowdy said, with a grin. "Like you."

Lark ignored that, too tired to engage in another battle of wits. And a part of her—the foolish, reckless, and very lonely part—would have liked to tell Rowdy Rhodes all her secrets and then demand to know his in return.

"You'd better go, Rowdy. I appreciate all you've done, but you're about to fall over."

A grin quirked the corner of his mouth. Then he cleared his throat eloquently. "I believe I'd like to have some of this coffee before I go," he said. "If you don't mind, that is."

Lark couldn't help reflecting on what a good thing it would have been to lie down next to Rowdy and sleep in his arms. But even if convention had permitted a schoolmarm such a wanton luxury—which it certainly didn't—Lydia and Pardner were occupying the only bed on the first floor. There was, quite simply, no place to commit that particular sin with any grace.

Rowdy curved a finger under Lark's chin, lifted and

placed a soft, brief kiss on her mouth. She wondered if he'd somehow known what she was thinking, and the possibility, remote as it was, made her blush.

"Maybe I'll go after all," he said. "Get some rest."

She wanted to plead with him to stay, and shamelessly, too, but she knew that wouldn't be wise. So she nodded and permitted herself the indulgence of laying both her hands against his strong chest, just for a moment.

He smoothed her hair, which was tumbling from its pins and badly in need of brushing. She probably looked like a madwoman, just escaped from some asylum.

"Good night, Miss Morgan," he said, without the mocking lilt he usually employed when he addressed her thus.

"Will you be leaving Pardner with us?" she asked.

Something like pain moved in his eyes, gone so quickly that it might never have been there at all. "Best not," he said. "You'll want to stay close to Lydia tonight, and there won't be room for all three of you in that bed."

She nodded again, and Rowdy gave a low whistle.

Pardner padded in from the next room, yawning.

Moments later he and Rowdy were gone.

Lark left the dishes for Mai Lee to wash when she returned, went into the bedroom she'd coveted with an unholy yearning, added wood to the fire Rowdy had built earlier, and pensively stripped to her bloomers and camisole.

Turning back the covers carefully, she crawled into bed beside Lydia, shut her eyes and tumbled into an instant and profound sleep.

"MAYBE THAT CHINAMAN could stick a bunch of those needles in Pa, so his nose would stop hurting," Gideon speculated the next morning, as he and Rowdy and Pardner approached the back door of the jailhouse, where the old man had spent the night. "I shouldn't have hit him so hard."

Rowdy smiled. "I wouldn't mind sticking a few needles in his hide myself," he said, thinking of the good set of clothes his pa had stolen from him and then ruined by bleeding all over them. Then there was the horse Pappy had almost helped himself to and the money pouch. "As for the sucker-punch, he had that coming."

For a lot more reasons than horse thieving, Rowdy thought.

They went inside.

Pa was ready with a list of complaints.

The fire had gone out.

He was hungry.

He had to piss like a racehorse.

Rowdy picked up the cell key and let his father out of jail.

"Your face," he remarked, taking in Pa's bruised cheek and swollen nose, "looks like somebody stomped on it."

Pa pushed past Rowdy, tossing Gideon an accusing glare, and made for the back door, probably heading for the outhouse.

"What if he steals your horse and runs away?" Gideon asked, looking worried as he opened the stove, bent on getting a fire going.

Rowdy grinned. "I'll send my deputy after him," he said.

Gideon flushed. "I know I'm not *really* a deputy," he told Rowdy. "You just said that because you didn't want me chasing after Pa on my own."

"You caught a man in the act of committing a crime and detained him," Rowdy said. "That makes you a deputy."

"I shouldn't have hit him," Gideon repeated.

"Maybe not," Rowdy answered. "But, the way you tell it, he meant to lead a horse over you, since you were blocking his way out of the lean-to. Short of shooting the old coot, I don't see what else you could have done."

"He said I'd never make an outlaw. That I don't have the stomach for it."

"That's a *good* thing, Gideon."

"I guess I didn't really think about what it meant, being an outlaw. Folks always chasing you, and a lot of hard riding and sleeping on the ground—"

"That and more," Rowdy said, taking up the coffeepot and heading for the door.

The weather was a little warmer, though the snow was still deep.

He'd just pumped water into the coffeepot when he scanned the street and saw Sam O'Ballivan riding toward him from one direction and Mabel Fairmont picking her way along on foot from the other.

He could deal with Mrs. Fairmont.

He'd hoped for a little more time—and for his pa to be long gone—before he had to face O'Ballivan, though.

He could just imagine the conversation they were about to have.

There's been another train robbery, Sam would say.

Yes, Rowdy might answer, *and I let the most likely suspect out of my jail five minutes ago. His name's Payton Yarbro. Did I ever mention that he's my pa, and I rode with him for years?*

Mabel reached him first. "I have just been to see my husband at the undertaker's," she said, "and he's *bent.* Poor Herbert is going to have to be buried *sideways.*"

"I'm sure there's a solution, Mrs. Fairmont," Rowdy said. Most likely the undertaker would have to break poor Herbert's bones or sever a few tendons to straighten him out for the coffin, but of course it wouldn't have been mannerly to say so.

Out of the corner of his eye, he saw that Sam was drawing nearer. He wasn't riding with any urgency, but he did look mighty serious.

"I'm not meant to live alone," Mabel said sweetly. "I'll need another husband. Are you single, Marshal Rhodes?"

Rowdy stared at her, forgetting all about Sam. He'd only met the woman once, and he'd disliked her instantly. Now, looking at her in the daylight, he was even less impressed. She was skinny, with dark hair and shrewd, greedy little eyes that seemed to pull perceptively at everything she saw.

And right now, she was seeing Rowdy.

"It's a little soon to be thinking about getting married again, isn't it?"

She bridled a little. "If you're worried that you'll have to raise Lydia," she said huffily, "you needn't trouble yourself. I've sent a wire to Nell Baker, down in Phoenix, and she'll be on her way here to fetch that little brat as soon as the roads are clear."

Well, there was some good news, anyway. Lydia had someone who cared enough to travel all the way from Phoenix to collect her.

"You've been busy this morning," Rowdy said dryly.

Sam was dismounting, near the hitching rail.

Mabel didn't seem to notice him. "If you don't want to marry me, just say so."

"I don't want to marry you," Rowdy complied.

Sam approached. Touched the brim of his hat to Mabel, though his gaze was fixed on Rowdy.

"I was sorry to learn of your sad loss, Mrs. Fairmont," Sam said.

Mabel didn't even acknowledge the man's condolences. She just gave a frustrated snort, hoisted her skirts and turned to pick her way angrily across the road, stepping high because of the snow.

"You thinking of getting married, Rowdy?" Sam asked, both of them watching her go. Sam seemed mildly amused, but Rowdy was seething.

"No," he snapped.

The irritation subsided, though, as he recalled the probable reason for Sam's ride into town, which must have been no mean enterprise, given the state of the roads.

Rowdy let out his breath. By now, his pa was probably back from the outhouse. He was a famous train robber, almost legendary—most likely, there'd be dime novels written about him anytime now. And there was a good chance that Sam, being an experienced lawman, would recognize Payton from some sketch he'd seen in the course of his duties, or even a written description.

And Pappy might just be spiteful enough to throw

himself in front of the train, so to speak, just for the pleasure of seeing his next-to-youngest son locked up in his own jail.

Yes, sir. Pappy would love that.

Rowdy sighed, remembered the coffeepot he'd just filled at the pump. "Come on inside, Sam," he said. "It's cold out here."

AFTER DRESSING as warmly as she could, Lark left Lydia in Mai Lee and Mrs. Porter's care and set out for the Fairmont house. No one answered her knock, and she was wondering if Mabel might be inside, stunned with grief, when a voice called tartly from the road.

"What do *you* want?"

Lark turned and saw Mabel striding toward her. Before she could say anything in response, Mabel spoke again.

"If you think you're bringing that girl back here," she said, "you're wrong. Miss Nell Baker is on the way to get her, and you can just keep her until then!"

Lark's mouth fell open, and her temper flared. *The woman is in mourning,* she reminded herself. *Be kind.* "I was just coming to tell you that Lydia is better, and to ask for some of her things, since it wouldn't be prudent to move her just yet," she said moderately.

"Well," snapped Mabel, "come in, then."

She shoved her way past Lark and opened the door.

Lark followed her over the threshold. She'd never been to the Fairmont house before, so she'd had no expectations, but if she had, they wouldn't have matched what she saw.

There was almost no furniture in the front room, and the floors were bare of rugs and dirty. Discarded clothing—or was it bedding of some sort?—lay piled in a corner, and something moved inside the heap.

"Go ahead," Mabel taunted. "Look till your eyes are full."

Lark blushed. She *had* been staring, and that was rude. "If I could just have Lydia's nightgown, and perhaps a warm dress—"

Mabel laughed and, quiet as it was, the sound had a screeching quality to it. "She doesn't have much, and what she does have might as well be burned. That's what snooty Nell Baker will do. Burn it all and tell the whole world how her dear brother-in-law, the *doctor,* married a slattern after her sainted sister died and brought up his *precious child* in a pigsty!"

Lark bit her lower lip, still reining in her temper, still trying to decide how best to respond. "Mrs. Fairmont, I know you're very upset over your husband's death, but—"

Mabel didn't let her finish. "In there," she said, jabbing a thumb toward one of two inside doorways. "That's where Lydia sleeps."

Just the other day Lark had walked Lydia home from school, and the child had rushed in to ask for last night's soup bone, so she could give it to Pardner. The recollection made the backs of Lark's eyes sting, and a lump formed in her throat.

What kind of teacher was she? She'd never dreamed the child was living like this.

Lydia was always cheerful, her face washed, her hair neatly braided. If her clothes were a little shabby, well, many of the other children wore hand-me-downs and patched garments, too. Most of them probably didn't even put on shoes until the weather turned cold, and often they'd already been worn out by an older sibling before the new owner inherited them.

When Lark didn't move, Mabel flounced through the indicated doorway and came out a few moments later with an untidy bundle in her arms. She thrust the things at Lark.

"Here," she said sourly. "It's what she has. Write it up in the newspaper. Have posters printed."

Lark barely heard her. Dr. Fairmont must have been the one to care for Lydia; it certainly hadn't been this impossible, wretchedly unhappy woman.

"You can leave now," Mabel said.

"Mrs. Fairmont, what are you going to do?" Lark asked. Mabel's surliness surely stemmed from shock over her husband's sudden death. And perhaps she was subject to melancholia, and that was how the house had fallen into such a state. She might be ashamed to let anyone, especially her stepdaughter's teacher, see the place, and therefore she was prickly. "How will you support yourself?"

"I'll marry somebody," Mabel answered blithely. "I already tried for a new husband, just this morning, but he figures he's too good for me, that Rowdy Rhodes. I don't know who he thinks he is. Some drifter, just riding into town with a dog sharing his saddle—"

Lark fought a strange desire to smile. Suddenly, despite all the struggles and the sorrows and the fear, she felt almost elated. "You proposed to Marshal Rhodes?" she asked.

"Yes," Mabel said petulantly, "and he practically spit in my face."

Lark bit the inside of her lip and tried to look sympathetic. "I'd better get back to Lydia," she said. "Thank you, Mrs. Fairmont, and if there's anything I can do—"

"You can get out of here and leave me alone," Mabel snapped. "I just lost my husband, you know."

"I know," Lark said mildly.

And she left.

WHEN ROWDY AND SAM stepped inside the jailhouse, Gideon was there, but Pappy was nowhere to be seen. Rowdy felt a curious mixture of relief and anxiety.

Where was the old reprobate?

Riding away on Rowdy's good horse?

Had he taken the money pouch and the saddlebags after all?

Gideon cleared his throat and put out his hand to Sam. "I'm Gideon Rhodes," he said, without so much as a hitch in his delivery. "Rowdy's my brother."

"Sam O'Ballivan," Sam said. "Glad to meet you." He must have noticed the slightly bent badge pinned to Gideon's shirt pocket, but if he did, he didn't say so.

Rowdy set the coffeepot on the stove, measured in some ground beans and spoke as calmly as he could. "Gideon," he said, "why don't you take Pardner out back for a little while?"

Gideon looked mutinous for a second or so, but he was a bright kid. He finally nodded and excused himself. Patted a thigh smartly so Pardner would follow.

And as soon as the dog and the boy were gone, Sam said the words Rowdy had anticipated he would.

"There's been another train robbery."

Rowdy kept his expression impassive. "When?" he asked.

"Day before yesterday," Sam answered. "I just got the telegram this morning. The man who brought it to me said you'd spent the night out in that blizzard, looking for Dr. Fairmont."

"I guess I didn't look fast enough," Rowdy said, and the rueful note in his voice was real. The doc had probably been only a few years older than he was, and despite a bad choice of brides, he hadn't deserved to die so early.

"Let it go, Rowdy," Sam said. "You can't save them all." He sighed. "Learned that the hard way myself."

Rowdy shoved some wood into the stove, hoping he'd get a chance to take a gulp or two of the coffee before he had to rush off in pursuit of outlaws he didn't want to find. Pappy was probably racing for Mexico, and Rowdy planned on heading in the opposite direction.

He didn't like doing things this way, though. Didn't like accepting pay for rangering that might go undone, and he surely didn't like lying to Sam, even if it was only by omission.

Especially not Sam.

Sam O'Ballivan had picked him out of a crowd, standing in front of the jailhouse down in Haven, and deputized him on the spot. Given him a badge and the first honest work he'd done in a long while, guarding a prisoner accused of a brutal murder.

Sam had trusted Rowdy, with no cause to do so.

"I guess you want me to track those train robbers," he said, resigned.

Fortunately, Sam seemed to take that resignation for plain weariness, but it was hard to tell with him. He'd gone to Haven and convinced everybody but Maddie that he was a schoolmaster, when he was really an Arizona Ranger, on the trail of a pack of outlaws that made Pappy look like a choir leader.

No one who knew Sam O'Ballivan for more than five minutes would risk underestimating him.

"There are a slew of rangers coming into Flagstaff," Sam said, in answer to a statement Rowdy had almost forgotten he'd made. "Once the trail is a little clearer between here and there, we'll join them."

"Any idea where we ought to start looking?"

Sam considered the question, considered Rowdy, too, but his expression was typically unreadable.

The coffee began to perk.

Rowdy's mouth watered, even as his heartbeat speeded up and something coiled in his belly, the old readiness to either fight or run like hell.

"I figure if we find Payton Yarbro," Sam said, at long last, "we'll have solved the problem."

11

"*OF COURSE* YOU'LL GO to supper at Sam and Maddie's tomorrow night," Mrs. Porter said, standing in the doorway as Lark helped Lydia into one of her own nightgowns, having just given the child a sponge bath. Directly after taking her leave from Mabel Fairmont, and coming straight home with the ragged bundle clenched in her arms, Lark had saved Lydia's aunt the trouble of disposing of the little girl's pitifully few clothes by stuffing them into the belly of the cookstove.

Lark sighed. She hadn't wanted anything, in a very long time, as much as she wanted to accept Maddie's kind invitation—except, of course, for Rowdy Rhodes, and that was a very different kind of wanting.

"Lydia will be just fine here with Mai Lee and me," Mrs. Porter insisted. "Won't you, dear?"

Lydia managed a little nod and drifted off to sleep.

"Come and have tea," Mrs. Porter told Lark, and though she spoke kindly, there was an underlying note of command in her voice.

Lark, her energy renewed after the brisk walk to and from the interview with the recalcitrant Mabel, felt restless. She wanted to march right down to the schoolhouse, fling open the door and ring the bell, announcing to all and sundry that classes were resuming *now*.

There would be no point to that enterprise, of course, since so few of the children—many of whom lived well out of town, along trails and roads buried under snow—could be realistically expected to attend.

So Lark followed Mrs. Porter into her kitchen and resigned herself to sitting down and sipping tea. This was inordinately difficult, since she was besieged by a strange, urgent sense that she needed to prepare for some impending crisis.

Mrs. Porter brought the teapot and the usual elegant cups and saucers to the table. Mai Lee was out on some errand, and they had the place to themselves, though Mr. Porter's coat, hanging on one of the pegs by the door, neatly brushed and aired, as though he might appear and put it on at any moment, belied the fact.

"Did you speak to Lydia?" the landlady asked, standing to pour tea for both of them and then sitting down. "About Nell Baker's coming for her, I mean?"

Lark sighed. Toyed with the handle of her teacup. "I asked her if she knew her aunt—though I didn't say the woman would be on her way to Stone Creek to fetch her as soon as there's a thaw—and she said she'd never met her. Apparently, Lydia's father and Miss Baker corresponded."

"What kind of person do you suppose she is?" Mrs. Porter fretted.

"I wish I knew," Lark said. Given her druthers, she

would have raised Lydia herself, but Miss Baker was a blood relation, the child's maternal aunt, and as such she would have a legal advantage. "She can't be worse than Mrs. Fairmont."

"Mabel Fairmont," Mrs. Porter said, "is nothing but a trollop."

"Was it—" Lark paused, bit her lower lip, then made herself ask the question, well aware that contained an implicit accusation. "Was it common knowledge in Stone Creek that Lydia was living in squalor?"

Mrs. Porter straightened her spine, and her gaze was direct. "Poverty is not unusual around here," she said. "I'm sure you've noticed that, even though you've been a member of our community for a relatively short time. Some of the children in your school don't have enough to eat, nor shoes or coats, either. We do what we can to help, people like the O'Ballivans and Major Blackstone—and me. But the need is very severe, and then there's the matter of pride. Most of these little ones would rather starve and go barefoot year-round than accept charity."

"I really didn't mean to imply—"

The landlady softened. Patted Lark's hand. "I know," she said. Then, after a pause, she went on. "I've noticed the quality of your clothes, Lark. Even the banker's wife doesn't have such fine things, nor Maddie O'Ballivan, either, and Sam is wealthier than most people think and generous with his wife. Rooming here, living as you do, well—"

Lark resisted an urge to bolt from her chair and flee, thereby forcing an immediate end to the conversation. She didn't, though, because Mrs. Porter, for all her little prejudices and intrusive ways, had been kind, taking Lark in as a boarder without references, seeing that the school board provided her with lunches she couldn't afford to provide for herself, and now even providing sanctuary for Lydia.

Wherever she went, and whatever happened to her in the uncertain future, Lark knew she would always be unceasingly grateful to Mrs. Porter for being so generous and helpful. Lark wouldn't have had the first idea what to do if her landlady had turned Lydia away. Tears burned behind her eyes, just to think of the desperation she would have felt and what might have happened to the child.

"There, now," Mrs. Porter said, probably misreading the expression on Lark's face. "You know I *hate* to pry—" at this, Lark had to hide a smile "—but it's obvious I've struck a nerve. Who *are* you, Lark? Truly? And what are you doing in Stone Creek, of all places, when you so clearly belong in Boston or Philadelphia or some other fancy city?"

Lark wanted to answer those questions. She yearned to. But she didn't dare. Her situation was simply too precarious and so was Lydia's, at least until Nell Baker arrived. "I wish I could tell you," she said, for that was the best she could do.

To her utter surprise, Mrs. Porter subsided. She'd been leaning forward, watching Lark's face avidly. Now she sat back and sighed delicately. "Perhaps one day you'll be able to confide in me. I do know this much about you, though—you are a good person, Lark Morgan. If you weren't, you wouldn't have stood by that poor little Fairmont girl the way you have."

"Thank you," Lark said quietly.

There was a brief, tremulous silence.

Then, glancing at Mr. Porter's coat and the date circled in red on the calendar, Lark said, "There's a story behind your husband's absence, isn't there?"

"I wish I could tell you," Mrs. Porter said, and though she'd tossed Lark's own words back at her, there was no flippancy in her tone or manner. Instead, she looked wistful, as though she truly *would* like to explain.

Secrets, Lark thought. *We all have them.*

She certainly did.

Mrs. Porter did.

And so did Rowdy Rhodes. She couldn't afford to forget that, not for a moment, but it was so perilously *easy* to forget. Especially when he kissed her.

BY THE TIME Sam O'Ballivan left the marshal's office, having conveyed a message from his wife that Rowdy ought to come to supper at their place tomorrow night, along with Lark Morgan, provided the thaw came, of course, Rowdy was practically sweating blood.

He and Sam had made plans to ride out for Flagstaff as early as Sunday morning, to meet up with the converging rangers, and while that was a prospect Rowdy dreaded, it had been nothing compared to his fear that Pappy might stroll into the jailhouse while Sam was there. He'd lived under an alias for a long time, Pappy had, but he was still Payton Yarbro, from the top of his obstinate head right down to the soles of his feet. He'd fooled a lot of people in his time, including himself, but fooling Sam O'Ballivan, now, that was something else again.

"Where's Pa?" Rowdy asked Gideon, who had been making a simple pot of coffee the whole time Sam was in the office.

"Hiding out in the lean-to," Gideon said, looking a little shame-faced to say it. Though he didn't have the time or inclination to pursue the thought just then, Rowdy wondered what it had been like for Gideon, growing up with Pa and Ruby.

Had "Jack Payton" been a different sort of father than Payton Yarbro?

Rowdy sure as hell hoped so.

Gideon moved to warm his hands at the stove, probably more because he was nervous than cold. "He said to let him know when O'Ballivan was gone. Pa, I mean."

"Let him sit in the lean-to awhile," Rowdy said, getting his mug off the desk and helping himself to some of Gideon's coffee. "A little reflection on his ways might do him some good."

Hesitantly Gideon grinned. "You're taking Lark—Miss Morgan—to supper at the O'Ballivans' tomorrow night?"

"If the roads are clear," Rowdy said, after a restorative sip of very hot coffee. "And if she's willing to leave Lydia for that long. There are a whole lot of ifs here, Gideon."

"You like her," Gideon said, still grinning.

"Of course I like her," Rowdy replied, after more coffee. "She's a nice person."

Gideon's eyes glowed, and Rowdy would have bet he was wishing he was older, so he might pursue Lark himself. "You're taking her to the O'Ballivans for supper," he repeated, good-naturedly stubborn.

"It's not like it sounds," Rowdy argued casually. "We're both heading to the same place, so it makes sense to travel together." He thought of the dance coming up Saturday night. He fully intended to go and have Lark on his arm, if he had to drag her out of Mrs. Porter's house. No doubt his younger brother would have a few things to say about that, too.

Rowdy sighed.

"You should have seen her with that little girl," Gideon said, turning wistful all of a sudden. "She'd have done practically anything to get her better."

Rowdy recalled the small grave outside that Flagstaff churchyard. "Tell me about your sister, Gideon," he said quietly.

Gideon averted his eyes for a moment, looking straight through Pardner like he was a window, then shifted his gaze back to Rowdy's face. "Rose died when she was only four years old," he said, his voice gravelly at the memory. "It was my fault."

Stunned and trying not to show it, Rowdy set his coffee aside on the desk. "How do you figure a thing like that?" he asked. "You must have been pretty young yourself."

Gideon's throat worked painfully. "I was six," he said, remembering. He found a chair, dragged it close to the stove and sat sideways on it, still staring through Pardner. "I was supposed to watch her. Ruby told me to watch her."

Rowdy debated a moment, then approached and laid one hand on his brother's shoulder. "What happened?"

Gideon braced his elbows on his knees and buried his face in his palms, his fingers raking through his thick, light-brown hair. "Rose had a kitten," he said bleakly, his voice muffled and hoarse. "We were playing on the sidewalk in front of the saloon, Rose and me. I got to looking at this horse that was tied up to a hitching post, and while I was doing that, the kitten must have wriggled out of Rose's hands." He paused, looked up at Rowdy with such abject misery that Rowdy would have gone back in time and lived that moment for him if he could have. He would have taken what he knew must have come next and all the pain that went with it, and borne it himself. "She chased the kitten into the street before I could stop her," Gideon went on, forcing the words out. "And she got run down by a wagon."

"I'm real sorry that happened, Gideon. I'm sorry it happened to Rose, and to you." And what about Pappy? Rowdy reflected, with a sudden and unaccustomed sorrow. How had the loss of his only daughter, at such a young age, affected him? "But it wasn't your fault. You were *six*. If you'd tried to run after her, you probably would have been killed, too."

Gideon swallowed again, tried for a smile and fell about a mile short of attaining it. "The kitten survived, though," he said, as if Rowdy hadn't spoken at all. "Ruby gave it to a rancher's wife, for a mouser. It's old now, for a cat, anyhow."

Rowdy squeezed Gideon's taut shoulder once before letting go. "You visit Rose's grave a lot, don't you?" he asked.

Gideon nodded. "Every day," he said. "It's hard, being so far away, but I figure I need to get used to that, if I'm going to be a deputy."

Rowdy's throat tightened, and he shoved a hand through his hair. He couldn't help recalling his last visit to his mother's grave—she was buried a mile or so from John T.'s resting place. He'd gone to tell her he wasn't riding with the Yarbros anymore. And there was another grave that came to mind, as well, outside Laramie, Wyoming. There were two people buried in that coffin, one of them younger than Rose.

"I guess a lot of us have a trail of graves behind us," he mused. "Ones we'd like to go back to but can't."

There was another silence.

"You reckon Pa's all right, out there in that lean-to? It's got to be cold, and his face probably hurts." Gideon paused, smiled wanly, maybe at the memory of yesterday's one-sided brawl, or maybe at some recollection of Rose.

"I'll go and look in on him," Rowdy offered quietly, because Gideon was red around the eyes, and probably needed a few minutes to collect himself. And because, suddenly, he needed to know how his pa was faring.

Pappy was sitting on an upturned crate, watching the three horses, Paint, Gideon's livery-stable mount and his own black gelding, chew on hay.

"Is that ranger gone?" he asked.

"He's gone," Rowdy said. "Gideon's worried about you. Says your face probably hurts."

"It hurts *plenty*," Pappy complained. "Thanks to him. Things have come to a sorry pass when a man's own son roundhouses him for no reason at all." But Pappy was nothing if not mercurial. In the next instant, a proud grin cracked the old outlaw's bruised and swollen face. "He packs a hell of a wallop, though. I've gotta say that for him."

"He told me about Rose," Rowdy said, taking up a grooming brush for something to occupy his hands and stroking the paint's back with it. "I'm sorry, Pap—Pa. That must have been a hard thing to get through."

Payton's expression changed. He looked away, but not before Rowdy glimpsed the old pain that had long since hardened in his eyes. "She was such a sweet little thing, our Rose. Full of mischief and bright as could be. It like to have killed Ruby, losing her, and I wasn't good for much of anything for a year afterward. Gideon was the strong one, but he's gone to that grave practically every day since. I wish he'd leave off from that."

"He blames himself for what happened," Rowdy said. "Did you know that?"

Payton looked glum. Nodded. "Ruby was wild with grief. She said some things to the boy that she shouldn't have—you know how people do when they're hurting."

Rowdy had to clear his throat before answering. "I know how they do," he confirmed. When his young wife, Chessie, had perished, and their two-year-old son, Wesley, had gone with her, both of them falling sick of a fever, Rowdy's mother-in-law had told him at the funeral that it was God's wrath. He'd been an outlaw, and Chessie had sinned by marrying him. And they'd both been smitten by the mighty hand of the Lord.

Rowdy didn't figure the Lord was anywhere near that mean-spirited, but some of His followers surely were.

"I've got to get out of here, boy," Payton said, jolting Rowdy out of a recollection he usually avoided. "I didn't rob that train. But I'm going to be blamed for it—you know I am. You have to get me a fresh horse or let me take this paint of yours."

"I won't stop you from going," Rowdy said grimly, "but you'll have to take your own mount. Even if you got out of Stone Creek without being seen, folks would notice I was riding a different horse, and they'd wonder why. When folks wonder, they start gathering into clusters to try and work it through."

"You'd think of something."

"No, Pa," Rowdy said. "Anyhow, I like this horse. It wouldn't be the same without him."

"No," Payton growled, back to his usual obstreperous self. "It *wouldn't* be the same, because I'd be miles from here, a free man, instead of being hauled up in chains by a bunch of Rangers." He stood, dusted off his pants, which were actually Rowdy's. "Samson can't make it to Mexico, Rowdy," he went on, patting the dark gelding. "He'll be fit in a week or ten days, but I can't wait that long. You know I can't."

Rowdy sighed. It would solve so many problems, for both of them, if Pa just vanished. But it wasn't going to help Gideon much, or Ruby, either. "All right," he heard himself say. "Take the paint. But I want you to leave him at the livery stable in Haven, Pa. You can buy another horse there and cross the river into Refugio—it's a little town just the other side of the border. Once you're across, you're on your own."

Payton considered the idea. "You'd come down there, when you could, and fetch back your horse?"

Rowdy sighed. "That's what I intend to do," he replied, still brushing Paint. "And if you try to steal him,

I'll track you to the far ends of hell. You've got my word on that."

"Sounds like you care more for this horse than your old pa," Payton lamented.

"I'd trust him a sight farther than I would you," Rowdy said. Damn, he hated to lose that horse, even for a few months. And it was a long trail down to Haven and back, one Pardner couldn't be asked to undertake again.

Explaining the black gelding wouldn't be easy, either. Once Paint and Pappy were gone, he'd say he'd swapped with some cowpoke passing through, but folks were bound to ask themselves, and each other, why he'd done it. Samson was aging, like Pappy, but Paint was in his prime, and Rowdy loved him almost as much as he did Pardner.

For a moment, he rested his forehead against the gelding's neck, saying a silent goodbye.

Pappy, meanwhile, slapped Rowdy on the back and made a stab at fatherly concern. "I'll leave the horse in Haven," he said. "You've got my word on it."

Rowdy glared at him. "He'd better be waiting when I get there, Pa," he said. "Because I'll stake you out on an anthill, naked and slathered in honey, if he isn't."

"I believe you," Pappy said, and he looked like he did.

"When do you plan on leaving?" Rowdy asked.

"Tonight, if this thaw holds," Pappy replied. He looked earnest now, even sincere, and his voice was low and quiet. "You look after Gideon. See he goes to college when the time comes. Ruby and me, we've already paid for it, and he can earn his keep doing odd jobs around the school. Don't let him play deputy past time, or fall in with bad companions."

"Bad companions," Rowdy repeated, raw because his horse was going away and he wasn't. Because Chessie and Wes were dead before their time, and little Rose, too, and because innocent children like Lydia had stepmothers like Mabel Fairmont. "Now, that's almost funny, Pa, coming from you."

"You're just bitter," Pappy accused, disgruntled again. "And it ain't very becoming, either."

"You're damn right I'm bitter," Rowdy replied, but he was already weary of sparring with his pa. His mother had been right, years ago, when she'd said there was "no salvation" in arguing with Payton Yarbro. The poor woman, she'd seen salvation everywhere she looked, it seemed, but as far as Rowdy could discern, she'd never quite reached it. Just the same, he wished he'd had the same gift.

He'd glimpsed his mother's true salvation once, though—in John T. Rhodes. Trouble was, both of them had been too upright to take what was offered them.

"Anything you want me to say to your brothers, should I cross paths with them?" Payton asked, eager to ingratiate himself in any way he could.

"Yeah," Rowdy answered. "Tell them not to rob trains."

ON FRIDAY MORNING, just after dawn, Lark awakened to a world so glittery and fresh-skyed that she wanted to sing with sudden joy.

The snow had softened to slush.

Exuberant at the weather change, and because she knew now that Autry had not crushed the music out of her soul after all, she crept out of the bedroom behind the kitchen, careful not to awaken Lydia, and found Mrs. Porter and Mai Lee already up and around. Mai Lee was unwrapping a parcel at the table, while Mrs. Porter poured copious amounts of what looked and smelled like rum into a huge bowl of batter.

"Mr. Porter liked lots of rum in his cake," she explained.

Lark was drawn to the package. "What's this?" she asked, drawing up alongside Mai Lee to look. Inside the sturdy brown-paper wrapping were two little flannel nightgowns and two equally tiny woolen dresses, one brown, one dark blue. Mai Lee must have purchased them the day before, when she was out of the house for several hours.

For a moment, seeing the dark, practical colors, Lark was reminded of boarding school, and some of the delight she'd felt on waking seeped out of her.

"For little girl," Mai Lee said, pleased. "Mrs. Porter, she pay. Put on account at mercantile."

Lark's gaze shot to Mrs. Porter, who lowered her eyes modestly.

"It was my Christian duty," the landlady said, blushing. "Nothing more."

"It was a very kind thing to do," Lark said, very softly.

"Nonsense," Mrs. Porter said, sounding brisk now as she went back to preparing her rum cake. "Mr. Porter always maintained that charity begins at home. 'Ellie Lou,' he would say, 'we must see to those less fortunate than ourselves.'"

Lark wanted to hug Mrs. Porter in gratitude, but she

sensed that the other woman would not welcome such a demonstration, so she simply said, "Thank you."

"You'd better hurry," Mrs. Porter responded, with a little sniff. "You don't want to be late for school." At Lark's hesitation, she added, "Mai Lee and I will tend to Lydia. And you've got your supper at the O'Ballivans' tonight, don't forget. The road out to their ranch will be muddy, to be sure, but probably no strain on Sam's team and wagon."

Lark's swooping heart rose skyward again at the reminder of her upcoming visit to Sam and Maddie's place. Until Mrs. Porter offered to care for Lydia in her absence, she'd been resigned to sending her regrets. "You're sure you won't mind—after all, Lydia still needs a great deal of care."

"You will go to that supper," Mrs. Porter said, cordially firm, "because I want to hear *all* about it when you get back. What was served. Whether there's real china, or tin plates, like Sam would have used if he was there by himself. What Maddie's done to that ranch house since she and Sam moved in. Are there curtains on the windows? And *especially* whether or not she plays Abigail Blackstone's spinet."

"Abigail Blackstone?" Lark frowned, searching her memory, but she didn't recall ever hearing the name before.

"The major's daughter," Mrs. Porter clarified. Another little sniff followed. "She died very tragically. Abigail was the *dearest* girl, though she never came to church."

Lark's heart took another dive, steep enough to leave her breathless, but she recovered quickly. She had to, for she had a long day ahead of her, classes to teach, followed by the journey to Sam and Maddie's ranch and an evening of gaiety.

She hurried upstairs to her old room to wash and dress and pin up her hair. She would wear her blue silk frock, she decided, even though it was unsuited for teaching. There might not be time to come home and change before Sam came to fetch her after school.

Forty-five minutes later, she unlocked the schoolhouse door, went inside, humming a song she'd once sung full-voiced, built a fire and proceeded to ring the bell, putting all her weight into pulling the heavy length of rope dangling from the little belfry.

To her disappointment, only four students came to school.

Gideon.

Susan and Mary Sommerville, whose father was the local undertaker.

And Roland Franks.

Roland glowered defiantly at Lark as he entered the schoolhouse, stomped over to her desk and set down her lard-tin lunch pail and lesson books with a condemnatory thump.

She smiled at him, determined to smooth his ruffled feathers and get him to wade through his *McGuffy's Reader* again. "Roland," she said cheerfully, "I'm so glad you changed your mind about coming back to school."

"I still think you ought to go to the dance with me," Roland said, unappeased.

Gideon sat up a little straighter in the chair behind a desk that was much too small for him. Before, his attention had wandered; now he was obviously listening.

"I had already accepted an invitation from Marshal Rhodes when you asked me," Lark lied patiently. "And, besides, it really wouldn't be right for you and me to socialize. After all, I'm your teacher. Such things simply aren't done."

Roland's neck flushed crimson. "A teacher down by Phoenix married my cousin Albert," he informed her. "Albert was in fifth grade at the time."

Out of the corner of her eye, Lark saw Gideon frown.

"Be that as it may," Lark said warmly, "I'm not interested in marriage, Roland—to you or anyone else."

"Not even that marshal?" Roland asked suspiciously.

Gideon sat up even straighter, and a little smile, reminiscent of Rowdy's, quirked at the corner of his mouth.

"Not even the marshal," Lark said. Then some imp of the perverse made her say, "I did hear that Mabel Fairmont was looking for a husband, though."

"Maybe I'll see if *she* wants to go to the dance with me," Roland said, ruminating. The change in his countenance was even more unsettling than his previous aspect had been.

"Roland, I was merely being—well, I shouldn't have spoken so lightly of such a serious matter. Mrs. Fairmont just lost her husband, and it would be highly improper to ask her to a dance when she's barely begun to mourn—"

As if Mabel Fairmont intended to waste any time mourning.

"I've got to go," Roland said decisively.

The Sommerville girls twittered.

Gideon watched the exchange between Lark and Roland with pensive amusement.

Roland strode out of the schoolhouse, bent on his mission.

Lark set her elbows on the top of her desk, buried her face in her hands and groaned aloud.

Within five minutes, Roland Franks would be pounding on Mrs. Fairmont's front door, with marriage on his mind.

What had she *done?*

12

For Autry Whitman that third train robbery was the final outrageous, insufferable insult.

When word of it reached him in Denver, he'd ordered his private car coupled behind a locomotive and stormed onboard. Now, on a bright Friday morning, he was steaming southwest, toward Flagstaff, with a trail of passenger and freight cars rattling along the track behind him.

The passenger cars were emptier than they should have been—word of the holdup had already spread, and folks were afraid to travel. Fewer passengers meant less revenue, a condition soon to be reflected in Autry's bank balances.

And that would not do.

He meant to meet with the Rangers and as many other law enforcement officials as he could corral, which was plenty, given the extent of his influence, political and otherwise, and demand immediate *action*. By God, this was America, and a man had a right to run a railroad without being molested by a pack of no-account hoodlums and ne'er-do-wells.

No one treated Autry Whitman like this.

No one save Lark McCullough.

Bile seared the back of Autry's throat, sour and scalding. He shifted uncomfortably in his seat and glowered out the window at a snowy landscape. He'd have an accounting from her, some fine day in the near future, and it would be a memorable one, too.

Especially for her.

Why, he'd found her in a San Francisco show house, cavorting for a lot of seamy strangers in a scanty getup, and he'd been *stricken* at the sight of her—not with love, Autry didn't believe in such fatuous sentiments as that—but with the desperate need to possess her. He'd given Cyrus Teede, the owner of the gentleman's club, twenty-five thousand dollars, and even at that price, Teede had been reluctant to sell.

He'd known what he had.

Lark. The golden songbird. The smiling Jezebel. On top of what he'd given Teede, Autry had spent a fortune to outfit her as a decent woman, befitting his station in life. He'd taken her home to Denver, knowing full well what she was, all her clever trickeries aside, and she'd played her part well.

For a while.

Then she'd begun the little rebellions. Talking back to him. Wearing blue when he'd specifically told her he liked her best in red. Giving his hard-earned money to street urchins. Finally she'd tried locking him out of her bedroom.

And he'd thrashed her for it, same as he would a disobedient hound or a balking horse. It was his right as a husband, as head of his household.

Three days after that, the songbird had flown.

Autry's right hand tightened into a fist. He'd find her, that was for certain. Divorce or no divorce, she was still his property. The little chit couldn't elude him forever—he had too many competent men out searching for her, spanning the whole West like a great, long-fingered hand.

Autry looked down at his fist.

He'd told the Pinkertons, and a few private agents, too, that he wanted to find Lark so he could tell her all was forgiven. Set up living arrangements for her, if she wouldn't come back to him.

But the truth was a little different.

Lark had humiliated him, far and wide.

And she would pay for it.

Once he'd taken care of business in that upstart cow town, he might even pay a call on an old friend, a local named Ruby Hollister. Ruby was a woman of singular talents, as he recalled, though he hadn't seen her in many years, and she knew how to lift a man's spirits.

Among other things.

Autry might have smiled in anticipation, if the trail of his thoughts, having turned a bend into the area of female favors, hadn't led right back to Lark.

Beautiful, golden-haired Lark, with a singing voice suited to her name.

She *owed* him. He'd rescued her from a seamy environment, willing to overlook all prior sins, and he'd been generous, too. Given her everything a woman could rightly want—starting with the title of Mrs. Autry Whitman—and plenty besides.

She'd lived in one of the finest mansions in Denver.

He'd hired a maid for her, and she'd never so much as washed a dish or made up a bed.

Her clothes were the best to be had, some sent from as far away as Paris, France. He'd decked her out in jewels, too, and asked only one thing in return—that she stand at his side, in public and private, as his wife.

Why, he hadn't even minded when she spurned his advances in the bedroom. There *was* a considerable difference between their ages—Autry would be seventy in May, while Lark had been just shy of twenty-five when he first laid eyes on her.

She'd done a lot of living by that time, though.

He'd known she didn't love him and, well, his intended assignation with Ruby aside, there were times when he couldn't do much besides set Lark on his lap and paw at her. She'd endured that for a long while, but Autry was no fool—he'd seen the revulsion in her eyes, even though, in the beginning, she'd tried to hide it.

When he *had* been able to attend to his husbandly duties, hoping to God to sire an heir, she'd lain stiff beneath him, like it was an ordeal. Considering where he'd met her, that was harder to take than the rest of it.

He could have accepted even that, so long as she played the part of an adoring wife in front of Denver society, and he had to admit, she'd done a good job of that—until the day she ran out on him during his best friend's funeral.

He closed his eyes, remembering.

He'd come home after the ceremony expecting consolation, and found her gone. *Gone*. At first Autry was too stunned to credit it. After some investigation, he discovered that Lark had told Phillips, his manservant, some cock-and-bull story about her sister taking ill, and the damn fool had driven her to the railroad station without a single quibble.

Trouble was, Lark didn't *have* a sister. She didn't have any family at all.

Except him.

Ten days after her departure, Autry had received divorce papers by courier, from some lawyer in San Francisco. Enraged, needing to take the shock out on somebody, Autry had sent Phillips packing, and he'd made sure nobody in Denver would hire him, too.

Then he'd wired the Pinkertons in California, and had agents dispatched to pick up Lark's trail there. But the lawyer hadn't parted with any information at all, save to say Lark had left the city days before and had not shared her intended destination.

When Autry protested, also by telegram, that *he* had not agreed to divorce, the lawyer had responded with such immediacy that he might have been standing right in the telegraph office when Autry's wire arrived.

"Divorce granted," the answer said. "Special circumstances. Mrs. Whitman asks nothing in the way of financial restitution and requests that you do not attempt to contact her again."

Autry still read that telegram sometimes, in the privacy of his study back in Denver, but only when he'd fortified himself with brandy and ire first.

"Mrs. Whitman asks nothing in the way of financial restitution."

As if he'd have given her one red cent, after what she'd done to him.

And he most certainly meant to "contact" her. It was

only a matter of time until he'd have the satisfaction of doing just that.

But first he'd deal with those robbers.

Autry leaned forward slightly in his plush seat, willing the train to go faster.

LARK SENT GIDEON and the Sommerville girls home an hour before school should have let out, but she stayed at her desk instead of going back to Mrs. Porter's, reading and waiting for Sam O'Ballivan to come and fetch her in a wagon, the way Maddie had said he would.

At four o'clock she heard the distinctive sounds of a rig and team, clattering up outside.

Eagerly, smiling a little at the things Mrs. Porter had instructed her to find out, she banked the fire, donned her spare cloak and rushed to the door.

A buckboard waited outside the gate, pulled by a pair of bay horses, but Mr. O'Ballivan wasn't holding the reins. Rowdy was.

The shadow of his hat brim, at which he promptly tugged with a practiced motion of one hand, covered most of his face. His impudent grin was clearly visible, however.

Lark froze on the schoolhouse steps.

Rowdy gave a visible sigh, climbed down from the wagon box and paused to open the gate.

Lark hesitated a few moments longer, then marched toward him, chin high, skirts swirling.

They met in the path, midway between the gate and the schoolhouse door.

"That's some dress," Rowdy observed, taking in the blue silk.

Lark had dined with the governor of Colorado and several congressmen in that dress, but she wasn't about to say so. "Thank you," she said stiffly. "And what are you doing here? I'm expecting Mr. O'Ballivan at any moment—"

"Plans have changed," Rowdy said easily, although now that she was standing up close to him, she saw signs of strain around his eyes and in the set of his mouth. "I'm invited to this shindig, too, and Sam asked me to bring you along. No sense in his driving all the way into town and then back again—twice—when I'm headed out there anyway."

Lark discovered, to her private chagrin, that she didn't entirely object to the prospect of going to the O'Ballivan ranch and then returning alone with Rowdy Rhodes. And that realization troubled her more than anything, made her want to dig in her heels and refuse to go at all.

She couldn't do that, of course, because Maddie had probably gone to some trouble to prepare for guests. And Lark wanted Maddie O'Ballivan's friendship.

Still, Rowdy could not be trusted. The bold look in his eyes implied that, as if the way he'd kissed her behind the jailhouse that day wasn't proof enough.

Lark blushed slightly at the memory, and her nipples pressed traitorously against the fabric of her best camisole and the bodice of her dress. Belatedly, she pulled her black velvet opera cape closed with both hands.

Rowdy chuckled, shook his head almost imperceptibly. Then he crooked an elbow at her. "Come along, Miss Morgan," he said, with the old note of mockery.

"Sam tells me it's an hour to the ranch by wagon in high summer, and it'll be slow going, with all the mud and slush."

Lark sighed. Then, with the greatest reluctance, she took his arm.

He had the audacity to touch her posterior while helping her up into the wagon, and when she turned to glare him to a cinder, he only smiled and tugged at his hat brim again.

His eyes made some very forward promises, and Lark's face went hot again with temper and—though she would have died before admitting it—a certain scandalous anticipation.

If he stopped that wagon somewhere along the lonely road to the O'Ballivans' and kissed her, she'd be a goner. Why, she might even let him do a lot *more* than kiss her.

Don't be a goose, she told herself, making a great fuss of settling onto the wagon seat, arranging the folds of her cloak, and generally situating herself for the long trip ahead. *It's the dead of winter, and even Rowdy Rhodes wouldn't have the gall to seduce you in a wagon.*

While Rowdy was climbing up to sit beside her and take up the reins again, she glanced back over one shoulder.

There were blankets in the bed of the wagon.

Lark's heartbeat fluttered in her throat, as though she'd swallowed a live butterfly and the poor thing was trying to escape.

Rowdy must have caught her looking and discerned her thoughts in that disturbing way he had, because he grinned as he released the brake lever and urged the team forward.

"Don't worry, Lark," he told her quietly, his voice moving like a caress under her skin. "When I make love to you, it will be in a warm bed. At least, the first time."

Delicious rebellion rose within Lark Morgan. He'd made her think about the things he planned to do to her in that "warm bed," which was exactly his intent. "I ought to slap you," she said, sitting up straighter on that hard wagon seat.

"You've tried that before," Rowdy observed lightly, "and you weren't quick enough."

"Now you're just being obnoxious," Lark accused, as he turned the team and wagon in the road. "Why do you insist on talking to me like this?"

"Because it riles you," he replied.

"If you actually believe I'm going to allow you to seduce me—"

"You'll allow it, all right," Rowdy said confidently, when she didn't finish the sentence. Then he leaned toward her a little and whispered loudly, "It's already begun, Lark. It's been going on since you and I first met, in Mrs. Porter's kitchen. One by one, I mean to strip away every objection, and when you ask me to—and you will—I'll have you."

Lark squirmed. Of course the seduction *had* begun—a word, a look, a touch. That soul-shattering kiss behind the jailhouse. "I will *never* ask you to make love to me," she vowed, in a furious undertone, as they drove straight through the center of town.

"Yes, you will," Rowdy countered easily. "Shall I tell you what it will be like?"

Lark's body went achy hot. *Yes,* it said. *Oh, yes.*

"No!" she gasped, and then smiled a wobbly smile at a woman on the sidewalk, fearing she might have heard.

Rowdy chuckled. "I figure you've been with at least one man in your life," he went on, just as if she hadn't protested—indeed, as if she'd *encouraged* him, which she had not. "But I'd bet anything you've never felt the things you're going to feel when I have my way with you."

"Stop."

"Stop what?"

"Stop seducing me."

"Way too late for that. You're almost there right now." He waved companionably to Jolene Bell, who scowled back at him from the doorway of her saloon.

"I most certainly *am not,*" Lark argued, but she wasn't all that certain, and Rowdy clearly knew it.

"Of course, after that first time, which will take place in a bed, like it should, I might have you just about anywhere, as long as we're alone. Against a wall, maybe, with your drawers down around your ankles—"

"Rowdy Rhodes," Lark said heatedly, "*stop it,* or take me home!"

"You don't want to go home," Rowdy told her. "You wouldn't want to disappoint Maddie like that. She's been snowed in awhile, just like you have, and she's probably looking forward to the visit." He paused as they passed out of Stone Creek, into the open countryside. The roads were deep with mud and slush, just as he'd said they would be. "And you don't want me to stop talking about making love to you, either."

"What makes you so sure of that?" Lark demanded, incensed.

And wickedly aroused.

"The way you keep squirming on the wagon seat, because you can't get comfortable, for one thing. The flush rising from your neck to your hairline for another, and the little throb at the base of your throat."

"This wagon seat is *hard,*" Lark protested, in her own defense.

"Not nearly as hard as I will be," Rowdy said.

Lark closed her eyes against an onslaught of feelings and images, but it was no use. Autry had been old and awkward and he'd smelled funny, too. Rowdy was her former husband's opposite in every way—he was young and virile. He was comfortable in his own skin, with a gunslinger's dangerous grace, and he always smelled of sun-dried laundry and strong soap.

He undoubtedly knew how to please a woman.

Think about Autry, she told herself sternly.

But she couldn't, because Autry was miles away in Denver, and Rowdy was right beside her, so close, in fact, that their thighs were touching.

"Inside," Rowdy went on mildly, "you're wound up tight as a watch spring when the stem's been turned too far. And I know just the way to make you let go. Won't even need a bed to do it."

Lark's heart hammered in her throat. Her stomach jumped.

And she parted her legs ever so slightly under the skirts of her blue silk dress.

"Rowdy," she pleaded.

"That's more like it," he said.

Her temper surged again. Where the devil had it been when she needed it? "That *wasn't* what I meant—"

"Wasn't it?" Rowdy teased.

She realized then that he was baiting her. Of *course,* he was merely nettling her, and she'd played right into his hands. So to speak.

"Go to hell, Rowdy Rhodes," she said.

"Yup," Rowdy said solemnly. "Tighter than a watch spring."

They traveled in silence for a while. Passed a farm-house or two, and copses of oak and cottonwood trees, bare-limbed and seeming to strain toward the sky, as if offering a desolate prayer for spring.

They'd probably been on the road for at least forty-five minutes, with the O'Ballivan place nowhere in sight, when Rowdy suddenly stopped the wagon.

"Horses need to rest," he explained, when Lark stiff-ened. "It's hard pulling for them, with the mud and all."

She let out her breath.

Nothing could happen here.

They were on the open road. It was broad daylight. And anyone could come riding by on a horse, or driving a wagon, at any moment.

She was completely safe.

Then Rowdy leaned into the back of the wagon and picked up one of the blankets.

"You're cold," he said, his eyes twinkling, when she started again.

He smoothed the blanket over her lap.

Lark tensed, closed her eyes, opened them again when he kissed her.

She wanted to resist.

She truly did.

But when he persuaded her to open her mouth for him, his lips warm and firm against hers, his tongue exploring—she couldn't help responding.

She whimpered softly and kissed him back.

She was dazed when he stopped, sweetly alarmed when he knelt between the wagon seat and the footboard and slipped beneath the blanket.

A molten shiver went through Lark as she felt him go under her skirts and petticoats, too. What was he going to do?

Autry had never done anything like—

He ducked under her left leg, set both her feet against the front of the wagon.

Oh, mercy. He was between—

She felt the delicate fabric of her drawers give way, right in the middle.

She sucked in a shocked, exultant breath.

And then his mouth was on her.

Lark gave a strangled cry, but it wasn't a protest, and Rowdy must have known that, because he chuckled, under the blanket and her skirts and petticoats. The sound echoed through her.

"Rowdy," she managed to gasp, clutching the edges of the wagon seat, "someone could come—"

He chuckled again. "Someone could," he agreed in a wicked drawl, his voice muffled by her garments and her skin. "In fact, I'd bet on it right about now."

Lark began to breathe harder, and more quickly. "Don't—" she whimpered.

"Don't what, Lark?"

"Don't—stop."

He feasted on her then. He tugged at her, and he teased, until she was wild with need, rocking in the wagon seat, her feet pressing hard into the footboard. Her nipples ached and perspiration broke out all over her body and she was climbing toward something, climbing and climbing—

And then the world shattered.

Lark threw back her head and shouted his name aloud.

He stayed with her, bringing her to several more releases, each one softer, and yet keener, than the one before.

She was dazed—melted—when Rowdy finally threw off the blanket, righted her petticoats and skirts, and shifted himself back onto the wagon seat. He wiped her wetness from his face with the sleeve of his trail coat, and Lark was suddenly, belatedly, mortified by what she'd allowed him to do.

She looked away.

He caught her chin in his hand and made her look back.

"That's what you ought to feel when a man makes love to you, Lark," he told her when she finally met his gaze. "It ought to make you moan and writhe and holler out his name when you come undone."

Tears sprang to her eyes. She'd *never* felt that way with Autry, never even known it was possible. With Autry lovemaking was something to be endured. Fumbling and sometimes painful, and always done in darkness.

Rowdy Rhodes had just—he'd just put his mouth to

the most intimate part of her body, on a public road, and she'd not only let him, she'd reveled in it, and she'd have done it again. And yet again.

She put a hand to her mouth, horrified by this realization. She'd always thought herself to be one kind of person, only to find out now that she was quite another. The next time she looked into a mirror, she'd see a wanton stranger gazing back at her.

She didn't know how to *be* this woman she had just become.

Rowdy smiled, pulled her hand away from her mouth, and kissed her again, lightly this time. Then he brushed the tears from her cheeks with his thumbs and turned to release the brake lever and take up the reins again.

Lark sat, baffled and damp, profoundly satisfied and conversely in greater need than before, still clutching the edge of the seat.

Suppose it showed, what she'd just done with Rowdy?

Suppose Sam and Maddie guessed, somehow?

"I'm going to have to mend my bloomers," she said.

Rowdy laughed. Shook his head. His blue eyes soothed her, even though they twinkled with mischief. "Where did *that* come from?" he asked.

She summoned up a little huff. "You tore them, remember?"

"I surely do. Leave them like that. It'll save wear and tear and be easier next time."

Lark stared at him, aghast. *"Next time?"*

"Tomorrow night, maybe," he said. "Before or after the dance." The mischievous glint in his eyes intensified. "Or maybe on the way back to town tonight, after supper."

Lark flushed again.

Rowdy chuckled.

"You wouldn't," Lark told him.

"You know I would," Rowdy answered.

Lark lapsed into sweet misery.

Half an hour later the O'Ballivan house came into view, nestled in a wide meadow beside a winding creek that had frozen blue in the cold. In fact, there were two houses on the property, at some distance from each other but enclosed by the same rail fence.

Smoke curled invitingly from their stone chimneys.

Rowdy seemed to know which place belonged to Sam and Maddie, and when Maddie came out onto the porch to smile and wave, Lark stopped worrying and relaxed.

Maddie wore a brown silk dress, and she was beaming. "Sam," she called, through the open doorway behind her, "they're here!"

Rowdy stopped the wagon, tipped his hat to Maddie and jumped down to come around to Lark's side and lift her from the seat. At the touch of his hands on either side of her waist, and for just the merest moment, she was back where he'd taken her earlier, at the height of ecstasy.

She crooned involuntarily, under her breath.

Rowdy winked at her and made sure she traveled the whole hard length of him before her feet finally struck the ground.

Sam came out of the house, and he and Rowdy unhitched the team, led the horses to the barn, so they could rest comfortably before the long trek back to Stone Creek later that night.

"I'm so glad you're here," Maddie told Lark, squeezing her hand and then pulling her into the house.

Mrs. Porter would have been impressed. It was a beautiful place, with paintings on the walls and bright Indian rugs gracing the wooden floors. The spinet gleamed in the light of a crackling blaze on the hearth of the big stone fireplace.

Lark took a step toward the little piano before she caught herself.

Mustn't touch the keys, the still, small voice reminded her. *Mustn't sing.*

Ever.

Those things were part of her old life, gone for ever.

"I thought I'd go mad, cooped up here during that blizzard," Maddie confided. "Sam was here, of course, but talking to him isn't like talking to another woman."

"Where's Terran?" Lark asked, remembering that she was a teacher and ought to inquire about her student.

"He's over at the major's, with Ben," Maddie answered, indicating that Lark should take one of the chairs near the fire. "And Sam, Jr., is already asleep." She sighed, glanced wistfully out one of the windows. "It gets dark so early in winter."

Inwardly Lark started slightly. It *was* dark.

When had the sun gone down. How could she have failed to notice?

"Would you like a cup of tea while we wait for Sam and the marshal to come back from the barn? Supper's almost ready, but they're likely to stand out there and talk awhile."

"Tea would be lovely," Lark replied gratefully. She

stood again, and was instantly aware of the ripped seam in her bloomers. She would mend them the *moment* she got home, she told herself.

She really would.

Supper smelled heavenly—Maddie had made chicken and dumplings, one of Lark's favorites.

The two women chattered as Maddie brewed and poured the tea.

Maddie was so obviously happy, through and through, that she glowed.

When Sam and Rowdy came in from the barn, entering by the back door, Sam introduced Rowdy to his wife. The look in Sam's eyes as he gazed at Maddie made Lark's heart catch painfully. Their love for each other was palpable, as real and eternal as the land the house was built upon.

Lark glanced at Rowdy, found he was watching her.

His expression was thoughtful, even a little solemn.

Maddie served supper in the kitchen, on sturdy dishes with flowers painted on the edges, and the meal was delicious.

Maddie and Lark laughed a great deal.

Sam and Rowdy were more subdued, though they exchanged the occasional word or two.

"Are you coming to town for the dance tomorrow night?" Lark asked Maddie, and then wished she hadn't brought up the dance, because Rowdy had said he was going to do *that* to her again, before or after.

If not on the way home that very night.

"If the weather holds, we'll be there," Maddie said. Mischief shimmered in her brown eyes. "I would surely *love* to make Sam O'Ballivan dance."

Sam grinned, shifted a little on his chair. But he didn't say he *wouldn't* dance. Lark concluded, a bit wistfully, that Maddie could probably get him to do almost anything.

Too soon, the meal ended, and the dishes were done, and Sam and Rowdy went back out to the barn for the team.

"I wish you'd stay the night," Maddie fretted. "Suppose another storm comes up?"

"We'll be fine," Lark promised. "And Maddie?"

Maddie paused, looked at her curiously. "What?"

"Thank you for tonight. It was wonderful."

Maddie smiled, approached and squeezed both Lark's hands in her own. "You'll have to come back," she said.

A few minutes later, when all the goodbyes had been said, and Lark and Rowdy were driving away from the ranch house, the lilting strains of the spinet reached Lark's ears, rippling over the melting snow like a silvery river.

She began to cry.

The moon was out, and they didn't need lanterns to see by, so she couldn't hide her tears from Rowdy.

"What is it?" he asked gently.

"The music," Lark said. She'd lied for so long, about so many things, that she wasn't sure of anything anymore, but she still mourned. "The music."

Holding the reins in one hand, Rowdy tucked the blanket around her with the other. Held her against his side for a long moment.

She felt dangerously safe there.

They'd gone a mile or two, perhaps, when Lark reached out from under the blanket to touch Rowdy's gloved hand.

He glanced at her, confused.

She swallowed.

"Lark?" he prompted.

"Do it to me again," she said, appalled at the brazenness of her words. "What…what you did before. Stop the wagon and make me feel all those things again."

Rowdy drew the wagon up alongside the moon-washed road, under the arching branches of an oak tree. Somewhere in the near distance an animal howled, the sound so lonely and forlorn that it stuck in Lark's heart like a nettle.

"You're sure?" he asked.

She nodded.

He climbed over the back of the wagon seat, made a little nest of the blankets there. Then, crouched, he held out his hand to Lark.

She let him help her into the bed of the wagon.

Let him lay her down.

He took off his hat, set it aside, and lifted her skirts.

This time, he removed her bloomers entirely. He bent her knees, parted them and lowered himself to her.

Lark gave a sob of welcome, and entangled her fingers in his hair, holding him close, seeking him with the motion of her hips.

He tongued her.

He suckled.

And she cried out to the wintry silver stars overhead as she spiraled up toward them and became a part of the night sky.

13

ROWDY RETURNED the hired team and wagon to the livery stable, after he'd seen Lark safely inside Mrs. Porter's back door and heard the lock turn behind it, and as he walked toward the jailhouse, he wondered why he hadn't kissed her good-night.

It wasn't as if he hadn't done plenty else.

He smiled at the memory of Lark's responses, still felt the press of her smooth, bare thighs against his ears. Damn, but it had been all he could do not to claim her in the back of that wagon, on that pile of scratchy blankets.

She'd have taken fire, pitched beneath him like a wildcat. He knew she thought she'd released all her passion—but she was in for a surprise. She'd barely scratched the surface of what burned beneath this first surrender.

But he'd made up his mind to have Lark Morgan in a bed before anyplace else, and until that sacred time came, he'd be content to keep unwinding that watch spring, every chance he got.

The jailhouse was dark, meaning Gideon had probably locked up for the night, so Rowdy made his way around back. He smiled, wondering if Lark would stitch up that tear in her bloomers or wear them as they were.

He'd find out tomorrow night, after the dance.

There were lamps burning in his house, the light glowing yellow at the windows, and he heard Pardner barking and clawing at the door. It opened, and the dog shot out and rushed him, galloping around him in gleeful greeting.

Rowdy bent and roughed up Pardner's ears.

Gideon loomed on the doorstep, a shadow rimmed in the glimmer of the lanterns. "Coffee's on," he called.

"Good," Rowdy replied. Thinking of Lark, and the way she'd shouted out his name when she reached her climaxes, he needed to walk around in the dark for a while. Cool off. "I'll be right in," he added. "Just want to see to the horses."

Gideon nodded and stepped back inside the house.

The lean-to was dark, but Rowdy could see his breath in the air. He reached for a lantern, struck a match to the wick.

And that was when he saw the paint, standing in his regular place.

Payton's black gelding was gone, and there was a note stuck through a nail on one of the weathered poles holding up the roof.

"Keep your damn horse," Pappy had written, in his curiously elegant copperplate.

When Rowdy had risen that morning, having slept on the cot in the jail cell, he'd known his pa was already gone, and he'd headed for the lean-to barn, right away, to confirm his suspicions and to mourn Paint's leaving, if not his father's.

The black gelding had been right where Paint was now. Gideon's livery-stable nag was still there, too.

Shaking his head, Rowdy ran an appreciative hand along the animal's side. Pappy had come back—God only knew when—and swapped Paint for his own mount.

What, exactly, did that mean?

With Pappy, it was hard to tell. He might have done it because he knew how highly Rowdy valued the pinto, but it could have been a petulant gesture, too. The note certainly implied the latter, but Rowdy wasn't sure.

And he decided not muddle his brain by debating the matter.

He made sure Paint and the other horse had plenty of hay and water, Pardner getting underfoot throughout the process, then headed back toward the house. He was fit to be seen now, but his groin still ached, heavy with the need to finish what he'd started with Lark.

The fire was high in the stove, and the coffee smelled better than good.

Rowdy hung up his hat, took off his coat and gun belt and glanced at Gideon, who was sitting at the table with a book open in front of him.

Pardner lay down where it was warmest and sighed.

"Was Pa here tonight?" Rowdy asked, and he watched his brother closely while he waited for the answer, because he knew Gideon might lie for a variety of reasons.

Pappy might have told him to, for one.

Or he could be covering for the old reprobate.

Gideon shook his head. No color rose in his face to refute the silent assertion. His gaze was direct, and there was no apparent restlessness in his hands or feet. "Me and Pardner, we been here ever since we shut up the jail at suppertime." He smiled. "Mai Lee brought a basket by, around sundown, and we had ourselves a feast. Fried chicken and biscuits."

"That's good," Rowdy said, instantly reminded that he'd had a couple of feasts himself that evening, outside the one at Maddie O'Ballivan's supper table.

In his mind he heard Lark's voice again, repeating a fevered litany with increasing desperation. Rowdy—oh, Rowdy, please—

He shoved a hand through his hair, turned his back to Gideon to pour a mugful of steaming-hot coffee. Maybe he should have stayed out there in the cold a little while longer and pondered the mysterious workings of Payton Yarbro's mind.

Gideon frowned. "Why'd you ask if Pa had been here?"

"Paint is back," Rowdy said.

"What?" Gideon asked, sounding surprised. "I went to the barn right after supper, and Paint wasn't there—only my horse and Samson."

Rowdy risked turning around. He was still so hard he hurt, but the lantern light was dim enough, and he was settling down a little.

"Pa *must* have come back, then," Gideon mused.

"And not very long ago, either," Rowdy agreed with a nod, after a sip of his coffee, "if it was around suppertime when you checked on the horses." He frowned.

Was Payton still lurking around out there in the dark someplace, he and the black gelding? "He left a note. 'Keep your damn horse.' That's all there was."

Gideon grinned. "I know you and Pa get along about like lamp oil and well water, but it sounds to me like he was trying to do something good for you."

Rowdy gave a contemptuous snort, but deep down he wondered if Gideon wasn't right. Even hoped, just a little, and against all good sense and reason, that it might be so.

Gideon's chair scraped against the floor as he shoved it back, and his grin was gone. "Why do you hate him like you do?" he demanded tersely. "He's your *pa*."

Rowdy considered that undeniable fact. Whether he liked it or not, and whatever he called himself to escape the fact, Payton Yarbro *was* his pa. Not John T. Rhodes. He'd never be his real self, for better or for worse, until he took back his right name.

And that, of course, was never going to be possible.

Suddenly he felt bleak inside. Hollowed out.

While Rowdy was pondering all these things, Gideon waited stubbornly for an answer.

"I don't hate him," Rowdy said, and realized in the moment he spoke that it was true. He didn't need the old man's admiration, or even his approval. If he never saw Pappy again it would be a month too soon, but he didn't hate him. Not even close.

"You act like you do."

"I'm not the one who knocked him clear back into the lean-to when he tried to leave the first time," Rowdy pointed out lightly.

Gideon reflected on that, sagged a little around the shoulders. "Was he really such a bad pa to you?"

Rowdy shrugged, took more coffee. "He could have been worse. The fact is, he wasn't around enough to tell what kind of pa he'd have made."

"Pa never laid a hand on me," Gideon said. "Not even once. That's why I feel so bad about breaking his nose and all."

Rowdy had known a much younger Payton, with a much hotter temper, especially when he began to get restless. Once or twice when he was little and his old man had hauled him off to the woodshed for a switching, Rowdy would have loved to break that arrogant Yarbro nose, just as Gideon had done.

"Pa wants you to go to college when you finish your schooling here in the territory," Rowdy said. "He asked me to make sure you do."

Gideon averted his eyes. He fancied himself a deputy marshal—Rowdy knew he'd worn that beat-up old badge to school that morning, pinned to the inside of his coat—and most likely he was about to argue that college would be a waste of time and money.

He ought to just get on with being a deputy.

Rowdy had a response at the ready. Gideon *would* make a good lawman, in part, ironically, because he had a streak of outlaw in him, along with that youthful idealism of his, but he'd be an even better one with an education.

Finally Gideon looked back at him. Swallowed hard. "I reckon I'll go when the time comes," he said. "To that college back east, I mean."

"Good," Rowdy said, surprised.

Suddenly Gideon grinned. "In the meantime, I don't mind looking at Miss Morgan every day." He gave a low whistle, one that would have raised Rowdy's hackles coming from anybody else but his kid brother. "She was *something* in that fancy blue dress she wore today."

Rowdy grinned into his mug, nodded. Lark had been something with that fancy blue dress up around her waist, too. Sweet and warm and juicy as a sun-ripened peach.

"Miss Langston—she was my teacher in Flagstaff—never wore anything like that blue dress. Folks would probably run her out of town on a rail if she did, and, anyhow, she's about a hundred and she's *square*."

"Square?" Rowdy asked, mildly confounded. In his experience, women were round, or they were angular, or something in between, but he'd never run across a square one.

"Ruby says it's because of her corset," Gideon said wisely.

"Oh," Rowdy replied, frowning. Still trying to work it out.

"I guess you'd have to see her for yourself to understand."

"Guess so," Rowdy agreed. "Speaking of Ruby—"

"I know," Gideon said, evidently anticipating what Rowdy had been about to say. "I've got to go back to Flagstaff, soon as I can, and let her know I saw Pa and he's headed for Mexico. And give back the livery-stable horse, too, so they don't hang me for a horse thief."

"I'll go with you," Rowdy said. "We'll leave in the morning, at first light, if the weather allows."

Gideon looked worried. "Do I get to come back here? Because I really like it better, even if I can't visit Rose's grave. I like being a deputy and going to school."

"If you want to come back," Rowdy told him, "you can." He liked having Gideon around, and Pardner clearly did, too. He just hoped he wouldn't have to leave them both behind, one dark day, to fend for themselves.

"You're not dodging that dance tomorrow night, are you?" Gideon asked forthrightly. "Miss Morgan told that big farmer you hauled out of the wagon the other day that she was going with you."

Rowdy had been about to raise his cup to his lips again, but at the mention of Roland Franks, his arm froze in midair. "He came to school?"

Now, why hadn't Lark mentioned that, when they were together all that time tonight? They hadn't been busy the *whole* time, after all.

Gideon nodded, frowning a little. "She wanted him to stay and take up his lessons again, just as if nothing had happened, but he stomped out of there meaning to ask Lydia's mother if *she'd* go to the dance with him, and Miss Morgan was upset after that. She put her hands over her face and made a real peculiar sound—I thought she was crying, for a second."

"But she wasn't?"

Gideon shook his head. "She got over it real quick, and started up the lessons."

Damn, Rowdy marveled silently. Lark still thought she could handle Franks. Get him settled right back into the third grade. For an intelligent, spirited woman, she sure had some sappy ideas.

Rowdy was briefly tempted to saddle up, ride out to the Franks place, wherever the hell it was, and convince Roland that his school days were over.

He was even *more* tempted to walk over to Mrs. Porter's, drag Lark out of her bed, try to get it through her boney little head that Franks wasn't longing for the delights of higher education.

He had another kind of delight in mind.

Rowdy sighed. Franks wouldn't be bothering Lark tonight, or even tomorrow, in the broad light of day, not after that scene in front of the jailhouse.

And if he, Rowdy, roused Lark out of a sound sleep and tried to reason with her, she might just be peeved enough to stitch up the seam in her bloomers.

Besides, he needed to get some sleep, especially since he and Gideon were making a fast ride to Flagstaff and back the next day.

He'd speak to Lark tomorrow, he decided.

Before the dance, since he had other plans for after.

LARK LAY RESTLESS beside a soundly sleeping Lydia, her face flaming in the darkness of the room they shared.

What had possessed her to throw herself at Rowdy the way she had?

All right, the first time, when he'd said all those things about watch springs, and ducked under her skirts, he'd taken her by surprise. She'd practically been in the throes of—she swallowed—*passion* before she realized what he was going to do.

But on the way back from Sam and Maddie's, she'd *asked* him to pleasure her again, like some hussy.

Mortification stung her cheeks at the remembrance of it.

She'd lain in the back of that wagon with Rowdy

willingly, even eagerly, for heaven's sake. And she'd carried on something terrible while he—while he—did what? Did it have a name, what he did?

Did other people do it?

She wished she could ask Maddie, but of course, that would be impossible. She'd die of embarrassment before she even got the words out.

And what if it happened again?

She stiffened, remembering her vow to mend the crotch of her best bloomers, the ones she'd worn tonight. Where was her sewing kit?

Should she get up, light a lamp, and see to the task right now, this very minute?

She simply couldn't.

It would be too terrible if Mrs. Porter, or even Mai Lee, got up for some reason, and caught her sewing up her drawers. Why, they might arrive at all kinds of wicked conclusions, and how would she explain?

No.

Better to do her mending another time.

Perhaps after she got home from the dance tomorrow night.

She could wear another pair of bloomers, after all.

But what if she succumbed to temptation again? Rowdy would surely tear the second pair, in just the same way, and she knew she wouldn't tell him to stop.

Her cheeks flamed with renewed heat.

She wouldn't tell him to stop.

Tonight she hadn't even been able to tell *herself* to stop, not with any conviction, anyway.

He'd said he was already seducing her. And then he'd proved it.

He'd also said she'd *ask* him to take her to his bed.

She'd been so sure she'd never do that.

That's what you ought to feel when a man makes love to you, Lark. It ought to make you moan and writhe and holler out his name when you come undone.

Was that what she was supposed to feel?

Lark wasn't sure.

All she knew for certain was that she wanted to feel all of it again.

SATURDAY MORNING DAWNED clear and fairly warm, for the twenty-eighth of January. It bothered Rowdy to shut Pardner up in the house, though he'd left him plenty of water and beef jerky to last. But he did it. Pardner was an old dog, and he might just fall over, same as John T. had out there in his cornfield, if he attempted to go all the way to Flagstaff and back. And carrying him in the saddle would have slowed them down too much.

Still, the dog's howls echoed in Rowdy's ears long after he and Gideon had ridden off.

They made good time, though. Arrived in Flagstaff at midmorning and tied their horses in front of Ruby's Saloon and Poker House, amid a flock of others.

Tinny piano music flowed out over the doors, proclaiming it was business as usual at Ruby's. Rowdy wondered how she was explaining Jack Payton's absence to curious customers and anyone else who might show an interest.

Gideon, he noticed, glanced toward the street. From the boy's expression, Rowdy figured he was watching Rose fall under the wheels of that wagon, as surely as if it was happening right then, and he wondered how many times the kid had relived that day over the ten years since then.

A chill ran down his spine.

It was my fault, Gideon had said.

Rowdy laid a hand on his brother's shoulder, nodded toward the saloon doors.

Gideon braced up, tore himself from his private reverie and followed Rowdy inside.

Ruby's place was like a hundred others Rowdy had seen in his many travels—there was sawdust on the floor, and the piano needed a tuning it was never going to get—but Ruby catered to local businessmen, not just cowpokes and drifters, as evidenced by all the suits he saw standing around.

The bar was fancier than most, made of some gleaming hardwood, intricately carved with curlicues and such. And the mirror behind it had none of the usual murky spots, where the silver showed through.

Someone must have alerted Ruby to their arrival, because she came sweeping out of a side room, her red skirts swirling around her, and headed right for them.

"Gideon Payton," she said, putting her hands on her rounded hips, "I've worried myself *sick* about you."

"I left you a note," Gideon reminded her. But he took his hat off and twisted it nervously in his hands.

Ruby was a force to be reckoned with, it appeared. She'd have had to be, Rowdy figured, to hold her own with Payton Yarbro all this time.

Her gaze sliced to Rowdy. They'd only met once, and briefly at that, but it was plain she remembered him.

"My office," she said summarily, and turned in a

flurry of skirts and expensive perfume to glide across the saloon toward the same door she'd just come out of a minute before.

Gideon followed right away.

Rowdy left him to it. He had no business with Ruby—he'd just come along because he didn't want Gideon making the ride alone.

He didn't want any whiskey, the day being so young, so he took a seat at an empty table, resigned to wait. A dancehall girl offered him a drink and whatever else he might enjoy, and he politely refused.

He tapped his fingers idly on the tabletop and scanned the room for a second time. There sure were a lot of suits in this saloon, he thought, for a cow town like Flagstaff.

Then, finally, it registered.

These weren't bankers or storekeepers.

They were rangers, hard-eyed and watchful, and there must have been a dozen of them.

Rowdy was glad he'd worn his badge, but truly it wasn't much comfort to him just then. There were Wanted posters all over the West bearing his description, and even his image, in a few cases, and some or all of these men must have seen them.

He'd known there would be an encounter, of course, but he'd expected to be in Sam O'Ballivan's company when the introductions were made. Even if some of the men were suspicious, Sam's presence would have automatically put a lot of their questions to rest.

Damn.

Why hadn't he *thought* of this?

Because he'd been thinking about Lark Morgan instead, that was why.

One of the men peeled himself away from the bar and approached, tall and spare, with weathered features and a dark handlebar mustache streaked with gray. His hair reached almost to his collar, trailing limp from under his round-brimmed hat.

"Robert Reston," the ranger said, putting out a hand.

Rowdy almost swallowed his tongue before he realized, in the split second between the first name—which was his own—and the last, that the man was introducing himself, not making an identification.

"Rowdy Rhodes," Rowdy replied affably. "Have a seat."

"Obliged," Reston answered, and pulled back a chair. His gaze rested a moment, thoughtfully, on Rowdy's badge. "You're a marshal," he said.

"Stone Creek," Rowdy confirmed.

"Stone Creek," Reston repeated. His eyes were brown, and luminous with the many sorrows he'd witnessed, but there was intelligence in them, too, and it was sharp as a razor fresh from the strop. "You know Sam O'Ballivan and Major Blackstone?"

Rowdy nodded, wishing he'd ordered a drink when he'd had the opportunity. He didn't need liquor, but he wouldn't have minded having something to do with his hands. No matter how good a man was at keeping his face impassive, his hands could give him away.

"I know them," he said mildly.

"You put me in mind of somebody," Reston told him, narrowing his eyes a little. "I can't say who it is, though."

Rowdy shrugged, even though his insides were jumping. Kept his hands still, and his feet resting easy on the floor. "Maybe you rode through Haven," he said, "while I was the marshal there."

"Haven," Reston echoed. "That's down south, isn't it? Around Tucson someplace? Never been there, far as I can recollect. Why'd you leave it to come to Stone Creek? If you don't mind my asking."

Rowdy knew it didn't matter to Reston whether he minded or not. "Sam O'Ballivan sent for me," he said.

"Made you a ranger?" Reston asked, raising an eyebrow so bushy that it could have served as a mustache had it been on another part of his face.

Rowdy hadn't planned on volunteering that he'd been sworn in as an Arizona Ranger, given that the major had asked him to keep it a secret, but Reston and the others would know soon enough. Tomorrow, in fact, when he and Sam rode to Flagstaff. They'd settled their plans the night before, while putting the team away in Sam's barn before supper.

"Maybe," he said, after a carefully calculated pause. "Officially, though, I'm just the marshal of Stone Creek."

Reston gave the slightest semblance of a smile. "If you're riding with O'Ballivan and the major," he said, "I'd allow as how you must be all right. But you sure do look familiar."

Rowdy didn't comment. He wished Gideon would come out of Ruby's office so they could return the rented horse to the livery stable, buy the kid another one and get the hell out of Flagstaff.

Sure enough, the side door opened again, right while he was wanting it to, and Gideon appeared, looking red-faced and anxious to be gone. Inside that office Ruby must have given him a dressing-down to remember for running off the way he had. Like as not, she had a spleenful for Payton, too, and Gideon had been unlucky enough to be the one to take it.

Gideon tucked some folding money into his coat pocket and looked around the place with an oddly confused expression, as though it had changed mightily since he'd been there last.

Rowdy nodded toward his brother and stood, easy and slow. "I guess I'd better ride," he said. "There's some ground to cover, between here and home."

Reston stood, too. "Good to see you again," he said, putting out his hand for the second time.

That "again" stuck in Rowdy's mind long after he and Gideon had left Ruby's place, paid a brief visit to little Rose's grave and turned in the white horse, dickered for a bay gelding to replace it and headed for Stone Creek.

14

AUTRY HAD JUST BEEN SERVED a king's breakfast at the table in his railroad car when the whistle shrilled and the wheels screeched, grabbing so hard at the tracks that his coffee and everything on his plate flew at him like they'd been sprung from a catapult.

Esau, his butler, who always traveled with him, was thrown clean to the floor.

Autry bellowed a curse, but it was barely audible over the shriek of those wheels, and out of the corner of his eye, he saw blue sparks shooting past the window, like a shower of strange, small stars.

Esau, an aging black man, portly and slow, groped his way to his feet, holding on to the edge of a seat to keep from being flung down again. "Lord have mercy," he cried. "This train done jumped the tracks!"

Furious, Autry grabbed a linen napkin and swabbed futilely at his egg-stained clothes. Spilled coffee, fresh from the dining car, burned his hide right through his pant legs.

The locomotive gave a great, teeth-rattling shudder

and stopped, and the shock of it reverberated right through Autry's car and on down the line. Cries of alarm echoed from behind him as he stood, shoving Esau aside to storm through to the engine room.

Up ahead somewhere, a gunshot cracked in the crisp air.

A robbery?

No. Impossible. Everything Autry Whitman did was news, given the extent of his financial empire, and that meant everybody capable of reading the papers knew he was onboard that train.

By God, no one would *dare* stop a train pulling his private car.

No one.

He blazed into the engine room like a wildfire, and found the engineer standing stock-still at the controls, face colorless, shoulders heaving, mouth working like a fish flopped up on a creek bank, staring out the little window above the levers and gauges.

Livid, Autry descended upon him, his big fists clenched at his sides. "What the *hell*…?"

The engineer turned, stared bleakly at Autry. "They blew the tracks up—see for yourself, boss—"

Autry blinked, stunned—as scalded as he'd been when his morning coffee cascaded into his lap. He stooped a little, being a tall man, peered out through the rectangular window and saw twisted, blackened track and railroad ties standing up in the ground, splintered and leaning.

Riders waited, three on either side of the ruined tracks, bandannas tied over their faces, rifles upraised.

Autry watched through a red haze as a glistening black gelding separated itself from the other horses.

Bold as you please, the bandit steered that critter right up alongside the locomotive and leaped deftly from the horse to the metal steps leading into the engine room, without ever touching the ground.

"If I hadn't stopped," the engineer lamented stupidly, apparently more afraid of Autry than the half-dozen train robbers bent on stripping every strongbox, every wallet and purse, every copper *cent* from that train, "we'd have jumped the rails!"

"Shut up, you damn fool," Autry growled.

Meanwhile the robber, a leanly built, agile-looking fellow, boarded the train, clad in rough clothes and muddy boots. His eyes were a vivid and strangely peaceful shade of blue.

Autry remembered the small but deadly pistol in his inside suit pocket and reached for it.

"I wouldn't," the robber said, lowering the rifle and cocking it, one-handed, in the same motion.

"This is an outrage!" Autry blustered.

"I reckon it is," the bandit replied, boldly relieving Autry of both the hidden pistol and his wallet.

Autry's gizzard rushed up into the back of his throat, and he was mad enough to chew it up and spit it out. "It'll cost me thousands of dollars just to fix those tracks. And I've got a trainful of passengers stranded out here, with no way to get to Flagstaff—"

The robber opened Autry's wallet, extracted the fat wad of bills inside and had the effrontery to toss the empty billfold straight into the furnace that powered the boiler, where it curled in the coal embers. "I reckon the good folks in Flagstaff will send help, once word reaches them," he said.

Autry saw the other riders trail, single-file, past the open doorway, set to board—and loot—every other car on that train. He seethed.

The bandit put the money—*Autry's* money—into the pocket of his coat. Nudged at Autry's chest with the tip of his rifle barrel.

"Rich man like you," he drawled, "with his own private railroad car, well, it just stands to reason there'd be a safe somewhere, doesn't it?"

"I do not have a safe!" Autry lied, perhaps a bit too vehemently.

"Move," the robber replied.

The engineer cowered in the corner, of no earthly use at all. Autry could only hope that Esau would have armed himself by now, from the small arsenal stored carefully in a discreet wooden chest behind the two rows of seats in the next car.

"Do you know who I am?" Autry demanded.

The rifle barrel poked into the hollow at the base of his throat, and the robber flicked the hammer back with a gloved thumb. The blue eyes above that mask were glacial. "I know, all right," the man answered, "and I'd just as soon shoot you as listen to another word."

"Do what he says, Mr. Whitman," the engineer pleaded. "You'll get us all killed if you don't—"

If Autry had been close enough, he'd have backhanded that yellow-belly hard enough to hit the wall and slide down it. But a sudden move would not be wise, with that rifle barrel shoved into his gullet.

Autry swallowed.

"Keep your hands out from your sides," the robber

ordered, as Autry turned to cross the coupling into his private car, his den, his sanctuary.

Autry obeyed, having no immediate choice in the matter. He'd left the door to the locomotive open in his haste, and the one leading back into his car as well.

The rifle jabbed hard into his spine as he navigated the coupling.

Esau sat, bound and gagged, in Autry's own seat, while two of the other bandits ransacked the place.

One of them found the store of guns and let out a whoop. "Pay dirt!" he yelled, and started tossing the rifles, two by two, to his partner, who caught them readily and relayed them to someone outside the train.

"Those weapons are *valuable!*" Autry protested.

"All the more reason to take them," replied the man at his back.

"You'll pay for this," Autry growled. "I'll have rangers and Pinkertons all over you—"

The rifle barrel skipped up Autry's vertebrae, one by one, to chill the underside of his skull. "Where's the safe?"

Esau's eyes were the size of wagon wheels. He was *sitting* on the safe, which was cleverly hidden beneath the seat cushion. Watching Autry, he made a pleading sound through whatever had been stuffed into his mouth before they'd gagged him with one of Autry's own monogrammed table napkins.

Without thinking, Autry shook his head.

The gunman behind him slammed him to the floor with such suddenness and force that, for a moment or so, Autry honestly believed he'd been shot. He waited for the pain, but all that came was a boot, pressing hard into the small of his back.

He gave a yelp, and that was when a weight came down on him, knocking the breath from his lungs.

The weight, which must have been Esau, was hauled off him.

Damnation, had they whacked Esau up alongside the head with a pistol butt?

Autry was significantly less concerned with that possibility than the safe hidden, heretofore, under Esau's black butt.

"Tie his hands," the leader said.

Autry groaned as his wrists were wrenched together behind his back and bound with what felt like a leather belt, cinched tight enough to cut off the blood flow to his hands.

"There's a real pretty woman in the third car back," a youthful voice said. "Can we bring her along?"

"Leave the women and the kids alone," the leader said coldly. It was a tone not even Autry would have defied with a gun in each hand and an army of Pinkertons standing with him.

He heard Esau moan, somewhere nearby.

Then they found the safe.

Dumped the cushion right on Autry's head.

He closed his eyes and silently damned all their souls to perdition.

"What's the combination, old man?" someone asked.

Autry clamped his jaws shut.

A shot splintered the air, frigid because of the open door between Autry's car and the locomotive, and Autry felt that bullet as surely as if it had penetrated his own flesh, instead of the lock on his safe.

"Well, now," the leader remarked. "That was worth the whole exercise."

Autry listened, helpless, while they looted personal funds.

"Just let me have the one woman," the young voice wheedled.

"Lay a hand on her," the boss replied, "and I'll kill you."

Someone else spoke up. "What's one female?" a man asked. "We been hidin' out a long, lonely while—"

The rifle barrel rose from the back of Autry's neck, and he felt a rush of relief—until he heard it go off with a bang that must have blown a three-foot gap in the teakwood-lined roof of his railroad car.

A tense silence fell, and Autry felt the first snowflakes drifting down through that hole above his head, coming to rest cold and soft on his nape.

"Mount up and ride," the ringleader told his men, apparently having made his point concerning the woman. "This train is due to roll into Flagstaff at two o'clock this afternoon. When it doesn't show, the rangers will follow the tracks right back here, and we're going to be hard put, with all we're carrying, to get clear of the place."

Suddenly there was a lot of scrambling, and Autry literally felt the blessed absence of everybody but Esau and the man who'd forced him onto his face in his own railroad car and robbed him blind.

"So long, Mr. Whitman," the robber said cordially.

Autry was draped in a sheet of snow before he dared get to his feet.

ROWDY KNEW, when Sam and the major met him and Gideon on the outskirts of Stone Creek, leading a fresh horse, that he wouldn't be taking Lark to the dance that night, and the state of her bloomers would remain a mystery.

"The two-o'clock train never arrived in Flagstaff," Sam said.

Without even dismounting, Rowdy climbed from Paint's back into the saddle of the chestnut gelding Sam had brought along as a spare.

"See to Pardner," Rowdy told an openmouthed Gideon, "and then go on over to Mrs. Porter's and convey to Miss Morgan my regrets concerning the dance. Tell her I don't know when I'll be back."

Gideon swallowed, nodded. "I don't reckon I could go along?" he ventured hopefully.

"Do as I asked you, Gideon," Rowdy replied.

"I guess, as deputy marshal, I ought to stay in town. Make sure things stay peaceful."

Sam gave one of his spare smiles, then bent to catch Paint's reins and hand them to Gideon. "That'll be a real help," he told the boy.

Gideon sat up a little straighter in the saddle, looking proud.

"We'd better ride," the major said, standing in his stirrups. "We'll be damn lucky to get to Flagstaff before dark as it is."

Rowdy shifted, adjusting himself to the new saddle and the prospect of a ride he didn't want to make, with a lot of things he didn't want to do at the other end of it.

Gideon tugged at his hat brim, out of deference to Sam and the major, and rode straight-spined for home.

Rowdy hoped to God there wouldn't be any real trouble in Stone Creek while he was away. If anything happened to Gideon, he'd bear the weight of it for the rest of his life.

THE RUM CAKE SAT, fragrant, in the middle of Mrs. Porter's kitchen table, with a fat candle stuck in the middle of it. There was to be a party of sorts, in honor of Mr. Porter's birthday.

Lark wondered if he might actually show up, in the flesh or as a specter, and put on the coat his wife had brushed and aired and hung on a peg beside the back door.

She glanced at Lydia, bundled in a quilt in a chair drawn up close to the stove, and smiled. The little girl was wearing one of the nightgowns Mrs. Porter had bought for her, and Mai Lee had braided her hair neatly for the festivities and given her a piece of rock candy to soothe her sore throat.

"If it's somebody's birthday," Lydia inquired, "why aren't there any presents?"

Lark was trying to think of a reply when a knock sounded at the back door. Her heart leaped a little.

Rowdy?

She'd have to face him eventually, of course, but at the moment she'd have preferred to hide behind a door, or even under a bed, until he left.

Since Mrs. Porter was in the study, and Mai Lee had gone out to run the usual errands, there was no one else to answer.

Lark drew a deep breath, released it slowly, smoothed her skirts and her hair and crossed the kitchen. Turning the knob, she closed her eyes for the briefest moment and felt color seep into her cheeks.

But it was Gideon who'd come calling, not Rowdy. Pardner was with him, wagging his tail in greeting.

Looking up into Gideon's solemn face, Lark was briefly, terribly, afraid. Had he come to tell her—

She caught hold of her imagination. Even managed a wobbly smile. "Come in, Gideon," she said. "And you, too, Pardner."

The young man, her newest pupil, removed his hat. Stepped over the threshold and shut the door behind him.

"Rowdy asked me to come," Gideon said shyly. "He can't take you to the dance tonight because he had to head straight back to Flagstaff, when we'd no more than got here."

Lark was both relieved to know that Rowdy was safe, and disappointed that she wouldn't see him that night. "Back to Flagstaff?" she asked.

"We had to go there so I could get a horse," Gideon explained, swallowing once and looking for all the world like a young man telling either a bold-faced lie or a partial truth. "The one I had was hired from the livery. Coming back, we met Sam O'Ballivan and Major Blackstone, and they wanted Rowdy to go on with them."

"I see," Lark said, still smiling even though a little frisson of alarm went through her. She knew Sam and the major had hired Rowdy to serve as town marshal, but what business could all three of them have in Flagstaff?

"Let me take your hat and coat, Gideon. And do sit down."

He hesitated, then nodded. Shed his coat and handed it over, along with his hat. His gaze strayed to the rum cake, and Lark smiled again.

In the meantime, Pardner had gone straight to Lydia, who was making a fuss over him, and Lark saw Gideon's regard move in their direction and soften slightly.

He approached Lydia's chair, crouched, looking up into the child's eyes.

"Feeling better?" he asked.

Lydia nodded. "I remember you," she said. "You brought me here on your horse. And it was snowing out, and very cold."

"That's right," Gideon said hoarsely.

Lydia was silent for a few moments. Then she said, "My papa died. His funeral is Sunday afternoon."

Lark's throat tightened around a spiky ball of pain.

"I know," Gideon replied. "I was real sorry to hear that."

"I'm going to Phoenix to live with my aunt Nell."

Lark sank slowly into a chair at the kitchen table, careful not to disturb Mr. Porter's birthday cake. She'd tried several times to broach the subject of Nell Baker's impending arrival, but always without success. Lydia would simply bite down on her lower lip and look away, sometimes giving her head a small, decisive shake. Now, perhaps because Gideon, big as he was, was in some ways another child, or perhaps simply because he'd rescued her and she was grateful, Lydia was ready to confide in someone.

Lark was desperately relieved.

"I went to Phoenix once," Gideon said quietly, and it struck Lark, once again, how like Rowdy he was, in his appearance as well as his manner and his countenance, but also in deeper ways. He was kind, and he didn't shrink from hard duties; he simply did what needed doing, efficiently and without complaint. "It's warm all the time there."

"Are there Indians?" Lydia asked, very solemnly.

"Pimas, *mostly,*" Gideon confirmed. "They're peaceful. Farmers. They've got irrigation ditches down there that are better than ten thousand years old."

"Ten thousand years?" Lydia marveled.

Gideon nodded.

Lydia considered that extraordinary length of time, which must have seemed like an eternity to an eight-year-old, then gestured, and Gideon obligingly leaned forward, so she could whisper in his ear. Even from halfway across the room, though, Lark, whose eyes were glazed with sudden tears, heard the child's words.

"I'm scared," Lydia said earnestly.

"I reckon your aunt Nell must be a nice woman," Gideon said, giving one of Lydia's pigtails an affectionate tug. "She'll take real good care of you."

Pardner looked on, turning his head toward Gideon, then back toward Lydia.

"Do you really think so?" Lydia asked, in a breathless tone, her eyes wide.

"Sure I do," Gideon answered. "She's coming all this way to get you, and that means she wants a girl to raise."

"I hope she's not like Mabel," Lydia said.

Lark sniffled and dried her eyes on the cuff of her dress. Straightened her back. Lydia would be safe with Miss Baker, almost surely, and she'd be fed and clothed. Was it too much to hope that the woman would *love* Lydia as well?

"I don't figure she could be like Mabel," Gideon mused.

"How come?"

"Well, because she's your aunt. That means she's got to be a little bit like you, anyhow. Maybe she's even a *lot* like you. And you're real nice, Lydia, so she must be, too."

"What if she's mean, though?" Lydia fretted.

"Then you just send me a letter," Gideon said staunchly. "I'll come right down to Phoenix, first thing, and fetch you back here to live with Miss Morgan." He turned his head, looking at Lark. "It's all right to promise that, isn't it?"

Lark could barely speak. "Yes, Gideon," she managed. "It's all right."

He turned back to Lydia. "See?"

"I don't know how to write," Lydia said, worried again. "I mean, I can write *some,* but my letters go every which way."

Gideon must have smiled, because, suddenly, Lydia smiled, too. "If Miss Morgan will give me a sheet of paper and an envelope, I'll write the letter for you. Make out the envelope and put a stamp on it, too. Then, if you ever have any trouble with anybody, all you'll have to do is mail the letter. Soon as I get it, I'll be coming for you."

After some searching—given that she was a fugitive, living under a partially assumed name, she didn't write letters—Lark produced a sheet of tablet paper, along with a pencil. The envelope was Mrs. Porter's.

She stayed close, watched over Gideon's shoulder as he wrote, "Please come and get me right away" in large block letters, slanted forcefully to the right. He read the message to Lydia, who nodded her approval, then carefully folded the paper, tucked it into the envelope and addressed it to himself:

Gideon Rhodes, Deputy Marshal
General Delivery
Stone Creek, Arizona Territory

Lark purloined a stamp from Mrs. Porter's supply and gave it to Gideon, who licked the back of it and ceremoniously pressed it to the envelope with the pad of his thumb.

"What if you aren't here when the letter comes?" Lydia asked.

"Somebody will forward it on to me, wherever I am," Gideon replied, with the kind of certainty only the young could offer so readily.

Lydia grasped the letter tightly. "When I grow up," she said, her gaze searching Gideon's face, as if to memorize his every feature, "can we please get married?"

Gideon patted Lydia's small hand. "If you still want me then," he replied easily, "we'll tie the knot. Chances are, though, you'll forget all about me, and when you're old enough, and pretty enough to have your pick of suitors, you'll marry somebody else."

"I'll *never* forget you, Gideon," Lydia said solemnly.

And neither will I, Lark thought. *Neither will I.*

THE RIDE TO FLAGSTAFF seemed longer this time, being so soon repeated, and when Rowdy, Sam and the major got to the railroad depot, it was full dark. Little splashes of lantern light stretched along the train tracks as men rode back and forth, ferrying women and children into town, then turning right around to head back out for more.

Clearly, there *had* been a robbery, and maybe something even worse.

Reston materialized out of the gloom to greet them as soon as they rode up—Sam first, then the major, then Rowdy, who was the last to dismount.

"They dynamited the tracks," Reston reported gravely.

Rowdy stiffened inwardly. He'd never known his pa to use dynamite, but there was always a first time. If a train was moving fast enough, it might roll right through a blaze laid on the tracks, even with logs the size of whiskey barrels.

"Anybody get hurt?" Sam asked Reston. He had to be thinking about an experience he'd had with a train down in Mexico, Sam did. God Almighty, Rowdy hoped this robbery hadn't been a calamity like that one.

"Nope," Reston replied, his gaze straying, measuring, to Rowdy, before shifting back to Sam. "No injuries to speak of, beyond a few bruises. Folks were scared, though, and they were a long time out there before we got to them. Soon as the train was late, though, we sent riders out to investigate."

The major scanned the darkness, as though he could see all the way to that train, stranded out there in the dark and cold. "I suppose the robbers were masked," Blackstone said, resigned.

Reston nodded. "According to Mr. Whitman—he owns this railroad and we brought him back among the first of the passengers, thinking he might have a heart attack, he was in such a dither—the leader had blue eyes and rode a black gelding. That's about all we know."

Rowdy's stomach pitched, then rolled over backward.

Blue eyes, striking enough to be memorable to a frightened old man.

A black gelding.

Payton Yarbro.

Damn if the old bastard hadn't lied through his teeth when he'd said he'd given up robbing trains. And when he'd claimed he was headed for Mexico, too.

"The old feller's over at Ruby's right now," Reston said. "You might want to talk to him yourselves."

"That can wait," Sam replied, "until after all the passengers have been brought in."

"We're almost done with that," Reston told Sam, but he was looking at Rowdy again. Probing at him in a way that made the small hairs rise on the back of Rowdy's neck. "No sense in wearing out your horses. Or yourselves."

Sam considered, then nodded. "Ruby's?" he asked.

Reston nodded. "Your friend here knows the way," he said, before peeling his eyes off Rowdy's hide. To Rowdy it felt like some of the skin came away with his glance.

Sam looked Rowdy's way, very briefly but in some

depth, then mounted up again. Rowdy and the major followed suit.

After he'd shaken off the effects of Reston's stare, Rowdy turned his thoughts to what little he knew about the robbery. Two details, that was all he really had. And all he really needed.

If he could have found his pa right then, he'd have done it. Handed the lying son of a bitch over to the rangers without batting an eye.

The lights of Ruby's Saloon glowed in the gloom as they rode up, but the piano wasn't playing. Out front, Rowdy, Sam and the major dismounted and found places for their horses.

Autry Whitman held court in the middle of the big, smoke-blued room, his white hair standing on end. A black man sat at the same table, as did Ruby herself, but everyone else kept their distance, staying on the periphery, lining the bar and claiming the far tables.

Whitman exuded power—and righteous wrath. He looked like some Old Testament prophet, and kept clenching his fists and mumbling, while Ruby, looking pale and jumpy, tried to ply him with free whiskey.

Rowdy knew what was going to happen. Knew there was no way to avoid it. So he resisted the urge to pull his hat brim down low over his eyes.

Sam was the first to speak. "Mr. Whitman," he said, evidently needing no introduction, "my name is Sam O'Ballivan. I'm an Arizona Ranger. This is Major John Blackstone and Rowdy Rhodes."

Whitman's stony gaze moved from Sam to the major to Rowdy, and stopped with a lurch as jarring as a train coming fast onto a gap in the tracks.

The old man narrowed his eyes.

"That's him," he said, flushing dangerously and starting to his feet.

Rowdy stood his ground, didn't move or speak.

He felt Sam and the major looking at him.

Whitman half rose, then sat down again, heavily. Shook his head, as if suddenly confused.

"It couldn't have been him," Ruby said evenly. "He was in this saloon when that train was robbed."

"Those blue eyes," Whitman murmured.

"Lots of people have blue eyes," Sam said quietly. But he glanced thoughtfully at Ruby, then turned his attention back to the railroad mogul, skipping over Rowdy entirely. "Do you know what time it was when the train was robbed, Mr. Whitman?"

"Ten-thirty," Whitman said, with an accusing look at the black man. "I'd just looked at my watch, to see how late Esau here was, serving up my breakfast."

Esau looked mighty uncomfortable, and didn't speak.

"At ten-thirty," Ruby said, "Mr.—Rhodes was right here in this saloon. I remember him because of the badge."

They were on dangerous ground, and Rowdy hoped Ruby knew that and would tread lightly. If she said Rowdy was her stepson, Sam and the major were sure to make the obvious connection. Then they'd want to know all about Jack Payton. And what Ruby didn't tell them they could learn by questioning anybody on the street.

Again Rowdy silently cursed his father. For robbing trains. For living a decade in one place, and a very public one, at that. For the pure, reckless arrogance of using his famous first name as part of his alias.

And then there was Gideon. He'd stood there in Mrs. Porter's kitchen, right after he'd shown up in Stone Creek, and said his name was Payton, not Rhodes. No one had commented at the time, or since, but Rowdy knew the landlady wouldn't have missed something like that, and neither would Lark.

Lark.

Rowdy ached inside. He didn't know which would be worse—leaving her behind with a hasty explanation or none at all, or seeing the look in her eyes when he was arrested for things Rob Yarbro had done.

Robert Yarbro. That was the name on all those Wanted posters, but in its way, it was as much an alias as Rowdy Rhodes.

Whitman studied Rowdy afresh. "He wasn't as tall as you are," he said.

For the space of a heartbeat, Rowdy didn't know what the man was talking about.

"Were you here today, Rowdy?" Sam asked quietly. "In this saloon, I mean?"

Rowdy nodded.

Gideon had been with him, when they'd all met up on the road earlier, outside Stone Creek. Suppose Sam and the major or—God forbid—Reston, decided to question Gideon?

Rowdy was an experienced liar, a thing he wasn't proud of but nonetheless had to acknowledge, at least to himself. Gideon, on the other hand, was bound to slip up.

He was just giving silent thanks that Reston was still

at the depot, when the man crashed through the swinging doors.

"We found one of them," he said. "He was facedown in the snow, shot through the forehead. Pockets stuffed full of other folks' money."

Having made this announcement, Reston turned and went out again.

Rowdy, Sam and the major all followed, with Autry Whitman not far behind.

The body was draped over the back of a horse.

Rowdy knew immediately that the corpse wasn't his pa, but there was something familiar about the man's form, just the same.

Reston stepped up, got the dead man by the hair of his head and lifted, so the lights of Ruby's Saloon fell on the blood-streaked face. The bullet hole was small and neat, except for the dried blood dribbling down from it.

Bile scalded the back of Rowdy's throat as he looked into the sightless eyes of a man who'd once been a trusted friend as well as an in-law.

It was Chessie's younger brother, Seth Alden.

15

"I KIND OF HOPED this Porter fella would show up for his own birthday party," Gideon confided to Lark, as the afternoon wore on toward evening. He'd just enjoyed his third slice of cake, and the honor of blowing out the candles had gone to Lydia.

Mai Lee and Hon Sing had left the table, Mai Lee to begin cleaning up after their early supper, Hon Sing to return to Jolene Bell's saloon. Mrs. Porter had gone down to the root cellar, after murmuring about some errand there, and Lydia, full of cake, had already been carried to bed.

"I believe Mr. Porter is dead," Lark whispered back to Gideon.

Gideon frowned. "Why would anybody throw a shindig for a dead man?"

"I have no idea," Lark said.

"Maybe he's not," Gideon mused quietly. Like his older brother, he apparently enjoyed a puzzle. "Dead, I mean. Maybe he's just away someplace, and Mrs. Porter figures he might come back anytime, and expect a cake for his birthday."

Mai Lee turned then, and cast an uncomfortable glance over one shoulder, but if she knew anything about Mr. Porter's whereabouts, be they above- or belowground, she revealed nothing.

It was cold, musty and dark in the root cellar—Lark had been there earlier in the afternoon herself, to fetch a jar of pickled beets for supper—and she couldn't imagine what her landlady might be doing down there. She'd been gone at least fifteen minutes, and Lark was getting worried.

"Perhaps I'd better check on her," she said, starting to rise. Only her dread of the place, she realized with some chagrin, had kept her from going earlier.

Gideon got up. "I'll do it," he said.

"I'm going, too," Lark said.

"Take candle," Mai Lee contributed, with a little shudder. "Dark like grave."

Lark found a candle in the pantry, along with a small box of matches, and she and Gideon made for the cellar, reached by way of a trapdoor in the far corner of the kitchen, opposite the cookstove. Dank air rose from what was essentially a hole in the ground, like the cold breath of some subterranean creature.

Lark shivered, handed the candle and matches to Gideon, and let him descend the steps first.

"Mrs. Porter?" she called tremulously, over Gideon's shoulder. Lark couldn't recall if her landlady had taken a lantern or a candle when she'd gone down into the dirt chamber earlier, but if she had, the flame had gone out.

There was no answer.

Gideon reached the bottom of the steps and stopped so suddenly that Lark nearly collided with him. The light from the candle he was holding wavered eerily against the damp, root-laced walls. A mouse skittered, somewhere out of sight.

"Mrs. Porter?" he said. "Ma'am? Are you—"

Lark strained to see around his broad shoulder—and spotted Mrs. Porter standing pressed into a corner, under a frieze of cobwebs, her eyes huge. She had brought a lantern—she clutched it in both hands—but the flame had guttered out.

Mrs. Porter blinked several times, as though coming back to herself from some great distance and arriving with a visibly jolting impact. In the next instant, though, she offered a fitful, distracted little smile.

"I was right," she said cheerfully. "There were no more walnuts. We used them up at Christmas."

Gideon handed the candle back to Lark, who hovered on the third step from the bottom, and went to Mrs. Porter. Took her gently by the arm.

Again Lark was reminded of Rowdy.

And for some new reason she couldn't have defined—she knew only that it had nothing to do with missing the dance, or the tear in her bloomers—she wished him back from Flagstaff with such an intensity that it wouldn't have surprised her if he'd materialized before her eyes.

Well, it wouldn't have surprised her *immediately*, anyway.

"You feeling all right, ma'am?" Gideon asked respectfully, at the same time steering Mrs. Porter toward the cellar steps.

"I *could* do with a dose of my medicine," Mrs. Porter admitted, sweetly confused again. "And perhaps a little rest."

Lark stepped back out of the way, glad to be above the kitchen floor again, away from the spiders and the cold and the inevitable mice. Waited as Gideon ushered Mrs. Porter up the steps, with the easy competence of those who are used to being strong.

Mai Lee and Lark escorted the landlady to her room on the second floor, each supporting her by an arm.

"My medicine," Mrs. Porter murmured, upon entering.

Mai Lee nodded and took a brown bottle from the bedside stand, which was illuminated by a beam of moonlight, while Lark helped Mrs. Porter to lie down on the bed.

With the older woman settled, Lark lit a lamp, watched as Mai Lee administered a dose of what was surely laudanum, which Mrs. Porter raised herself half off the mattress to receive.

Across the bed Mai Lee's and Lark's gazes caught, held, broke apart.

Lark unlaced Mrs. Porter's shoes and removed them, then covered her with a blanket, found folded at the foot of the bed.

Having never been in the room before, Lark stole surreptitious glances, here and there, taking in the heavy velvet drapes, the massive furniture, the cold stone fireplace. She saw an exquisite mantel clock, its case of painted china, and numerous knickknacks. But there were no photographs or paintings and no visible evidence that Mr. Porter, or any other man, had ever shared these quarters.

Still, Lark felt strangely anxious, as though the master of the house might step out of one of the shadowy corners and demand an explanation for their presence, hers and Mai Lee's.

"I'll just close my eyes for a few moments," Mrs. Porter said, with a benign little sigh. Perhaps she was used to the heavy, almost ominous atmosphere of that room—and it was equally possible, of course, that Lark was merely imagining these disturbing aspects.

Mrs. Porter was soon snoring.

Leaving the lamp burning, Mai Lee and Lark slipped out of the room, moving as quietly as they could, Mai Lee pulling the door shut behind them.

"How long has Mrs. Porter been taking laudanum?" Lark asked, when they were alone in the corridor.

Mai Lee sighed. "Long time," she said. "Not take Hon Sing's medicine. It better. Have herbs, brought all way from China."

They moved toward the rear stairway, leading down into the kitchen.

Lark thought of Hon Sing's glistening needles, and the way he'd used them so skillfully to help Lydia. Mrs. Porter probably wouldn't have submitted to that treatment, any more than she would have taken the herbs, and it seemed a shame to Lark.

"Mai Lee," she said, suddenly able to keep the question back any longer, "what happened to Mr. Porter?"

Mai Lee's eyes widened. "He gone," she whispered.

"Dead?"

Mai Lee shrugged. "Not know. One day, here when Mai Lee make breakfast. Put on hat and go to bank. Not see again."

"You must have heard something," Lark insisted, but

carefully, thinking of Mai Lee's celebrated ability to gather all the local news and bring it straight home to Mrs. Porter. "Surely people talked, and if there was a funeral—"

"No funeral," Mai Lee said. "No talk. Just gone."

"But surely—"

"Just *gone,*" Mai Lee repeated firmly.

Downstairs they found Gideon standing by the door, wearing his hat and coat, Pardner waiting patiently at his side.

"If you don't need me to go for someone," Gideon said, "Pardner and I had better be on our way." His chest swelled slightly. "With Rowdy gone, I figure I ought to make his rounds for him."

Lark's heartbeat quickened slightly at the prospect of Gideon patrolling the streets of Stone Creek, alone and unarmed. It was, after all, Saturday night, and there was a dance at the Cattleman's Hall. Even though she'd only lived in the community a short while, she knew cowboys came from outlying ranches to attend these soirees, and they sometimes visited one or more of the town's saloons beforehand.

She scrambled for an excuse, some words to persuade him to stay, but nothing came to her, beyond asking him to fetch Hon Sing back from Jolene Bell's place to look in on Mrs. Porter and Lydia.

He'd guess what she was doing and, besides, Hon Sing might get into trouble if he was called away from his work.

"Be careful, Gideon," Lark said.

He smiled. Nodded. "Obliged for the fine supper and the cake," he said. And then he opened the door and went out, Pardner hesitating to look back at Lark, then turning to follow.

Lark immediately grabbed her everyday cloak from its place on the row of pegs near the door, swung it around her shoulders.

"Where you go?" Mai Lee asked, right away, and with a note of alarmed suspicion in her voice. "It dark. Dance tonight. Maybe trouble."

Lark was already tying the cloak's ribbon laces under her chin. "I need a little fresh air," she said, and hastened out, taking care not to slip on the icy back steps.

Gideon and Pardner were just ahead, on the sidewalk, visible in the glow of a streetlamp.

Lark was careful to move quietly, hoping not to attract Gideon's attention. Pardner turned once, though, and started toward her at a trot.

Lark ducked into the shadows of a neighbor's lilac bush.

Gideon whistled, and Pardner, after a brief hesitation, obeyed his summons and went on.

The saloons along Center Street were virtually deserted and, after looking that way, Gideon changed directions. Headed for the Cattleman's Hall, which was behind Stone Creek's only bank, in the middle of a weedy lot.

Horses surrounded it, in a great, shadowy horde, and the lively strains of a fiddle and a washboard spilled out the open doors of the hall, along with laughter and the stomping of feet.

Gideon proceeded toward the hall.

Lark followed, staying close to the clapboard wall of the bank. She ought to just go home, she told herself.

Look after Lydia and Mrs. Porter and perhaps mend her torn bloomers. Instead, she kept going, filled with a mysterious urgency that literally drove her on.

The squeal of a horse made her draw in a sharp breath. At first she thought the animal was hurt, but then she saw it rearing onto its hind legs, its forelegs pawing at the air, monstrously big in the moonlight and the glow of the lanterns inside the hall. The rider on its back was no more than an outline of a human form.

Gideon sprinted toward the hall.

Lark ran after him, no longer caring if he saw her.

The rider ducked his head and rode through the doorway at a gallop.

Pardner began to bark, and streaked after Gideon, who was running full-out now.

Screams and shouts rang from inside the Cattleman's Hall.

Gideon disappeared through the opening.

Lark ran faster, breathless now. She reached the doorway just in time to see several men trying to catch hold of the horse's bridle—the animal was terrified, its eyes rolling, its nostrils flared as it kicked and skidded on the dance floor. The rider on its back, obviously drunk, threw back his head and let out a bellowing whoop.

Gideon managed to grasp one of the reins, tried to soothe the horse with his free hand.

The rider swung the horse around, meaning to see Gideon trampled, but he moved swiftly, slipping under the animal's lathered neck to the other side.

"Willie!" a man yelled. "You get down off that horse before somebody gets killed!"

Lark put a hand to her mouth, frozen in the doorway, trying to see Gideon, but he was behind the horse now, and men were converging cautiously from all sides of the room.

The horse began to kick hard with its hind legs, and everyone jumped back, and in the confusion of all that, the rider called Willie must have drawn his gun. A shot exploded in the breath-hot, fear-heavy room.

Several women shrieked, and Lark would wonder, ever after, if she'd been one of them.

Willie spurred the horse into a run, and Lark barely got out of the way before they shot through the doorway.

And there was Gideon, lying on the floor, with blood pooling through his coat, wounded in the left shoulder. Pardner slinked close and bared his teeth, snarling ferociously at anyone who tried to approach.

Lark hurried toward them.

Pardner whimpered when she landed on her knees beside Gideon, cupping his pale, blood-spattered face in both hands.

"Gideon!" she cried. "Gideon!"

He didn't open his eyes.

She laid her head to his chest, felt it rise and fall against her cheek, heard the faint, thready beat of his heart.

She looked up. Pardner was pressed up close to Gideon's side, vicious in his intent to protect the boy from further harm. Lark had no doubt that, mild-mannered as he usually was, that dog could have torn out someone's throat.

"Get Hon Sing," Lark ordered, stunned by the calm, reasonable sound of her own voice. On the inside she was screaming hysterically.

"That Chinaman over to Jolene's?" a man asked, from the blur surrounding the little circle of floor that stayed open around Lark, Gideon and Pardner.

"He's a doctor!" Lark must have shouted the words, because they left her throat raw. "Get him—tell him what's happened—"

Several men ran out of the hall.

A woman tried to bring a ladle of drinking water, shaking in her hand, but Pardner, still fierce as a wounded wolf guarding a cub, growled dangerously and poised himself to lunge.

Lark, still on her knees, tears trickling down her cheeks, leaned forward and rested her forehead against Gideon's.

"Don't die," she whispered. "Please, don't die."

Rowdy arrived in Stone Creek at sunup on Sunday morning, riding low over the saddle and pushing Sam O'Ballivan's spare horse to the limit. Word of Gideon's shooting had reached him at Ruby's by telegram, two and a half hours before.

The words of that wire were burned into his mind as surely as if someone had heated an iron until it glowed red orange and branded them there.

"Gideon shot. Come quickly. Lark."

Supposing Gideon had been taken to Mrs. Porter's, Rowdy was headed that way, but Pardner suddenly ran out from beside the jailhouse, barking frantically.

Rowdy reined for home.

There were lights burning in the windows, and three or four horses stood out front. Pardner darted for the door and scrabbled at it with his forepaws, even as Rowdy swung down out of the saddle and sprinted after him.

The door opened just as Rowdy caught up to Pardner, and Lark stood there, her hair all atumble, one cheek and the front of her dress smudged with blood.

"Rowdy," she said.

Rowdy gripped her shoulders, heard Sam and the major ride in behind him but didn't look back. "Is he—Is Gideon—"

She shook her head. "But it's bad," she whispered raggedly. "Oh, Rowdy, it's bad—"

He half thrust her aside.

Gideon lay, stripped to the waist, on the long kitchen table. The Chinaman from Jolene's place stood beside him, with a scalpel gleaming in his right hand. Needles protruded from various parts of Gideon's still body, shining in the lamplight.

"What the hell—?" Rowdy rasped, about to go for the Chinaman.

But Lark stepped in front of him. Placed her cool hands on either side of his face and made him look into her eyes.

"Rowdy," she said, very slowly, "*listen* to me. Hon Sing is a surgeon. And without him, Gideon hasn't a chance of surviving."

"The needles—"

"They'll control the pain and keep Gideon from bleeding too much," Lark said in the same steady, careful tone of voice.

Rowdy recalled something about Hon Sing and his needles—something Gideon had said—but the gist of it eluded him. "That's crazy, Gideon needs a doctor—"

"Hon Sing *is* a doctor," Lark said, gripping

Rowdy's shoulders now. "Let him work, Rowdy. Please, *let him work*."

Rowdy shoved a hand through his hair, pushed gently past Lark to approach the table and stand looking down at his brother. His eyes burned, and his throat felt like a fist, gripping so tight that he wondered if he'd ever breathe again.

Across the table stood Hon Sing, still holding the scalpel. The Chinaman's gaze met Rowdy's and held.

Rowdy looked down at Gideon again.

And then, very slowly, he backed away.

Lark was there to meet him when he turned. She took his hand, squeezed. Through a haze he saw Sam and the major standing just inside the door. Heard Sam say, "Everybody out, except for the doctor and Rowdy and Miss Morgan."

People filed past, all men—Rowdy had seen their horses out front, but not really registered their presence inside the house. But now he just stared down into Lark's eyes, sure he'd splinter into fragments if he looked away; that outside her notice, he didn't exist at all.

"What happened?" he ground out. He knew the Chinaman had begun cutting on Gideon, and couldn't bring himself to look.

Couldn't leave, either.

Couldn't move.

Lark was holding him upright, with only the look in her eyes. "We can talk about that later," she said gently. "Right now we're just going to wait."

Sam appeared behind Lark, solemn and trail worn from the hard ride out of Flagstaff. "Rowdy," he said, his voice quiet, "the major and I will stay and make sure the boy's looked after. You go with Lark and sit down someplace, let her help you wait this through."

Rowdy nodded, though what Sam said didn't make any real sense to him.

He turned and stumbled toward the door, trusting Lark to follow him.

She gripped his hand again and headed him in another direction.

Next thing he knew, he was sitting on the edge of his bed, with his head in his hands, while Lark occupied a straight-backed chair nearby.

"I never should have let him come here," he said, after a long, long time spent groping his way through a thicket of regrets. He looked into Lark's eyes and gave a gruff, mirthless laugh. "He thought he was a deputy. And *I* let him believe it—even gave him a badge."

Lark didn't speak. Maybe she knew he needed to talk, say what was inside him.

"He's *sixteen* years old, Lark," he went on.

She nodded, looked as though she wanted to close the space between them and take him into her arms, but didn't.

"He's supposed to go to college next fall, back in Pennsylvania. It's all paid for. I gave my word I'd keep him safe. And now he's lying on a kitchen table, with needles stuck in him everywhere, while a saloon-swabbing Chinaman whacks at him with a knife."

Lark's mouth tightened briefly, but her eyes were compassionate. "I told you," she said, very softly. "Hon Sing is a doctor. A surgeon."

"Then why's he working for Jolene Bell?" Rowdy

demanded, as some of the shock subsided, and he began to think a little more clearly.

"Because he and Mai Lee have to earn a living," Lark said moderately. "He'd never be allowed to practice medicine here."

"I should have been here."

"You weren't. There's no point in torturing yourself."

He thrust out a sigh, rumpled his hair again. Wondered where he'd lost his hat. "If I could be out there on that table, if I could take Gideon's place, I would," he said.

"I know," Lark replied.

"Tell me what happened."

"I'm not sure you're ready to hear it."

"I'm ready. Tell me, Lark, because I'm going to go crazy if you don't."

She told him.

Gideon had come to the rooming house for supper and birthday cake. Afterward, he'd announced that he had rounds to make, because he, Rowdy, was away. Lark had been unsettled by his going and decided to follow him.

In an effort to protect Gideon's pride—the kind of thing only a woman would do—she'd stayed out of sight.

He'd looked toward the saloons, Gideon had, and, evidently satisfied that all was well there, headed on to the dance at the Cattleman's Hall.

Rowdy saw the rearing horse in his mind's eye, and the rider on its back, just as clearly as if he'd been there himself. Saw the man bend low to ride a panicked horse inside the dance hall. Heard the screams from inside.

Closed his eyes.

"Gideon tried to stop him," Lark finished. "He must have gotten hold of the bridle, on the side where I couldn't see. And then there was a gunshot, and the man rode out, and Gideon was—Gideon was just lying there...."

"Who was this rider?" Rowdy asked taut with the need to know.

"Someone called him Willie," Lark said carefully.

"I'll kill him," Rowdy said, and he'd never meant a thing he'd said in his life more than he meant that. His brain hitched back to his first day in Stone Creek, when he and Pardner had availed themselves of Jolene's bathhouse. Two men had come in—one named Harlan, one named Willie.

The second man's features came clear in Rowdy's mind.

"No," Lark replied. "You'll let Sam handle this."

"I'm the *marshal*."

"You're also Gideon's brother. You can't possibly be objective."

"I don't *want* to be objective," Rowdy protested. "I want to shove a .44 down the bastard's throat and blow his stomach out through his—" He stopped, remembering that this was Lark he was talking to, not Sam or his pa.

Her face was pale, her eyes wide. A faint shimmer of gold showed at the roots of her lush brown hair, now falling from its pins.

"Why did they bring him here, and not to Mrs. Porter's?"

"Because of Lydia," Lark said. "She's been through

a great deal as it is, and she's very fond of Gideon. I didn't want her to see him like this. And, anyhow, since you live here, this is Gideon's real home."

Gideon's "real home" was Ruby's Saloon and Poker House, but it was miles away and thick with rangers. Ruby might have seen to the boy, but without Pa there to insist, it seemed almost as likely that she wouldn't have wanted the bother.

He thought of Rose's small grave outside the cemetery fence, and imagined a new one being dug beside it for Gideon.

His stomach threatened to come up, right along with the contents.

"Why did you have to go back to Flagstaff in such a hurry?" Lark asked. "Gideon said Sam and the major met you on the road, and you rode right out again."

I don't reckon I could go along? Rowdy heard his brother say.

God, if only he'd said yes.

If only he'd said yes.

None of this would have happened. Gideon would be safe.

"There was another train robbery this morning," Rowdy said. "Maybe an hour's ride outside Flagstaff. And old Autry Whitman himself was a witness—"

Lark's eyes rounded, and her wan face went white. "Autry Whitman?" she repeated, gripping the sides of her chair with both hands. *"He was there?"*

Rowdy watched her, ready to spring off the bed and catch her before she tumbled forward in a swoon and hit the floor, if it came to that. "Do you know him, Lark? Autry Whitman?"

She shivered at the name, but shook her head violently. "No!"

She was lying, of course, but Rowdy didn't call her on it.

She stood up, sat down again.

And then tears brimmed along her lower lashes and spilled over.

Oh, yes. She knew Autry Whitman, all right.

He might even be the man she was running from.

Whatever Whitman was to her, she was scared to death of him.

16

SITTING THERE IN ROWDY'S bedroom, precisely the place she shouldn't have been, Lark reeled at the revelation he'd just made.

Autry was in Flagstaff—Rowdy had seen him, spoken to him.

Her former husband would be furious about the train robbery, of course, and because he'd been aboard when it happened, the affront would be magnified to Biblical proportions. Worse, if he was dissatisfied with the investigation, he might well come to Stone Creek, chasing after Sam and the major, meaning to cajole and threaten until they returned, tracked down the criminals and restored whatever had been stolen.

Rowdy was watching her closely, from where he sat on the edge of the bed, and she knew he wouldn't buy anything but the truth.

She had to run.

But she couldn't. Because Nell Franks still hadn't come to fetch Lydia back to Phoenix. And because of

Gideon. How could she leave and never know if he'd fully recovered—or even survived?

She could not go, not even if it meant coming face-to-face with Autry Whitman.

"Let me help you, Lark," Rowdy said quietly.

Tears stung her eyes. "Autry is a dangerous man," she replied woodenly. "You have no idea how powerful he is, how far his reach extends, and what people will do for him because he pays them—"

She paused, shuddered.

Once, in a moment of anger, Autry had grabbed her hard by the hair, pulled her face close to his and spat out the words, "Defy me, Lark. Go ahead. You'll find yourself inside a pine box, like all the others!"

Like all the others.

Lark had known he wasn't bluffing; Autry had surely ordered murders, and beatings, as well. He employed a network of thugs and never dirtied his own hands. But to cross him was fatal business, especially when money was involved.

She'd injured him in a far worse way; she'd damaged his formidable pride. If Autry got her alone, cornered her somewhere, he might well kill her, and personally.

She swallowed, simply unable to contain the secret any longer; whatever the consequences, she had to tell one person, and that person was Rowdy. "Autry Whitman," she said, "is my former husband."

Rowdy leaned forward, rested his forearms on the thighs of his muddy trousers. He did not look horrified, or even particularly surprised, though the look in his blue eyes was as sharp as the point on any of Hon Sing's needles. "Former?" he asked, very quietly.

Outside that room, Hon Sing was operating on Gideon, and the boy's life hung in the balance. Inside, the air seemed to quiver.

"Former," Lark confirmed. "I divorced Autry a few days after I left Denver. I've been hiding ever since."

Rowdy nodded. "I thought it must be something like that," he said. "It isn't an easy thing, getting a divorce, especially when it's the woman who goes after it. How did you manage it so quickly?"

Lark let out a long breath. Wished she could go and sit beside Rowdy on his bed, feel his arm slip around her, steely strong. But she was too afraid he'd shun her. "If you have enough money," she said evenly, "you can do almost anything."

"Were there any children, Lark?" Rowdy put the question gently enough, but she could see by the flicker in his eyes that the answer was important to him.

"Of course not," she said, feeling mildly indignant. Given all that had happened during the night, Gideon's shooting, seeing him moved from the Cattleman's Hall here, in the back of someone's wagon, she was mostly numb. "I wouldn't have left my own child behind. And besides, Autry couldn't—"

"Couldn't what?" Rowdy prompted, when she fell silent. "Couldn't make love to you?"

She trembled, bit down so hard on the inside of her lower lip that she tasted blood. "He tried. He put his hands on me—and sometimes, he even—" She closed her eyes.

"It's all right, Lark," Rowdy said, though he still gave no indication that he wanted her beside him, that he'd ever touch her again. "You were married to the man. Naturally, you shared his bed."

Lark tried to blink away her tears, but more came, and then more, until her face was wet. She sat rigidly in her chair, yearning to be held, fearing she'd perish, at least on the inside, if Rowdy spurned her. "I didn't feel—I didn't feel any of the things I felt with you." She gave a slight shake of her head, and a bitter little sob of a laugh. "I didn't even know it was *possible* to feel those things."

The corner of Rowdy's mouth tilted up, but the grin came nowhere near his eyes. He looked so worn down that, even in her own extremity, Lark suddenly wanted to offer him consolation more than she wanted to receive it from him. She ached to lie down with Rowdy Rhodes and wrap her arms around him, and hold him tightly until everything was all right.

"Whitman is old enough to be your grandfather," he said. "What possessed you to marry him in the first place? And don't say you loved him, because I know you didn't. Was it the money, Lark?"

Lark straightened her spine. She'd thought the hardest part of all this would be telling Rowdy that she'd lived two horrid years as Autry Whitman's wife, a plaything to be fondled and spoiled and petted—and used. But, no, she had yet to say the most difficult truth.

She shook her head. "It wasn't the money," she said. "I was singing in a saloon in San Francisco when I met Autry."

"Go on," Rowdy said. His voice hadn't changed, nor had his manner, but his eyes were hard as he waited for the rest.

"I was the 'swing' girl," Lark reflected, looking back in her mind, seeing herself on that ridiculous crimson velvet contraption, suspended from the high ceiling of Cyrus Teede's show house by golden ropes, soaring out over the upturned faces of leering men in one of several scant costumes, singing and smiling just as though she *enjoyed* being the center of all that lascivious attention.

Instead, she'd lived in fear.

Whenever the box office receipts were down, Teede, a hoodlum in gentleman's garb, threatened to send men to her room. They'd be willing to pay handsomely for a visit, Teede had said, and she wouldn't even have to sing.

Lark had been well paid for performing in the show house, but Cyrus "invested" most of her money. She'd tried to leave twice. On both occasions Cyrus had found her and dragged her back. Slapped her into submission.

She realized, as she was remembering all this, that she was telling it to Rowdy, too. Saying it right out loud.

"Then, one spring evening, Autry came to see the show. Everyone kowtowed to him, the famous railroad owner. Teede had already told me he was planning to sell my favors, and I knew that was going to be the night, because I'd seen him talking with some of the regulars, all of them looking at me. I saw money change hands. I was so afraid, I could barely sing—I knew Teede meant what he'd said, and all the doors were being watched by his henchmen. I wasn't going to get away, and I'd be beaten senseless if I tried—*after* Teede's customers had their way with me."

Rowdy's jawline tightened, but he didn't speak. He simply waited.

Lark swallowed. "Autry immediately let it be known that he wanted me, the way he might have wanted a bauble in a storefront window. He believed I was a…a prostitute, but he was willing to marry me, just the same." She blew out a breath. "Oh, he was so *noble* about it. He must have paid Teede an astronomical sum of money to let me go—"

Rowdy shifted, watching her, resting his elbows on his thighs now, his fingers tented beneath his chin. "What happened then, Lark?" he asked, his voice as still as deep waters sheltered from the wind on all sides.

Lark dashed at her cheeks with the back of one hand, raised her chin a notch. "Autry and I were married that same night, by a justice of the peace, in Teede's back office. I'd escaped being thrown to those men like a carcass to wolves—but I *hadn't* escaped. I still spent the night in a rich stranger's bed."

Rowdy closed his eyes against the images, but Lark knew by the bunching of a muscle in his cheek that he hadn't evaded them.

Having begun the tale, Lark couldn't seem to stop. Words tumbled out of her mouth, truths long withheld, even from herself. "I was a virgin when Autry took me the first time, but, like I said, he never believed that, even when he made me bleed. I guess he thought it was some kind of whore's trick. By morning, I was so raw and bruised, I could barely get out of bed—the only reason I did, the only reason I didn't just lie there, waiting to die, was the fear that Autry would pounce on me again."

Rowdy muttered a curse, and Lark felt condemned by it.

"Do you know what he did the day after we were married?" she went on, partly out of spite, because she was sure Rowdy was judging her, and partly because she still couldn't stop the flow of confession. "He bought me a new wardrobe and all sorts of jewelry—oh, I was a showpiece, to be sure. Back in Denver, he installed me in his mansion and presented me as his pristine young bride, who'd married him for love. I played the part until I couldn't stand it anymore."

"And then?"

She told Rowdy about the funeral she'd attended with Autry. Said how she'd pleaded a sick headache and asked to leave. Then she'd told the carriage driver she'd gotten word that her sister was sick—dear God, how many times had she longed for a *real* sister, someone like Maddie O'Ballivan, to turn to for help?—and taken the next train out of town.

She'd gone to San Francisco first, even though it was Cyrus Teede's territory, because she had a few hundred dollars there, money she'd saved while singing for a living, mostly given to her by men hoping for more than a song, tucked into a safe deposit box in a bank. It had taken every penny to end her marriage to Autry, and she'd paid it gladly.

She'd gone to a special shop, immediately after securing the divorce, certain that Autry had already hired Pinkertons to search for her, and had her blond hair dyed brown. Then, clutching her copy of the decree of divorcement, she'd boarded another train, the first one leaving San Francisco that day, not caring where it was headed, as long as it wasn't Denver.

She'd gotten off in Phoenix, bought a newspaper for a penny and read the classified advertisements. Thus she'd learned there was a teaching position open in Stone Creek, and that Mrs. Porter had clean rooms to let for a reasonable price.

She'd gone without meals on the long stagecoach ride north from Phoenix, a journey of several days, for her money—now amounting only to what she'd stolen from Autry's humidor in the study—was nearly gone. It had taken the last of it to secure room and board at Mrs. Porter's, and even then she hadn't had enough. Mrs. Porter had taken pity on her and let her pay the rest when she received her first month's salary.

Having related all this, Lark felt dry and empty inside. She had nothing more to tell, so she just sat there, her back straight, waiting for some reaction from Rowdy.

When it came, it startled her so that she nearly bolted.

He rose off the bed, with a creaking of mattress springs, crossed to her, and pulled her to her feet. And then he began unbuttoning the bodice of her ruined dress.

When he'd removed the dress, Rowdy threw back the covers on the bed and laid her down on them. Took off her shoes. Drew the quilt up to her chin and bent to kiss her forehead.

"Get some sleep," he told her. "We'll figure out what to do about Whitman and the rest of it later, when you're rested. Right now I'm so worried about Gideon, I can't think about anything else."

Lark ached to be held, and at the very same time, she prayed Rowdy would leave her alone. Prayed he didn't think, as Autry had, that she was a whore, ripe for using. As much as she wanted Rowdy Rhodes, she couldn't have borne it if he used her.

Fresh tears sprang to her eyes, and it was all she could do not to reach for Rowdy, not to pull him down onto the bed beside her.

He left the room, closing the door quietly behind him.

Lark lay stiff in the cool, wintry light streaming in through the window. She would never sleep again; she was sure of that.

But in the next moment she nodded off.

Hours later she awakened, stirred from the depths of slumber by some sound, and knew that Rowdy was back. It must have been early afternoon, she concluded, but she couldn't be sure she hadn't slept round the clock, either. If she had, it was Monday, and she was late for school.

Lark watched, her heart pounding, as Rowdy sat down on the side of the bed to remove his boots.

"I know you're awake," he said. "No sense pretending you're not."

Lark sighed. "Gideon?"

"He'll be a while mending, but he'll be all right. Sam and I brought the cot from the jailhouse, and Gideon's sleeping on that. Mai Lee came to sit with him, once Hon Sing finished the surgery."

Tears of relief rushed to Lark's eyes, but she blinked them back.

"What time is it? Is it still Sunday?"

"It's about three-thirty in the afternoon, and, yes, it's still Sunday."

"I'm not a whore, Rowdy," she heard herself say.

"I know that," he replied, standing to haul off his shirt, unbutton his pants, strip till he was naked.

Lark blinked, at once thrilled and alarmed by the sight of him. "You do?"

He chuckled, lifted the covers and got into bed beside her. He felt hard and solid and blessedly warm, and she resisted an urge to draw closer to him, slip into his arms.

Had the time come?

Was he going to make love to her?

Or was he there simply because he was exhausted and there wasn't another bed?

As if in answer, Rowdy rolled from his back onto his side. Laid a hand boldly over Lark's left breast. She was wearing only a camisole and a pair of drawers—left from when he'd undressed her earlier.

"This is the day, Lark," he said, caressing her, chafing at her nipple with the side of his thumb until it jutted against the thin fabric of her camisole and she groaned. "You can still say no. I swear I won't touch you again, if you do, but if you want me as much as I want you, then I'll have you."

She couldn't speak. So she simply nodded.

Rowdy sighed, a deep, masculine sound, and worked the tiny buttons on her camisole until her breasts were bared to him.

Her breath was already fast and shallow. "She'll hear," she fretted. "Mai Lee will hear—"

"She's asleep," Rowdy said, and bent to suckle at her nipple even as he hooked a thumb under the top of her drawers and began pulling them down. "There'll be plenty to hear, though, if she isn't."

Lark moaned again.

And then Rowdy's hand slipped between her legs, and he found the tear in her bloomers, chuckled as he worked his fingers through to play with her. "So you wanted to be ready for me," he said.

Lark whimpered as he teased her most sensitive spot. Shook her head. "I must have put them back on by mistake—" she protested, but even that much was so hard to say, given what he was doing to her, that she couldn't go on.

"Liar," he said. He went back to suckling at her breast, and she gasped softly and started when he thrust his fingers inside her. Her hips surged up off the mattress, seeking more.

He brought her quickly to that first release, sharp and keen, but not assuaging her terrible need. Instead she wanted him more.

He shifted onto his knees, removed her drawers, tossed them aside, along with the camisole. He spread her hair out around her head on the pillows and then, gently, he guided her hands to the rails in the headboard, closed her fingers around them.

Confused, feeling deliciously vulnerable, Lark tightened her grip.

"I'm not a whore," she said again.

"I wouldn't do this if I thought you were," he answered, and kissed his way down her belly until he reached the place where his fingers played. He parted her, took her into his mouth.

Perspiration slickened Lark's palms as she gripped the headboard railings. She moaned his name, pleading.

He took his time with her, took his pleasure, now feasting upon her, now barely flicking at her with the tip of his tongue.

Finally, when the need was beyond bearing, Lark exploded, her entire body convulsing in a spasm so sweetly violent that she couldn't hold in a long, lusty wail of release.

Mai Lee must surely have heard, she thought, but then Rowdy was on top of her, lying between her spread legs, prodding at her, causing her to open for him, and she couldn't think of anything else but the way it felt.

He entered her with one swift motion of his hips. Went deep.

Lark's eyes rolled back in her head, and her grip on the headboard felt slippery. She dared not let go, though, because she needed anchoring, needed some way to keep her mind tethered to her body—her quivering, anxious, seeking body.

Rowdy pressed his hands into the mattress on either side of Lark, and paused, his head thrown back. She felt him restraining himself, knew he was savoring the feel of her around him, even exulting, in some elemental male way, in possessing her.

She began to move beneath him, very slightly and very slowly, and the power shifted. Rowdy groaned hoarsely, whispered her name.

They found a rhythm then, moving in concert, with a savage grace.

He brought her to the brink, brought himself to the brink.

Then he stopped again. Without withdrawing from her, he lowered himself to kiss her, conquering her as thoroughly with his tongue as with his manhood. She was breathless when their mouths parted, and could only make a low, guttural sound when he began to take her in earnest.

He moved more and more quickly, though each stroke was as smooth as a sword thrust into a scabbard. Lark drew up her knees and thrashed under Rowdy, pummeled him wildly with her body, let go of the headboard at the final moment—and soared.

She felt Rowdy stiffen, long moments after her own climax, and spill himself into her, moaning her name, over and over again, as he gave himself up.

He fell to her, and they lay entwined for a long, silent while, breathing raggedly, and as one.

"Do you think Mai Lee heard?" Lark asked, worried.

"No," Rowdy said. "But she might hear this." And then he turned her onto her stomach, and set her hands back on the rails above her head, and glided into her from behind, one hand cupping her right breast, the other under her, stroking the nubbin of flesh between her legs. She felt the walls of her femininity convulse around him.

Lark climaxed, hard, within three thrusts, and buried her face in Rowdy's pillow to muffle her throaty cries. She was still reeling from that when Rowdy, who hadn't given in to pleasure yet, raised her onto her hands and knees. After pausing, kissing her shoulders, her spine, the back of her neck, he rammed into her, like a stallion taking a mare, catapulting her into a daze of new and wholly unexpected ecstasy.

This time, there was no muffling her cries.

And no muffling his.

Half the town must have known what they were doing, let alone Mai Lee, Lark thought, in some small, lucid part of her mind, as she quivered at the peak of a shattering surrender. And she didn't give a damn.

Let them know.

Let them know Rowdy Rhodes was having the schoolmarm in a squeaky bed in the house behind the jailhouse, having her thoroughly. And she was loving it.

17

ROWDY WAS GONE LONG before Lark awakened in a strange bed much later, confused and a little disoriented. Then, remembering what had transpired there, she felt her cheeks burn, even as she set aside her own embarrassment, by force of will, to consider more pressing matters.

Gideon. Was he alive? Had Hon Sing's surgery succeeded?

She sat bolt upright, desperate to know.

And Lydia. How was she faring? Lark had not seen the child since before she left Mrs. Porter's to follow Gideon to the Cattleman's Hall, and though she'd been on the mend, a relapse was certainly possible.

Finally, there was Autry. He could be on his way to Stone Creek even at that moment, or, worse, he might already have arrived. Suppose he'd installed himself at the Territorial Hotel, bent on harrying Sam and the major to pursue the train robbers with every available resource?

He might see her, at any time, or hear her name by chance. Most people addressed her as "Miss Morgan"—Autry wouldn't recognize that, because she'd made it up out of whole cloth—but someone might refer to her as "Lark," and that would be disastrous.

Why hadn't she called herself Susan or Mary, names common enough to escape notice?

But she knew the answer, of course. She'd given up so much of herself, running and lying and dying her hair. She'd kept the name her mother had given her because she hadn't wanted to abandon herself completely—because she *was* Lark.

Filled with sudden urgency, she looked frantically about for her clothes, but they were missing. Everything was gone—the dress stained with Gideon's blood when she'd knelt beside him after the shooting, and when she'd held him in her arms in the bed of a wagon as he was being transported to Rowdy's house. The drawers and camisole had vanished, too. Everything had been taken away except her shoes, which still lay oddly askew where Rowdy had tossed them when he took them off her feet.

Lark snatched the quilt off the bed, wrapped it around herself like a coronation robe, and opened the bedroom door just a crack. Peered out.

Gideon lay sleeping on his cot. Lark squinted, examining him from a distance. His shoulder was bandaged, seeping a little, but his color was good, and he seemed to be breathing normally, and with relative ease, considering what he'd been through.

There was no sign of Mai Lee or of Hon Sing, but Rowdy sat near the stove, reading a book, fully clad, one booted foot braced against the chrome rail, and Pardner was stretched out on the floor, midway between him and Gideon, keeping his canine vigil.

"Where are my clothes?" Lark whispered anxiously, and with a peevish note in her voice.

Rowdy grinned, closed the book. "I burned them," he said, as though it were a perfectly reasonable thing to do. "They were pretty well ruined."

"You *burned*— What am I supposed to wear? I can't leave this house in a quilt!"

He smiled a private little smile, as though relishing the thought of Lark parading through Stone Creek clad only in the covering from his bed, then nodded toward the table, where a bundle waited, wrapped in brown paper and neatly tied up with twine. "Mai Lee fetched some things for you from the rooming house. Shall I bring them to you?"

"No!" Lark replied quickly, and rushed out to snatch the package off the table, nearly losing her grasp on the quilt in the process.

Rowdy smiled. "Bathing room's that way," he said, nodding toward a nearby door. "I lit a fire under the boiler a while ago, so the water ought to be hot."

The very thought of a real bath restored Lark considerably. She took her fresh clothes, the edge of the quilt dragging behind her with a homespun kind of elegance, and scurried in the direction Rowdy indicated.

The tub was a thing of gleaming splendor, the likes of which Lark had not seen since before she'd fled Denver. There was a flush commode, too, and a pedestal sink made of real porcelain, though it only had one spigot. Even at Mrs. Porter's, surely the best-appointed house in Stone Creek, she had used chamber pots and the privy, and taken shivering baths in her room, with only a basin, a cloth and a towel.

After closing the bathing room door carefully behind her, Lark set the clean clothes Mai Lee had brought her on the lid of the commode, still in their parcel, put the plug in place in the bathtub and turned on the spigots.

Gloriously plentiful, steaming water poured out of the faucet, thundering into the tub, and Lark was so overcome with gratitude and joy that she nearly wept.

She let go of the quilt, letting it fall into a pool of faded color at her feet, stuck a toe in to test the water. It was perfect—hot, but not scalding—and best of all, it soon filled the tub nearly to the brim.

Settling in, Lark soaked awhile, then used the soap and washcloth Rowdy must have set out for her, scrubbing herself squeaky-clean from head to foot. The feeling was so heavenly that she almost forgot that Autry was bound to come to Stone Creek, if he hadn't already, and discover her there. Even if she hid out, which she fully intended to do, she couldn't remain entirely invisible. She still had to teach school, after all, and she would need to look in on Gideon often, while he recovered.

She slipped down into the water until it reached her chin, frowning.

Common sense argued for leaving. She could enlist someone, surely, to escort her as far as Phoenix in a wagon or a buggy—she couldn't risk getting aboard the stagecoach, because its arrival and departure were events in Stone Creek, and her going would arouse considerable notice. Once she'd reached Phoenix, which seemed an impossible feat in itself, even if Autry didn't send riders after her, she could…what?

Board a train? Autry could have agents on all of them, looking for her.

Buy a stagecoach ticket? Where would she go, and what would she do when she got there—wherever "there" was? She had no friends, no family and no money.

All these things compounded the problem, of course, but they weren't the real reasons she couldn't leave Stone Creek.

She was bound to the place by ties of caring—for Gideon, for Lydia and all her students. The school term wouldn't be over until early June, and honor required her to complete her contract, informal though it was.

And there was a still greater reason.

It would mean leaving Rowdy.

Before he'd made love to her, she *could* have gone somewhere else, given herself a new name and started over, entrusting Gideon and Lydia to others. Sam O'Ballivan, busy as he was, had worked as a schoolmaster in Haven—he could have finished out the term for her or found someone else. But from the first moment of intimacy—not in Rowdy's bed just hours before, but on the way out to Sam and Maddie's place, when he'd made her shout his name to the sky—she'd been lost to any plan that didn't include him.

Rowdy might well vanish one of these days, she knew, because he had dangerous secrets of his own. If that happened, assuming she managed to deal with Autry and hold on to her job after the truth came out—she'd been married *and* divorced, and those things were considered unacceptable in a teacher—she'd stay on in Stone Creek, she decided, and live out her best years as a spinster schoolmarm. But at least she would have known passion, and the memory would sustain her through otherwise lonely nights.

She would find a way to survive, even to thrive, with or without Rowdy.

What she would *not* do was run away again.

She meant to stand and face Autry, if it came to that. She knew Rowdy would help her, and in the event that he'd already gone, she would seek Sam O'Ballivan's assistance.

Having come to terms with these things, Lark felt renewed, though her fears certainly hadn't diminished. She completed her bath, dried herself off with a flour-sack towel and donned her clothes, smiling when she found her hairbrush, toothbrush and powder tucked in the folds of her green woolen skirt.

Silently she blessed Mai Lee for her thoughtfulness.

She brushed out her hair—it wanted washing, but that was an undertaking that required several hours—plaited it into a single braid and tied it with a bit of the twine Mai Lee had used to bind the parcel closed.

She must have looked quite presentable when she stepped out of the bathing room, because something sparked in Rowdy's eyes as he watched her. She looked away, embarrassed to remember just how completely she'd surrendered to him.

She stood over Gideon's cot, leaned a little to touch the boy's forehead.

He opened his eyes, looked up at her in bafflement. "Miss Morgan?" he ground out. "What are you doing here?"

Rowdy all but overturned his chair getting to his feet, coming to stand beside Lark. While he'd seemed calm, at his reading, he'd been waiting for Gideon to wake up, and probably fearing that he never would.

Lark watched, smiling through tears, as remembrance dawned in Gideon's face. "I was shot," he said, very slowly.

"Yes," Lark answered. "But you're going to be all right. Hon Sing took very good care of you."

"Did he stick a bunch of needles in me?" Gideon asked, grinning wanly.

"He did," said Lark with a nod. "And he performed surgery on you, too. That's why you have bandages. The bullet came very close to your heart."

He shifted on the cot, sought and found Rowdy's face, where a lecture was brewing, his expression both obstinate and chagrined. "I was only trying to be a good deputy," Gideon said.

Rowdy's voice was hoarse when he answered. "It was a damn fool thing, what you did. But it was brave as hell, too. Do anything like it again, though, and I'll shoot you *myself*."

Gideon tried to sit up, fell back down onto the cot again. Pardner stepped up to lick his cheek, and he chuckled and reached out, shakily, to ruffle the dog's ears.

Lark remembered the fierce way Pardner had guarded Gideon after he was shot, and smiled. When Gideon felt better, she'd tell him all about it. Tell him how she'd had to spend long minutes calming the dog before he'd allow anyone besides Lark to get close, and how Pardner had jumped into the back of the wagon, with her and Gideon, to make the ride with them.

"Are you hurting?" Rowdy asked his brother. "Hon Sing left some stuff here—to take for pain. Powder, folded up in a piece of paper."

Gideon shook his head. "I just feel numb, pretty much everywhere." He looked at Lark again, searched her face. "You followed me to the dance, didn't you?"

Lark drew up a chair, took Gideon's hand in both of hers. He'd been unconscious, from the time of the shooting until just a few minutes before. If he'd awakened at any point, she would have known, because she'd been watching him so closely. "How did you know that?"

"I saw you," he said. He glanced sheepishly at Rowdy, but his eyes were clear and solemn when he turned back to Lark. "I saw Rose, too." Gideon paused, swallowed. Rowdy went to get him some water. He drank from the ladle, then nodded, as if to confirm his own words to himself. "I saw Rose. You were kneeling beside me, Lark, and Rose was standing right behind you. She was wearing the dress she died in."

"Who is Rose?" Lark asked, moved.

"My sister," Gideon said. "She died when she was four years old."

Lark was confounded, her emotions stirred in some deep and inexplicable way, and Rowdy remained silent.

"You don't believe me," Gideon accused, looking from one of them to the other. "You don't think I really saw Rose. But I did…I *did*."

"I do believe you, Gideon," Lark said.

"You only *thought* you saw her," Rowdy said. "You were *shot*, Gideon, and you had some kind of dream. Drink some more water."

"Be quiet," Lark told Rowdy, holding Gideon's hand tightly now. "Did you speak with…with Rose?" she asked softly.

Gideon shook his head. "I wanted to," he said sadly, "but there wasn't time. She was there, and she said some things I can't remember now, and I wanted to go with her when she left, but she shook her head. Then she was gone."

Lark bit her lip. "After my mother died," she said, smoothing Gideon's blankets gently, "I was inconsolable. My grandfather was lost in his own grief, and he wouldn't have known what to say to me, anyway. But the night after her funeral—" she paused, aware that Rowdy was listening intently, and straightened her spine "—well, I would have sworn Mama came and sat on my bed. I didn't see her, though—I wish I had."

Gideon looked somewhat mollified. Then his gaze shifted to Rowdy, standing behind Lark. He changed the course of the conversation. "Did you find Pa? Did he—?"

Lark felt the swift tension in Rowdy's body, even though they weren't touching, perhaps because some unseen, mystical factor of their lovemaking still connected them. She looked back at him just in time to see him shake his head, not in denial, but in warning.

The reminder was sobering. She might have shared her secrets, but Rowdy still had plenty of his own. She'd bared her soul to him; he'd told her nothing at all.

No, he'd undressed her and put her in his bed. Later he'd returned and ravished her so completely that her body still pulsed with the aftershocks of truly cataclysmic satisfaction. But he'd made no promises, certainly. And he'd withheld the truest part of himself from her, for all the physical intimacy they'd shared.

"I'd better go out and make my rounds," Rowdy

said, suddenly uncomfortable. "If Lark—Miss Morgan—wouldn't mind staying with you for a while…"

Lark nodded. "I'll stay," she said. *For Gideon's sake, Rowdy Rhodes, not yours.*

"Obliged," Rowdy said, as though they were two polite strangers, almost colliding on a sidewalk, then cordially sidestepping each other. As though they had not been lovers only a few hours before. "I'll get back as quick as I can."

Lark nodded, a little tersely.

Gideon closed his eyes and drifted back into the solace of sleep, perhaps hoping to find his lost sister, Rose, waiting there.

Bent on going out, as much to escape any questions she might ask, she suspected, as to fulfill his duties as town marshal, Rowdy crossed the room, strapped on his gun belt, reached for his hat and coat.

In a moment of stark clarity, Lark recalled what he'd said, after she'd recounted the events leading up to Gideon's near-fatal shooting, and how, in the midst of the chaos, someone had called out the name "Willie."

I'll kill him, Rowdy had vowed.

Lark rushed to catch him before he went out the door.

"You're not going looking for the man who shot Gideon, are you? Not yet—not without Sam and a posse?"

Rowdy eyes were blank, veiled from within. He'd closed himself off to her, stepped behind some invisible barrier, through which she could not pass. "He's one man," he said grimly. "What do I need with a posse?"

"It's almost dark, Rowdy. At least wait until tomorrow!"

"I mean to ask some questions of the folks that were

at that dance, among others." His jaw tightened. "Just the same, if I happen to run across the bastard, I might just have to invoke Rhodes Ordinance."

When I need a law, I just make one, he'd told her the day of the blizzard.

That was Rhodes Ordinance.

Lark gripped Rowdy's arm. "Don't take the law into your own hands," she whispered. "Promise me you won't!"

"I can't make that kind of promise," Rowdy said. "I've lied every day of my life since I was fourteen years old, and I won't do it anymore. If I find Willie—or meet up with Autry Whitman—well, the truth is, I don't know exactly what I'll do, but I'm sure as hell going to do *something*."

Lark clung to Rowdy. She felt Pardner press between them, squirming to be noticed.

"Stay here with us," she said to Rowdy. "Just for a little while. I'll make some coffee, find something to fix for supper…"

Rowdy smiled almost imperceptibly and placed a light, tantalizing kiss on her mouth. He would share himself with her only when they made love, she realized, and it wasn't enough. *It wasn't enough.*

"I'll be all right," he said.

"You *won't*. Autry is vicious, Rowdy, and, worse, he's a coward. And the man who shot Gideon *must* be an outlaw, or he wouldn't have done anything like that."

"I can be pretty vicious myself if the situation calls for it," Rowdy said, gently removing her hand from his arm. A cold wind blew in around them, through the partially open door. "And I can handle any outlaw. I know how they think, Lark. I know the places where they hide, everything they're afraid of, how to track them." He paused, looked away for a moment, then met her gaze again. "After all, I'm one of them."

Lark's mouth dropped open.

Rowdy smiled again, his eyes bleak, and went out the door.

Pardner tried to follow, and Rowdy sent him slinking back inside, dejected, with a stern word. The animal plopped down in front of the stove, with a disconsolate little whine low in his throat.

Lark shut the door, leaned against it, pressing her forehead into the wood. Rowdy was an *outlaw?*

That *couldn't* have been what he said—she must have misunderstood him. He was the marshal of Stone Creek—Sam O'Ballivan and Major Blackstone thought highly enough of him to give him a badge. And he was too strong, too honorable, too *good* to be a criminal.

Surely she'd heard him wrong.

JOLENE'S SALOON WAS CLOSED for business, that being Sunday, but Rowdy found a side door and went in anyway.

All the tables were empty, but Hon Sing was standing on a chair in back of the bar, swabbing down the long mirror with water that smelled pungently of vinegar. Hearing Rowdy enter, or maybe just seeing his reflection in the glass, he turned, paused in his work.

"Boy has fever?" the Chinaman asked.

Rowdy shook his head. "Gideon's doing all right, thanks to you."

Hon Sing dropped the rag he'd been using into the

bucket set among the whiskey bottles and dingy glasses under the mirror and stepped down off the chair. Came around to stand facing Rowdy.

"You not come for whiskey," Hon Sing said solemnly.

Again Rowdy shook his head. Took a folded sheet of paper from the inside pocket of his trail coat and extended it to the Chinese doctor who'd been reduced, through circumstance and casual prejudice, to washing mirrors in saloons and cleaning up after whores and gamblers and drunken cowboys.

Hon Sing just looked at the paper, puzzled.

"It's the deed to the place behind the jailhouse," Rowdy said. "I've already signed it over to you and your wife."

Hon Sing blinked, and his hand shook as he took the deed, examined the writing on it, which was probably incomprehensible to him, as highly educated as he undoubtedly was. "Too much," he said warily, though a light of cautious hope glinted in his eyes.

"You saved my brother's life," Rowdy replied. "Seems to me, he and I got the better end of this trade."

Almost reverently Hon Sing tucked the document inside his black cotton shirt. And he smiled. "Thank you," he said, and bowed his head slightly.

Rowdy inclined his own head in response. "I'm grateful, Hon Sing. Truth is, I wouldn't have let you stick those needles in Gideon, let alone cut on him, if Lark hadn't stepped in."

"Miss Morgan fine woman. Good to Mai Lee. Good to Hon Sing." The Chinaman paused, frowned. "Very afraid, though."

Rowdy nodded. He knew now, at least, who Lark

feared and why. From what he'd seen of Autry Whitman, not to mention the man's reputation, she'd had good reason to be scared.

He'd deal with Whitman, that was a grim certainty. Right now, though, it was Willie he wanted to find. It was a common name, Willie, but he'd heard it in the bathhouse behind this same saloon, the first day he was in town, and he remembered the man it belonged to. He also remembered that Hon Sing had been present, summoned by Jolene to empty dirty bathwater through the floorboards.

"Do you recall those two cowpokes, or drifters, who came in when my dog Pardner and I were here? One of them was called Harlan, and the other was Willie."

Hon Sing hesitated, then nodded decisively. Smiled, probably at the memory of Pardner sitting in soapy water up to his chest. "Hon Sing remember," he said, and instantly sobered a little.

"Do you know anything about them? Last names? Whether they work around Stone Creek someplace or were just passing through?"

"Not work," Hon Sing said, pondering. "Drifters. But Hon Sing see before."

Rowdy hooked his thumbs in his gun belt. Waited, because he knew there was more. He could practically see the gears turning in Hon Sing's mind as he weighed the implications of speaking or remaining silent.

Hon Sing looked around, probably on the alert for Jolene and then hurried behind the bar, returning with what looked like a ledger book.

"Jolene write names," he said, in an anxious whisper. "Everyone who bathes. Everyone plays poker."

Rowdy took the book, laid it on top of the bar and

opened it. Ran his finger down pages of names—coming across that of the mysterious Mr. Porter numerous times, up until about two years back.

Impatient, and worried that Jolene would appear and hand Hon Sing some grief for giving Rowdy access to her private records, he flipped forward until he saw his own name. Grinned slightly at the terse connotation added beneath it.

"And dog."

Below that were the two Rowdy sought—Harlan Speeks and Willie Moran.

Rowdy closed the ledger, handed it to Hon Sing, who quickly put it back in its normal place. "Is Jolene around?" he asked.

Hon Sing looked worried. "In back," he said. Then he patted the deed, standing out against the fabric of his shirt, and smiled very slightly. "Jolene in back, with womans. I get for you?"

Rowdy stopped the man with a glance when he would have rounded the bar to head off on the errand. It would be a while before Mai Lee and Hon Sing could grow a garden on that acre, and the house was still uninhabitable. He didn't want Jolene to get her hackles up, thinking the help had betrayed her, and give Hon Sing the boot.

"You've done enough," he said. "And I'm much obliged. Best you get back to washing down that mirror, though."

Hon Sing nodded, climbed back up on the seat of the chair he'd been standing on earlier and commenced to swabbing again.

Rowdy made for the back of the saloon.

Heard Jolene's cackle before he spotted her, through

the doorway of a cramped, dirty kitchen. She and two of her girls were seated at a cluttered table, smoking cheroots and swapping yarns.

Rowdy's entrance caused a little stir.

Jolene immediately sobered and sent the scantily-clad girls scurrying for the back stairs.

"Both of them are available for a price," Jolene said, cocking a thumb toward the steps. A mingling of stale perfume and body odor made the room rank. "Which one do you want?"

"Neither," Rowdy said. He was standing up and dressed, in contrast to the last time a conversation between him and Jolene had taken this turn, and he felt no compunction to hide his distaste. "I don't use the services of whores."

"Just schoolmarms," Jolene said shrewdly.

Rowdy felt the familiar muscle bunch in his jaw. It was the curse of the Yarbros, that muscle, the one part of his body he couldn't control.

Jolene grinned lasciviously. "Whole town knows the high-and-mighty Miss Lark Morgan was all night in your place," she said. "And I'll wager when she leaves, she'll be wearing different clothes than she had on yesterday. Oh, I could make me a fine dollar if I had *that* bit of baggage in my stable—but she's all yours, isn't she, Marshal Rowdy Rhodes?"

As much as Rowdy would have liked to claim Lark for his own, he knew he couldn't. He was wanted, an outlaw chasing outlaws. One of these days the past was bound to catch up with him, and he had a gut-clenching hunch it would be soon.

Lark deserved a good husband, a home, children of her own.

With a price on his head, he couldn't give her those things.

And there was one other thing he knew for sure: he wasn't about to discuss Lark with Jolene Bell or anybody else.

"I came here to ask about a couple of your customers," Rowdy said, taking some satisfaction in the look of irritated disappointment on Jolene's face when he didn't take the hook. She'd been hoping he'd let something slip about Lark, who'd probably stirred up a lot of speculation in Stone Creek, even before he came along to complicate matters. "I'm looking for Harlan Speeks and Willie Moran."

Jolene's eyes narrowed. "What do you want with them?"

"You know damn well what I want with them," Rowdy said. "The man who shot my kid brother was called Willie."

"Every third boy in this town is called Willie," Jolene asserted. "It's right common."

Rowdy acknowledged that with a terse nod. "It's also a place to start."

"I reckon you could ask the folks who were at the dance," she said.

"I can," Rowdy answered, "and I will. But right now I'm asking you."

Jolene sighed. "You can't say where you heard it. Harlan's all right, but Willie's got himself a nasty temper, especially when he's been celebratin'."

"Wild horses couldn't drag it out of me," Rowdy said.

Jolene looked uncertain. "Last I knew," she said, "they were sleeping in the barn out at the Franks place, the pair of them. Doing a few chores to earn their grub."

"Thanks," Rowdy said, turning to go.

"Rhodes?"

He stopped, looked back at Jolene. Waited.

"I seen your face once before. On a poster that come across Pete Quincy's desk, back when he was still marshal. I used to look at them, when I could, to make sure I wasn't harborin' no outlaws, either at my poker tables or upstairs with my girls. I just don't need that kind of trouble. Anyhow, I don't recollect the name on that poster, and it sure as hell wasn't Rowdy Rhodes, but it was you, all right. You tread light around me, *Mr. Town Marshal,* and you won't have no cause to worry. You bother me, though, and you'll have worries aplenty."

Rowdy stood absolutely still. He didn't deny anything Jolene had said—that would only have aroused her suspicions further—but he didn't confess, either. "Thanks for the information about Speeks and Moran," he said, and then he left.

Went straight to the lean-to, back of his place, and saddled Paint.

He was just leading the horse out into the dusky gloom of nightfall when he realized Lark was standing a few feet away, clutching her cloak around her and watching him. Her long braid rested over her right shoulder, and he felt an unholy need to unplait it and comb his fingers through.

"Is Gideon all right?" he asked.

She nodded.

Rowdy put a foot in the stirrup and swung up into the saddle.

Lark looked up at him. "You're going after Willie, aren't you?"

"Yes," Rowdy said. "If I'm not back by morning, see if you can have Gideon moved over to Mrs. Porter's. Take Pardner along, too, and ask the man over at the livery stable to put up Gideon's horse. I'll settle up with everybody when I get back."

Her throat worked visibly. "Rowdy—"

He resettled his hat. "I've got to go, Lark."

She stepped directly in front of Paint, took hold of his bridle strap. "Gideon needs you. *Stone Creek* needs you. And you're chasing off on some—on some *vendetta*—"

"Lark," Rowdy said reasonably, but with an edge of temper, "taking a horse into a public building is against the law, and so is shooting somebody down in the process. I'm still the marshal. And even if Gideon hadn't been the one to take the bullet, I'd be making this ride."

"At least tell me where you're going, so I can tell Sam," she insisted. "You may need *help,* Rowdy, even though you seem to think you're invincible!"

Rowdy nodded. "I'm not invincible," he said. "And I'm not the man I made you think I was, in there in that bed today. For now, let's just leave things at that."

"Rowdy, what are you saying?" She put the question tremulously, and let go of the bridle strap. "That I shouldn't care what happens to you? That you didn't mean any of the things you told me?" She paused, and her chin wobbled as she gazed up at him, moonlight catching in the tears glazing her eyes. "Oh, I know you didn't say you loved me. I didn't expect that, didn't even hope for it. But your body said plenty, Rowdy. It said *plenty.*"

Rowdy tried to rein the horse around her, but she

moved again, forestalling him. "I've made love to a lot of women," he told her, hating himself for the coldness in his voice, underscoring the lie he was about to tell. "I reckon my body 'said' pretty much the same things to them."

She gasped, and even in the thick twilight, he saw her face go paler than exhaustion had already made it.

He'd hurt her. He'd probably lost her, which was an ironic insight, considering that he'd never had any real claim on Lark Morgan, even when she was pitching beneath him, clawing at his back like a wildcat and sobbing out his name.

It was hard, treating her this way. But in the long run, it was all for the best.

He had nothing to offer Lark, save the tenderness of his lovemaking and a whole lot of trouble and heartache. Precisely because she'd touched him so deeply, in places even Chessie hadn't been able to reach, and because he had to keep her safe, he needed to set her away from him.

Trouble was, he didn't know if he could do that.

Even then, with the ride to the Franks place ahead, and Pappy and the train robberies and all the rest of it, he wanted to stay. He wanted to tell her everything—about Chessie and the baby, about his years as an outlaw, all of it.

He wanted to stay.

And that scared him more than anything else that might lie ahead.

"I'm going, Lark," he said, more for her sake than his own. "Step aside."

Her spine went rigid, but she moved out of his way.

And he knew, without looking back, that she watched him until he was out of her sight.

LARK STOOD OUTSIDE long after Rowdy had gone, crying like a silly schoolgirl.

He'd said he believed her, when she told him she wasn't a whore, but now she feared he didn't, any more than Autry had. She was a plaything to him, an amusement, not someone he'd listen to or confide in. Not someone he'd trust—

Or love.

She sniffled. Dried her cheeks with the back of one hand.

Rowdy *was* an outlaw—it was just awful enough to be true.

One of these days he'd leave Stone Creek for good.

And she was in love with him.

Desperately, irrevocably in love.

Knowing this, the future sprang up stark ahead of her, dark and empty and endless. She'd be like Mrs. Porter in a few years, bravely pretending she wasn't alone, surrounded by unseen mementos of Rowdy, as real as Mr. Porter's coat, and books lying open everywhere, and the stub of his cigar in the ashtray on his desk in the study.

She'd remember the way Rowdy was with his dog.

The way his mouth quirked up at one side when he wasn't inclined to smile but couldn't help it.

She'd remember how he'd pulled that wagon to the side of the road, on the way to Sam and Maddie's place, and again, on the way back, and brought her into a whole new realm, a whole new sense of herself as a woman. He'd awakened an unquenchable passion inside her, another reality, another existence she hadn't dreamed was possible.

And it would all be wasted.

She'd have nothing tangible, though.

No coats or books or cigar stubs.

Heading back toward the house, where Gideon and Pardner were waiting for their supper, Lark made a strangled little sound, meant for laughter, but too raw in her throat to be anything but sorrow.

She wouldn't even have her bloomers, with the tear in the seam, to remember Rowdy by, because he'd burned them.

Wadded them up, with her blood-stained dress and her camisole, stuffed them into his stove and let the flames take them.

He might as well have thrown her on the fire, too.

All the things she hadn't quite dared to hope for had gone up in that blaze.

All the dreams, budded tight but straining to bloom.

With a last sniffle and a lift of her chin, Lark went inside the house.

She made a supper of scrambled eggs and toasted bread.

Gideon woke up long enough to eat, thank her and then immediately fell asleep again.

She served Pardner the leftovers—having barely touched her own food—and washed the dishes.

And when Mai Lee came, kindly circumspect, with knowing in her eyes, Lark greeted her warmly.

"Mai Lee stay with boy," the woman said. "You go home." She fluttered her hands, like the wings of some tiny bird. "Mrs. Porter ask, where Lark? Where Lark?"

"How is she?" Lark asked, remembering the incident in the cellar and the strong dose of laudanum her landlady had taken later. "And Lydia—"

"Lydia fine," Mai Lee said, bending to inspect Gideon, who hadn't stirred at her arrival. She had a lidded basket over one arm, and took out strips of cloth and a jar half-filled with some strange-colored poultice, probably intending to change the bandages Hon Sing had applied after surgery. "Mrs. Porter, she—" Mai Lee paused, searching for some elusive word "—walk-sleeping."

Lark, in the process of putting on her cloak and trying to ignore Pardner's mournful aspect at her going, stopped. "Mrs. Porter has been sleepwalking?"

Mai Lee nodded. "Find in cellar, hour ago. She digging in floor, with kitchen spoon." More fluttering of hands followed. "Digging. Digging. I stop her. She not know Mai Lee."

Lark frowned. "Did you ask Hon Sing to examine her?"

"She not let," Mai Lee said, without rancor. "Say heathen."

"I'm sorry," Lark said. Pardner whimpered and tried to squeeze through when she opened the door, perhaps wanting to walk her home as he'd done for Lydia, but more likely in an attempt to follow Rowdy.

She patted him on the head. "No," she said, gently but firmly. "You have to stay with Gideon."

Pardner sat down heavily and gave a low, mournful howl.

Suddenly Lark felt tears threatening again. Because she wasn't the only one who'd be left behind when

Rowdy went away—Pardner would be, too. As ferociously as he'd protected Gideon at the Cattleman's Hall the night before, and the trip to Stone Creek from Haven notwithstanding, he was an old dog, graying around the muzzle.

He simply wouldn't be able to keep up out there on the trail.

It was all Lark could do, in that moment, not to drop to her knees on the kitchen floor, wrap her arms around Pardner and weep wretchedly into his ruff—weep for both of them.

You can be my dog, she told him silently. *When Rowdy goes, and Gideon is off to college, you can be my dog.*

Pardner looked up at her, his brown eyes luminous with sorrow.

He knew what was coming as well as she did.

Swallowing her heart, which had surged up into the back of her throat and swelled there, hurting as if it would surely and literally burst, Lark closed the door between herself and Pardner and hurried through the darkness, headed home.

And a fancy carriage, drawn by six matching horses, stood directly in front of Mrs. Porter's house.

18

LARK STOPPED, staring at the carriage from just outside the golden cone of light from the nearest streetlamp.

It was precisely the sort of vehicle Autry might have hired; as strenuously as he guarded his pennies, he loved to make a show of wealth and, by extension, power.

She slipped up closer behind the carriage, noted the mud on the sturdy wheels and the doors. Could such a rig be had in Flagstaff, for any price?

Lark was debating between summoning up the courage to go into the house and fleeing wildly into the night when a man stepped out of the shadows, near Mrs. Porter's front gate, and cleared his throat.

He was tall and slender, dressed in livery and a top hat. Lark didn't recognize him; she was still poised to bolt, but curiosity stayed her.

"May I help you?" he asked.

"Do you work for Autry Whitman?" Lark countered, backing up until she bounced off Mrs. Porter's picket fence.

The man chuckled. "No, madam," he replied. "I'm in the employ of Miss Nell Baker."

Lark let out the breath she'd been holding, swayed slightly with the heady relief of drawing another. "You've come for Lydia," she concluded aloud, and felt the backs of her eyes begin to burn.

The coachman studied her for a long moment, then nodded. Of course he would be reticent concerning his mistress's business in Stone Creek; he didn't know Lark from Adam's third cousin, Bessie Sue.

"I live here," she explained, with a nod toward the big house behind her, and then felt utterly foolish for saying something so inane. What did Nell Baker's carriage driver care where she resided?

The combination of relief—this carriage *hadn't* brought Autry Whitman to Stone Creek, as she'd first feared—and sadness, because Lydia would soon be going away, left her dizzy-headed.

He smiled benignly and with some amusement. "Then you might want to go inside. It's cold out here." He gave a shiver. "Not at all like Phoenix."

"You could come in, too," Lark suggested, suddenly sorry for the man. "I'll put on a pot of coffee, or tea, if you'd prefer, and you can warm yourself by the stove."

"And get a flaying from Miss Nell for not staying with the coach?" the driver replied. "No, thank you."

"Is she—Miss Nell Baker, I mean—is she…unkind?"

The man frowned. "Unkind?"

Lark hesitated. "I'm Lydia's teacher, you see," she said. "And I've become quite fond of her. So, naturally, I'm concerned with—"

Just then Mrs. Porter's front door banged open, and

a woman appeared on the porch, more shadow than substance, but sturdily built and with imposing posture.

"Evans!" she called. "Who are you talking to out there? Why are you dawdling? I require your assistance to bring my niece out to the carriage!"

Lark opened the gate, moved cautiously up the walk.

"I'm on my way," Evans said, hurrying past her and on toward the house. "And I was speaking to Miss…?"

"Lark Morgan," Lark said, reaching the bottom step, looking up at Nell Baker. "Lydia has been my pupil at Stone Creek School, and I board in this house."

Nell Baker stepped forward, into the light of the moon and the faint reach of the streetlamps. She was plain, with quick, dark eyes, her hair pulled severely back from her face. Her dress was black bombazine, and her aspect precluded nonsense in any form or fashion. "Are you the one who looked after my niece when she took ill? God knows, it couldn't have been that trollop, Mabel, though she did show the grace to inform me that poor, foolish Herbert had managed to turn himself into a block of ice."

Lark opened her mouth. Closed it again.

Nodded.

"Speak up!" Nell Baker ordered. "And why are you standing down there on the walk like a ninny?"

Lark, intimidated at first, gathered her forces and marched up the steps, forcing Miss Baker to make way for her. "I helped take care of Lydia," she said. "A lot of other people did, too—Hon Sing and his wife, Mai Lee, especially. Mrs. Porter and a young man named Gideon Rhodes, too. And I am *not* a ninny."

Except with Rowdy, chided the damning voice of Lark's conscience.

She moved past Lydia's aunt and into the house. Only a single lamp burned in the entryway, glowing dimly on a side table.

Miss Baker came in, closed the door smartly. "Mrs. Porter," she huffed, in a loud whisper. "Loony as a goose flying north for the winter when the whole flock's headed south."

Lark set her hands on her hips, prepared to do battle on her landlady's behalf. But before she got a chance to lay into Miss Nell Baker good and proper, Lydia appeared in the dining room doorway behind her, dressed in a somber but costly little black velvet dress, surely provided by her aunt.

Herbert Fairmont's funeral had been held that afternoon, Lark realized, thunderstruck. She hadn't even remembered when Miss Baker referred to her late brother-in-law, quite callously, as a "block of ice." While she had been thrashing about in Rowdy Rhodes's bed, Lydia had been mourning her father.

"Aunt Nell says I can have a pony when we get back to Phoenix," Lydia announced. She looked pale and fragile and oddly stalwart, too.

Lark went to the child, crouched to look into her eyes. "Darling, I'm so sorry I missed your papa's funeral. It was this afternoon, wasn't it?"

"Lots of people came," Lydia said. "Mabel carried on something terrible, till Aunt Nell put her hands over my ears." She paused. "I guess you had to take care of Gideon. Mrs. Porter said he got shot." Her eyes grew enormous, and her lower lip wobbled. "Is Gideon going to die, like my papa did?"

Lark took the little girl's hands in hers, squeezed them. "No, sweetheart. Gideon will be fine."

Lydia leaned close, whispering now. "I still have the letter he wrote for me," she confided. "It's in my new reticule, the one Aunt Nell brought me. If I ever need him, he'll come for me, won't he? Like he said he would?"

Lark's eyes filled with tears. "Yes," she said. "I'm sure he will."

"Lydia," Miss Baker said gently, "you're taxing yourself. Let's get you into your cloak, and Evans will carry you out to the carriage."

"We're going to stay at the Territorial Hotel tonight," Lydia said, clearly impressed. "I've never stayed in a hotel before."

Lark hugged the child, kissed her cheek, then rose, looking back at Nell Baker.

Miss Baker took a small, blue woolen cape from where it rested over the stair banister, draped it gently around Lydia's shoulders, raised the hood and fastened the cloth buttons. Kissed her forehead. "You're the image of your mother," she said quietly, "and she was as beautiful as a princess."

Looking on, Lark knew by the woman's words and manner that Lydia would be safe with her and loved. She swallowed a lump in her throat.

"Evans!" Nell Baker called. "What *are* you doing?"

Evans appeared, dusting the crumbs of Mrs. Porter's rum cake from the front of his fancy coachman's coat. "The lady of the house offered me refreshment," he said, clearly unhurried. "And it would have been rude to refuse."

"Carry Lydia to the carriage, please," Miss Baker said moderately.

Evans scooped the little girl up into his arms. "Off to the ball, Cinderella," he said.

Peering out from under the hood of her new cloak, Lydia waved goodbye over Evans's broad shoulder, and they were gone.

Lark watched them go, feeling much as she had earlier when Rowdy rode out, figuratively trampling her heart under his horse's hooves. She cared about all her pupils, but she'd come to love Lydia somewhere along the way. Lydia and Gideon and Pardner—and Rowdy.

Unexpectedly Nell Baker laid a hand on her shoulder. "Lydia is my own dear sister's only child," she said quietly. "I'll raise her well, Miss Morgan, and bless God every day for the gift of doing so."

Lark swallowed. Nodded.

Nell smiled. "And she'll never need to send that letter, either," she said.

"You knew?"

"I heard her telling Mrs. Porter about it," Nell answered. "He must be quite a young man, this Gideon."

"He is," Lark said.

Nell opened the door, paused briefly on the threshold, ready to leave. "Life is peculiar, isn't it?" she asked reflectively. "Why, from what little I know of Gideon, I wouldn't be one bit surprised if he came knocking at my door, in ten years or so, just to see how Lydia was faring."

Lark smiled, imagining that faraway day, when Lydia would no longer be a child, but a beautiful young woman. Nell Baker had already gone when she replied, alone in the entryway, "Neither would I."

LYDIA SAT OBEDIENTLY on a settee in the lobby of the Territorial Hotel, where she'd never expected to be if she lived to be as old as Noah, and watched as Aunt Nell spoke with the clerk behind the desk. Mr. Evans, meanwhile, carried in reticules and a small trunk, winking at her once, when she sagged a little for missing Miss Morgan, and making her smile.

"Our best rooms are taken, I'm afraid," Lydia heard the clerk say to Aunt Nell. Then, dropping his voice to a loud whisper, which Lydia clearly heard even though she was some distance away, he added, "Mr. Whitman arrived this afternoon, you see. The *railroad* Mr. Whitman. He's out at the O'Ballivan place right now, taking a strip off Sam and the major both for not catching the men who robbed his train yesterday morning."

Just then the big front doors slammed open, and a tall, gray-haired man strode inside, followed by another man dressed much like Mr. Evans. He had shiny black skin.

Lydia tried not to stare, but she couldn't help it. She didn't take particular notice of the black man—Charlie, who ran the livery stable, was the same color, after all, and so were several of her papa's patients. No, it was the other man who intrigued her. He looked like a big, mean lion, an *old* one, with his hair bushed out around his head like a mane.

"Thunderation!" he roared. "Isn't there a decent place to eat in this backwater town?"

Aunt Nell gave him a long, disapproving look, which he noticed, but ignored.

Lydia got up off the settee and approached him.

Tugged at the sleeve of his coat. "My teacher says it's rude to shout," she said, "in public or in private."

The lion-man looked down at her, scowling. "Sometimes," he said, "it's the only way to get anything accomplished."

Lydia shook her head solemnly. "Miss Morgan says it's rude," she insisted.

"Lydia," Aunt Nell said firmly, turning briefly from her business with the clerk, "sit down."

"I'll be right with you, Mr. Whitman," the clerk called.

Lydia returned to the settee, and was surprised and strangely gratified when Mr. Whitman sat down right beside her.

"And what brings a child like you to the hotel?" he asked her.

"My papa got buried today," Lydia told him. "And Lark—Miss Morgan, I mean—couldn't be there because she had to take care of Gideon. He got shot trying to keep a horse from trampling people right in the middle of the Cattleman's Hall. I'm going to marry Gideon someday. I've got a letter I can send him from anyplace, if I ever need help, and when he gets it—" She fell silent. Mr. Railroad Whitman looked as though he might be fixing to behave rudely again and yell. His face was all red, and his eyes looked like marbles stuck into the sockets, all gleaming and hard, same as the ones the boys played with at school.

"Your teacher's name is *Lark?*" he asked, and though he didn't raise his voice, he splashed spittle in Lydia's face, the way Mabel had sometimes, when she was vexed.

"I'm not supposed to call her that," Lydia said, watching as Aunt Nell collected keys from the clerk and handed them to Mr. Evans. She hoped she wouldn't have to sleep in a room all by herself; she was afraid she might have bad dreams about her papa. Mabel had told her once that sometimes people got buried when they weren't really dead, and then they woke up and tried to claw their way out of the coffin and through six feet of ground, too. "But that's what Marshal Rhodes calls her—Lark, I mean—and I like to say it sometimes because it's so pretty. Don't you think it's pretty, Mr. Railroad?"

"Lydia," Aunt Nell said, coming to stop in front of where she and the lion-man sat, side by side, "our room is ready."

Belatedly Mr. Railroad remembered his manners and stood. "Miss Morgan said a gentleman always stands when a lady is present. She made Terran O'Ballivan and Ben Blackstone and all the other boys do it once, at school, even though she'd just come out of the cloakroom."

Lydia's throat tightened. She was going to miss Terran and Ben, and *especially* Lark. Not Beaver Franks, though. She hoped she'd never see *him* again.

"I hope my niece hasn't been a bother," Aunt Nell said, taking Lydia's hand, starting toward the big staircase.

"Marshal Rhodes?" the man muttered, as though Aunt Nell had not spoken to him at all.

Lydia looked back at him. "His name is *Rowdy,*" she called. "Not 'Marshal.'"

Mr. Railroad Whitman looked even more consternated than before. "Wait," he blustered, hastening across the room.

Aunt Nell paused, and her hand tightened around Lydia's, fair crushing the bones.

"This woman—your teacher—where does she live?" He said to Lydia. "Here in Stone Creek?"

Lydia nodded. Perhaps he had children who needed a school to go to and someone kind to teach them. She was eager to help. "She lives at Mrs. Porter's house," she said. "But she was at Rowdy's since clear last night. I'd have had to sleep by myself if Mai Lee hadn't put a cot in my room. Lark missed my papa's funeral, and I almost didn't get to say goodbye to her."

"Lydia," Aunt Nell said. "Do stop prattling." Her voice was cool as buttermilk fresh from the spring-house when she spoke to the railroad man. "My niece is recovering from a very serious illness, Mr. Whitman, and she has had a trying day. We'll bid you a good evening, now." With that, she turned and started up the stairs in earnest, and Lydia had no choice but to follow, since her hand was still locked inside Aunt Nell's.

She looked back once, though, over her shoulder, and saw Mr. Whitman turn to his companion, the one dressed like Mr. Evans. The two men conferred, in voices Lydia couldn't hear, and then Mr. Whitman turned right around and went outside, pushing the hotel doors open hard with his outstretched hands.

ESAU HURRIED AFTER HIM. "Mr. Whitman, sir," he said hastily. "What is it?"

"She's here," Autry said, the knowledge buzzing through his middle like a steam-powered mill saw, fit to cut him clean in half.

Esau blinked, glanced nervously up and down the cold, empty Sunday-night street. "*Who* is here, sir?"

Autry drew a deep breath, suddenly famished for air. He filled his lungs, felt revived. Even exhilarated. "*My wife, Esau. My wife is right here, in Stone Creek.*"

"How do you know that?" Esau asked, moving as though he wanted to take hold of Autry's arm and pull him back into the hotel.

Autry jabbed a thumb toward the building. "That little girl I was just talking to in there happened to mention that her teacher's name is Lark."

Esau had been jittery ever since the robbery yesterday morning. "At least come up onto the sidewalk, sir," he fretted. "We could be run down by some passing horseman."

"Esau," Autry said, "do you *see* a horseman? Or a *horse,* for that matter? This is Stone Creek, not Denver."

Esau appeared willing to concede that they were in no immediate danger of being trampled, but he was still jumpy as a frog in a frying pan. "It's probably just a coincidence," he said. "That the little girl's teacher is called Lark, I mean."

"How many Larks do *you* know, Esau?"

Esau gulped.

Autry began to pace in front of a horse trough. There was a green scum floating on top of the water. *Lark.* The kid had clearly said *Lark.* And she'd mentioned another name Autry knew, too—Rowdy Rhodes.

The marshal who'd come to Flagstaff with Sam O'Ballivan and the major the day before.

She lives at Mrs. Porter's house, he heard the child say. *But she was at Rowdy's since clear last night—*

Autry seethed, wanting to tear at his hair, wanting to rip the doors off houses, one by one, until he found the Porter place. Until he found Lark.

So she'd spent the night with the lawman, had she? The one with the train-robber eyes. Damn, but he'd *seen* those eyes—above the mask of the man who'd entered his railroad car and stripped it of everything valuable.

"Mr. Whitman," Esau pleaded. "Please come inside, before you catch the pneumonia."

Images rushed into Autry's beleaguered mind.

He saw the contemptuous amusement in the azure eyes of the train robber.

He saw Lark—his Lark—naked, with her golden hair down, whoring with that marshal.

And his blood seared its way through his veins, thumped in his temples, turned his vision to a fiery haze. He put his hands to the sides of his head, sure it would burst open.

"Mr. Whitman," Esau pleaded. "*Please* come inside."

Autry forced himself to breathe slowly and deeply.

It was dark out.

He was overwrought.

He wanted to be clearheaded when he found Lark. He'd looked for her for so long, spent so much money, suffered an agony of humiliation every time some Denver matron patted his arm and made some pitying remark. He wanted to see her face clearly when she realized he'd caught up to her—not in the glow of a lamp. Not in a stray beam of moonlight. No, he wanted to see her in the clear dazzle of a winter sun.

He would wait until morning.

And when the morning came, he would head for Mrs. Porter's first, then the schoolhouse. If he didn't find her in either of those places, he'd head straight for the marshal's place, damned if he wouldn't.

Turn over Rowdy Rhodes's bed and see who fell out of it.

MRS. PORTER SAT ALONE at the kitchen table, her hands folded prayerfully, gazing into empty space. Lark hung up her cloak, went to the stove for the teakettle and pumped water into it. Mai Lee was at Rowdy's, looking after Gideon, and Hon Sing was probably still at the saloon. The house seemed hollow without them.

"I'll miss Lydia," Lark said, because it was true, and because she wanted to get a conversation started. The change in Mrs. Porter was disturbing, if not alarming. When had it begun?

"He's going to kill me," Mrs. Porter murmured.

Lark set the teakettle on the stove with a bang and hurried to the table. "Who, Mrs. Porter?" she asked.

"I saw him today. After Dr. Fairmont's funeral. He was standing in front of the Territorial Hotel, smoking a cigar. I know he thinks I didn't recognize him, but I did."

A chill danced down Lark's spine. She pulled a chair close to Mrs. Porter's and gripped the other woman's hand. It felt cold as a corpse's. "*Who,* Mrs. Porter? Who did you see?"

Mrs. Porter looked at Lark, blinked, and her eyes cleared a little. "Why, Mr. Porter, of course," she said. "My husband."

"You saw your husband at the Territorial Hotel?" Lark spoke calmly, but she wished Hon Sing would come home. On the other hand, there probably weren't enough needles in the whole of China to fix what ailed Mrs. Porter.

The landlady nodded. Tears welled in her eyes. "He looked so handsome," she said. "In spite of all of it, I must admit my heart skipped a beat."

The teakettle began to rattle slightly on top of the stove.

"Didn't you speak to him?" Lark asked. The cozy kitchen seemed eerie all of the sudden, and she stopped wishing for Hon Sing's return and longed for Rowdy's instead. Rowdy would know what to do. He'd be able to charm Mrs. Porter out of whatever reverie she'd tumbled into.

"Speak to him?" Mrs. Porter echoed, befuddled.

Lark smiled determinedly. "You could have told him about the rum cake you made for his birthday."

"But I told you, dear," Mrs. Porter argued, her voice light with pleasant indulgence now. "He means to kill me. Anyway, the rum cake's all gone."

"Surely not," Lark said gently, meaning that Mr. Porter could not possibly intend to commit murder. Especially when the victim would be his own wife.

"Of course it is," Mrs. Porter said. "Gideon ate three pieces, and that Mr. Evans, the one who came to get little Lydia, finished off the rest."

Lark took a breath. "So much has happened," she said, in her most soothing voice. "Lydia being so sick. Gideon getting shot. You're exhausted, that's all. You'll feel ever so much better in the morning."

"Wait and see," Mrs. Porter replied. "He'll crush my head with a shovel. Splatter my blood all over the walls." She paused, smiled brightly. "Is the tea ready?"

IT WAS AFTER NINE when the Franks place came into view, a run-down, hardscrabble dirt farm that would probably look worse in the daylight than it did under the moon. Seeing a cluster of horses out front, Rowdy drew rein under a shadow-draped oak tree to consider the situation.

Wished he'd asked for more than directions, when he stopped at the livery stable on the way out of Stone Creek. He'd only met one Franks, and that was Roland. Now he wondered how many of them there were, and if the shack was some kind of watering hole for other drifters besides Speeks and Moran.

He'd been so busy thinking about Lark, he'd let some things slip.

He shifted, stood in the stirrups to stretch his legs and nearly jumped out of his hide when somebody landed behind his saddle, clasped a rock-hard arm around his middle for balance. He was still trying to control the startled horse when a pistol barrel was pressed into the base of his skull.

"God *damn* it, Pappy," he growled, hoping the riders at Franks's hadn't heard Paint whinny in alarm. "I *hate* it when you do shit like that!"

Payton laughed and lowered the pistol. "You'd better wake up, boy," he said. "Stop mooning over that schoolmarm and pay attention to business, before you get yourself killed."

"What are you doing here?" Rowdy demanded. "I thought you were headed for Mexico."

"I was waylaid by a discovery," Pa said. He nudged Rowdy's foot back out of the stirrup and used it to dismount. Stood grinning up at him, the usual unlit cheroot poking out of one side of his mouth, caught between his white teeth.

"What kind of discovery?" Rowdy asked tersely. What was the penalty for trampling your own pa? Would it make a difference that he was wanted in four states besides the Arizona Territory? Was there a reward?

"I found out who's been robbing those trains."

"That should have been easy enough. All you had to do was look in a mirror."

Pa looked hurt. Even laid a hand to his chest, fingers splayed. "It grieves me sorely that my own son, my own flesh and blood, doesn't believe a single word that comes out of my mouth. I *told* you, Rob. I *didn't* hold up those trains. But I know who did."

"Who?" Rowdy asked testily. And how had Pappy known about him and Lark? Damnation. He'd been back to Stone Creek, of course, and talked to Gideon.

"Never mind that now. Where the hell were you when that yahoo shot your little brother?"

"I was in Flagstaff," Rowdy said, swinging down from the saddle to face his pa. "Sam and the major and I went because of the holdup on Saturday morning." He paused. "You were right about the rangers. Ruby's place is full of them."

"You hate admitting I'm right about anything," Pa said, jabbing at Rowdy's chest with an angry forefinger.

"Pappy," Rowdy said, "I don't have time to talk

about this now. The 'yahoo' who shot Gideon is probably inside that farmhouse over there, right now."

"Of course he is," Pa replied, like it was old news. "How many horses do you see in front of that place?"

"Five," Rowdy said, without looking. "Why?"

"How many riders were waiting when that train stopped for twenty feet of dynamited track?"

"Six," Rowdy answered, annoyed. Then some of the steam went out of him. "One of them was Seth Alden."

"Chessie's brother," Pa said. He didn't sound anywhere near surprised enough to suit Rowdy.

"He took a bullet in the forehead."

Pa heaved out a sigh. "Never figured that kid for an outlaw," he said. "I thought he'd turn out to be a circuit preacher or something."

Rowdy changed the subject, because Seth was at the end of a long line of things he had to think about. "There were a lot of witnesses this time, Pa. One of them was Autry Whitman, the railroad magnate. And he said the man who held him at gunpoint and stripped his car of everything worth a plugged nickel had blue eyes. *Real* blue eyes."

"So you just automatically decided I was guilty." Pappy threw out his arms and slapped them against his sides, disgruntled.

"Go figure. You're a famous train robber. Three trains have been stopped and stripped in six months. And God help me, you're my pa, so I've got the bad luck to have your eyes."

"They thought it was you, didn't they? Those rangers? But Ruby got you out of it, didn't she?"

"*Damn* it, you haven't just been to Stone Creek to

see Gideon, you've been to Flagstaff, too. Are you crazy?"

Pa shrugged. "There's been some debate about that—my sanity, I mean—for as long as I can remember," he said. "Anyhow, I needed money and a decent horse. So, yes, I went to see Ruby. What the hell business is it of yours, anyhow?"

"I'm trying to keep you from spending the rest of your natural life in the prison at Yuma, you cussed old bastard." Rowdy grabbed his pa by the front of his coat, yanked him up close. *"Who robbed the trains?"*

Pa inclined his head toward the farmhouse. "They did."

Rowdy let go of his pa. "How do you know that?"

"I just do. For once in your life, you're just going to have to take my word for something."

Rowdy shoved a foot in the stirrup, pulled himself back up into the saddle.

"You can't go in there by yourself," Pa protested, catching hold of the reins. "Go get Sam O'Ballivan and the major and whoever else you can find."

Since he couldn't pull the reins out of his pa's hand without the bit hurting Paint's mouth, Rowdy sat still. "That's a hell of an idea, Pappy," he scoffed. "And, in the meantime, of course, you'll warn them and they'll be up in the hills in some hideout before I get back."

"I might warn one of them," Payton said.

Rowdy's heart missed a beat, started up again with a painful thud. "What are you trying to tell me, Pappy?" he asked.

But he already knew.

"It's Levi," Pa answered, after a long silence and a

sad look toward the farmhouse. "Or Ethan. One of the twins. Hellfire and spit, I never could tell those two apart."

Rowdy closed his eyes. *No,* he thought.

And inside the farmhouse, a gun went off.

19

PAYTON HELD FAST to Paint's bridle, even as the report of the gunshot reverberated in Rowdy's ears. "Don't do it, boy," he said. "Don't ride into that nest of outlaws by yourself. Go get Sam O'Ballivan. He doesn't live but a few miles from here, and he's been palavering with a whole pack of rangers ever since this afternoon."

Rowdy leaned in the saddle, broke his pa's hold on the bridle strap.

Shouting erupted inside the farmhouse—or the barn. He couldn't tell which.

He wondered, feeling strangely detached, if the shot he'd just heard had gone into Levi or Ethan, stopped one of their hearts. Wondered if either one of them wouldn't be better off dead than held to account for three train robberies—and whatever else they might have been up to lately.

"Think about Gideon," Payton persisted, his voice quiet, but urgent, too. "Think about that pretty schoolmarm. Hell, think about the damn *dog*. All three of them need you, in their own ways. And they need you *alive*."

The hinges of Rowdy's jawbones ached. "You must have a horse around here somewhere," he said evenly. "Why don't *you* make the ride to the O'Ballivan place, since you know right where it is?"

"Because I'm Payton Yarbro, that's why!"

Rowdy shrugged. Waited.

"All *right,*" his pa said, forcing the words between his teeth. He whistled softly, and the black gelding trotted out of the darkness, reins dangling. "But if they shoot me on sight, it will be your fault."

"Get out of here," Rowdy said. He took his pocket watch from the inside pocket of his coat, flipped open the case, checked the time. "You have an hour," he told Pappy, watching as he mounted the gelding and gathered the reins. Through all that, the old man still had the cheroot poking out of the side of his mouth. "Unless they try to ride out—or there's more shooting—I'll wait that long. No longer, though."

Pappy glared at him, reined the horse around and rode for Sam's.

The shouting had died down inside the farmhouse, but there was a charge in the air, the kind that precedes a deafening roll of thunder.

Rowdy considered climbing onto the roof and stuffing something into the chimney pipe to smoke them out. Discounted the idea, because they'd hear him tromping around over their heads for sure, and probably pepper the ceiling with bullets.

So he waited.

And then he waited some more.

He consulted his watch again. Barely ten minutes had gone by.

A cloud drifted across the moon, casting the world into darkness, except for the wavering lantern light shining from the windows of the farmhouse.

Rowdy decided two things in that moment. One, that he couldn't just sit there for another minute; and two, if he or the horse had to get shot, it wasn't going to be the horse.

He got down from the saddle, left Paint to graze on what grass he could forage from the hard, winter-ravaged ground. He made sure the .44 was loose in his holster, then headed for the farmhouse, staying wide of the windows in case the clouds didn't cooperate.

The walls of the farmhouse were thin, and Rowdy leaned lightly against the one closest to the barn.

"You hear something?" an unfamiliar voice asked.

"Hell, who could hear anything?" somebody else replied. "My ears are still ringin' from you shootin' that rat!"

Rowdy let out his breath. Wanted to shut his eyes for a moment, too, but he didn't dare.

"I'm tellin' you, I *heard* something!"

"It's just the wind."

This time Rowdy recognized the voice. It might have been his own.

The pit of his stomach pitched, as if he'd just mounted a bronc set to buck.

"I'm goin' out there and see—"

"I'll do it."

A chair scraped against the floor. The door opened.

Rowdy, having crept to the corner of the house, watched as the man stepped out, standing in a stream of lantern light. His hair gleamed in it, straw-gold. He paused, lit a cheroot, Pappy-style. Shook the match out and cast it aside.

"It's a fine night," he said easily. "Believe I'll take a little stroll."

Oddly, nobody protested. Thieves, in Rowdy's experience, were easily distracted.

He waited.

His brother turned, looked in Rowdy's direction.

The cloud passed, and moonlight poured down on both of them, as sure as if it had been dumped from some celestial bucket.

Levi.

His cheek dimpled as he smiled.

Rowdy didn't smile back. He just inclined his head toward a copse of spindly cottonwoods, not far from the house.

Levi nodded, fell into step with Rowdy as he walked toward the trees.

When they were both safe in the thick shadows, Rowdy turned, grasped Levi by the lapels of his shirt and flung him hard against a tree trunk.

"You," he growled.

Levi's dimple flashed again. He made no move to retaliate, but simply put his hands between Rowdy's and broke his hold. "It's good to see you again, little brother," he said. "But then, you're not so little anymore, are you? Taller than me by a good three inches."

"Did you shoot Seth Alden, Levi?" Rowdy demanded, in no frame of mind for brotherly reminiscences.

Levi looked affably regretful. There was a coldness in him Rowdy had never credited before, steely hard. "I had to, Rob," he said mildly. "He defied my orders.

Tried to take a woman off the train, after we robbed it. So I shot him."

"Just like that? You *shot* him, like he was a rabid coyote? God damn it, Levi, he was *Chessie's brother*."

"He wasn't the kid you remember," Levi said reasonably. His gaze, ice-blue even in the shadowed moonlight, slid to Rowdy's badge. "You ought to cover that thing up or something. I looked out the window twenty minutes ago, and saw a flash of silver. That must have been what it was."

"You weren't worried?"

Levi grinned. "I might have been, little brother, if I'd known it was you."

"Spare me the bullshit," Rowdy said, once he'd unclamped his jaw again. "I'm pretty sure that one of your men, Willie Moran, shot my—*our*—brother, Gideon. I don't give a damn if the rest of you get a start, but I want Willie Moran."

Levi raised one eyebrow. "You don't give a damn if the rest of us get a start on *what?*"

Rowdy sighed. "Rangers. Pappy went to get them, and they're probably headed this way right now."

"Suppose I'm weary of running, right down to the soles of my boots?"

"Run or stand, that's your choice. But they're coming. And I'm going to have to take their side, Levi."

"Why? Even with that badge pinned to your coat, you're still a Yarbro. And you've got a price on your head, just like I do."

"You said it yourself," Rowdy replied, thinking of Lark and Gideon and Pardner. "I'm fed up with running."

Levi half turned with an easy grace and glanced

toward the house. "Willie shot Gideon?" he asked. He held a hand at waist level, palm down. "The kid was that high the last time I saw him. There was a little girl, too. Followed him around like a pup."

"She died," Rowdy said. "The little girl, I mean. Her name was Rose."

Levi absorbed that. "Damn," he said, finally.

Rowdy heard the sound of approaching horses then, traveling fast, and knew Levi had, too.

"There's a woman," Levi said. "Her name's Polly. I promised I'd get back to her."

"Then you'd better ride," Rowdy replied.

Levi nodded. Then his face changed. "I'm real sorry, Rob," he said.

That was when something struck the back of Rowdy's head—in the split second before he pitched forward into a pit of darkness, he figured it for either a sledgehammer or a pistol butt.

When he came to, all hell had broken loose; bullets ripped through the air, all around him.

Somebody got him by the back of his coat, hauled him roughly to his feet and behind a tree.

It was Payton. "Damn it, I *told* you to pay attention!" the old man rasped.

Rowdy looked around, still a little dazed, saw Sam, Reston, the major and several other rangers, off their horses, returning fire from in front of the house. The horses had scattered, but their riders were trying to mount them, and flame shot from over the saddles.

"Did he get away?" Payton whispered hoarsely.

Rowdy touched a hand gingerly to the back of his head, looked at the blood on his fingers. "Yeah," he said.

"Which one was it? Ethan or Levi?"

"Levi," Rowdy answered, trying to get his eyes to focus. "But Ethan might have been with him. *Somebody* sure as hell bashed the back of my skull in." There was a brief cease-fire, as more clouds parted and the moon came out again.

"Willie!" Pa yelled, and one of the riders stopped, stared at him. The stillness was profound. "Did you shoot my boy, Gideon?"

"I did!" Willie yelled back, defiant. "And now I'm going to shoot you, you old fool!"

And all of a sudden, before Rowdy could grab hold of him, his pa ran forward, both .45's blazing like the fires of hell.

Sam raced after him.

Willie took a bullet in the arm, courtesy of Payton's wild spray of gunfire, but held the saddle and shot back.

Payton went down, still whooping like a wild Indian racing to glory.

Willie raised his rifle and took aim at Sam, who was right out in the open, trying to get to the old outlaw sprawled facedown on the ground.

Before he'd even made sense of it all, Rowdy drew and put a bullet between Willie's eyes. He flew backward off his horse, arms spread, flailing for balance even as he fell.

The two remaining outlaws threw down their guns and put up their hands. One was Harlan Speeks, and Rowdy didn't recognize the other. He knew, in a spark of detached logic, quite apart from everything else that was happening, that Roland Franks had been the one to knock him down from behind and ride out with Levi.

Sam crouched beside Payton, apparently unaware that he'd almost been shot, and rolled the old man over onto his back.

Rowdy knelt across from him, at his pa's side. Watched as blood gurgled up out of his mouth.

"Damn it," Payton said, spitting. "I'm hit."

"Lie still," Sam told him gravely, before looking up at Rowdy.

Rowdy saw pity in the other man's eyes, and something else, too. Something he'd known was there all along, but had chosen to ignore, because he didn't want it to be true.

"I'll have your gun, Rowdy," O'Ballivan said.

Rowdy, having shifted his gaze back to his pa's face, didn't look away again. He just handed over his pistol, butt first, to Sam. The barrel was still hot.

Sam stood, very slowly, and walked away.

"Why'd you do a stupid thing like that, Pappy?" Rowdy asked, his voice harsh as gravel in his throat.

"The bastard shot Gideon," Payton Yarbro choked out. "He shot my boy."

Rowdy closed his eyes for a moment, opened them again.

"I'm dying, I figure," said the old outlaw. The man Rowdy had loved—and hated—by turns. The man he'd wanted to be other than what he was. A father, like John T. would have been, if he'd ever gotten the chance.

Rowdy nodded once. "I figure you are," he agreed.

Pappy gave a strangled laugh, groped for Rowdy's hand. "Damn, if this isn't a hell of a way to go," he said. "Thought I'd die in my bed when I was pushing ninety."

Rowdy was silent. His eyes burned and the back of

his head hurt like a son of a bitch and his stomach threatened to roll right up out of his mouth.

His pa squeezed his hand, hard. "I was the best man I knew how to be, Rob," he said.

"I know, Pa," Rowdy answered, running the back of his free hand across his face. "I know."

Payton stiffened slightly, expelled a last rattling breath, and then closed his eyes. Rowdy didn't move, just stayed there on one knee, wondering how it was that he could wish things were different, even after it was too late for anything to change.

Reston approached. Waited.

Rowdy got to his feet. Put his hands together and lifted them a little.

Without a word, Reston snapped a pair of cuffs on him.

Sam brought a blanket out of the farmhouse, laid it over Payton.

"You knew all along?" Rowdy asked him.

Sam nodded, taking no discernible pleasure in the triumph. At some signal from him, Reston turned and walked away.

"When?" Rowdy prompted.

"After the first robbery I gathered all the posters I could with the name Yarbro printed on them," Sam said, looking down at Payton's still, shrouded form with something like regretful admiration. "And there was your face. It was just a sketch, but I knew it was you. So I sent for you. The major and I figured you'd lead us to your pa if we gave you a chance."

"And I did," Rowdy said bleakly. Even Jolene Bell had seen that poster. What had he been thinking, staying in Stone Creek when he knew the danger, could feel it, like the eyes of a stalking panther, raising the small hairs on his nape?

The answer was simple. He'd been thinking of Lark, and not much else.

Sam nodded. "I'm sorry," he said. And he sounded as though he meant it. He looked down at Payton again. "I didn't expect it to turn out like this."

"I need to talk to Lark Morgan," Rowdy told him.

Sam gave a second nod. Started to walk away.

"My pa wasn't in on any of those robberies," Rowdy said to Sam's back.

Sam stopped. Turned around. "I know," he said.

And Rowdy knew then why Sam had run after Pappy the way he had. Payton Yarbro hadn't been innocent—far from it—but he'd gone for the rangers, at considerable risk to himself, and he'd brought them back. He'd finally done the right thing, the old man had, and he'd paid for it with his life.

LARK STARED through the peeling bars of the cell, brought there by Sam on that Monday morning, unable to credit what she was seeing.

Rowdy was locked up, a prisoner in his own jail. He looked haggard, his eyes bleak.

Without a word Sam brought Lark a chair, set it facing the cell, and she slumped onto it, shaking.

When the outside door shut, she started a little but didn't look around.

"My name," Rowdy said, "is Robert Yarbro."

Lark swallowed, blinked back tears. Put a hand over her mouth.

"I'm sorry, Lark. Sorrier than you'll ever believe."

"You're…you're a train robber?"

"I was," Rowdy said.

She swayed, caught hold of the chair seat on both sides, in an effort to steady herself. "And now you're going to prison?"

Rowdy nodded. "Probably," he said.

Lark thought she'd be sick. "What's going to happen to Pardner?" she asked.

"I'm hoping you'll look after him," Rowdy answered.

Lark nodded, began to weep.

"I love you, Lark."

She looked up at him, stunned.

One side of his mouth quirked upward, but his eyes were filled with sorrow. "I know I picked a hell of a time to tell you that, but it's true. And there are some other things I have to say, too."

Lark waited, dazed.

Rowdy *loved* her.

He was going to prison, if not to the gallows.

And everything that might have been glowed in Lark's heart, then dissipated like smoke.

"I never killed anybody," he said. "Except for my loving you, that's the most important thing for you to know."

She believed him, believed he'd never ended anyone's life, maybe because she couldn't bear not to, but more because she knew killing simply wasn't in him, and nodded again. Tried to dry her face with the back of one hand, but it was hopeless, because more tears came.

"I was married once, too," Rowdy went on. "Her name was Chessie, and I loved her. When she had our son, Wesley, I stopped riding with the Yarbros and tried to settle down. Make a farmer of myself. But then Chessie and the baby both took sick of a fever, and they died. I buried them together, and then—" he paused, swallowed "—and then I went back to robbing trains. After six months or so, I gave it up. Drifted around, punching cattle mostly, until I ended up in Haven, and Sam appointed me marshal."

"Not Gideon?" Lark whispered. "He wasn't—?"

Rowdy shook his head. "No," he said quickly. "Gideon never knew. Thought his pa was a saloonkeeper."

It was something, at least. Gideon was innocent of any crime; he still had a future. Lark clung to that while the rest of her world collapsed around her, post upon beam, brick upon brick.

"When...when we made love," she began miserably, "were you using me, Rowdy?" Things would have been easier if he said yes, whether it was true or not, and they both knew it. If he'd used her, thought she was a whore, the way Autry had, she could hate him.

And hatred would be a relief in this case, compared to the love that yawned inside Lark like some unfathomable chasm of the soul.

She saw the struggle in his face.

"No," he said, after a long time. "I wasn't using you, Lark. I'd have asked you to marry me, if my past was different. I'd have given anything to be an ordinary, honest man and have you to come home to every night. I knew I oughtn't to have touched you, but the truth is, I wanted you so much I couldn't help it."

She stood, faced him through the bars.

"I love you, Rowdy Rhodes," she said, "or Robert Yarbro, or whoever you are. And I'd have married you gladly, if you'd asked. I'd have learned to cook and sew and I'd have carried your babies under my heart, and I'd have sung again, too, just because I couldn't hold it in, for being so happy. But none of that is going to happen, is it?" She leaned forward, pressed her face between the bars, touched her tear-wet mouth to his, lightly and very briefly. "Is it?"

"Not with me," Rowdy said. "But you're a beautiful woman, Lark. You can have all of it—the husband and the songs and the babies, too."

"No," she said, shaking her head. "I don't want anyone else."

Behind her the door opened and closed again.

The time Sam O'Ballivan had allotted to them was up.

The world was ending.

Rowdy looked past Lark, then back at her face, deep into her eyes.

"Go teach school, Lark," he said. "Once you walk out of that door, put me out of your mind. Whatever it takes, do it."

She *couldn't* put him out of her mind, much less her heart, but she nodded anyway, turned away, and dashed past a solemn-faced Sam O'Ballivan into the cold, bright sunlight of the worst day of her life.

HE WAS BACK.

Sitting right there at her kitchen table.

She'd known he would come, of course. Sent Mai

Lee out on her errands early, sighed with relief when she shut the door behind Lark, off to the jailhouse with Mr. O'Ballivan.

Now he was pretending they'd never met. Sitting in his own chair again, where he'd always sat. Asking a lot of questions about Lark, trying to confuse her.

But Ellie Lou Porter *wasn't* confused. Not now. The clarity was so keen, in fact, as to be painful.

"I made a rum cake for your birthday," she said.

He frowned, looked convincingly puzzled. "Where is Lark?" he asked.

"I don't know," Mrs. Porter said, for she was "Mrs. Porter" even to herself. She hadn't been Ellie Lou for ever so long—certainly not since she'd become a wife, when she was just sixteen.

She'd had such hopes as a young bride. Such hopes, and every reason to entertain them.

Mr. Porter was prosperous. He'd built this lovely house for her. Founded the Stone Creek Bank. Made a name for himself in the community, hardly more than a cluster of homesteads, when they'd first come here from Chicago.

She'd waited for babies to come.

But a year passed, and then another.

Mr. Porter became anxious. He needed an heir, he said. Couldn't she give him even one son, after all he'd given her?

She'd cried.

He'd slapped her for the first time.

Started spending his nights at Jolene Bell's soon after that, not caring who knew.

Not caring that people whispered and pointed and pitied her.

Still, she'd brushed his coats and lighted his cigars and made him a rum cake every year on his birthday, because that was his favorite. If she just tried hard enough, she reasoned, he'd love her again. He'd stop hitting her, leaving bruises on her where no one could see.

But he never loved her, and he never stopped hurting her, either.

She'd grown to accept his rages. Mr. Porter was an intelligent man, respected in Stone Creek, even though he went awhoring on a regular basis. So did a lot of other husbands, after all, though no one ever talked about it.

She must have deserved it all, she thought.

She must have done something very wrong.

Then one night he'd come home from the bank, very late, and calmly announced, right here in this kitchen, that he was leaving her. Taking up with some tawdry woman he'd met at Jolene Bell's. She could have the house, he told her grandly—take in boarders to make ends meet.

She'd be fine.

And then he'd opened the trapdoor in the floor and gone down to the cellar. He'd kept spare money there, a considerable sum in a metal box with a lock on it, thinking it was a secret.

But of course she'd known. Hoped he was saving it for that Grand Tour he'd promised her, long before, on their wedding night. It had sustained her, that dream, even though some part of her always held it false.

And now he meant to spend the whole of it on a saloon whore.

She'd crept after him, picked up the shovel she used

to turn over the soil for her garden every spring. He'd laughed—*laughed*—when he turned around, with the box in his hands…his big hands that he'd closed into fists so many times to pummel her spirit, as well as her body.

She'd swung the shovel then, hard.

And he'd looked so surprised when blood spouted from his broken nose. He'd called her a name, and started toward her, and she'd bashed in the top of his head with the edge of the shovel. Heard it crack like a melon under a cleaving knife.

It had taken her almost three days to dig a hole in the cellar floor big enough to bury him in, working frantically whenever Mai Lee was out of the house.

And now, here he was back.

She'd known he would come.

Oh, yes, she'd known.

LARK RUSHED through Mrs. Porter's back door, her eyes glazed with fresh tears, and stopped when she saw Autry Whitman rise slowly out of the chair no one ever sat in.

He smiled. "Your hair is different," he said. "But that's what whores do, isn't it, Lark? They dye their hair and paint their faces."

Instinctively she turned to run, then stopped.

Mrs. Porter was sitting calmly at the kitchen table, murmuring to herself.

"What have you done to her?" she demanded, turning back and finding Autry standing directly behind her.

"Not a thing, *Miss Morgan,*" Autry said. "But I plan to do plenty to you, you little slut." He reached out, grasped her hard by the hair.

Lark cried out from the pain.

"Did you really think you could get away from me?" Autry snarled, flinging spittle into her face.

"Let me go," Lark said.

He backhanded her so hard that she would have fallen through the open doorway if his fingers hadn't still been deep in her hair, the nails tearing at her scalp.

"You gave yourself to that marshal, didn't you?" He tightened his grasp, shook her. *"Didn't you?"*

Still recovering from the blow, Lark gasped at a new rush of pain.

She tried to kick him, bite him. Flailed at him uselessly with both hands.

He hit her again, nearly rendering her unconscious.

He was going to kill her.

She spat in his face. Screamed at Mrs. Porter to run.

Autry shoved her against the door frame with an impact that forced the breath from her lungs in a single whoosh of air. Her knees gave out, but he wouldn't let her fall.

"You *liked* spreading your legs for the marshal, didn't you, Lark?" he growled.

She nodded, fiercely, proudly. It was the only way she could hope to hurt him, and *by God* she wanted to do that.

Autry's voice turned to a croon. "You'd be with him right now, if you could, wouldn't you?"

"Yes!" she cried out. *"Yes!"*

He drew back his hand, and Lark waited for the blow to land.

But it never did.

There was a loud boom, thundering against the very

walls like a blast of dynamite, and Autry's eyes went blank. He let go of Lark, his hand opening slowly, with a peculiar languor, and crumpled heavily to the floor.

Mrs. Porter stood behind him, holding Mr. Porter's shotgun—usually stored in the broom cabinet—in a tremulous grip. "Quickly," she said, looking at Lark but not seeming to see her. "We've got to bury him again. This time we'll put the flour barrel on top of him, and he'll stay put."

Lark closed her eyes, leaning against the door frame, drawing in one quick, shallow breath after another. The cold from outside revived her a little, and she straightened, looked down at Autry.

There was no question that he was dead. The shotgun blast had ripped through his back and splintered his chest from the inside.

Lark whirled out onto the step, gripped the edge of the door with one hand and vomited until her stomach was empty. She heard excited voices—blessed voices—in the distance, and then pounding of horses' hooves.

Help was coming.

Lark turned, stared at her landlady in disbelief. Mrs. Porter had set the gun aside and raised the cellar door, and she was dragging Autry's body toward it.

20

IT WAS GIDEON who let Rowdy out of the cell, when the blast of a shotgun disturbed the peace of that Stone Creek morning, threw the door open wide and stood back. Gideon, with a sling supporting his left arm and a look of hollow desolation in his eyes.

"Ride, Rowdy," he said. "Paint's saddled and ready out back."

Rowdy stared at him. "Did you—?"

Gideon shook his head. "I didn't fire the shot," he said. A wan, Pappylike grin stretched his mouth. "I just took advantage of the opportunity."

Rowdy laid a hand on Gideon's good shoulder, in no hurry to grab his chance and leave. "If you didn't shoot that gun," he asked, "who did?"

The Yarbro muscle bunched in Gideon's jaw. "It came from somewhere around Mrs. Porter's place," he said. "At least, that's where everybody headed. *Get out of here,* Rowdy. I'll see to Pardner and look after Miss Morgan, too, as best I can."

It came from somewhere around Mrs. Porter's place.

Rowdy rasped a curse and bolted. Autry Whitman. Good God, with Pappy dying and all the rest of it, he'd forgotten all about him and the threat he represented to Lark.

"Not that way!" Gideon yelled. "Out the back!"

Ignoring his brother's protests, Rowdy hit the sidewalk at a dead run. Pardner, lying a few feet to the side of the door, leaped up and streaked ahead.

The rooming house looked as though it were under siege when Rowdy reached it, what with all the horses outside.

Lark, Rowdy thought, vaulting over the picket fence after Pardner, who had bunched his haunches and made the jump without so much as a pause.

Reston was blocking the doorway, Sam just inside.

"What the—?" Reston gasped, when Pardner shot between them, closely followed by Rowdy.

Lark sat in a chair in the kitchen, staring blankly at nothing.

Rowdy stepped over Whitman's body with no more than a downward glance and went to her. Crouched in front of her chair, took her hands in his.

"What happened?" he asked.

She blinked, evidently startled to see him there. "Mrs. Porter shot him," she said. "She shot Autry. She thought he was Mr. Porter—"

Rowdy looked around, his gaze briefly connecting with Sam's before swinging back to Lark's face. "Were you hurt?"

"Autry was going to kill me," she told him. "Mrs. Porter saved my life. And now she's…she's…" Tears rose in her eyes, eyes that were already red-rimmed and swollen. Of all the things he regretted, and there were many, giving Lark reason to cry was the greatest. If he could take back only one thing, of all the things he'd done, it would be that. "She collapsed, Rowdy. Mai Lee and Hon Sing are with her, but I think…I think—"

He stood, pulled Lark into his arms, held her with the fierce closeness of those who must soon let go. "It'll be all right," he murmured into her mussed, fragrant hair. "Everything will be all right."

She clung to him, shook her head against his chest. "Not without you," she said. "Not without you." She stopped then, looked up into his face. "How did you get out of jail?"

"I was about to ask that same question myself," Sam put in, from somewhere nearby, "though I'm pretty sure I know the answer."

Gideon.

He'd been willing to risk his own freedom, risk college and possibly years of his life, just to turn Rowdy loose.

"I'm right here, Sam," Rowdy said, still holding tightly to Lark. "No harm done."

"We'd better move this body," Reston put in. He was one of those restless sorts, the kind who always had to be doing something, setting things right. No doubt he'd rather have thrown Rowdy back in the cell, personally, with Gideon for company, but failing that, he'd settle for loading a bloody corpse in the back of a wagon.

Sam ignored Reston, spoke to Rowdy instead. Rowdy and, by proximity, Lark. "The major sent for a territorial judge," he said. "He'll decide your fate when he gets here, after consulting with the governor, but meanwhile you've got to stay behind bars."

Rowdy sighed. Nodded.

There was no undoing his past. It was as real and as deeply carved as letters chiseled into a tombstone.

"You could have been clear of Stone Creek by now," Sam went on quietly, speaking to Rowdy though his gaze touched on Lark once or twice, pondering. "I guess I don't need to ask why you stayed."

Lark gripped the front of Rowdy's shirt as if she was never going to let go. "Rowdy saved your life, Sam O'Ballivan," she said, with sudden spirit. "I heard you say so to Mr. Reston, just a few minutes ago."

Sam nodded. "That's true," he replied. "Under the circumstances Mr. Robert Yarbro here might have shot me himself, out there at the Franks' place. Thrown in with the outlaws, instead of the rangers, and ridden out with the others. A lot of men in his position would have done just that."

Lark sagged a little, pressed her cheek into Rowdy's chest.

He eased her into a chair, prepared to go willingly back to jail now that he knew what he'd come to find out—that she was safe. Still whole. Still Lark.

"Stay right here where I can keep an eye on you," Sam told Rowdy, waving Reston away when he came forward with his trusty handcuffs. "I've got enough to think about, with a dead man on the floor and another one buried in the cellar. I can't be chasing after you on top of it."

Rowdy grinned slightly. The matter of Levi's escape still lay between them, perhaps never to be resolved. He hadn't tried to stop his brother from getting away, he'd even encouraged him to run. He'd been wrong to do that and he knew it, but short of shooting Levi, he hadn't had a choice. And much as he hated the idea of doing a stretch in Yuma, maybe it was a chance to do penance not only for himself, but for Levi, too.

Gideon appeared in the open doorway just then, swallowed hard after assessing the scene. Stepped over Autry Whitman's body to come inside, weaving his way between a half-dozen milling rangers and townsmen.

He came face-to-face with Sam O'Ballivan, almost first thing.

Sam thumped a forefinger in the middle of Gideon's chest. "Don't you ever do a damn fool thing like releasing a prisoner again, boy. Even if he *is* your brother."

Gideon swallowed visibly, but stiffened his Yarbro backbone. His chin jutted out. "I'd do it again," he said stubbornly, with all the conviction of youth. It was because of that, because of his inherent strength, that he was up and around so soon after taking Willie Moran's bullet. Just looking at him gave Rowdy a strange, throbbing hope that *one* Yarbro, at least, might amount to something. Might serve as the living answer to all those prayers their ma had offered, always believing, against all evidence. "If I had my way, Rowdy would be a long ways from here by now."

Sam simply shook his head, gave a rueful chuckle and went back to the bloody business of rangering.

"Where's Mrs. Porter?" Gideon asked, drawing near the table. In the short time Rowdy had been acquainted with his younger brother, Rowdy had sized him up for an attendance taker, among other things. He liked everybody accounted for, and if somebody was missing, he'd probably turn over the whole territory looking for them.

Lark answered the question. "Mai Lee and Hon Sing took her upstairs," she said. "She's…she's not well, Gideon."

It was then that Hon Sing appeared on the back stairway. He paused, midway down, looked at Lark and shook his head.

She began to cry.

And Rowdy, not giving a damn that half the population of Stone Creek seemed to have crowded into that kitchen, pulled her onto his lap and pressed her head gently to his shoulder. She trembled in his arms, and he grieved for the parting that would surely come.

One Week Later

A BITTER WIND HOWLED through the streets of Stone Creek, as well as Lark's own raw and wounded heart, heralding the imminent arrival of another snowstorm.

The schoolhouse was temporarily closed.

Autry's body, accompanied by Esau, had been placed in a pine box the day before and freighted to Flagstaff in the back of a wagon, there to board a train bound for Denver.

Ruby Hollister had come, in grand style, to retrieve Payton Yarbro's remains, and Gideon had gone with her when she left, though he vowed to return, finish the school year and take up his duties as deputy again. He did not seem to register that Rowdy would be going away, no longer the marshal of Stone Creek.

That very morning, Lark had received a long telegram from Autry's lawyers—"Darned if you don't own a railroad, Miss Morgan!" the clerk had beamed, upon delivering the message—but sudden wealth was the furthest thing from her mind as she waited, with Mai Lee and Hon Sing, in front of a blazing fire in Mr. Porter's study.

She couldn't even think about Mrs. Porter's funeral, from which the three of them had just returned. Mr. Porter had been laid to rest beside her, a skeleton stacked and sealed into a wooden box, hastily constructed by the undertaker's son, almost as an afterthought.

No, there was no room in Lark's mind for anyone or anything, save Rowdy. He was still in jail, and Sam and the major and the territorial judge, just arrived from Phoenix, were meeting at that very hour, at the Cattleman's Hall, to decide what would happen to him.

Lark listened to the ponderous ticking of the mantel clock, felt her heartbeat adjust itself to the rhythm. Pardner lay at her feet, or more properly, *on* them. He hadn't been far from her side since the day Mrs. Porter had shot Autry. Every time she looked into his eyes, she saw the same question.

Where is he?

"I get you tea?" Mai Lee asked, breaking the silence.

Lark smiled, shook her head. "You're the mistress of the house now," she reminded the other woman. "You don't have to wait on anyone."

Incomprehensibly, considering her blithe prejudice, Mrs. Porter, having no living relatives, had left her house and property to Mai Lee and Hon Sing. They'd probably made plans—to sell out and move away on the proceeds, or stay and take in boarders, as Mrs. Porter had done—but they had yet to share them with Lark.

"I get tea," Mai Lee insisted, and hurried off to the kitchen.

A moment later she was back.

Pardner was instantly on his feet. He gave an uncertain woof.

"Someone to see you," Mai Lee said to Lark, a smile shining in her eyes. "In kitchen."

Lark stood slowly, her heart outstripping the pace of the mantel clock now, racing.

Pardner barked and ran for the back of the house.

Lark followed, wringing her hands. She dared not hope—the price of disappointment was too high.

And he was there.

Rowdy stood in the kitchen. He'd hung his hat and coat on the pegs beside the back door, bent to ruffle Pardner's ears in greeting.

He straightened at Lark's entrance, and his gaze caressed her, summer-sky blue.

She stopped, afraid to go any closer. Afraid he wasn't real.

She'd had so many dreams in which he came to her, and awakening to reality was like dying, over and over again.

"Did you escape?" she finally asked, befuddled.

He chuckled. "No," he said. "I've been pardoned, thanks to Sam O'Ballivan and the governor of the territory."

"P-pardoned?"

"And I can keep the marshal's job, if I want it," Rowdy said.

Lark started toward him, stopped again. *If I want it.* Had he come to get Pardner, and say goodbye?

"Do you?" she dared to ask, because everything depended on the answer. "Do you want to stay?"

"That depends, Miss Morgan."

Lark could barely hear, for the pounding in her ears. For the silent hope clambering and scrambling in her heart, groping its way into her mind. "On what?"

"On whether or not you'd be willing to marry a former outlaw, live in a house behind the jail and be called Mrs. Yarbro."

Lark swallowed painfully. For a moment the kitchen floor seemed to tilt beneath her feet. She fully expected to awaken in her bed upstairs, rummy from the rigors of her dreams. "Oh, Rowdy—"

He waited, hooked his thumbs under his gun belt.

"Or is it Rob?"

He chuckled, shook his head once. "I've always been called Rowdy," he said. Sadness rested briefly in his clear eyes. "Pa figured it suited me."

"Yes," Lark said.

"Yes, it suits me, or yes, you'll marry me?"

She let out a joyous sob. "Yes, I'll marry you." She laughed. "And yes, it suits you."

He still didn't close the space between them, but there was a tender watchfulness in his eyes. "Right now? Today? Because I'm bound to bed you, well and truly, before the sun goes down. And I want it to be honorable this time. I want it to be right. And that means we have to be hitched first."

Lark flung herself into his arms then—barely touched the floor but flew to him, threw her arms around his neck and held on. "Right now," she agreed, weeping and laughing at the same time. "Today."

He kissed her, a deep, celebratory kiss, full of all that had so nearly been lost. "Good," he said, when he let her go, and she stood, breathless, within the circle of his embrace. "Because the major is right behind me, with a Bible in one hand and a marriage license in the other. Sam'll be a witness, and Mai Lee and Hon Sing, too."

Lark smiled up at him. "You were pretty certain of my answer, weren't you, Mr. Yarbro?"

He grinned. "Pretty certain," he admitted. "But you never can tell with a woman. I figured you might have changed your mind about me, with all that time to think."

She stood on tiptoe and touched her mouth to his. "I thought about *you,* and nothing else."

Rowdy tasted her lips, made them tingle. "I'll be a good husband to you, Lark," he said gravely. "And if you ever have cause to shed tears again, it won't be on my account."

They were still standing there, exchanging a covenant too deep for words to express, when Sam and the major arrived a few minutes later, and Maddie, too.

Mai Lee and Hon Sing were summoned, and the marriage took place right there in the kitchen, where so much had happened. Lydia had been brought there, sick unto death. Autry had died there, and violently.

But it was also where Lark and Rowdy had met and looked into each other's eyes for the first time. It was where Rowdy had taken Lark on his lap, that night, and held her until she slept.

She'd been in the worst danger of her life there.

And felt safest.

Oh, yes. It was fitting indeed that the ceremony was held in the Porter kitchen, with Pardner standing between the bride and groom, listening raptly to the solemn and holy words Major Blackstone read from the Good Book.

Lark wouldn't have swapped it for the finest cathedral in the world.

LARK CROONED HOARSELY, her body straining under Rowdy's as she gave herself to him, fully and without reserve, in the bed where they had every right, before God and man, to make love. To make babies. To share secrets they'd kept even from themselves.

His eyes burned, even as he struggled to keep from joining her in the sweet maelstrom of release. *Lark.*

She stilled, sighing, and looked up at him. "Let go, Rowdy," she whispered. "Let go."

And he did, with a groaning shout, throwing his head back, emptying himself into her. *All* of himself, not just his seed, but his spirit and his mind and everything he'd never dared hope for.

She soothed him, during and in the sacred aftermath, her fingers playing in his hair. Murmured gentle, nonsensical words. Granted him a solace he'd never known he was seeking.

"I love you, Lark Yarbro," he said, much later when he had the breath for it. He moved in her, hard again, and she gave a soft gasp of pleasure and arched her back to receive him more deeply.

"Prove it," she teased.

"Our bathwater's getting cold," he said, enjoying the way her eyes widened. "You're going to have to wait."

"I don't *want* to wait. I want you now, because you're mine, and I can have you. I can have all I want of you."

He chuckled, withdrew from her, delighted in the look of rebellious disappointment on her face.

He got out of bed, and scooped his wife—*his wife*— into his arms. Carried her into the bathing room and lowered her carefully into the lukewarm water he'd run earlier, right after they'd come back to the marshal's house as Mr. and Mrs. Robert Yarbro.

He'd needed a bath, having been in jail for a week, where he'd had to be content with a basin and a rag, when he wanted to wash. But Lark hadn't been willing to wait, and he hadn't been able to resist her.

Now he joined her in the water, and they sat cross-legged, facing each other, like a couple of naked Indians at a powwow.

She pouted.

He rubbed soap between his hands and lathered her breasts.

She moaned.

He lifted her onto her knees, lathered another part of her, playing with her until she tilted her head back and closed her eyes, the temptress, surrendering.

He rinsed her, and that was almost as much fun as the washing had been.

She began to quiver, whimpering his name.

He bathed himself, got out of the tub and left her kneeling there, staring up at him in baffled defiance.

"If you want what I'm about to give you, Mrs. Yarbro," he said, "you'd better get yourself back to bed."

She flushed, stubborn and flushed with arousal, but she got out of the tub. Let him dry her off with a towel, watched as he dried himself. Saw just how much he wanted her.

Biting her lower lip, Lark ducked out through the doorway, and he swatted her lightly as she passed.

He took his time getting back to the bedroom, and the wait was excruciating, but when he got there, Lark was lying in the middle of the mattress, in a tangle of covers, wearing a pair of bloomers with a tear in just the right place, and nothing else.

She grinned mischievously.

He laughed and shook his head.

And then he went to her, and in a slow, smooth tumbling roll, turned her, so that she was kneeling on the pillows, clutching the top of the headboard in both hands.

Rowdy slid between her legs, parted the ripped in the bloomers, and grasped her hips to lower her onto his waiting mouth. She groaned and rocked and, finally, pleaded.

He teased her.

She ground herself against him.

He suckled hard, brought her to the edge of satisfaction. But when she tensed to let loose, he turned her again, laid her down, and entered her with a hard thrust. Watched as her eyes rolled back and she came unwound slowly and silently, a thousand different expressions flitting across her face in the space of a few moments.

In the next instant Rowdy's own release came, consuming him in a silver fire, blinding him to everything but her.

"DID I MENTION that I own a railroad?" Lark asked her husband—*her husband*—the next morning, while she fiddled with the stove, trying to figure out how one went about cooking, exactly. Snow drifted past the windows, and the world seemed blanketed by peace.

Rowdy, who had been admiring the way she looked wearing only his shirt, and idly sipping coffee he'd brewed himself before she was even awake, shook his head. "No," he said mildly. "I don't think you did."

She smiled at him, over one shoulder. Stepped over Pardner to take a skillet from a shelf. "It's ironic, isn't it?" she asked, testing him a little. Would it matter to him, the money and the railroad? "Autry was so busy trying to find and kill me, he forgot to change his will."

"Imagine that," Rowdy said, glowering a little.

"I'm very, very rich," she told him. And she was rich, but not because she'd inherited a fortune from Autry Whitman. She was rich because Rowdy Yarbro loved her.

He frowned.

"I have a mansion in Denver."

He shifted uncomfortably.

"We could live there," she said, watching his face. "You'd never have to work again. Instead of robbing trains, you could send them here and there, at a whim."

"Wherever there were tracks," he pointed out, still looking serious. And then he said precisely what she'd hoped he would. "I don't want to live in Denver, Lark. And I sure as *hell* don't want to run a railroad."

She went to him, sat astraddle of his lap.

Kissed the sides of his strained mouth. "You mean you didn't marry me for my money, Marshal?"

He began unbuttoning the shirt she'd thrown on after getting out of bed.

"Last I knew," he said, looking thoughtful as he concentrated on the task at hand, "you were a schoolmarm, without two nickels to your name. And you intended to keep on teaching as long as the town council would allow."

She was bared to him. Goose bumps rippled over her flesh in anticipation of his touch.

He cupped her breasts in his hands, looked into her eyes.

She squirmed slightly, gasped as he chafed her nipples with the sides of his thumbs. "Well," she murmured, between little catches in her breathing, "maybe our sons will want to run a railroad."

He tilted his head to one side, nibbled at her. "Sons," he said, clearly not listening.

"Or even…our…daughters," Lark gasped.

He suckled, even as he moved to open his pants.

Paused long enough to ask, in a low, rumbling rasp, "Do you want children, Mrs. Yarbro?"

"Yes," Lark managed.

"Then be quiet, so we can get one started."

She bit her lower lip, nodded.

He lunged inside her, claiming her so fully that she cried out in shameless welcome.

And then she was instantly, utterly, deliciously lost.

ROWDY YARBRO WALKED the streets of Stone Creek that night, with his badge pinned on the outside of his coat and Pardner trotting happily at his side.

He tested shop doors, to make sure they were locked.

He counted the horses in front of the saloons.

He checked on the schoolhouse.

He stood awhile outside the Porter house, and thought what a fine thing it was that Mai Lee and Hon Sing owned it now.

Passing the only church in town, a small, white clapboard structure, he stopped and looked up at the steeple, with its plain wooden cross stark against the night sky, trimmed in soft-falling snow.

For a brief moment he was a boy again.

Bless my boy Rob, he heard his mother say.

He knew she'd asked for a lot of things on his behalf—a loving wife, a home and an honest road to travel from one day to the next.

Those things had been a long time coming, but here he was, a marshal, sworn to uphold the law, with a strong, smart woman to partner with. He had a clear conscience, friends like Sam O'Ballivan and Major John Blackstone, Mai Lee and Hon Sing. He had a good dog and a fine horse.

He reckoned his ma would count all those things as answers to her prayers, and who could say if she'd be wrong?

Standing there in the silent, drifting snow of a February night, looking up at that cross, Rowdy lifted his hat.

"Much obliged," he said.

* * * * *

THE BUSHMAN WHO CAME BACK

Mysteries by Arthur W. Upfield available as Scribner Crime Classics:

An Author Bites the Dust
The Bachelors of Broken Hill
The Battling Prophet
The Bone Is Pointed
Bony and the Kelly Gang
The Bushman Who Came Back
Death of a Lake
Death of a Swagman
The Devil's Steps
Journey to the Hangman
Man of Two Tribes
The Mountains Have a Secret
Murder Down Under
Murder Must Wait
The Mystery of Swordfish Reef
The New Shoe
No Footprints in the Bush
The Sands of Windee
Sinister Stones
The Torn Branch
Venom House
The Widows of Broome
The Will of the Tribe
Winds of Evil
Wings Above the Diamantina

Arthur W. Upfield

THE BUSHMAN WHO CAME BACK

A Scribner Crime Classic

COLLIER BOOKS
MACMILLAN PUBLISHING COMPANY
New York

Collier Books
Macmillan Publishing Company
866 Third Avenue, New York, NY 10022
Collier Macmillan Canada, Inc.

Library of Congress Cataloging-in-Publication Data
Upfield, Arthur William, 1888–1964.
The bushman who came back.
I. Title.
PR9619.3.U6B75 1988 823 88-16189
ISBN 0-02-025911-5

First Collier Books Edition 1988

10 9 8 7 6 5 4 3 2 1

Printed in the United States of America

THE BUSHMAN WHO CAME BACK

CHAPTER I

A BEGINNING FOR LINDA

THE DAY was the 7th of February, and it was just another day to Linda Bell. Of course, the sun was blazing hot at six in the morning, another morning when the wind sprang up long before six and was a half gale when the sun rose. It sang when crossing the sandy ground, and roared farewell as it sped through the line of pine trees guarding the Mount Eden homestead from the sprawling giant called Lake Eyre.

For Linda this day began like all other days. First she slipped from bed and gazed at the large calendar on the wall above the dressing-table. Later she would be asked to name the day, and already she knew that to remember it would be conducive to happiness.

Linda was most self-dependent although she was only seven years old. She needed no rousing, no instructions on how to begin a new day. Taking a towel from a rack, she tripped daintily through the open french windows to the veranda, and along the covered way to the shower recesses. She sang a little song to the accompaniment of the wind under the iron roof as the tepid water from the great tanks high above the ground sluiced down her white body. Now and then into the song crept the word 'seven', and the same word occurred when she was still singing, on regaining her room and proceeding to dress. She was making her bed when the breakfast gong without defied the wind, to call the Boss and the Hands.

The homestead kitchen was large, already hot, filled with the aroma of coffee, frying mince-balls and grilling steaks. At one end stood the small table where Linda and her mother

ate, and at the other end was the annexe in which the men ate. The men appeared and sat at the long table, and Mrs Bell asked each what they chose, and served them. That done, she served a cereal to Linda without consulting her, and then carried Mr Wootton's breakfast tray to the inner dining-room.

Mrs Bell was plump, fair, thirty, and pleasing to behold. It was said that her husband was a horse trainer, and that she had once been a school teacher. She believed that children were no different from horses—that they needed to be trained with firmness and kindness, and that if training is left too late, the child becomes a useless adult, precisely as belated training is wasted effort on a horse or a working dog. Thus she spared herself no trouble, but saved herself much worry.

"You have done your hair nicely this morning, Linda," she observed as she sat at table with her daughter. "Saves time to do it nicely in the first place. What is the date today?"

"February Seven, One Nine Five Seven," intoned Linda, her grey eyes wide and faintly impish.

"That's my girl," approved Mrs Bell. "Mr Wootton says he's going to town today, and I see that your comb has lost two teeth. What colour would you like the new one to be?"

Linda chose blue, but her mind was on the slight noises made by the hands leaving the meal annexe. Her mother asked her to tell the time by the wall clock.

Hurrying now to finish her breakfast, Linda's jaws slowed while she gazed at the clock. Then she guessed a little, as she always found it difficult to be sure whether before or after the hour. This morning she guessed correctly by answering:

"Seven minutes to seven, mother."

"Good for you, Linda. Now I suppose you want to run out to see the men off to work. Well, you may go. When the men have left, come in and do your lessons. It's going to be a nasty day, and we'll get through as quickly as you've a mind to, shall we?"

The homestead buildings at Mount Eden formed the sides of a large square. The main house occupied the east side, the men's quarters the side opposite. On the flanks were the office and store shed, the horse yards, the trade shops, the well and reservoir tanks. In the corner of the square was a round house, constructed entirely of canegrass.

When, a trifle too hurriedly, Linda said grace and skipped from the kitchen, she stepped right into the open square. Already the early morning shadows were deepening in sharp contrast with the sunlit ground, and squadrons of dust horses ridden by riders of the west wind were racing from the men's quarters to the house, passing by and speeding up the slope to the line of pine trees and the vast open Lake Eyre beyond them.

The men were coming from the quarters to receive their orders for the day. There were four, all white men. Three wore spurs to their riding boots. One was a heavy man, two were lean, and the fourth a young man darkly handsome, and, compared with the others, almost flashily dressed in the ultra-stockman style.

They halted just outside the office door. The young man waved to Linda, and the big man called the morning greeting. Then Mr Wootton appeared from the house side veranda. He was short and stout, red of face, when the complexion of his men was uniformly nigger-brown. His clipped moustache was dark. His hair was worn short and was plainly grey at the temples. His eyes were small and distinctly green, and always kindly for Linda. To her he was the Big Boss, the King of Mount Eden. Unfailingly he must be called 'Mister Wootton'. Invariably he wore a soft-collared shirt and a tie, gabardine trousers and shoes, instead of riding boots.

As usual, Mr Wootton slipped a key into the office door lock and entered. He was invisible for two to three minutes and Linda knew he was studying a big book kept on his desk, and knew, too, that he looked into the book to tell him all about the station, and what needed to be done.

On reappearing, he stood in the doorway and called for Arnold.

Arnold was the very large man who could do anything from blacksmithing to making a motor engine go. Because of the wind and the cawing of passing crows, Mr Wootton had to speak loudly.

"Want anything from town today, Arnold?" The big man shook his head, saying:

"Don't think so, Mr Wootton. Not for the station, anyway."

"All right. The wind oughtn't to be strong out at Boulka. You might take the truck and go for another load of iron. And take your time to get the iron off without tearing holes in it. You know."

"Good enough," drawled Arnold, and Linda asked:

"May I go with Arnold, Mr Wootton?"

"If your mother says so," he assented, and called Eric.

Linda raced to the house. Eric was lanky, raw-boned, slow. When Linda returned he was saying:

"The mud'll keep 'em from crossing for another six weeks even if it don't rain, which ain't likely. Them steers know enough to shy off getting themselves bogged. 'Sides, before the lake is hard enough to take 'em, the flood oughta be right down the Coopers and the Georgina, an' spilling over from the Diamantina."

"Could be, Eric," agreed Mr Wootton. "Well, take a ride out to Number Fourteen and look over the stores. Anything you want from town today?"

Eric chuckled dryly, and winked at Linda.

"Well," he drawled, "you might bring me a box of them lollies with the nuts on 'em. Seems like I got to give a present to my girl. Must keep in with her, y'know."

"Yes, you must get a present for your sweetheart," agreed Mr Wootton, seriously. "Is her name Linda, by any chance?"

"That's tellin', Mr Wootton," and again the wink which produced beaming adoration in the little girl's face.

The next man called to receive orders was the young man named Harry. He came forward with rolling gait, and even the wind could not drown the tinkle of his spurs. He was sent out to ride a section of the boundary fence. The fourth man, named Bill, was instructed to ride into White-Gum Depression and report on the feed. To him Mr Wootton put questions concerning the aborigines.

"Any sign of Canute and his people, Bill?"

"Sort of local? Naw, Mr Wootton. They're never to hand when wanted. They'll be away up on the Neales by now, living on lizards and ants, going for corroborees and such like, and putting the young fellers through the hoop."

"Charlie promised he would come back early to give a hand with the muster."

"You'll see Charlie when you see Meena. And that'll be when Canute says so. He's their boss. You can send 'em to the Mission Station, teach 'em to read and write and sing hymns, but in the end they do just what old Canute tells 'em."

"Yes, yes, I know," Mr Wootton agreed explosively. "All right, Bill. Want anything from town?"

"Well, you could bring me a coupla pairs of them grey pants you got me last winter. Oh, an' what about a couple of ladies' handkerchiefs? Small ones with lace round the edges, and the letter 'L' in the corner. The store'll have them kind. I got a sort of sister called . . . why, hullo, Linda, I didn't see you."

"You did so, Bill," argued Linda, from whose face disappointment had been banished by joy.

"Oh, Linda!" said Mr Wootton. "Will your mother allow you to go with Arnold?"

"Mother says not to, Mr Wootton. Mother says I have to stay and help her because Meena and the others are still away."

"I didn't think of that, Linda. Of course you must help your mother. All right, Bill, I'll not forget the handkerchiefs and the box of nut chocolates."

Mr Wootton re-entered his office, and Linda accompanied Bill to the yards, where the other riders were saddling up. She watched them leave, and then went back to the house, and demurely dried breakfast dishes for her mother.

After that, lessons at the kitchen table until nine o'clock, when Mrs Bell sounded the house gong, made tea and provided buttered scones. Mr Wootton came to the kitchen for morning tea, standing the while, and noting on a pad the items Mrs Bell needed. Linda accompanied him to the car shed, and stood watching as the dust and sun-glare took the car up into the sky over the track to Loaders Springs.

She was now free for the remainder of the morning, free to be herself, free to chide and scold and love, instead of being chided and loved. There beside the car shed was her own house, a circular house having canegrass walls and a canegrass thatched roof, and a wood floor three feet above ground to keep the snakes and ants out; a little house for a little girl, built by the girl's sweethearts.

Thus far, just another day for Linda Bell.

She ran up the two steps and through the thick grass doorway to enter her house, leaving the buffeting wind outside, and meeting with calm silence. There was a real window set in the thick grass wall, and the window faced to the south, from which the cool winds of winter came. There was a table with the legs shortened, and a chair with the legs shortened. There was a rough bookstand and real books on the shelves, and on top of the stand were four dolls.

One doll was the exact likeness of her mother. Another was the image of Mr Wootton. The third was a lovely young woman with straight black hair and large dark-brown eyes, and the fourth was an elderly man with weak blue eyes, a long face, and drooping grey moustache.

Linda stood before the dolls, and said:

"Meena! What's the date? No, it's not February 10th, Meena. You should know the date. You went to Mission School. All right. Ole Fren Yorky, you tell me the date. February 9th! Of course it isn't February 9th." Linda

glared at the doll with the weak blue eyes and the absurdly drooping grey moustache. She mimicked her mother: "Ole Fren Yorky, I'm asking you to tell me the date today. Oh dear! Won't you ever learn!"

So the converse with the four dolls continued over a wide range of subjects, including a box of chocolates with nuts on top, and lace-edged hankies with the letter L in the corner. She was seated in the chair, the dolls on the table before her. She had straightened Mr Wootton's tie, and had combed Meena's hair, and was intently trying to twirl points of Ole Fren Yorky's moustache when the report of a rifle obliterated the low buzzing of the blowflies.

"Now, Ole Fren Yorky, stay still," she scolded. "Your moustache is getting disgraceful. That'll be Mr Wootton out there shooting the crows. You know very well how naughty they are, and have to be shot sometimes."

Ole Fren Yorky wouldn't be still, and Linda had to concentrate on gaining compliance with her efforts. Minutes later, she remembered that Mr Wootton had left an hour before for Loaders Springs. A tiny frown puckered her dark brows. She pushed Ole Fren Yorky to one side, and had put her hands to the table to push her chair away from it, when there appeared in the doorway the original Ole Fren Yorky.

Terror leaped upon her. The man's weak blue eyes were now hot and blazing. He ran forward, a light swag at his back, a rifle in his left hand. Linda sprang out of the chair, and then found herself unable to move. A bare arm gripped her about the waist and she was lifted. She opened her mouth to scream, and her face was pressed hard into a sweaty chest, and no longer was it just another day.

CHAPTER 2

MURDER IN EDEN

UNTIL FOUR o'clock it was just another day for Arnold Bray.

Like many big men, Bray was deliberate in thought as well as action, and this led people to believe him to be slow in both. Under thirty, he received the respect of men of his class much older than himself, and from men much younger who noted his powerful physique.

He was that asset to all pastoral properties—the man of all trades, and it was quite unnecessary for Wootton to advise him how to remove iron sheets from a roof. The building to which he drove this day was situated some twelve miles from the Mount Eden homestead, and had been used as a shearing shed in a period when sheep were reared, only to be severely attacked by wild dogs. In this land where rust is reduced to a minimum by the dry atmosphere, the roof iron was worth salvaging.

By three o'clock Arnold had removed enough iron for a sound load, and, having lashed it securely from the high wind he would encounter on leaving this shelter amid tall blue gums, he took time to boil water and brew a quart pot of tea. It was three-thirty when he called the dogs into the truck cabin and started for the homestead.

Once beyond the trees, the wind buffeted the load and made steering on the narrow and little-used track something of a task. The truck hummed powerfully as it moved up a long and gradual slope to the summit of the highlands, which were never more than two hundred feet above the lowlands marked so clearly by creek and swamp and depression. Here on the bare slopes lay vast areas of ironstone gibbers, closely packed like cobbles, evenly laid into the cement base of earth-clay, and so polished by the wind-

driven sand grains that they reflected the sunlight in a glassy glare.

Here, this day, earth and sky merged without an horizon. Arnold could not have seen the summit of the long slope had he looked for it, so masked was this world of open space and wind and dust by the distortion of sunlight. A tall solitary tree became a mere broken sapling; a boulder reached in a few seconds had appeared to be a dozen miles distant; what had seemed to be a barrier of sand was actually a faint fold in the earth.

Abruptly, in front of Arnold's truck was the homestead; the square of buildings, the line of pines, the braked windmills, all like a picture left upon the floor and covered with the dust of years-long neglect. Yet the homestead was two hundred feet below the truck, and a mile away.

The wind was blowing to the truck, a gusty wind which stockmen would find slightly unpleasant, not unbearable. The two dogs squatting on the seat beside the driver were happy until but half a mile from the homestead. Then, at the same time, both tensed, began sniffing, finally joined in a chorus of low lament.

Arnold could see Eric mounted on his horse, and the horse was standing almost motionless in the centre of the square fashioned by the buildings. The animal's legs seemed a hundred feet high, and Eric appeared to be sitting on a barrel, causing Arnold to chuckle, because never was he bored by the tricks played by this remarkable land.

Attracted by the dogs' behaviour, wondering at the stockman's most unusual stance, Arnold pressed on the accelerator, arriving at the motor shed, where the iron was to be stacked, in a cross cloud of dust and squealing brakes. Eric dismounted, and led his horse to the man standing beside the grounded dogs.

"Been hell to play," he said, the slow voice failing to hide shock. "No one here but her. The kid . . . I can't find the kid. Mrs Bell's over by the kitchen door. I covered her up. I . . ."

"What happened?" asked Arnold, his steady voice not matching the concern in his eyes.

"Don't rightly know. Exceptin' that Mrs Bell's been shot dead. The boss . . ."

"Was set to leave for town," supplemented Arnold. "Let's look-see. How long you been back?"

"Quarter hour, half hour, I don't know. I got to the yards and saw the crows by the kitchen door where no crows oughta been. So I rode over and saw what it was. I yelled and screamed for the kid, but she didn't come out from nowhere. And no one else either. I don't get it. I tell you, Arnold, I don't get it."

"We will. Anchor that horse somewhere. Wait! Keep the horse. May want it in a hurry."

Arnold glanced at his shadow, subconsciously noting the time, recalling that his employer usually returned from town between five and six. A great number of crows were circling about, dozens more were perched on the house roof and on the round roof of Linda's playhouse. What they had done to the dead woman's neck and arms. . . . It was Mrs Bell without a shadow of doubt. Arnold gently replaced the bag over the body and stared into the troubled eyes of the rider. The dogs slunk away. Eric said:

"I did right covering her? Then I got back on my horse and shouted for Linda. Got the jitters sort of. Expected someone to shoot me. What're we to do?"

"Find the kid. Where have you looked?"

"Nowhere. Just shouted. Them crows! She musta been shot this morning."

"Take a hold, Eric." Arnold's voice was quiet, and it calmed Eric Maundy. The slight twitching of his lips firmed to grim anger. "We'll look-see in the house first; there's no one else around, accordin' to them crows."

Inside the kitchen, they called for the child, waiting for her reply. Here, where the wind was baffled, the silence was hot and familiar. Their shouts fled away into the rooms beyond, to crouch in corners and wait for them. When they

entered the spacious living-room they were halted by the wreckage of the expensive transceiver, and by the smashed telephone instrument. It was the first time Eric had been there, but Arnold had often serviced the telephone.

There was no further damage. Nothing had been disturbed. Eric found the axe with which the instruments had been destroyed, lying under a chair where it had been carelessly flung.

The dust was crossing the open square, tinting the buildings, brazing the hard clay ground. Above, the crows were streaking black comets against the glassy roof of white flame. Eric said:

"More ruddy crows than when we kill a beast. Blast 'em!"

Arnold made no comment, and Eric followed him in a further systematic search, beginning at the canegrass meat-house, trying the locks of the office and the store room, proceeding to the playhouse.

The four dolls were on the table, Ole Fren Yorky toppled and lying on his back. The place was in its usual tidy disorder, familiar to both men. There was nowhere here for Linda to hide. Leaving, they looked under the floor, knowing they could see beyond the structure, hoping against vanquished hope. They had finished with the men's quarters, a building containing four bedrooms and a common-room, when Arnold saw young Harry Lawton dismounting at the stockyard gates.

His shout stopped the young man from freeing the horse, brought him to them, large spurs jangling, red neckerchief flapping.

"You'll want your horse," Arnold said. "There's been a shooting. Mrs Bell is dead and Linda has vanished."

"Hell!" exploded Harry. "Linda couldn't have shot her ma. What else happened?"

"Ain't that enough?" demanded Eric, and waited for instructions from Arnold.

"You fellers get going. Ride around. Look for tracks.

Look for . . . you know. Look for Linda. Somebody came after the boss left for town. The bloody crows didn't shoot Mrs Bell."

They obeyed without question that steady authoritative voice, and Arnold went back to the quarters and leaned against the front wall and chipped at a tobacco plug. He was cold deep down in his mind, so enraged that, now no one was near to see, his grey eyes were wide and blazing.

The question tormented him. Who had done this grim thing? A traveller? Hardly. No tracks went beyond Mount Eden, save the little-used track to the old homestead called Boulka, and he himself had just come in by that track. A traveller was as rare as an iced bottle of beer on the centre of Lake Eyre. All the blacks were away on the Neales River, fifty miles to the north. The nearest town, Loaders Springs, was more than forty miles to the south-west, and the nearest homestead was something like a hundred and ten miles away round the southern verge of the lake.

There was left . . . what? Five white men who had eaten breakfast here at Mount Eden, and any one of those men, including himself, could have returned, unknown to the others, and murdered the woman. And the kid? No . . . no! That Arnold wouldn't accept. Every man of them loved Linda. Knowing he would find no tracks, Arnold yet sought for the tracks of strangers, or tracks betraying unusual movement out of time.

He was trudging about the hard, sand-blasted ground when Bill Harte joined him. Neither spoke, both staring into the eyes of the other. Harte was small, wiry, bow-legged and iron-fisted. Under the weathered complexion lay the barest hint of mixed ancestry. The tight lips parted in what could have been a snarl, but his voice was low and clipped.

"Met Eric on the way in," he stated. "Told me. No sign of the girl?"

"No sign of anything, Bill. You see around. You're better than I am at it."

They walked to the body, and Harte lifted the bag.

"She was running when she was shot," he said. "She was running from the kitchen door, and whoever shot her was standing in the doorway. Betcher on that. Prob'ly was runnin' to grab up Linda. Linda musta been in her playhouse when it happened. You looked there, of course?"

Arnold didn't reply to the obvious. Harte moved away, almost at the run, crouching to bring his eyes closer to the ground, and the big man, watching, realised that he was a mere amateur tracker beside Bill Harte. All the others were superior to him, too, but then all of them together knew less than he of welding iron or repairing a pump.

What to do now? Something had to be done with the body. It had lain there for hours, and the ants were investigating it. Arnold judged by his shadow that it was close to five o'clock, when Wootton's return could not be far off. Harte was running about the outbuildings like a distraught dog. The others were nowhere in sight. Yes, something had to be done beside just standing about. The boss might be late, mightn't get back till after dark.

From the carpenter's shop he brought several wooden pegs and a hammer. The pegs he hammered into the hard ground so that they outlined the body, then he dusted the ants from it, turned it over, and for a space looked down upon the pained face and the wide grey eyes in which revolt against death was so plain.

Without effort, Arnold Bray took up the body and carried it to the woman's bedroom, where he placed it on the bed and then found a spare sheet with which to cover it. Cover the Dead. . . . She had been a good woman, above him in so many things, a woman he had admired humbly when there had been women he had admired, but not humbly. The possible motive for this thing, so much worse than mere murder you read of in the papers, persisted in entering his mind, although he fought it back with savage anger. And so preoccupied was he by the futility of it all that without

conscious animation he drew the blind, and then passed from room to room to draw down every blind.

Bill Harte called from the rear door, and Arnold went to him, hope reborn, and slain again when he looked into Bill's eyes.

"Come with me," Harte said, harshly. "You check."

He led the way to the underground tank which had cemented floor and walls and a canegrass roof rising to a pyramidal summit. From this place he proceeded a dozen steps to the rear of the meat-house, where he halted and stared at the ground against the grass wall in the lee.

"What d'you see?" he demanded.

Arnold saw nothing at first, save the imprints of a dog. Then larger prints appeared to grow on the light-red ground, so that the dog's prints faded into insignificance. What now he was seeing were three prints made by a man's boots. They were unusual in that there were no heel marks.

"You musta seen those prints some time or other," Bill stated.

"If I did I don't recall them," admitted Arnold. "Still, they look like the prints of a man running. No heel marks. I know! Ole Fren Yorky walks like he's always running. They're his tracks."

"Yair. Yorky made 'em."

"But Yorky's in town on a bender."

"Couldn't be. Yorky made them tracks four-five hours ago. That right what Eric says about the telephone and the transceiver?"

Arnold nodded. He said with sudden determination:

"I'm driving the truck to meet the boss. He'll have to go back to town to report to Pierce and bring men out to join in the hunt for Yorky. Yorky's got Linda . . . if he hasn't killed her. Yorky's got to be nabbed, and quick. If he's killed Linda you keep him away from me."

CHAPTER 3

THE DECEITFUL LAND

WITHIN MINUTES of a crime being reported in a city, a superbly organised Police Department, backed by modern scientific aids, goes into action. It was not to the discredit of Senior Constable Pierce that he was thwarted by inability to see without lights over an area of something like ten thousand square miles of semi-desolation; because the weather was against him in a land where the weather can aid or baffle keen eyes and keen brains.

He arrived with the doctor from Loaders Springs shortly after nine on that night following the murder of Mrs Bell. It was then black night, the stars blotted out by dust raised all day by the mighty wind. Before dawn a new transceiver was working at the Mount Eden homestead, and a new telephone installed. At dawn two trucks left to locate the aborigines and bring back all the males, to be put to tracking. Soon after dawn cars and trucks began to arrive, bringing neighbours from homesteads fifty, sixty, a hundred miles distant, and at dawn other men rode out from homesteads still farther distant to patrol possible lines of escape for the murderer of Mrs Bell, and the abductor of her daughter.

The man called Ole Fren Yorky, born in Yorkshire, brought to Australia when he was fifteen, outwitted bushmen reared in this vastness of land and sky, and the native trackers of whom the world has no equal. His tracks were discovered at the vacated camp of the aborigines situated less than a mile from the homestead, and beside the canegrass meat-house within yards of the house kitchen door; those two places sheltered by the wind. He carried a Winchester .44 repeating rifle, and the woman had been shot by a bullet of this calibre.

Men discussed the motive, but more important was the

finding of Linda Bell, alive or dead. Her fate was of paramount importance, for until the child's body was found, hope remained in the hearts of the hunters.

The initial verve of the hunters gradually degenerated into doggedness. The aborigines lost interest, rebelled against the driving of the white men, as though convinced that Yorky, with the child, had won clear of their ancient tribal grounds.

The white force dwindled, men being recalled to their homesteads to attend chores which could no longer be neglected, and at the end of four weeks the organised search was abandoned.

Three days after Constable Pierce informed Wootton of the official abandonment of the search, the station owner was told of the coming of another policeman. Wootton had engaged Sarah, from the aborigines' camp, as cook, and Sarah's daughter, Meena, as maid, and the routine of the station was as though interruption had never been when this morning, as usual, Meena brought to the living-room table the large tray bearing Mr Wootton's breakfast. Cheerfully he said "Good morning", and, shyly demure as usual, Meena responded.

Meena was in her early twenties. She had lost the awkward angularity of youth, and was yet distant from ungainliness reached early by the aborigines. Not a full blood, her complexion was honey, and her features were strongly influenced by her father, even her eyes being flecked with grey. Wearing a colourful print dress protected by a snow-white apron, her straight dark hair bunched low on her neck, and with red shoes on her feet, she was an asset to any homestead, and, in fact, was appreciated by Mr Wootton. Her voice was without accent, soft and slow.

"Old Canute say for me to ask you for tobacco in advance. He's been giving too much to Murtee, and Murtee says he used his to stop old Sam's toothache."

"Sam's toothache, Meena!" exclaimed Mr Wootton. "Why, old Sam must have lost his last tooth fifty years ago."

"Old Sam lost his last tooth before I was born. But old Canute's run through his tobacco. He says if Mr Wootton won't hand out, then tell Mr Wootton what about a trade."

"A trade! Explain, Meena."

"Canute says for you to give him a plug of tobacco, and he'll tell you something you ought to know."

"Oh," murmured Mr Wootton. "Sounds like blackmail to me. D'you know what this something is I ought to know?"

"Yes, Mr Wootton. I know. Canute told me."

"And you won't tell unless I promise to give that wily scoundrel a plug of tobacco?"

The expression of severity on the cattleman's face subdued Meena. For the first time she shuffled her feet on the bare linoleum. She spoke two words revealing the unalterable position she occupied.

"Canute boss."

Wootton's experience of aborigines was limited, but he did know the force and authority wielded by the head man of a native clan, and thus was aware that the girl was behaving naturally, was merely a go-between as the messenger between Canute and himself. Severity faded from his green eyes.

"All right, Meena. I'll trade. Pour me a cup of coffee."

The girl poured the coffee, then, standing away from the table, she said:

"Old Canute say to tell you big-feller policeman come soon."

Again Mr Wootton did not scoff.

"How does Canute know that?" he asked quietly. "I was talking with Constable Pierce on the phone less than an hour ago, and he knew nothing about another policeman coming here. Canute's only guessing, Meena. Not worth a plug of tobacco."

"Him and Murtee sit-down beside little fire all last night," Meena said seriously. "Little fire. By themselves. The lubras not allowed to look."

"But you did, eh?"

"I am not a lubra."

"But you believe this silly magic?"

"Canute, Head Man. Murtee, Medicine Man."

Wootton sensed the utter finality of this statement.

"I'll advance the tobacco, Meena. Tell Canute it will be a plug short next ration day. And tell Charlie and Rex to come back to work. Mustering to be done. They've been loafing around too long."

Meena looked down at the seated man, encountering frankly his hard green eyes and sensing the powerful magnetism of the white man. She smiled as though because of his surrender, but knew there had been no surrender.

When in Loaders Springs next day, Wootton mentioned the tobacco incident to Constable Pierce, who seemed less sceptical than the cattleman, but agreed it was a good tale to spin for a plug of tobacco.

However, the aborigines were right on the mark. At the third dawning following the announcement made by Canute per Meena, Detective Inspector Napoleon Bonaparte was seated against one of the pine trees overlooking the Mount Eden homestead, and down in the horse yards was a riding hack and pack-horse which had brought him from the south two hours previously.

The stars were fading, and from the abyss below the ridge appeared a pavement of molten lead. Then it was as though lead ran in streams and rivers, was poured into bar-moulds, and soon all these isolated sheets of metal fused into a great plane of lead, spreading to the east, the north and the south, until the vast slate supported the dome of the greening sky. When fan-tails of light further illuminated the sky, the sheen of the leaden expanse beneath faded, cold, ugly, inert.

There before Napoleon Bonaparte was The-Sea-That-Was; its headlands and its bays and its inlets, the coast stretching to the south and to the north, its level, silent surface of mud destitute of vegetation all the way to the far horizon, and farther still. Lake Eyre! The last puddle,

sometimes to be filled with river water from the north, of The-Sea-That-Was, a puddle sixty miles wide and a hundred long.

Down in the viscous mud lie the bones of monstrous reptiles and animals, and man-catching birds. Along the curving shores, buried by drifting sand, are the mounds of shell fish gathered by the ancestors of Canute's tribe for feasts that kept them fat for generations.

What is geographically named 'the Lake Eyre Basin' roughly comprises two hundred thousand square miles, and most of it is below sea level. Save along the western edge, where run the rare trains northward to Alice Springs, the white population is less than two hundred, and the aborigines number but a hundred more. The rivers, when they run every decade or so, run uphill. Sand dunes float in the air, and kangaroos leap from cloud to cloud. The horizon is never where it ought to be. A tree one moment is a shrub, and the next a radio mast. A reptilian monster sunning itself on a mountain ridge is, after all, a frilled lizard sprawled on the dead branch of a tree partially buried in a sand dune.

In this deceitful land a man and a child had vanished.

That had been an Everest of a problem for Senior Constable Pierce, and Bony, who came five weeks later, had to concede much to the policeman's reputation as a bushman and to all those many white men who had joined in the search. A deceitful land, yet it would not deceive any one of them to whom an area of two hundred thousand square miles would be on a par with a square mile of city blocks to the city dweller.

A man must eat, and during the hot summer months could not live a day without water. He dare not move a mile from water without carrying a supply, and water sources, other than the bores and at homesteads, were few indeed, after eleven rainless months. Every remaining supply had been watched by men whose eyes wouldn't fail to register the tracks of wild dogs, aborigines, cattle, and, if unable to decipher smoke signals, would note the

whereabouts of aborigines, either in their wild state or semi-civilised. Were Ole Fren Yorky still alive, and there was no expressed doubt that he was, he had achieved remarkable success in eluding the finest desert men on earth.

They had been the prospectors trying to locate a man and a child. Now that Bony was arrived, he was, perforce, the mining engineer who would have to delve beneath the surfaces of this deceitful land.

So that when he came to Mount Eden after all prospecting had been done, he didn't fork a horse and race it here and there, or board a jeep and add to the normal dust, because it was apparently assumed that Yorky and the child were not lost, and, because of Yorky's bush experience, were not dead of thirst. Therefore, lives and planes hadn't been risked.

There were facts that could not be denied, and facts that could be assumptions, and assumptions that could be facts. A woman had been shot with a .44 rifle, and her daughter had been abducted from the homestead. A man seen near the homestead on the morning of the crime had left tracks within a few yards of the position of the body. When last seen, he had been carrying a .44 Winchester rifle.

The weekly windstorm raged that day, and those few tracks were sheltered from the wind by the homestead buildings. The man, with the child, had gained a lead over the searchers of some twenty hours, and over D. I. Bonaparte, five weeks.

Not a man had seen them since that day. Not one searcher had found a track left by either man or child, no tell-tale fire site, no sign of them whatsoever. Facts were few, assumptions many. One was that Yorky hadn't shot the mother and abducted the child, but that one of the five white men had returned that day, had shot the woman, with Yorky as witness, and the child also. Then had taken Yorky and the child to a distant place, and buried the bodies at the front of a moving sand dune, so placing the full responsibility on Ole Fren Yorky.

The all-seeing eagles knew the answer, as did the crows. The eagles this early morning came low to espy the stranger seated under the green tops of the pine trees, and the crows were equally interested, but quickly gave up when knowing he was alive. They indulged in insatiable curiosity in the stranger's horses down in the yards, and in two women who were trudging towards the house from the direction of the aborigines' camp. Some of the crows flew out a little way over Lake Eyre, and returned as though fearful, while several others continued on over the lake until Bony wondered if they intended to cross to the hidden shore beyond.

When smoke issued from a house chimney, Detective Inspector Bonaparte walked from the ridge down to the homestead of Mount Eden.

CHAPTER 4

MOUNT EDEN WELCOMES BONY

Of all Canute's subjects, numbering forty-three, only Sarah had not the slightest fear of him, and what fear, engendered by inherited instincts, she had of Murtee the Medicine Man was rarely manifest. She was one-fifth white, and four-fifths black, and all that her father contributed was a softening of the aboriginal lines of her features, and an acute sense of humour. It is told that before Canute was blinded by a grass fire, she laughed at him when in a towering rage, and that when Canute rushed at her, brandishing a waddy, she took it from him and knocked him cold, then stood over him and hugged herself tightly while laughing down at the silent one. It is also told of Sarah that in punishment Canute put the ban of silence on her, and she kicked him in the stomach and laughed right heartily.

Now that Sarah was cooking at 'government house', she and Meena rose early and arrived at the kitchen near enough to six every morning. It was her job first to prepare the morning tea which Meena took to Mr Wootton, whom she would surely find seated at the transceiver and talking with a neighbour.

This morning the fire had been lit and the water was simmering in the wide-bottomed kettle, and Meena was busily tidying the living-room, when there stepped into the kitchen one Sarah had never seen. She noted his lean dark face, the deep blue eyes, the white teeth and the smile, the clean white shirt tucked into brown gabardine slacks. She said:

"No feller 'lowed here. What you want? Brekus not ready yet."

"*I* am allowed here," he told her, adding as though an afterthought, "*I* am allowed anywhere. Have you made morning tea yet?"

Without invitation he seated himself at the scrubbed table, stretched his legs, smiled again at Sarah, who was undecided whether to be pleased or angry. It was the blue eyes which brought the indecision, they and the voice more than hinting at authority. Meena appeared, paused in the doorway to the living-room. Sarah swayed the teapot violently to assist the brewing, and, with the pot held by the handle and the tip of the spout, she asked:

"You big-feller policeman, eh?"

"Yes. You knew I was coming?"

Sarah nodded, placed the pot on the side of the stove, took cups and saucers from the dresser. The boss was forgotten. First she served the stranger. Standing before the visitor, Meena came to stand beside her, and Bony said:

"You are Sarah. And you are Meena. I shall be here some time. Is Mr Wootton up and about?"

"He's inside waiting for his tea," replied Meena, recalling Sarah to her duties. "What's your name?"

"Napoleon Bonaparte. If we ever become friends you

may call me Bony. Meanwhile, please tell Mr Wootton that Inspector Bonaparte is here."

"Inspector Bonaparte," she repeated, and giggled. She cupped her hand about her breast, thrust forward her tummy, and again giggled. Sarah looked at her and dug an elbow hard into the ribs, which cut the giggle. She gasped, and managed to say: "I thought you would be old, have grey hair, look fierce. You married?"

"Mr Wootton . . . tell him I am here," Bony urged gravely.

White or black, it makes no difference. Meena smiled at him, her hips swaying as she walked to the living-room. Once she looked back at him, and Sarah exclaimed:

"That Meena!" But there was pride and affection on her broad face.

Meena returned and nodded for Bony to enter the living-room, and, passing her, he tilted her chin and said:

"You will not be so saucy when I leave Mount Eden."

The cattleman was standing with a tea-cup in one hand and a biscuit in the other. His expression was one of incredulity. His hair was tossed, and his moustache needed clipping.

"Inspector Bonaparte?" he questioned, with emphasis on the rank. "Of what?"

"Of detectives, Mr Wootton," suavely replied Bony. "It seems that I am famous in some quarters and not so in others."

"But we know nothing about you. The policeman at Loaders Springs knows nothing."

"I asked him to know nothing," calmly announced Bony. "In fact I am ten days late, having been delayed on a case at Boulia."

"In south-west Queensland? You came here by . . . ?"

"Horse. I needed to meditate between murders, Mr Wootton. My credentials."

Wootton placed cup and biscuit on the table and leaned forward to examine the open wallet, and the copy of the

letter instructing Bonaparte to investigate the murder of Mrs Bell, for and on behalf of the South Australian Police Department. Frowning, the cattleman straightened and stared into the blue eyes, so predominant in the dark face. He said:

"You have no objection to my contacting Senior Constable Pierce?"

"None whatever. By the way, your cook gave me a cup of tea which I left on her kitchen table. May I?"

"Meena!" called Mr Wootton. "Bring Inspector Bonaparte another cup of tea and biscuits."

Meena came in with the tea. Bony's eyes were directed to the polished panel of the transceiver, and her employer was at the wall telephone. Her gay mood had given place to one of curious watchfulness, and for a second or two she gazed at the slim figure with the squared shoulders, the straight back, before withdrawing with a rustle of her starched apron.

Bony was looking over the titles of the books, of which there must have been a hundred on the shelves beside the transceiver, when Wootton said:

"Pierce said he expected you. He said, also, that he told no one of your coming, in accordance with your instructions. And yet the blacks knew. The maid told me three days ago that a high-ranking policeman was coming. Doesn't add up, does it?"

"Oh yes, it adds up," countered Bony. "They communicate, you know. Smoke signals, telepathy. I've been associated with them on the Boulia case."

"On the killing of that aboriginal stockman? I've heard about it. You found the killer?"

"Of course."

"Otherwise you would not be here now?"

"Naturally. I locate a killer once I start on his tracks."

"I am afraid you won't get on the tracks of our murderer, Inspector. The wind wiped them out, bar at two places, and that a month back."

"I was speaking metaphorically."

"Oh! Well, anything I can do, we can all do, to help, you can be assured. . . . What d'you suggest?"

"I am in possession of the frame of this Mount Eden crime, and have to resurrect the flesh. That will take some time, in view of the reputation of Constable Pierce, and the thoroughness of his efforts. As you ask me to make suggestions—a room, a shower, breakfast."

"Of course. Meena! I'll have the room prepared for you. Your things . . . where?"

"On the pack-horse I left in your horse yard."

"Good! Meena! Call Charlie to fetch Inspector Bonaparte's gear from the pack-horse in the yards. And see to it that the corner room is ready for the Inspector. Tell Sarah about the extra breakfast. And, Meena, don't dally with Charlie."

Meena smiled faintly and departed. She was both impressed and subdued.

"Pardon me remarking on it, Inspector, but your arrival indicates very early travelling."

"It surely does, Mr Wootton. I came down the Birdsville Track on the mail truck to Maree, caught 'The Ghan' to Coward Springs, where I contacted Constable Pierce and borrowed the horses. I made north and looked over the country southward of Lake Eyre. When day broke this morning, I was meditating on the long ago of the aborigines. Always I have been interested in anthropology."

"Sometimes I wish I had studied the subject," Wootton said. "You know, I've been here only five years, and it's my first experience of the country and the blacks. They defeat me. I hope some day to defeat the country."

"You never will. No man ever has. But I know what you mean. Could you spare your men for the day?"

"Yes. I had work set for them, but it can wait."

"Thank you. After breakfast, could we have them gathered somewhere that I may talk to them?"

"Of course. My office is large enough."

"Kind of you. I will try not to inconvenience you more than necessary. This part of the Eyre Basin needs rain. When was the last rain?"

"Five months back. We want rain all right, but the ground feed is holding out. See anything of the floods up in Queensland?"

Bony could add nothing to Wootton's knowledge received over the radio, excepting to add his opinion that the water might reach Lake Eyre via Coopers Creek and possibly down the Warburton River. The cattleman sensed the determined avoidance of the subject in both their minds, and escorted Bony to the guest room.

At breakfast Bony raised the subject of Yorky's singular title.

"Oh, that!" Wootton said, chuckling. "It happened years ago, before my time, anyway. I think Yorky is known, by repute, all over the back country. He's quite a character, or was before his mind must have become unhinged. No horseman, and useless as a stockman, but handy to have in dry times managing a pumping station, or riding a boundary fence.

"Like most of his type, he'd stick to a job for months, then suddenly leave with his cheque and make for a town. After drinking a cheque at Loaders Springs at the time I'm talking about, Yorky humped his swag out this way, intending to ask my predecessor for a job. The next thing was that the policeman at Loaders Springs—not Pierce, of course—rang through to say he'd received a report that Yorky was living with the blacks down on the creek, and would the owner of this place go along and bring him out. You know how it is, the law against a white man living in an aborigines' camp.

"Anyway, the cattleman, name of Murphy, rode to the camp. There was no one about excepting Chief Canute and a few of the lubras, including Sarah, now cooking for us. Sarah being more civilised than the rest, he called her and she came out of her humpy. Murphy said: 'They tell me

you got a white man in camp, Sarah. Tell him to come out at once.' Sarah denied she had a white man in the camp, but Murphy persisted, until Sarah said: 'No white feller in my camp, Boss. Only my ole fren Yorky.' It appeared that Yorky turned up suffering badly from the booze, and Sarah took him in and was nursing him with soups and things."

"Hence the Ole Fren Yorky," supplemented the amused Bony. "How old would he be, d'you think?"

"Difficult even to guess," replied Wootton. "I'd say in his early sixties."

"Did you employ him ever?"

"Oh yes. He left here with his last cheque three weeks before he shot Mrs Bell. He'd been on another bender then, you see, when I found him at the blacks' camp. There were no aborigines there then. They were all away on walk-about."

"Tell me about finding Yorky there."

"Well, you see, it's my custom to go to Loaders Springs every week, and always on a Thursday. On that particular Thursday, I left about half past nine, per car. Half a mile along the track there's a gate, and just under another half mile there's a creek. The creek's always dry except after heavy rain, but between the road dip and the creek mouth with the Lake there's almost a permanent waterhole. They tell me the blacks have made it their headquarters for generations. Murphy let them fence it in from the cattle, and I've never interfered with them or the water.

"Well, that morning when I got there, I saw Yorky squatting over a bit of fire and drinking tea from a jam tin. I wondered why he'd camped there, when he had only to tramp another three-quarters of a mile to get here, and stopped to speak to him. He said he was sick, and he certainly looked it. He'd hoped the blacks would be there so's Sarah could look after him. And he pleaded for a drink—just a small reviver.

"I had a bottle of whisky in the car, and I gave him a hefty nobbler and told him to get along to the homestead

and ask Mrs Bell to give him a feed. He said he would, and I drove on. A minute later, when I looked into the rear-vision mirror, I saw him on the track, swag up, even his rifle strapped to the swag."

Bony pushed his empty plate a little from him, and drew closer the second cup of coffee.

"How did he appear to you . . . mentally?"

"All right, I think," replied Wootton. "Of course he was shaking a little, having been on the spirits for three solid weeks. The nobbler I gave him certainly bucked him up but no one will ever make me believe that drop of whisky drove him off his rocker enough to shoot Mrs Bell and clear out with the child. It's something I don't understand."

"We shall," Bony said, and rolled a cigarette.

CHAPTER 5

DIGGING

THE FOUR hands were invited into the office, Charlie and another aborigine being told they could take the day off. All four were familiar with the interior of this large room, and so noted that on the wall behind the desk had been tacked a large-scale map of Mount Eden.

Wootton occupied the chair behind the desk. Bony stood beside the desk, almost lazily smoking, while the four men sat and made themselves comfortable, at the invitation of their employer. Finally, obviously wondering what this was all about, they regarded Bony with deep interest.

"As you know, it is now several weeks since Mrs Bell was killed and her daughter abducted," he began. "Five weeks ago a man and a small child vanished, and both man and child were known to you better by far than I am known to you.

"Since that tragic day, you and many others were engaged in an intensive search for Ole Fren Yorky. You know the details of that search, and the balance of human effort within the extent of the country about Lake Eyre. No doubt you have assessed the chances of locating two human beings on an area of country many people outside would think to be a limitless world, in which fifty, a hundred, men could easily be lost. Thus you will agree with me that, despite all the hunting, all the planning, the chances of Yorky getting away, or holing up somewhere, were good from the beginning. The hunters held four kings, but Yorky held four aces. Correct?"

"Could be, and could not be," doubted Arnold Bray. "I don't reckon Yorky planned it. He was too sozzled to plan much. I said, and I still think, that the blacks helped him."

"Knowing that Yorky was fairly close to the aborigines," Bony proceeded to argue, "knowing that all the aborigines were camped on the Neales River, the first thing Constable Pierce did was to send riders at top speed to cut off that line of retreat for Yorky. When the trucks for the trackers arrived at the Neales River, they made sure that every aborigine was there. As you say, Arnold Bray, Yorky never planned the murder. It was committed on impulse."

"And then he was lucky enough to find he held four aces," interrupted withered William Harte. "In the first place, Yorky knows this country better than any of us, and, better than us, he can think closer to the abos. Put yourself in his place. . . . He done a murder before he even thought about it. He knows we're all away, that no one ain't likely to come around till middle afternoon. He's shot Mrs Bell, and he can't shoot the kid 'cos the reason he shot the woman ain't strong enough for him to shoot the kid. So he's got the kid on his hands 'cos the kid seen him doin' the shootin'. He's like a bloke having to walk with one boot on and the other off. So he looks over his cards, and decides he holds better cards than anyone else."

Seated on the floor with his back to the wall, Harte paused to roll a cigarette, and Bony prompted him, the others apparently conceding his superior knowledge and experience.

"When he shot Mrs Bell," resumed the ageless man, "Yorky knew the country was wide open to him. He knew just where all the abos were . . . fifty miles something up north. He knows them abos pretty well, knows how their minds work, and the reason why he didn't shoot the kid was stronger than the reason why he ought to have shot her, to give him the best chance of getting clear out of this country. As I said, he knows the blacks better than any of us. He knows that once they're put to his tracks, even if them tracks is bits of dust in the air, they'll catch up with him. If they wants to, that is. He knows that if he kills the kid they'll want to; if he don't, they won't. That was his cards."

"The aborigines thought much of Linda?" pressed Bony.

"They surely did. Like everyone else. One time we was playin' poker over in the quarters, and I drew a Queen of Hearts and snaffled the jackpot, and I said without thinking: 'That's my Linda for you, fellers. The Queen of Hearts.' And that's what she was around these parts."

"The aborigines, however, did try to track Yorky," Wootton reminded him, and Bony was delighted at the course his conference was taking.

"Too right," agreed Harte, who then had to go to the doorway for another spit. "What happened? They're up on the Neales, half-starved, livin' on goannas and flies. They get brought back, and they're given lashings of beef and flour and tobacco to start 'em off right. Instead of huntin' a perenti or another feller's gin, they're set to huntin' Yorky.

"But do they hunt for Yorky? I got me doubts, and I got 'em because they knew he got aces. 'Good ole Yorky,' they'd say. 'We'll look around, sort of, and feed up on the boss's beef, an' smoke the boss's baccy.' But they didn't just look around, as you said, Mr Wootton. They set to work all right, but not because they hate Yorky for killing Mrs

Bell. They set to work like bloodhounds to make sure Yorky hadn't killed Linda and planted her body somewhere, and when they reasoned that Yorky hadn't been that ruddy stupid, that he'd got clear away with the kid, they sort of got tired, and gradually eased up till they quit. That's why I say Ole Fren Yorky knew when he collared Linda that he held all the aces."

"And he will continue to hold them while he keeps Linda Bell alive?" encouraged Bony.

"That's so. While he's got Linda with him, it's Yorky's game."

"And you still don't think that the blacks know where he is?" drawled lanky Eric Maundy.

"No, I don't think they do, Eric. To find that out would mean work, and they'd be satisfied to know that little Linda was safe enough. They'd say Yorky and the kid was around somewhere, that Yorky would come out of smoke when it suited him, and meanwhile Charlie will be chasing Meena, and Canute will scratch his neck 'cos he's too old to take her even though she was promised to him when she was born. You gotta know them abos, Eric."

"Reckon you know 'em?" jibed the young man named Harry Lawton.

"If you think you know 'em better, put up a better yarn," advised Arnold with asperity.

"If we accept your idea," Bony contributed, "where is Yorky obtaining food for himself and the child?"

"At his camps," replied Harte. "Perhaps you don't know that when Yorky left here for a bender, he had a job riding the boundary fence."

"That's so," added Wootton. "The boundary fence is some hundred and fifty miles round the station, bar where it cuts into the Lake. Yorky rode it with camels. He had a camp every twenty miles, with water at every second camp."

"And them camps were stocked with tucker," inserted Harte. "You know, flour and tea and sugar kept in tins and tinned dog and fish if he was stuck. I asked him once about

the abos getting down on his tucker and tobacco, and he laughed and said they wouldn't steal from him."

Bony studied the wall map of Mount Eden Station. To Wootton he said:

"Mark the camps, please, and mark additionally those camps where the water is." To Harte he said: "What's outside the boundary fence?"

"Nothing. Open country, excepting down south and south-east."

"Wild aborigines?"

Harte shook his head, saying:

"Not till you get up about the Simpson Desert, and they ain't as wild as they used to be."

"The country . . . dry all the way up north and west?"

"Same as around here. Haven't had no rain for months, and that fell at the wrong time. Still, there's water if you know where to find it. Water in holes up on the Neales. Water under the Lake mud, if you can stomach it."

"H'm! We seem to be going somewhere." Bony looked at each in turn. "I want you to mark on this map where each of you went that day Mrs Bell was shot, and note also the time when you were farthest from the homestead. That is, as close as possible. A blue pencil, Mr Wootton, please."

They did as requested. Then Bony said:

"I understand that you four men have been in this part of Australia for many years, much longer than Mr Wootton. You have been most co-operative, and I ask you to continue so. It is good to know that you believe Linda is still alive, and that rescuing her must take priority. I would not have expected such full co-operation, were it not for the possibility of recovering the child.

"You will see clearly that the actual rescue could well be attended by grave danger to her from the man who abducted her. To save himself he might kill her. It is of vital importance to know exactly the kind of man he is, or was, before he shot Mrs Bell. First, let us try to under-

stand why he shot Mrs Bell. Had he ever expressed dislike of her?"

"Not that I ever heard," replied Arnold. "He was one of them inoffensive poor bastards. Never hardly spoke unless spoken to. You had to get him alone, and sort of talk soft to him, before he'd open up. He'd talk fast enough to Linda, and the black kids."

"When drunk or recovering from a bout, did he think of women, talk about them?"

"No."

"Did Mrs Bell ever express dislike of him, ever strongly criticise him?"

"Just the opposite. Mrs Bell sort of liked him, I think. Patched his shirts more than once."

"After he'd washed 'em," chuckled young Harry Lawton. "She'd do that for any of us."

"You're too flash to have old shirts to be patched," drawled Eric.

"She never objected to Linda talking to Yorky?"

"Don't think. Had no reason to. He was harmless enough."

"Yorky must have gone wonky to have shot her," insisted Eric.

"All right! Then let us get down to his association with the aborigines," pressed Bony. "You have said he was close to them. In what way? Did he live secretly with a lubra?"

Harry Lawton broke into laughter, and was silenced by the glare in Arnold's grey eyes. It was Harte who replied.

"Look, Inspector. Yorky was older than me. Not much, but still he was so. I remember Yorky coming into this country about thirty-five years back. Not much to look at but real rough: always small and a bit wispy, if you know what I mean. And I can't say he'd had much education, less, sort of, than Meena and Charlie and the other abos who went down to Mission School for a spell.

"Yorky could read the papers, follow the races and all that. But he got to know more about the ants and things

than I ever wanted to, and he got to know the ways of camels when he was frightened of horses. I don't think he was more taken up with women than most of us. Camped for a night or two with one down at Loaders Springs. You know the sort. Some say that there was times when he camped with Sarah, and I have heard that there was times when he had a young lubra with him on the boundary fence. A long time ago, though."

Harte went again to the door to spit.

"But this is what I am trying to get out. Yorky was more interested in watching ants and birds than he was in talking about cattle and horses like the rest of us. He'd get the black kids to take him out and show him things. All the kids took to him, and they run like hell from me. Gradually he got in with the blacks. And I'm sure it wasn't to get at the lubras. He was sort of interested in them like he was in the ants. He'd give them things. Fork out tobacco, buy a dress or some such."

"I once told him he oughta write a book about 'em," interrupted Harry Lawton. "He knows more about 'em than the perfessors and them sort of blokes."

"He could have done, too, if he'd had any education," agreed Harte. "Well, that's how it is with Ole Fren Yorky. You heard how he got the name?"

"Yes. And what you have said supports what I already know of him," replied Bony, and bending over the desk he jotted a note on a slip of paper. "It does seem that Yorky must have lost his balance through the booze to have shot Mrs Bell. Could you say he tended to be mentally childish?"

"No," said Arnold with conviction. "Yet he wasn't . . . I don't know how to put it. He reminds me of a nephew of mine down in Adelaide. Used to moon about when other kids were playing or larking. Got so when he grew older that he went around dreaming. But he had brains. Ended by being a first class commercial artist with a publishing firm in Sydney. No, Yorky was never wonky. The way he plays poker proves that."

"He had what I'd call low cunning," commented Lawton. "You could never tell what cards he held."

"So that all of you actually find it hard to believe that Ole Fren Yorky did shoot Mrs Bell?" asked Bony.

"That's about it," agreed Arnold, and the others nodded agreement. "There's times when I won't believe it."

"You are sure those were his tracks you picked out?"

"Too right! Couldn't mistake 'em," replied Harte.

Bony presented his note to Arnold, and said:

"When I locate Yorky, we shall know all about it. The motive will be interesting; the way of his escape will be interesting, too."

Arnold nodded to Harte, and they left the office. The others watched them leave, knowing they did so at the behest of Bony's note. Wootton cleared his throat preparatory to saying something, and was stopped by a screech from without.

Struggling figures appeared in the doorway, and the men brought in a furious lubra.

CHAPTER 6

THE ART OF REASONING!

"LEMME GO, you Arnold Bray. Lemme go, I say," shouted Sarah, and, having inserted the large woman into the office, Arnold and Harte freed her arms and blocked the doorway. Either Sarah was in excellent form, or the struggle hadn't lasted long, but she now stood with fists balled into her hips, a glare in her eyes, and requiring only a broomstick or a rolling-pin to ape her white counterpart.

"She was round at the back wall with her ear to a crack," announced Arnold. "Just listening in."

"I was only sittin' in the shade outside that hot ole

kitchen," shouted Sarah, and Wootton would have spoken had not Bony said, placatingly:

"Well, there's no harm in that, Sarah. It's deep shade here, and you are entitled to it. Still, there's house shade outside the kitchen door, and I saw only an hour ago a nice chair. You go there and sit in that easy chair, or even better, what about morning tea?" Again Wootton attempted to speak, but Bony waved him to silence. The lubra's black eyes encountered the blue eyes of the slim Napoleon Bonaparte, blue eyes hinting at laughter, friendliness, and abruptly she smiled:

"Mornin' tea! Crikey! I forget about it. That Meena! She should of told me."

Nodding to Bony, she turned about, scowled at the men and went out like a cork down a drain.

"Well, what d'you make of that?" demanded Wootton, his face flushed. "Eavesdropping for sure. You should have made her tell us why she was doing that, Inspector!"

"You cannot make those people do anything they don't wish to do," Bony said, coldly. "That she was listening is a point, but only that. We have to remember that she and Yorky were friends, and that she must be interested in his fate, as we are. I think you men may leave. Perhaps this afternoon or this evening we could get together again and talk. All right with you?"

They assented: then as they were about to go, young Lawton asked:

"Mind telling why you wanted us to mark that map with where we were that day Mrs Bell was murdered?"

"Not at all. It was mere police routine. You see, any one of you four men could have returned after Mr Wootton left that day, then shot Mrs Bell and taken the child away and killed her. Even you, Mr Wootton, could have done just that."

"But what about Yorky? Yorky was known to come here that morning," pressed Lawton, and the others nodded quick agreement.

"As I told you, it is merely police routine to establish the whereabouts of everyone at the assumed time the crime was committed. In fact I think Constable Pierce asked for that information, and that it is recorded in his report."

"He did make a song and dance about it," admitted young Lawton. "Looks like we're all sort of suspect, don't it?"

"Pierce acted rightly," patiently continued Bony. "Look at it this way. Not one of you is supported by a witness as to what you did between the time you left the homestead and the time you returned. No one saw Yorky at the blacks' camp other than Mr Wootton. To be sure, Bill Harte found Yorky's tracks back of the meat-house, and showed them to Arnold Bray, who agreed they were his. To be sure, Yorky's tracks were found at the homestead gate. Pierce took plaster casts of those tracks. Before Yorky is put on trial, if he is, the casts must prove that he actually made those tracks, that he was, in fact, at this homestead on that morning. A good policeman, and Pierce is a good policeman, leaves nothing to chance."

"Fair enough," supported Wootton. "All right, you men can take the day off, and if you think of anything, I'm sure the Inspector will be happy to talk it over."

They were drifting across the square to the quarters when the morning tea gong was beaten, and they about-turned and went back to the meal annexe. Tea and buttered scones were served by Meena to Bony and his host on the house veranda, and when she had withdrawn, Bony questioned about her.

He learned that a religious body conducted a Mission Church and school a few miles out from Loaders Springs. Aborigines, both adults and children, were warmly welcomed. A large number of children chose to live at the Mission, chose to because there was no compulsion. They were taught the elementary subjects—drawing and painting, basketwork, needlework, woodwork, and in return assisted the pastor and his wife with the stock and the garden.

"I visited the place one afternoon," Wootton said.

"Surprised me, the work the children were doing in class. And how they sang, too! I had only just come here, was still raw to the country, and I asked the pastor what happened to the children when they left. He said: 'Oh, the lads become stockmen, and the girls do domestic service round about. That's when it suits them. We do our best, as we hope you can see, but after they leave us, the old ones get them back.' "

"I can understand that," Bony agreed with the pastor. "Meena, though, seems to be an excellent maid."

"I think so. Yes, she's good in a house. But then neither she nor Sarah will stay here overnight, and there's no telling that they'll turn up in the morning, or go off with the others on a walkabout. That girl can sew and mend as good as Mrs Bell could. And Charlie—you saw him this morning—is a damn fine wood carver."

Wootton stretched his thin, short legs and lit his pipe.

"You ought to see the dolls he carved for little Linda Bell. One is the dead spit of Ole Fren Yorky, and there's another you'd say was my image. The one supposed to be Mrs Bell isn't so good, but another one, of Meena, to my mind, is the best of the lot. We'll go and see them if you like. They're over in the playhouse."

"Yes, I'd like to see them. I understand that the men built the playhouse. Which reminds me: did Linda spend much of her days there?"

"A good deal, Inspector," replied the cattleman reflectively. "You know, you can't wonder that we worshipped that child. Every Sunday afternoon she'd invite us all there for tea. Had her own tea set and her mother filled the teapot. I went sometimes. She'd have her visitors squatting on the floor, and she'd hand down her small cups and saucers and plates of scones and cake; and the men would talk to her with exaggerated politeness, and she would be the little lady." Wootton sighed. "Only that last day I was commissioned to buy a box of chocolates and special handkerchiefs for her."

A few minutes later they left the house for the canegrass playhouse. It was noticeable how the thick walls shut out the noises of the crows, the windmill raising water, and the soft hissing of the gusty wind over the ground. Standing within the entrance, Bony surveyed the interior, noting the cut-down furniture, and the fact that objects were not positioned as described by Constable Pierce. Almost at once Wootton exclaimed:

"Why, two of the dolls have gone! They were set up on the shelf bench. And those presents. The comb and the box of handkerchiefs have gone too. Now, what the hell!"

"When did you last see them?" asked Bony.

"Oh, about a fortnight back. The men wanted to tidy up the place, having the idea of making it nice for Linda's return. I obtained permission from Pierce, and they went to work. Swept the floor, cleaned the window, put the dolls side by side on the bench, and the presents on the bench, too. I'll call them."

Bony heard Wootton shouting. He surveyed this room, and was saddened by its emptiness of personality. The cut-down table and chair, the books, the old trunk, and small dresser with the bright chintz curtain only hinted at a life which once had warmed this place. Oddly enough, he felt himself to be an intruder.

They came crowding in, Wootton and his men, silently taking in this well-remembered place.

"Ole Fren Yorky and Meena gone off on walkabout all right," exploded Harry Lawton.

"And the handkerchiefs, and the comb, the blue one," drawled Eric with fierce breathlessness. "Left the chocolates. They was no good anyhow. Heat melted 'em."

Harte quietly went forward and gazed along the surface of the shelf bench. His voice was cold.

"Who was in here last? I was looking in Sunday, week back, and them dolls was all there where we put 'em in a row. I remember how Meena was sort of turned to look at the boss. It wasn't yestiddy, nor the day before, they were

took. There's plenty of dust fell on the places where they were sitting."

They talked. They pondered. Finally they agreed that the last man to look into the playhouse had been Bill Harte and that had been nine days ago. All remembered that the dolls were then on the bench, and that the presents Linda was to have received that day her mother was shot were also set out on the bench.

"Them ruddy blacks have raided the place," Harry Lawton accused.

"We'll find out right now," decided Eric. "Come on, let's argue it out with old Canute. He'll make the thief part up . . . or else."

Anger charged the quiet air, and then Bony spoke:

"I would like you to leave the matter to me, and to say nothing of it in the hearing of Sarah and Meena," he said with easy authority. "Now just see what else has been taken . . . books, from that dresser, anything?"

Arnold examined the books, shook his head. He lifted the curtain in front of the dresser, disclosing a dainty tea service, a box containing coloured wools, and material. Again he shook his massive head and dropped the curtain. Eric cried:

"Wait on, Arnold! Them cups and things."

He sprang forward and lifted the curtain. Then he straightened, paused to be supported on his discovery, finally shouted quite unnecessarily:

"There was six cups and saucers. Now there's only five. Look! A cup and saucer has been pinched, too."

Men swore. Bony said:

"Keep on looking. Be sure if anything else is missing."

Dolls to comfort a little girl. A china cup for her to drink from instead of a tin mug, perhaps a jam tin. Handkerchiefs and blue comb taken, but not a box of chocolates spoiled by the heat.

Aboriginal children would not have ignored the chocolates, although ruined by heat.

"Her Kurdaitcha shoes," drawled Bill Harte. "They don't seem to be here, either."

The Kurdaitcha Man of legend, the fabulous being who walks by night, his feet covered with emu feathers glued with blood so that he leaves no tracks for aborigines to follow when it is light. Harry Lawton withdrew from the search to tell Bony that Charlie had fashioned imitation shoes for Linda.

"Yes, those pretty pieces have gone, too," Arnold declared. "All decorated with feathers and pictures drawn on 'em with hot wire. Old Murtee could have taken them for his collection of magic things."

Eventually it was agreed that nothing else had been removed. Eric again suggested 'arguing it out' with Canute, and it was Arnold who told him, "That's out," because Inspector Bonaparte said so. It was noticeable that their first reaction of cautious familiarity towards Bony was replaced by firming respect, for, as it had been with so many others in the past, his eyes, his voice and speech caused them to forget his mixed race. He was saying:

"It is often wise to set aside the act in favour of the motive. Just now when we found Sarah listening to us, the act might be of smaller importance than the reason prompting her. So it is with these missing articles belonging to Linda Bell. Who took them is of lesser interest to me than why they were taken. Assuming, of course, that they were not removed by the aboriginal children, or by someone intending to give them to the children."

"I think I see your point, Inspector," observed Wootton. "Someone could have taken them to Linda, wherever she is with Ole Fren Yorky."

"Proving that Linda is still alive," added Arnold with satisfaction.

"That Linda wanted them things to play with," hopefully supplemented Eric. "Could of been that Yorky came here himself to get 'em."

"We'd have seen his tracks," Arnold said.

"Not if he came last Sat'day, or yesterday week," objected Bill Harte. "Them two days it blew like hell, and blew all night too, remember."

"It could be more likely that one of the aborigines stole them to take them to Yorky for Linda," contributed Wootton.

"So we come back to the abos," crowed young Lawton.

"Yair, the abos, Harry," agreed Eric. "We'll get it out of them. Who pinched the dolls and things, and what was done with 'em. Now what-in-'ell you smiling about, Inspector?"

"I'm beginning to wonder who is the detective," Bony replied. "Inductive reasoning must keep to specified rules, and often to indulge in such reasoning is unwise until all the available facts and probable assumptions are marshalled. There is an assumption which has not yet occurred to you, an assumption which we have authority to examine. We may assume that the presents and the dolls were removed by someone with the intention of putting into our minds the idea that Linda is still alive. The motive for that is obscure, but still reasonable to accept."

From Bony they looked at each other, bewilderment plainly evident. To make confusion stick, he went on:

"Recall what I said about the tracks you believed were left by Yorky. Until proved, we may only assume he made them, and we may assume someone else falsified them, knowing that most people see what they want to see. So there is one assumption we may add to another, and those two to yet a third, and then we have a faint glimmer of a theory.

"Crime investigators are trained minds. I have been trained to think along lines of deduction and induction. These are two separate processes of thinking, as doubtless you know. Or perhaps you don't know. Which is why I require you not to question the aborigines, or to mention this matter to the domestics over the way. Is that understood?"

Eric coughed and nodded. Young Harry nodded and looked vacant. Arnold was thoughtful, and Bill Harte's bright dark eyes were curious. Mr Wootton blinked and spoke for all.

"I think we follow you, Inspector Bonaparte. You may depend on us not to interfere."

"I was sure I could depend on you," suavely returned Bony.

CHAPTER 7

SAVAGES AND BYRON

THE FIRE was like the red and flickering eye of Ganba, the Great Snake. Tall white pillars encircled the fiery eye, and between these pillars the sweet notes of Ganba's snoring floated on to warn the aborigines in all Australia that he was out from his chambers under the earth.

The fire burned redly amid the white gums surrounding the waterhole. Ganba's snoring was coming from a length of hollow tree branch called a dijeridoo and played by an aborigine whose hair and beard were white, whose naked chest and back were cicatriced in fantastic designs and marks.

The audience of men stared into Ganba's red eye. Behind them sat their women, the young girls and the children. All the babies were either asleep or watching with large and rounded eyes. Only occasionally did one move, and then slightly, so engrossed were they by the voice of the dijeridoo.

The dijeridoo was as thick as a man's leg, and so long that the end rested on a sheet of bark beyond Canute's outstretched feet. The mouth end was but little smaller than the far opening, and from it issued sounds, which, to ears accustomed to white man's music, would be meaningless.

Canute was telling a story which was first told when Lake Eyre was part of a great sea.

There was a woman who lived in a cave on a hill, a wise woman who could see far and who heard the birds talking. With her was her son, a stripling, a beautiful youth. Now the day came when a party of the woman's people were to leave for a distant country to trade magic churinga stones for spear shafts. These men came to the woman and asked that her son might go with them, and so begin to become a man.

The woman consented, and the youth departed with the traders, and they were away for a long time, until the woman, anxiously watching from her cave, saw them come over a ridge far away. Slowly and often she counted them, and the number was short by one.

The traders said that a great man-bird had swooped down upon them and taken the youth into the sky and given him to its fledglings in a nest on a pile of stones. They hid themselves in hollow trees and dared not come out till night came.

So, as custom dictated, all the men cut into themselves the mourning marks, and all the women cut their breasts and lamented for five days. On the sixth day the woman called the traders to sit before her cave. She spoke soft words to them, and gave them honey ants on palm leaves to eat, and sweet water in little gourds to drink. And one by one they fell over, and told her they had killed the beautiful youth because all the maidens rejoiced over him, and would not look upon them.

They died, and the woman made a big fire and burned them, and she raised her arms to lift the sky high and permit a tall willi-willi to sweep over the world and kick the bones to dust.

Was it Canute telling this story? How can a story be told unless with words? You may say that music can tell a story for those with ears to hear, but you would be the last to say that Canute was producing music. Shall we compromise, agree that Canute was passing on the old old stories for those

with ears to hear and minds to interpret them? For from that dijeridoo issued no tune, no rhythm, no note to be even imagined as musical.

Detective Inspector Napoleon Bonaparte listened raptly to the story of the woman and the beautiful youth. None was aware that he stood behind one of the white pillars.

A lean old man sat beside Canute. His arms rested on his knees, his face resting on the crossed arms. Bony saw Sarah, who was nursing a naked baby. Her face was lifted as though pictures were strung between two of the white gums. Meena was there, wearing a blue skirt, her body naked above the waist, the soft firelight shimmering like golden dew on her untapped breasts. Like many of the others, she was gazing into the heart of the fire. The young man Bony knew as Charlie was there too, watching Meena.

Bony had listened to more than the outline of the story. He had heard the tramp of the willi-willi coming across the world, the clash and crash of pounded bones kicked to dust. He had seen the cave, the very stones of its entrance, the woman tall and graceful, and the stripling son as he walked down the hill to pass into the keeping of his murderers. Bony had felt the wind, heard it in the trees and in the grass. He had watched the lie swoop down from the sky, the lie which was a giant bird with a man's head. He had shrunk away from the evil of the bird's face, and he had thrilled as he watched the agony of the poisoned liars.

He was but half way from the white man toward these descendants of the ancient inhabitants. He heard, and saw the pictures, because he knew the story. Thus he could follow and interpret the sounds issuing from the dijeridoo. But when Canute told another story of which he was ignorant, the sounds were of no help, told him no story, but did create pictures of flat water, waving tobacco bush, wind stirring sand grains. The story was told and another begun, and he received pictures sometimes blurred, sometimes sharply clear, in rapid alternation.

He fancied, for it could have been nothing more than

fancy, that he saw a white man heavily burdened. The load he carried was larger than himself. Later, he saw a white man crawling on hands and knees. The noises from the hollow instrument filed past his ears, each one isolated. It was as though one laughed as it passed, another cried, another whispered something he couldn't hear. He saw a man, a slim man. His hair was black and straight. His face was pale. He was groping to identify this man and did identify him when he was struggling to look, as through fog, upon a child whose skin was white, and then was black, and in whose arms snuggled a spirit baby created by mirage water.

Another picture commanded his mind, stayed there for a fraction of a second, fled into the darkness behind his closed eyes. The flash picture was of a ghost, a woman running from him, and on her back a question mark.

And then he was following another remembered story, this time of two young aborigines who robbed the nest of an eagle and were captured by a dingo with an eagle's head, and who made them carry him because he had a burr in his foot.

The last note of a musical instrument is emphasised by the vacuum of silence, like the bottom of a well receiving a stone. When the sounds of the dijeridoo ceased, there was no silence, the minds of those listening continuing to hear what the ears no longer registered.

Bony could not be sure when the dijeridoo stopped, nor when he realised that it had done. On opening his eyes, he saw that Canute was rolling a cigarette, the dijeridoo was lying on the ground at his side, and the audience was still captive. He noted, too, that Meena was the first to be conscious of her surroundings, and immediately after her, a woman and a young man. Meena rose and soundlessly departed to the deeper shadow of a humpy before the others broke from the spell, and those closest in blood to the pure aborigine were the last to be released by Canute's 'art'.

Stepping round the trunk of the tree, Bony leaned against

it and brought fingers to work making a cigarette. Someone tossed wood into Ganba's red eye, and the initiated men moved nearer to Canute and his chief henchman, Murtee. Then Bony struck a match and applied the flame to his cigarette.

Those about the fire turned at the sound, save the Medicine Man and the Chief. Bony went forward, ebony images now frozen, waiting inscrutably. He passed round a right flank of them, and seated himself crosslegged when the Elders were directly to his front. Dark eyes reflected the firelight, not unlike black opals.

Bony smoked his cigarette, and not a word was said, nor a gesture made. It was as though they occupied one side of a gulf and could be reached only by him who had wings to fly. Slowly, Bony made another cigarette, and casually smoked that to the last half-inch, and still no word was spoken.

All of them, and there were seventeen, were in excellent physical condition, several being positively fat. Canute wore good cloth trousers and no shirt. Murtee wore a blue silk shirt, trousers and tennis shoes. Two were smoking good-quality pipes. Knowing he would have to attempt the flight, Bony spoke.

"You are Orrabunna men. I am Worcair man."

He knew his assessment of the degree of their nearness to the whites was accurate when Canute said:

"My mother was emu totem and my father was jerboa. I am emu man."

"My mother! I don't know her totem. My father was a white man. My other father is my brother and my son, my uncle and my grandfather. His name was Illawallie. He was head man of the Worcair. The marks of the Worcair are on me."

Canute stood, saying:

"Let me know with my hands."

Bony stood, removed his shirt, and the old man's fingers traced the cicatrices on his back and chest. Then his fingers

traced his features, and finally his hands to each fingertip. That being done, Bony resumed his shirt and they sat.

"Long time ago you sealed to Worcair people. Now you white-feller policeman," pronounced Canute. After a long silence he asked: "What you want from Orrabunna men?"

"Two spirit people made by Charlie and given to Linda Bell."

Canute again fell silent, and before Murtee spoke Bony knew that to the Medicine Man the buck had been passed.

Murtee stroked the thin grey beard falling from his lean face.

"Ole Fren Yorky and Meena have gone up to the sky. Mr Wootton and Missus Bell no good for sky. They make sky fall down."

"Who took them from the playhouse along at homestead?"

"Kurdaitcha Man. I look into little fire and Kurdaitcha Man tell me. Kurdaitcha Man and spirit Meena and Ole Fren Yorky, all go up into sky."

"Kurdaitcha Man liar, eh!" charged Bony. "Ole Fren Yorky go up into sky maybe, but Meena still here. What for Kurdaitcha Man not take Meena up into sky, but take Spirit Meena up into Sky?"

That was as far as he progressed. First Murtee and then Canute pushed him back over the gulf separating the two races, and began to treat him as a white visitor.

Murtee laughed as though amused. Canute chuckled mechanically. The other men smiled and joked among themselves. They wiggled their toes, bunched shoulders, scratched their arms. They occupied their side of the gulf, and Bony the side where stand the white men who actually believe the aborigines are ludicrous savages.

"What say you hand those dolls back to Mr Wootton to look after for Linda?" Bony suggested, and old Canute chuckled again and cheerfully denied any one of his people had taken them. Murtee shrugged, stroked his beard.

"Charlie's ole dolls not in this camp. The ole dolls belong to Linda. Perhaps some day Linda come back, then she want them," observed Murtee, laughing, without the slightest cause to laugh. Canute almost rolled over, such was his spurious front, and the others copied his lead. Bony laughed with them, making them uneasy because unsure if his merriment was real or mockery. Their faces grew swiftly serious when he leaned forward to the fire and withdrew several burning sticks, which he placed with flaming ends together, to form a separate fire.

Before this small fire he squatted, and across his bunched knees he rested a forearm, and with a metal tobacco box he rubbed his forehead, as though it were a magic churinga stone, before sinking his face to the forearm. They became distinctly uneasy, for Bony's spirit might well be about to leave his body and talk with the Kurdaitcha Man up in the sky. Murtee whispered, and Canute thus followed the act. Referring to the Medicine Man living near Boulia where he had but recently been on investigation, Bony lifted his head, saying:

"Boulia feller, called Eruki, he been tell me he told you long time ago I was coming to Mount Eden. So you been talking to Eruki up in the sky. What say you now talk to Ole Fren Yorky and tell him to bring Linda Bell back to Mount Eden? All you blackfellers good fellers. You all been looking for tracks. Now you sit down and talk magic, like you talk magic to Eruki. You send your spirit, Canute, and your spirit, Murtee, up into sky to talk with Kurdaitcha Man. Tell him to come down and into Ole Fren Yorky and make him bring Linda back."

They were again images, ebony images with opal flashing eyes. As he had confused five white men that morning, so now he left the black men equally confused. Rising to his feet, he stared down into each pair of flickering eyes, and then left the camp and passed into the wall of dark night.

If you cannot create a tree, plant a seed.

As soundlessly as he had approached the camp, he departed from it, and he had almost gained the road when a singular noise halted him. It was followed by another he could not tab, and, crouching to the ground to gain a skyline, he saw two figures under a low tree bordering the track. A man and a woman were facing each other. They were holding hands and swaying backward and forward like children playing.

Silhouetted against a dull screen, they were sharply etched nevertheless. The man freed the woman's hands and then thrust his hands forward, palms upward like cups. The cups touched the woman's breasts, and she lashed out and smacked the man's face. The man laughed, though the blow must have been painful, and then he sprang forward and clasped the woman, whose face was tilted to take his kisses.

Bony veered to the left, silently walked parallel with the track until he was sure his retreat was unobserved.

"Well, well, and well, well!" he breathed. "Romantic Byron! Who listens once will listen twice; her heart be sure is not of ice, and one refusal no rebuff."

CHAPTER 8

MUCH ADO ABOUT A BLOODSTAIN

THE FOLLOWING morning when Meena waited at the breakfast table, she placed the food before Wootton and Bony efficiently and with no trace of either nervousness or servility. Her large dark eyes never once met those of the guest, however, and yet there was no apparent avoidance, no revelation of consciousness of the visit to her camp. When she had departed for the kitchen Wootton asked:

"What's your programme today?"

"Oh, I have to contact Pierce," casually replied Bony. "First, though, I would like to talk with William Harte before he leaves for the day's work. You won't mind?"

"Not at all." Wootton brushed his moustache with his napkin. "As I said yesterday, anything any of us can do. Did you enquire about the missing dolls at the blacks' camp last night?"

It was a natural question, Bony having been absent from the homestead, and in view of the talk in the playhouse about the dolls.

"Yes, I did," he replied. "I talked to Canute and his Medicine Man. Put it to them straight about the dolls. They both said they knew nothing, and were sure no one of their people had stolen them."

"It must have been one of them, or one of us five white men," argued Wootton. "No one else has been around the place since Harte last saw the dolls on the bench. As someone said yesterday, Yorky could have come back for them, but that would have been rather risky for him, wouldn't it? Wouldn't the blacks have known?"

"Likely enough to both questions."

"Then you think the blacks know where Yorky is hiding out?"

"Yes and no to that one, Mr Wootton." Bony smiled disarmingly, adding, "You have not been long enough in this country to know that to hasten is to crawl, and to crawl is to hasten."

"But the child, Inspector."

"Her condition will not be bettered or worsened at this point. Permit me to ask the questions. Tell me, Mrs Bell was shot on February 7. Late that night the policeman and the doctor arrived. When was the body taken to Loaders Springs?"

"Next day. The doctor took it in his station wagon. She was buried at Loaders Springs."

"Did he leave before or after the aborigines came in the trucks sent for them?"

"He left after lunch, and the trucks didn't return till after sundown. Why all this?"

"Now, now! I ask the questions. Charlie carved the dolls' heads and tinted the faces. Who made the clothes?"

The cattleman frowned, obviously uncertain.

"Couldn't rightly say. Mrs Bell, I think. Might have been Meena. Shall I call her?"

"Please do."

Without rising, Wootton called, and the girl came, to stand placidly awaiting his orders.

"Meena, who made the clothes for Mr Wootton, Mrs Bell, and Ole Fren Yorky?"

"I did."

"All of them?"

They could see that Meena was wriggling her toes in her red shoes, although to them her feet were not visible. She giggled, and the small white teeth momentarily pressed down on the lower lip. In that moment she was remarkably attractive. She said:

"I didn't make Mr Wootton's trousers, or Ole Fren Yorky's. The ones I made, Linda didn't like because she couldn't take 'em off. So Mrs Bell made new ones that Linda could take off and put on."

"And what happened to the trousers you made?" asked Bony.

"I don't know what Linda did with them."

"Who stuffed the dolls' bodies?"

"Mrs Bell tried hard." Again Meena giggled—a delightful sound. "I did first. Then Linda tried. Then Mrs Bell had a go. Arnold did it in the end with sawdust in the carpenter's shop."

"And Charlie carved the heads, painted them, and put the hair and whiskers on the men?"

Meena's eyes rested steadily on Bony, who could then see the grey flecks in the dark irises. She nodded, and Bony buttered a piece of toast.

"Did he carve them when supposed to be working for Mr Wootton?"

"No. No time for anything when station work going on. He did them any old time."

"How much was he paid for them?"

This question brought a change of expression. Indignation gleamed in the dark eyes, shadowed the voice.

"Nothing at all. Charlie work for nothing . . . for Meena."

"Did them for nothing!" echoed Bony, and now the honey skin darkened, and once again came the joyous giggle.

"Well, I paid Charlie," she said. "I give him one kiss for Mr Wootton, one for Mrs Bell, and one for Ole Fren Yorky. Not till he done them and gave them to Linda."

"Oh! And how many kisses did you pay for Meena?"

"Why you want to know? But I'll tell. I'm not scared. I let him kiss me twice for Meena, 'cos he worked double as hard on her."

"When are you going to marry that feller?" asked Wootton, and Bony was surprised by the firmness in his voice.

"I belong to old Canute," replied Meena, swift rebellion in her eyes and voice.

"Rubbish! Young woman like you unclaimed because of that stupid old custom."

It was a pity that Wootton said that, because it banished the girl's natural frankness, and reverted her to the normal evasiveness of the aborigines, whose greatest weapon, as with all, is laughter. To further questions, Meena answered with giggles which were not the genuine reflection of her mood, and presently Wootton dismissed her.

"Can't make her out," he complained to Bony. "Good-looking wench like that. Any white man could have done worse than marry her. I'd marry her myself if I'd half the chance."

"You are not married?"

"Was. Been a widower for fourteen years. Joking, of

course. Those Indian Summers I read about once don't work out. Besides . . ."

"Go on," urged Bony, laughing. "An Indian Summer could be an improvement on Hoary Winter."

"Not for me. I know what the heat's like. I lived in hell for twenty-two years. I know all about temperatures. Well, I'd better go along and give the men their orders. I'll tell Bill to wait about for you."

Wootton left by one of the two pairs of french windows, and Bony dallied on at table, sipping coffee and smoking.

He wasn't happy about Wootton. He was an odd man out in this setting of Lake Eyre. He was like a newly cut diamond in an old-fashioned gold ring, and what was that saying about new wine in old bottles . . . exploding? Five years he had been in this country, and he wasn't assimilated by it as fully as some immigrants in much less time. It could be a streak of pomposity. He would dig into the background.

There was the question of Mrs Bell's body. Rising, he crossed to the chair under the wall telephone and called for Constable Pierce.

"You, Inspector!" Pierce said from Loaders Springs. "Yes, sir, what can I do? Run out there to report?"

"Perhaps. I have the copies of your reports and the statements, and I am edging myself into the picture. I am speaking softly in order not to be overheard. You hear me all right?"

"Quite clear, sir."

"You have still in your possession the plaster casts you took of Yorky's tracks?"

"Yes, a copy. The originals, and the bullet from the body, I sent down to Adelaide."

"When first you saw the body it was in the woman's room?"

"Yes, on the bed."

"Did you touch the body? Then or subsequently?"

"No. Dr Crouch was with me."

"Could you fetch Dr Crouch to your phone?"

"Expect so. Shall I send for him?"
"Yes, do. I'll hold the line. See that I'm not cut off."
Bony was waiting when Meena came in with her clearing tray, and Bony waved her out. He left the instrument for the few seconds necessary to cross to the door and close it, and smiled at the picture of Meena's face. He hadn't long to wait before a deep voice spoke.
"Dr Crouch speaking, Inspector."
"Ah! Good morning, doctor! I won't keep you long. Recall to mind, please, what happened on your arrival here. You found the body of Mrs Bell in her room. Who was with you?"
"Pierce and Wootton."
"Finding the woman obviously dead, you turned the body over to examine the wound, I presume. Who was then with you in the room?"
"I told Pierce the woman was dead. Wootton looked ill. I asked Pierce to take Wootton away. He did so. No one was with me when I examined the body. You make me curious."
"I'll satisfy your curiosity one day, doctor. Meanwhile, be patient with me. You found the body lying on its back under a sheet?"
"Yes."
"How did you leave the body at the termination of the examination? I mean position."
"On its back . . . under the sheet as I found it."
"Later that day it was removed to your station wagon. Who conveyed the body to the car?"
"I don't know, Inspector. I gave orders for it to be transferred from the house to the car."
"Tell me this. To examine the bullet wound in the woman's back you had to cut away the clothing?"
"Yes."
"Tell me just what you did do."
A little impatiently, Crouch described how he had with scissors cut the white linen blouse from the back of the neck

to the band of the skirt. The wound was such that it wasn't necessary at that time to examine the body further for secondary wounds, as the wound between the shoulders was obviously fatal. And Dr Crouch was by now even more curious. Suavely, Bony asked him to stand by to permit Pierce access to the telephone. To Pierce he said:

"When you first saw the body, Wootton was with you. What exactly did you do? Don't tell me what the doctor did. I know."

"Well, I entered the room, having been informed by Bray that Mrs Bell's body was there. The doctor was with me, and so was Mr Wootton. I turned down the sheet to establish the fact that the body was actually there on the bed. Mr Wootton gave a sort of moan, and Dr Crouch told me to take him out. Which I did."

"The body was lying . . . in what position?"

"On its back, Inspector."

"No other person entered the room while the doctor was there?"

"No; Wootton sat on a chair in the hall, and I was with him."

"Now we come to the removal of the body to the doctor's car. Who supervised that task?"

"I did. I had Arnold Bray and Eric Maundy with me."

"What did you do?"

"Well, the body was under the sheet again," Pierce said with slight stoicism. "I tucked the top sheet about the body, and turned up the edges of the under sheet about the body, and the men carried it out."

"No one of you three men saw the body?"

"No. It was as I said. No one looks at a body unless he has to."

"That'll be all for the moment, Pierce. Come out today. Better make it for lunch. I'll tell Wootton you'll be here."

"I'll be there, sir."

"Good! And bring those plaster casts."

Bony left by the window, and, crossing the square, found

William Harte on the narrow veranda of the quarters. Harte was attaching a new silk cracker to his stock-whip, and his bright eyes gleamed with shrewd expectancy at Bony's approach. Having seen Arnold in the open motor shed, and the other two stockmen riding from the yards, Bony knew that he had Harte to himself, and, nodding the day's greeting, he leaned against the veranda rail, and fell to rolling the inevitable cigarette.

"How long have you been in this Lake Eyre country?" was his opening.

"All me life. Was born away over on Clifton Hills."

"You must know it well," conceded Bony. "Is there any shadow of doubt in your mind that those tracks behind the meat-house were made by Yorky?"

The bright eyes became mere dark spots in the leathery face.

"If them tracks were imitations, then they were ruddy good, Inspector. You're raisin' the doubts, not me. I don't think . . ."

"Supposing I told you that those tracks hadn't been left by Yorky, would you gamble your way?"

Harte took time before replying:

"No, I don't think I would, Inspector. Not now."

"Even though Wootton saw Yorky at the blacks' camp that morning? Knew he was to head this way?"

The slow grin twitching the corners of the man's mouth supported the shrewdness Bony had already attributed to him.

"I'd say Yorky made 'em, but I wouldn't do no betting on it. There wasn't enough of those particular tracks to make me bet me shirt they was made by Yorky."

"We'll leave it, Bill. Another matter. You saw Mrs. Bell's body lying on the ground near the house. Can you recall the size and shape of the bloodstain on her blouse?"

"Too right. I won't forget that ever. The crows had made a mess of her neck and shoulders, but the blouse wasn't torn."

Dark brown eyes and deep blue eyes held steady for a long moment.

"Between ourselves," Bony asked, slowly.

"It's your hand," agreed Harte.

"Draw me a picture of that bloodstain."

Harte crouched to the earth floor of the veranda and with the point of his clasp knife granted the request.

CHAPTER 9

TO RUN IS TO CRAWL

CONSTABLE PIERCE came, lunched with Wootton and Bony, teased Meena and complimented Sarah, and after two hours in conference with Bony, departed for Loaders Springs. The journey homeward seemed to him of short duration, so much was his mind occupied by impressions which confounded all preconceptions of the man he had met.

Bony was waiting in the shade of the ridge pine trees for the men to come in from the duties assigned to them that morning. He could see them, stringing down the background slopes, riding tired and thirsty horses, and he watched them free their mounts to drink or take a sand-bath. In addition to the four white men there were now four aborigines. There was no fraternising, the aborigines taking buckets to the reservoir tanks and washing in readiness for dinner.

Pierce had left food for thought as well as the plaster casts duplicating those he had sent down to Adelaide. Bony had gathered much to add to the policeman's tersely written reports, especially material assisting him to fill in mere sketches of people and places.

Now Old Fren Yorky stood clear to Bony, who had never seen him. Pierce had revealed the man in a light less shadowed than he had been in a report of a murder suspect,

for the policeman living in a small community is able to be far less isolated than when he lives in a large community. The few are neighbours; the many animated units.

Pierce had been stationed at Loaders Springs for eleven years. He was able to say that Yorky was well behaved when in town, and this opinion was not affected by Yorky's weaknesses, one being that although he had a room at the hotel, he could be found sleeping on the bench outside, and on two occasions in winter had been discovered sleeping in a station cell.

Bony was informed of matters he would not without necessity enter into a report. He said that the previous owners of Mount Eden were confident that Meena, Sarah's daughter, was begotten by Yorky. He said, too, that long before he came to Loaders Spring, Yorky had been a participant in several brawls, and he drew the picture of a man who, although of small physique, had been dynamite in his prime. People are so apt to see a man as he is, and forget what he was.

It is obvious that a man in Pierce's situation would have opinions and theories which he could not reveal to a superior unless asked to do so. And Bony had seldom found co-operation withheld by such as Constable Pierce, who found pleasure in giving it.

"There's men who tease Yorky about his height," Pierce had said. "Tales told about him like this one. Yorky carried a swag bigger than himself, and once when he was walking to Loaders with a swag up, he passed right through the place because he couldn't see it for the swag! There's another story of him being in a crowded bar all evening, and towards closing time a feller said to him: 'Hullo, Yorky! Haven't seen you in years!' And Yorky said he'd been standing before him for the last two hours.

"So what have we? A wisp of a man who once could fight his way out from under a heap of he-men, and had become old and conscious of his loss of physical strength. A little man always resentful of chipping about his size. Of

late years he had to bottle up what at one time had been released with fists and boots. Gradually he turned more to the aborigines and farther from the whites. He could have resented something Wootton said quite innocently, or something said by the men, even something said or not done by Mrs Bell. They're all agin' him. So he decided to steal something loved by everyone . . . young Linda. And when Mrs Bell stepped into it, he killed her."

"Tell me about the men. Anything against them?" Bony had asked, and Pierce had replied:

"Nothing much. Young Lawton's been in trouble once or twice. Fights over the young lubras, chiefly. The last time Canute complained about him, I told Lawton that if it happened again I would advise Canute to sool all his bucks on to him and compel him to leave the district. Once I had to serve a summons on Bray for not complying with the Taxation Regulations, and Bill Harte took to a couple of roughs passing through town who held him up for money." Pierce chuckled. "You should have seen them. Crouch had to nurse 'em for a couple of days before he could turn them loose."

"Ah! Dr Crouch!"

"Yair. A character. Three-bottles-of-whisky-per-day man. Bets on flies crawling up a window. Tall, powerful man with a grouch agin' the Government, no matter what government. And is such a doctor that, did I arrest him, the entire district would set out to tar and feather me."

"And Wootton, Pierce?"

"Told me he'd been a general storekeeper in New South. Came to Australia forty-odd years ago. Made good. Married and had two sons. Both of them joined the Army, and both were killed in action. That killed the wife. Wootton wanted to be a pastoralist, always wanted to be the big landowner, so he sold his business and bought Mount Eden."

"And Mrs Bell?"

"Nice little woman. Wootton engaged her through an agency in Adelaide. We found out that her husband had

left her a couple of years before. My wife liked her. But then my wife likes everyone. She lets out my prisoners sometimes if they spin a good tale, and I've got to go after 'em and bring them in again."

So, over to Bony. The Law had had no troubles worth telling with Canute and his people. Canute and several of the elders, including Murtee, wore clothes but were almost as distant from white influence as are the wild abos. The younger people, like Meena and Charlie and Rex, were civilised and reasonably well educated, thanks to the Missioner, but nevertheless were rigidly controlled by their Elders.

Although it was now late and Sarah would ring the dinner gong any minute, the afternoon continued hot and still. The crows were waking into activity, and Bony idly watched three of them coming from across the lake while he continued to ponder on the character sketches presented by Constable Pierce. A willi-willi, red and dense and powerful, its column of dust and debris revolving at terrific speed, marched down the western dunes to the lake. Lake Eyre refused to feed it. It first cut off the willi's feet, then its legs, then masticated the swaying body, working upward until only the head was left wagging stupidly a thousand yards high.

Here, in this land, to run was to crawl. In this land, the ancient legends were reality; the lake was dead, but the surrounding land was sleeping under the hot sun, waiting for the water to return and transform its dust into verdancy.

Another night came to comfort men as a cloak for the naked, and when another day dawned, Bony was astride his horse and travelling northward from Mount Eden.

He followed the cement-hard white beach, flanked on one side by embankments of red sand, and on the other by the sea of rusty mud. Here and there the tracks of cattle told where animals had ventured on to the mud a few yards to lick the salt from its crust. He came at long intervals to the mouth of an ancient river, or to the lip of an inlet. The

land constantly changed for him; the sea of mud never. The only thing lacking in this picture was water. Given water to hide the mud, to cool the breeze, this beach could be named Crescent Parade, and this one ahead Little Cove, and the one traversed a natural for a Nudist Colony.

When Yorky with the child had left Mount Eden, he would have kept to this iron-hard shore, knowing that even the aborigines could not track them, and knowing, too, that he would have to step from it at some place or other, and that the aborigines would know that as well. He had certainly won a remarkable victory. He would have been guided by the Universal Controller of Life, Water.

Bony found no sand-soakage in the creek beds. Once he walked out on the mud, when his feet sank ankle-deep into it, and with a digging stick he holed down to the clay bed, and found no seepage.

Towards sundown he saw ahead a line of dots extending on to the lake. The dots grew to black columns, collapsed to become a row of drunken aborigines, and finally became fence posts, extending for a mile out, and the fence must have been hastily erected years back, following the swift slaughter of this inland sea. However, near the 'coast' new wires had been strung to keep Mount Eden cattle within the boundary, for this was the boundary fence once patrolled by Ole Fren Yorky, and which Bony now determined to follow, to examine Yorky's camps.

This night he spent beside a small iron hut near a bore. There was a gate here giving egress to the unfenced country to the north. Inside the hut were several thirty-gallon oil tanks now containing weevilly flour, and small tins of tea and sugar, matches and plug tobacco, light rope, tar in bottles, and kerosene in a tin; without doubt a camelman's camp.

The following night Bony spent at another of Yorky's camps, this time a three-sided shed constructed with tree branches, and situated on the bank of a creek where water lay a foot deep above coarse sand. Long after the water had disappeared, it could be obtained by digging.

At neither of these two camps was there sign of human visitors. Bony had seen no human tracks beside the netted fence. He had observed no smoke signals, no suspicious movement amid the prevailing mirage, which hemmed him all day long.

Next morning, the first warning stirred the hairs at the back of his neck. During the afternoon he was convinced that he was being followed. And when he camped again at one of Yorky's old camps he was elated by this first evidence since he began this investigation, of the sand dune coming to him.

It was the third night from the homestead, and he slept in a single blanket on a claypan some hundred yards from the glowing embers of the camp fire. He was undisturbed, and started the following day before sun-up, keeping to the fence, his destination the next watering place but a mile from the road to Loaders Springs, the fence having followed a great arc.

At noon he was still being trailed, and knew that the tracker was keeping several miles behind him. It was unnecessary for the tracker to see what he did, where he went, for the tracks left by his horses, and his own when he dismounted, would be easily read.

In a city, of course, you slip around a corner and wait to see who comes after you. But how to deal with an Australian sleuth who maintains his distance from you by many miles?

On coming to a mile-wide flat bearing nothing but foot-high tussock grass, Bony decided to wait for the tracker beyond the low sand ridges on the far side.

As anticipated, the terrain was suitable. He tethered his horses on a patch of wild rye amid a small area of wait-a-bit and box trees, and himself lay at ease in the shade cast by a cotton bush. Before him was the flat, gently pulsating in the ground mirage. He could see the opposing ridges over which he had crossed to ride down to the flat.

An eagle came low to prospect him and the horses. He waved a hand to tell the bird there was nothing dead, and

the eagle soared aloft to continue its eternal aerial patrol. Bony was lucky that the crows hadn't followed him from the last camp, and that no others had yet taken up their espionage.

It is ever an advantage to know what the enemy knows and does not know. The tracker knew that Bony was travelling from one of Yorky's water camps to the next. Therefore, he would not know that Bony was now waiting for him. On the other hand, he would not know if Bony decided to deviate, chose to make temporary camp to brew tea, or take a nap, and so he would proceed with extreme caution, and when coming to the first flat he would watch for signs that his quarry could be lingering just beyond it.

As usual at this time, the day was hot, and humidity low, the shade temperature at the distant homestead being in the vicinity of 120 degrees. There was no wind, and against the golden-dusted sky individual clouds were born, grew to giants, dwindled to dwarfs and died. They first appeared as white dots, swiftly extending, thus creating great shadows laden with cool air, and bringing about the disturbances fashioning the strictly local windstorms called willi-willies.

The favoured march of the willi-willies is from north to south, and they were travelling this line, not many being in sight at the same time, seldom more than three. One passed close to Bony, whipping his hair and drying the perspiration on his face. It moved with steady speed at about thirty miles an hour, whirling sand and debris upward into its red body, roaring like a beast when passing over scrub. Yet another halted on the flat, performed a jig, rocked as if about to collapse with fatigue, finally became thrice in size and reached high speed as though a living thing.

What with the heat, the sticky flies, the eagles and the willi-willies, Bony was left with no cause for boredom. With the patience of his maternal ancestors, he waited, and was beginning to believe he would still be waiting the next day when a feminine willi-willi came tripping to the distant sand ridges. She paused there, seemingly shrinking from the

open space, a little fearful of venturing farther. Then, mustering courage, she advanced cautiously.

Wisps of dead grass and herbage formed her feet, shimmered her red gown with gold to the waist. Her slim body rose to several hundred feet, swaying gently in a swooning waltz as she proceeded. A gambler here would be in paradise, for he could back his hunch without taking into account pulled horses or stacked cards, and Bony was backing this willi-willi to pass on his left, when the unpredictable happened.

As they are conceived by a gentle eddy, so the willies die in an eddy. This one began to die when but a hundred yards from Bony. Something gross and unsporting punched her in the tummy, but she staggered onward in increasing tempo as though striving to keep up with the orchestra.

Bony betted she wouldn't reach his side of the flat, and won. Suddenly she lost her feet, and lifted her skirt as though to cover her shamed head.

Absorbed in the fate of the female, he saw not the male, for there was Charlie racing to cover, he having almost crossed the flat in the centre of a revolving column of sand.

CHAPTER 10

IN EFFORT TO TRADE

BETRAYED BY the willi-willi, Charlie gained the nearest cover at Olympic speed, ending the spring with a dive for Bony's cotton bush.

Following the dieting of the walkabout to the Neales River, Charlie had fattened on Sarah's white-man tucker, and was now in excellent condition, his arms and legs of Grecian proportions, his tummy less to be admired. All he wore was a pair of dark-brown shorts; his only equipment a

hessian bag subsequently found to contain a small calico bag of tea and a gnawed leg of fire-charred kangaroo. On coming to rest under the cotton bush, his head was within fifteen inches of Bony's head. When their gaze clashed, Bony said, mildly:

"Good day-ee, Charlie! Are you travelling?"

Charlie grinned, genuine humour associated with astonishment in his black eyes.

"Day-ee, Mr Bonaparte. Bit hot in the sun, eh?" Then realisation of the situation smote him and he shrank away without thought of the sunlight burning his feet beyond the bush. "Crikey! This your bush, eh? I'll get going."

"We go together," purred Bony, standing with Charlie. "We have much to talk about, and three miles' travel to the next camp. We go that way, to my horses."

Charlie found dislike of the hard blue eyes and of the automatic directed to his stomach, and ultimately disliked the hard smile on Bony's face. He was ordered to unhitch the pack-horse and lead it to Yorky's next camp, and on glancing backward now and then, it was to see Bony mounted, the pistol in his right hand. Escorted occasionally by an indifferent willi-willi, they moved over the flats and the low sand ridges, through the swamp gums, across dry creek beds and narrower gutters, to arrive at a bough shed erected beside a lake of shallow water maintained by a bore half a mile away.

Here Bony told Charlie to remove the load from the pack-horse. Then with his left hand he unstrapped one of the pack-bags and took from it a pair of handcuffs. They were not of the kind Charlie had seen previously, which are manacles rather than wrist-cuffs. Still, he knew their purpose, and he offered no resistance. The heavy pack-saddle was lifted into the shade of the bough shed, and then, before he understood what was going on, one of the cuffs was unlocked from a wrist and re-locked to the iron structure of the pack-saddle. Thus he had one hand free with which to protect his face from the flies, and if he wanted to run, well,

the saddle went with him, and he wouldn't run far and never fast.

Save for its proximity to water, the camp site was unsatisfactory, open to the westerlies, unprotected from the dusty ground churned by the hoofs of nomadic cattle. Although brackish, the water was good enough for tea if taken with plenty of sugar, and the closer to the bore, so was the water more heavily laden with alklai, hot almost to boiling point at the mouth of the L-shape iron outlet pipe. Day and night gushed the water from the depths, year after year since the bore was put down.

Bony made tea, gave Charlie a pannikin of it, opened a tin of beef for each of them. He tossed the charred kangaroo leg to the already gathered crows, and then when they were smoking and the sun had gone down, he began the interrogation.

"You're a rotten tracker, Charlie. Too much Mission learning, eh? You learn to read and write, but you're no tracker."

"I followed you all the way from Mount Eden, anyway," reminded Charlie, cheerfully, and yet with wariness in his eyes. "I done no wrong. Free country. Mr Wootton go crook when he knows about this." He raised his cuffed wrist, and for the first time anger glowed. "I got my School Certificate, like Meena and the others. I'll write to the Chief Protector of Aborigines in Adelaide."

"Do that, Charlie," Bony said kindly. "Ask him to call on you in jail. You see, Charlie, I'm a terrible liar. I'm the worst liar you ever met. I may—it will depend on you—arrest you and put you up on a charge of interfering with a police officer in the execution of his duty, obstructing the police, assaulting a police officer, taking unlawful refuge inside a willi-willi, and several other matters I could think of."

"You got to prove all that."

Charlie was as yet unimpressed, because his respect for Constable Pierce was due to that policeman's tolerance,

and also to the result of a little learning and association with a Missioner. Evil white men hadn't entered his ken. On the opposite side, Bony knew all too well that you cannot abstract with violence information from an unwilling aborigine. He was sure that Charlie hadn't tracked him of his own volition, that he had been ordered to do so, and most likely was instructed not to divulge who issued the order.

"You know Constable Pierce, Charlie," Bony went on. "Some other place boss policeman over Constable Pierce, and some other place bigger boss policeman. Now I am a Big Chief policeman. I'm like Chief Canute. What I say goes. I tell lies about you and everyone believes me, not you. You tell the judge I'm a big-feller liar, and he'll add six months more jail. I say you did all these things, and you go to jail for three years. Better for you to tell me where Yorky is, and then instead of jail Constable Pierce will make you his tracker."

"Sez you," scoffed Charlie, and Bony was dismayed because Charlie now appeared to be more sophisticated than he had thought.

"You must have been to the pictures," he said.

"Too right! Down at Loaders Springs. Us Mission abos was allowed by the Missioner every Sat'day night. Took us to town in his truck. We seen Bob Mitchum and Gary Cooper and all them."

"You astonish me, Charlie. The cinema on Saturday night and hiding in a willi-willi on Sunday morning. Singing in church on Sunday evening, and pointing the bone on Monday afternoon. Still, you'll be seeing films in jail once every month, and singing songs when locked in a nice cold cell all night. And, Charlie, while you're in jail, do you know what will happen?"

"What?"

"Some other aborigine is going to take Meena."

With boosted confidence, Charlie countered with:

"Meena belongs to Canute. No blackfeller can take Meena."

"But you tried, Charlie. I saw you the other night. She slapped your face, and then let you kiss her. She let you kiss her twice when you made the doll of her and gave it to Linda. I know you like Meena. I know that she likes you, too. But you're afraid, aren't you? You're afraid of old Canute. You know that if you run away with Meena, the bucks will track you and catch you, and you will be speared, and Meena's knees will be broken so that she can't run away another time."

The scenting nostrils were flaring, for love and desire are not the prerogatives of the white man. Almost dreamily, Bony went on talking.

"You want to marry Meena, Charlie, and old Canute say: 'No, you don't. Meena's my woman. I got her when she was a baby. I bought her from her father.' D'you know who Meena's father was?"

Charlie frowned, then shook his head.

"Does Sarah know?"

Now Charlie grinned, saying:

"She'd know nothing like that for sure."

"Then who did Canute get Meena from when she was born? I don't think Meena was promised to Canute ever. I think it's a yarn. Having visited the white man's halls of culture called 'the pictures', you'll have heard the word 'sucker' and will know just what it means. You, Charlie, Sucker Charlie.

"Long time ago, and when I look back I'm astonished how far back on my tracks it was, I met my Meena," continued Bony, and instantly Charlie's interest was increased. "My Meena was lovely and soft and warm, just like your Meena could be for you. But my Meena made out she didn't want me. You know, let me kiss her on the tip of her nose and only that. You know what these Meenas are, I'm sure.

"Well, a long time went by, and I only ever got as far as kissing my Meena on the tip of her nose. Then one day the Missioner came, and I asked him straight if he'd marry me

to my Meena. When he said 'Yes,' I grabbed my Meena and ran her to the Missioner, and he read out the words, and when he asked me if I would, I said, 'Yes,' and when he asked my Meena if she would, and she wouldn't answer, I pinched her bottom till she did. D'you know what I did then?"

Celibate Charlie was caught.

"I dragged my Meena away from the Mission, and away from the camp, and soon she didn't have to be dragged any more. She ran with me, and presently we came to a creek. Beside the creek was a great place where tobacco bush grew all round a billabong, and among the bush were ducks laying eggs, and waterhens mating, and ibis standing in the water catching silver bream. Then I made a humpy of bush and gathered leaves to make the ground soft and warm. And d'you know what, Charlie?"

"What?" pressed the entranced Charlie.

"Why, now I've got one son who's a doctor missioner away up in Queensland, and two more sons as well. Of course, you won't have any sons, and you won't have any Meena in a nice warm humpy. Because you'll be in jail. That's if you won't tell me what I want to know. Then what? Why, Meena will be looking for Charlie, and Charlie will be locked up in jail, and then she'll come to thinking she'd like to have babies, and some other blackfeller will be waiting for her, and he won't be so silly as to make me lock him up in jail."

By no means without imagination, Charlie pictured his Meena in the arms of a rival while he himself languished in durance vile. He had never been in a whitefeller's jail, but he knew there were no women in them, and once there he couldn't go on walkabout whenever inherited instincts commanded.

Seated on the ground, he rested his back against the pack-saddle, and by bringing his free hand close to the cuffed one, he managed to roll a cigarette and strike a match. It was almost dark, but the air was still heated by the

hot earth. The stars were dancing their summer jig. A wedge of ducks whirred low, decided that the artificial lake was too small, and sped upward and away into the profound silence. Now and then Bony fed the small fire from Yorky's reserve woodpile, and the reflection of the lazy flames shimmered upon both faces, framing them within the shape of the bough shed.

Wise in the ways of the bush and its inhabitants, yet Bony was tricked. He had thought it possible that Charlie would be tracking him in company with a mate, but as the hours passed, and as Charlie had evinced no confidence in rescue, Bony dismissed the thought. His mind being intent on manœuvring Charlie into a mood of co-operation at least, and full confession at most, he was unaware of the stalker.

And, as it turned out, so was Charlie.

Bony's task was not an easy one. He could meet a white man and know exactly how to deal with him. He could have met a wild black man and would have known how to deal with him too. In either case, a matter of plain psychology based on the race and character of the subject. Although Charlie was a pure-blooded aborigine, he was a complex being, occupying a place between the wild aborigine and his inhibitions and superstitions, and the fully civilised aborigines who in many districts near the cities of Australia are justly entitled to 'Mister' and 'Missus'.

Therefore: how much was Charlie influenced by Canute and the Elders supporting the chief, and how much by the Missioner and Mr Wootton and Constable Pierce? Bony believed that by placing Charlie midway between these two groups, then moving him half way to the left towards Canute and his Elders, he would have Charlie correctly positioned.

"I tell you something, Charlie," he said, when Charlie gave no sign of co-operation. "Suppose you say you are my friend. Then I can't tell old Canute how you made a mess of tracking me, and I won't say anything about that to anyone else. Then all the lubras and the little gins won't laugh

like hell at you. So we say nothing about that, and you tell me why you been tracking me, eh?"

Charlie mutely shook his head, with a faint sign of reluctance, and Bony added to the bribe.

"Suppose I tackle old Canute, Charlie. Suppose I tell him I know he and Murtee been pointing the bone, and that I'll have them put into jail for it. Who did they point the bone at last time?"

"Dunno," replied Charlie. "Perhaps it was at old Moses over on Titigi. Perhaps it was up on the Neales. Anyhow, old Moses he died pretty quick."

"That's it," agreed Bony. "Well, I tell Canute he and Murtee pointed the bone at Moses. Old Moses died. That's murder, Charlie. So I tell Canute like this. I say: 'Look you, Canute, old feller, you're too old to take Meena, and Charlie loves Meena, and Meena loves Charlie, and they want to be married by the Missioner, all straight and square." Then old Canute he say: 'You go to hell. I got Meena when she was born. Meena's my woman.' And I say: 'All right, Canute, then you go off to jail for all your life. I know you murdered old Moses by pointing the bone at him, and I'll tell the white-feller judge all about it. Then you'll be hung.

" 'Now I'll tell you what, you silly old coot. You let Charlie have Meena, him being a young feller and able to look after her, and I'll say nothing about you pointing the bone at Moses.' " Bony smiled at Charlie, and Charlie was seeing a little of the light of common sense. "Do we trade?"

"No," countered someone behind Bony. "You take that thing off Charlie's wrist. Go on, take it off."

Swiftly Bony turned. He found himself looking into the barrel of his own automatic. The barrel was wavering, and the safety catch was still on. Above the hand holding the pistol was the face of Canute's Meena.

CHAPTER II

BONY'S GUESTS

ACCORDING TO persons who are brought to trial for murder, guns go off of themselves, and quite often a jury actually believes it. Anyone who has the slightest acquaintance with firearms knows that you must pull the trigger to discharge such a weapon, and to do that you have to curl a finger about the trigger. Still fewer people appear to understand that many types of firearms are fitted with a safety device, and that if the safety catch is in position no amount of trigger-pulling will bring about the desired explosion.

When Meena pointed the automatic pistol at Bony, it was instantly obvious that either she was ignorant of this type of weapon or had no intention of permitting it to go off of itself and commit murder. Her wide eyes and stern mouth, although presenting a new facet of her dark beauty, warned Bony that he was fortunate that the weapon she held was not a waddy, for waddies are also claimed to rise and fall of themselves, but are much less lethal.

"Why, Meena!" he exclaimed. "What a pleasant surprise."

"You loose that Charlie," she commanded. "Go on! I'll count three, and then . . ." threatened Meena.

Lazily Bony turned to one side and took the cuff key from his side pocket. Tossing it to Meena's feet he said:

"You loose him. I'm tired."

Her left hand went down for the key, and from a crouching position she knelt, and on her knees made the short journey to Charlie. Arrived at the saddle and his imprisoned wrist, she put the pistol on the ground, and the next instant it was whisked away by Bony. Meena was up on her feet, enraged and shouting, and the pistol was pointing at her. Her shouting faded to a whimper of fury, when Bony said:

"You must never place a delicate weapon like a pistol on the dusty ground. Look at all the dust and sand on it. I'll have to spend half an hour cleaning it. Now you free Charlie, then put more wood on the fire and boil the billy for tea. And don't let the sand get into those handcuffs. Put them into the pack-bag, and give me the key before you lose it. Women!" Charlie stood, perplexed as was Meena, and Bony went on:

"Sit down again, Charlie, and roll a cigarette. We have a cook now, remember. She makes the tea."

From staring at each other, they stared at Bony, who was squinting down the barrel of the pistol as though the weapon was his most precious possession. Then Charlie grunted and the tableau ended by the man sitting down and the girl looking about for the billycan.

"What d'you think of my plan to tackle old Canute?" nonchalantly enquired Bony. "Ought to make him come to heel and give you Meena. In fact, I'll guarantee that it does. Or else, Charlie. Or else he goes to jail."

Charlie grunted again, and looked at Meena. She had placed the filled billycan against the red fire coals and was standing and gazing at the flames in obvious amazement. Unconsciously she was now Bony's firm ally in the scheme to soften Charlie. She wore only a pair of shorts, dark blue in colour and an admirable fit. Silhouetted against the firelight, her figure was tantalising, her naked breasts, her slim neck, her profile and the crown of curly hair all totalling the love call to Man. It stirred even Bony.

Charlie, although young, possessed wisdom. Negatively he shook his head and winked, thus advising 'no see' tactics. The girl continued to watch the flames, and Bony began to hum a tune and apply himself industriously to the pistol-cleaning. The water in the billy boiled, and the girl dropped a handful of leaves into it, then lifting the billy with a short stick under its handle, she set it down to cool, and turned to look at the two men.

"Charlie, stir yourself and open a tin of meat for Meena,"

ordered Bony. "Come and sit down, Meena, and let Charlie look after you. You must be hungry and thirsty."

Charlie scrambled off to obey, and Meena sank to the soft earth, sat tailor-wise, and looked at Bony as though he were the man that never was. Carefully, Bony wrapped the pistol in the rag.

"I should not have left this on the blanket roll behind me. It might have gone off when you picked it up, Meena. I don't like pistols. Dangerous things to handle. How did you know that Charlie and I were camped here?"

"Tracked you easy enough," boasted Meena. "Saw where you caught Charlie just off the flat and made him lead the pack-horse." She accepted the opened tin of meat from Charlie without looking at him, and when he brought her a pannikin of tea, still she ignored him. "You're a cunning feller, Mr Bonaparte. You catch Charlie like he was a little gin."

"He had bad luck, Meena. You see, he was crossing that flat inside a willi-willi, and just before the willi got to my side it fell apart, and there he was in the open. Very nearly tricked me. I've heard of it being done, but not seen it before, and I've never tried it. What's it like, Charlie, inside?"

"All right," chuckled Charlie. "Air's clear. Sand rushing round and round that fast you can just see out. Meena's done it. I watched her. That time she went along good till the willi went faster and faster, and she run and run to keep with it, and then she fell down, and there she was."

"And here she is," added Bony. "Who were you tracking, Meena? Charlie or me?"

"Charlie? What for you track Mr Bonaparte? Go on, you tell. I saw you start after him at the homestead, and I said to Sarah I'd find out for why."

Charlie was now an ebony image. The firelight on the girl's face and body was reflected as from gold dust. That she was famished for food and drink was plain, and Bony sought information.

"You have been on Charlie's tracks for three days, Meena?"

She nodded, and continued to glare at Charlie.

"And no tucker?"

Still glaring at Charlie, impatiently she shook her head. To her lover she said:

"You're a cunning feller, too, but not properly cunning. I heard what Mister Bonaparte said he'd do to Canute about me, and I seen you go all softy-softy thinking about it. You're going to say what Mister Bonaparte wants, and you're not going to get me off of Canute for doing it, see?"

Charlie looked embarrassed, and began pouring sand from one hand to the other. He employed the old, old stratagem of laughing to cover up, and Meena threw the meat tin with deadly aim, the tin smashing into Charlie's mouth.

"But Charlie is happy, Meena. He and I were having a little talk before you butted in."

Blood showed on the man's lips where the jagged edge of the tin had connected. He licked off the blood and stood, for now primitive man was set upon his dignity, and primitive woman was to pay forfeit. Perhaps.

"Before you begin, put more wood on the fire," Bony requested calmly.

"I'll do that," roared Charlie, and Meena yelled: "And I will, too."

"All right, but don't put all of Yorky's woodpile on," Bony shouted.

They calmed, both panting less from exertion than from consuming anger, and they regarded Bony, who still reclined at ease on the warm earth. The look in his eyes probably reminded them of the Missioner, and something of the Missioner's teaching, for with downcast eyes Meena dropped her load of wood and returned to sit close to Bony, to torment Charlie, rather than for protection, of which she wished none. The lover flung his wood on the flames, which quickly grew, and sullenly he sat down with his back to the saddle.

"Now we are together again," murmured Bony, "let us be at peace and talk friendly. True, Meena, that you tracked Charlie to find out why he tracked me?"

"That's right." From the pocket of her shorts she took a tin, from which she produced tobacco and papers and began making a cigarette. He waited, and then leaned forward to offer the flame. She leaned nearer to bring the cigarette to the match, and smiled provocatively at Charlie.

"And why have you been tracking me?" Bony hurriedly demanded of Charlie.

Charlie took refuge in sullenness, and Meena said brightly:

"That ole Canute feller sent him, I bet."

"Like to know, wouldn't you?" Charlie asked with a feeble imitation of a sneer, and Bony now decided to break up this lovers' tiff.

"Now listen, you two. Playing about tracking each other and running around inside willi-willies is over for today. There's Yorky and Linda Bell. There's the policeman and Mr Wootton and me. You are supposed to be as anxious as anyone to locate Yorky. Now, Charlie, you answer questions and no more silliness. What we all say to one another goes no farther than the firelight, I promise you. And don't forget, you two have been playing each other too long. You have to get married by the Missioner, settle down, have children, be happy. I'll fix Canute, don't worry. All right, Charlie, why have you been tracking me?"

"Murtee tell me I track you, I see where you go and what you do," replied Charlie, still sullen.

"But you were working for the station."

"I told Boss I was sick."

"What did Mr Wootton say?"

"Nothing. But he put Bill Harte on to tracking me, see if I was sick." Charlie laughed. "Soon lost Bill Harte."

"How do you know Mr Wootton put Bill Harte on to you?"

"I seen Bill ridin' slow-like behind me. He was keeping to cover."

"And Mr Wootton told Bill Harte to track you? How do you know that?"

"He musta. Bill never heard me tell Boss I was sick."

"All right, leave that. Murtee told you to track me along. Why did he tell you to do that?"

"Dunno. Murtee Medicine Man."

"Has Murtee got Linda's dolls?"

The question certainly surprised Charlie, and Meena said:

"Course not. Linda's dolls are in her playhouse."

"Two of them are. Ole Fren Yorky and Meena are not. They're gone. Someone took them. Who?"

"No blackfeller took 'em," asserted Charlie, and Meena watched him like a suspicious wife. She said:

"I'll tell Sarah. Sarah'll find out. Maybe Mr Wootton, or one of the men took them. Them dolls belonged to Linda."

"Too right," agreed Charlie. "I made 'em."

"Where are Yorky and Linda? You tell me."

Reaction to this question satisfied Bony for the moment. He put another searcher.

"How many trucks went up to the Neales for your trackers?"

"Two. Arnold and Jim Holly from over Wandirna."

"You all came back on those trucks?"

"All the men, and some of the lubras. Meena and Sarah and others."

"Well, then, who stayed behind, to walk back?"

Charlie rolled off a dozen names, including Canute, and further questioning disclosed a doubt in Charlie's mind that Murtee was in the camp when the trucks came. He had not returned to the homestead on either of the trucks, both Charlie and Meena were sure. They saw Murtee two days afterwards in the camp by the creek. Canute was there, too, and they spent most of every day rubbing churinga stones against their foreheads and squatting over a little fire well apart from the others.

"When you got back, Meena, what did you do? Go tracking for Yorky, too?"

"No. Sarah was put to cooking at the homestead, me to help her and look after the house. Plenty of people about then."

"You don't know where Yorky and Linda went?"

Meena shook her head.

"Does Sarah know?"

Again the girl replied negatively.

"Does Canute know?"

Shutters fell before her eyes. One moment they were expressive, the next moment they were blank. Charlie was frowning, and when Bony looked his way, the shutters had dropped too. Silence reigned about the fire. Above, the heavy silence was disturbed by the conversation of a wedge of ducks.

Bony pretended not to notice the fallen shutters, and went on with his questions. At once the shutters were raised and he was again receiving co-operation. He learned that Mr Wootton had not been chasing Mrs Bell. That Arnold hadn't been making up to her. That William Harte had 'put it on her' to marry him, and that Harry Lawton said he was going to push his luck. He learned, too, that Wootton had threatened to sack Harry Lawton if he went on baiting Ole Fren Yorky, imitating his voice and his peculiar manner of walking. Knowing the answer, he asked:

"Did you see Mrs Bell after she was shot?"

Both shook their heads vigorously.

"Wasn't she shot in the back?"

Both brightened at being able to answer in the affirmative.

"Made a nasty mess on her blouse, so Constable Pierce told me."

They agreed with Constable Pierce, and, nonchalantly, Bony made a mark on the ground—a question mark. On looking at them, his brows raised, they nodded.

"You never saw her," he said. "How d'you know?"

And the shutters fell again.

CHAPTER 12

PRODDING THE ENEMY

ON ROUSING from an early cat-nap, the Three Sisters told Bony the time was about midnight. There were wild ducks on the bore-created pond, and he was puzzled by what could possibly interest them in water where no weeds could grow, and spent a lazy moment in reaching the conclusion that they were resting. Far away a cow bellowed, and, even farther than the cow, a pack of dingoes broke into a howling chorus.

The night was still and warm. Nearer him than the fire, Meena lay sleeping on her side, her head resting on an arm. By the pack-saddle, Charlie slept, lying on his back, his head resting on the ground. Bony dozed off again, and when he stirred next time, the Three Sisters said it was five o'clock, and dawning was tinting the east pale sea-green.

The billy was half full of the last tea brew, and this Bony heated by placing the can on the broken-open fire embers. Sipping the blue-black tea, and chain-smoking what he had the audacity to call cigarettes, he squatted over the red embers as his maternal ancestors had done, feeling about him the influences of five hundred generations of Canutes and Murtees, and their Charlies and Meenas.

He was concerned this early morning by the points of conversation of the previous evening, for all the points when welded strongly indicated aboriginal participation in what appeared to be a crime in which only white people were involved.

It could be claimed that no crime committed by a white person on or against another white person in this Lake Eyre Basin could be unknown by the aborigines, for there are many who believe that nothing can happen without aboriginal knowledge, whether it be the death of an eagle or the

changed shape of a sand dune. In strong support of this contention was the fact that Canute, blind as he was, saw with the eye of his mind the shape of the bloodstain on the back of the murdered woman. Canute had passed that knowledge to others of his tribe by, or with the assistance of, his dijeridoo, at the same time passing it to Bony, who had been present. Before that moment of receiving the blurred picture, which to others nearer to Canute would be clear as crystal, Bony had seen no photograph of it, nor read a description of it in any report.

It was an item of information known by Canute when he and his tribe were all supposed to be fifty miles from the scene of the crime, and as nothing can reside in a man's mind unless drawn into it from outside, from whom had he received the description of a bloodstain roughly in the form of a question mark?

When Bony had bluntly asked the man and the woman still sleeping nearby how Canute knew of that mark, shutters fell. They might not know how or from whom Canute was informed, but they did know he had been so informed, and they could have gained their knowledge in the same way and at the same time that Bony had. They would not question Canute, would accept the fact that he knew, and be content to ignore something which did not concern them.

Then why had Canute passed the knowledge to his followers? Was it to impress upon them his authority, and to confirm a ruling he and his Medicine Man had proclaimed? Where are Yorky and Linda Bell, those two sleepers had been asked, and the shutters had fallen swiftly as though he might read the answer in unguarded eyes.

This would account for lack of evidence of concern about the fate of Linda Bell. It would support the opinion that the interest of the aborigines in tracking the man and the child waned long before it could reasonably be expected to do so. For your aborigine is the greatest child lover of all human races, and Bony was sure that Yorky would have been

tracked right to the tip of Cape York had he murdered Linda Bell.

The rested ducks skittered across the glass-like surface of the small lake, to take off on the next leg of their journey, and within minutes it would be full light. Standing, Bony gazed on the sleeping lovers who dared not defy the authority governing their hearts and minds, and he was compelled to admire the degree of discipline to which they had been brought, and to pity them for the freedom thus denied them. He took a towel to the water, stripped and walked to the centre of the small lake, when it but reached his knees, and lowered himself into it and watched the changing lights in the sky above.

To question Charlie and his Meena further would be unfair to them, as well as futile. They had consciously and unconsciously given him something to aid his investigation. They knew a little of the much known to Canute and his Grand Vizier. They were sure in mind that Linda was safe enough. And that meant the child was still within the Lake Eyre Basin. By tracking him, Charlie was merely obeying an order. By tracking Charlie, Meena had acted on impulse prompted by one of several reasons. Neither could be rushed; both could be led to further co-operation.

Towelling himself, he dressed and returned to the camp, where he was shaving when the girl stirred and stood, stretched her arms and opened wide her shoulders. Seeing him, she turned to the fire and replenished the fuelling, then filled the billy from the pack-drum and set it against the flames.

On completing his toilet, Bony crossed to stand with her.

"After we have eaten you had better return to the homestead," he said. "You will remember that you didn't catch up with Charlie, and he and I will wipe out the tracks about this place to prove it."

She turned to face him, her large dark eyes gentle, the grey flecks soft and distinct. He saw himself in her, and she herself in him. Each of the same duality of race, each was of

neither one race nor the other. There was a faint tremble about her mouth when she said:

"Did you speak true last night when you told Charlie about your Meena, and being married and running away to that place among the tobacco bush?"

"Yes. You heard that?"

She nodded, her face downcast.

"You would like the Missioner to marry you and Charlie, wouldn't you?"

Again the slight nod, the dark eyes hopeful, and Bony wished that Marie, his wife, was there to help the girl to break the chains of tribal taboos.

"Canute is blind and old," he reminded her. "Murtee is old. I'll tell them to free you from the birth promise so that you can marry Charlie. When I tell them, they will. And then the Missioner can marry you, and you can go away and camp somewhere among tobacco bush where Charlie can love you."

"True?"

"Bet?"

She watched him break unequally two match sticks, watched him wave his hands, then present the sticks in his clenched fist, the tops on a level.

"Long I will; short I won't," he recited.

She pulled one of the sticks, and he opened his hand and she found her choice to be the longer. She remained so still with her head bent to look at those sticks, that he wondered if she had detected the trick which removed the gamble from the act, and then was rewarded by the smile on her face, a smile which, like the day, was slowly born.

"Better wake that Charlie," he advised, and turned away to re-pack his shaving gear.

She wakened Charlie by nudging him with her toes and calling him a lazy black bastard. Charlie grunted, stood, stretched as she had done, grinned and lunged at her. She turned and fled, fled to the lake, and he raced after her and joined battle with splashing water. She danced about him,

shouting with laughter at his attempts to grab her, shrieked with pretended terror when he succeeded. Together they fell and writhed amid foam, and eventually came walking back to camp hand in hand. And as they ate the food presented by Bony, the heat of the fire raised steam from their shorts.

Later, the two men silently watched the girl skirting the lake, and Bony thought that if white girls had been there to watch Meena, they would never wear shoes. For a moment she stood on the crest of a red dune, then turned and waved before disappearing beyond it.

"How far is the Loaders Springs road?" Bony asked, and was told some four miles. Eighteen miles beyond the road gate was the next of Yorky's camps where water lay in a rock-hole. "You can follow on after me, Charlie. You know, make believe you are still tracking me, eh?"

Charlie laughed, and there was no doubt he was pleased at this way out of admission of failure. They discussed the matter of erasing Meena's tracks, and Charlie said it couldn't be done under two days, and predicted wind later on this day which would do the job for them. He brought the belled horses, helped to load the pack-animal, and squatted over the dying fire while giving Bony a lead of several miles.

Sitting easy in his saddle, the pack-horse trailing behind, Bony began soon to doubt that Charlie's weather prediction could be correct. The sky gave no sign of wind, and if no wind came to wipe away Meena's tracks, they would be read by another aborigine, who would report them. Noon found Bony still riding. The willi-willies were again on the march, the sun-heat powerful, and the necessity of creating a diversion from those camp tracks became ever stronger.

One of Bony's rules of crime investigation, and one which more often than not brought results, was to stir up those opposed to him when it seemed they were standing still. Canute and Murtee were reclining in the tree-shade and content with the counter-move they had made by sending

Charlie to find out what the big-feller policeman was doing. Charlie and the big-feller policeman were following an endless boundary fence in the heat of a late summer, a fence lying along the perimeter of a great circle centred by Mount Eden homestead. In three days Bony and his follower would again reach Lake Eyre, this time to the south of the homestead, and so far the only gain for Bony was what he had set out to achieve, proof of interest by the aborigines in his investigation.

He decided to create a diversion from Meena's tracks which also would spur those wily aborigine leaders into action of some kind.

He would smoke-signal to them!

At four o'clock the wind was still absent, and the sky was wiped clean of clouds.

The place for the signals was found in a narrow gully where grew young tobacco bush amid sapling gums. Bony heaped dry bush and sticks at three widely separated points, and beside the rubbish he deposited other heaps of green tobacco bush and green tree boughs.

In general, smoke-signalling is done to convey simple messages, and in particular is used to draw a distant medicine man or head man into telepathic communication. It was not Bony's intention to send a message, but to create confusion, curiosity and alarm.

He fired a heap of rubbish, and the rubbish burned brightly without smoke. On to this fire he tossed green bush, and at once dense smoke rose straight upward. When the column was high and the green stuff almost consumed, he fired the second heap, and when it was bright, blanketed it with green boughs. Thence from one fire to another, he sent up three columns with varied spacing of each, the weather being perfect, and he patted himself with justifiable satisfaction. Canute and his followers couldn't read the message, because there wasn't one, and what poor bewildered Charlie, now plodding along the horses' tracks, would think of it was subject for quiet merriment.

The aborigines in their camp, and Charlie on the tramp, would most certainly be perturbed by the signals they couldn't understand.

Aided by memory of the wall map in Wootton's office, Bony estimated he was then nine miles direct from Mount Eden homestead. That the smokes would be seen by the aborigines there, he was confident, and that Canute would despatch some of his bucks to investigate would be certain.

An hour later he was riding up one of the gibber-armoured slopes over which Arnold had to pass to reach the old homestead for the iron, and on arriving at the summit of a tabletop he was amused and gratified to see smokes going up from Canute's camp.

He was about to begin the long descent to a wide belt of trees and a windmill, when he saw an answering signal rising from the place at which he had created both diversion and confusion. Charlie was informing Canute that a debil-debil was playing hell in general.

Throughout the night, Bony sat with his back against a tree some three hundred yards from the rock-hole near which was based Yorky's camp. He waited for Charlie, but Charlie failed to materialise from the encircling darkness.

CHAPTER 13

BALANCING RESULTS

SIGNS OF wind were not disturbing until noon the next day, when the sky was streakily washed with slacked lime and the sun's rays were tinged with red. Bony rode a hundred yards from the fence to accept the meagre shade of a patch of bull-oaks which, when first seen, appeared to be ten miles distant when actually they were within a mile, and

looked to be thriving British oaks on a mountain top when they were half dead on the slope of a shallow rise.

The flies were in festive mood. Slightly smaller than the common house fly, Bony had kept them at bay with a leafy switch, like a pasha riding a small donkey, and now they followed him into the shade, to attack again as he removed the saddles from the tormented horses, not bothering to tether them as they were not so stupid as to wander into the sun-glare. At once they sought his company, when he, having made a small fire to boil water, found refuge in the rising heated air that he might convey food to his mouth, and the horses stood either side of him, their heads also in the hot air. Better the heat than flies drowning in the eyes.

Of Charlie he had seen nothing since the morning of yesterday, and so far nothing resulted from his trick smoke-signalling. He had observed no puzzling tracks, and since leaving Mount Eden homestead had found no sign of Ole Fren Yorky.

Still, in this country, the wise do not hasten to peer beyond the crest of a sand dune, but rather await the dune to come to them. And it indicated its intention of so doing when, later this day, Bony was continuing his journey along the endless boundary fence.

He and the fence were crossing a vast area of gibbers. Fortunately he was proceeding eastward, because it was impossible to see anything westward for the glare of reflected light from the ironstone armour covering the ground. Ahead some few miles, the fence would terminate at Lake Eyre, seventeen miles south of the Mount Eden homestead.

He saw the first of the smokes rising west of north, and so distant that they looked like gold straws sprouting from the mirage. There were three. One was continuous, one was broken at long intervals, and the third broken at short intervals. They lasted for about ten minutes and ended in a flat-top of dark-grey fog. Then four smokes rose from near or at Canute's camp. Two were unbroken.

That was all, this day, and when night masked the heated earth, and Bony hadn't reached Yorky's next water-camp, he hitched his horses to scrub trees, sat with his back to another, and dozed fitfully until the first ray of dawn.

Before the sun rose, during those magic moments when this Earth is pure and without deceit, smokes rose from Canute's camp, from far to the west, far to the south, and far beyond Mount Eden's northern limits.

As Bony rode, a grim little smile puckered his firm mouth, and he said to the horse: "When everyone even remotely concerned in a crime sits down, then do something to make them stand. My smokes have certainly made someone stand."

Before noon he came to a bore languidly spouting water on the far side of the fence, and remembered having camped here when journeying to Mount Eden. Passing through a gateway, he watered the horses and was filling the drums when he heard on the Mount Eden side of the fence a succession of shots sounding like rifle reports produced by a stock-whip. Minutes passed, then he saw the rider cantering to the gateway. He rode through to Bony's camp fire, vaulting off the animal before it stopped.

"Day-ee, Inspector. How you doing?" asked Harry Lawton.

"So-so," replied Bony. "Have a spot of tea?"

"My word."

Young Lawton unstrapped the quart pot from his saddle, removed the cup-lid and filled it from Bony's billy. He raised the cup and said:

"Good hunting! Flamin' hot, isn't it? Going to blow like hell before night by the look of that sky."

The brown eyes bespoke casual curiosity. The shaven face, the neck and chest revealed by the open shirt and the bare forearms had the smooth firmness of flesh possessed by Charlie, and were almost the same colour. Lawton's trousers were of grey gabardine, his riding boots of quality kangaroo hide, and his spurs were goosenecked and fitted with six-

pences to make them jingle. He displayed the art of sitting on his heels without sitting on the spurs.

"What are you doing out this way?" asked Bony.

"Me? Oh, riding the ruddy fence and turning the cattle back towards the homestead. Cattle will hang around trying to get to the water this side of the boundary. You been missing some fun."

"Oh!"

"My word!" Lawton grinned. "Been hell and low water down at the abos' camp. Best riot come ever. You oughta see some of 'em. Rex is dragging an ear over his shoulder. Sarah's lost half her teeth somewhere. Meena got hanks of her hair pulled out, and somebody wielded a waddy against old Murtee and outed him."

"When did all this happen?" sharply enquired Bony.

"Night before last. Heck of a good go. We seen only the tail end of it. Bodies lying all over the joint when me and the boss and Arnold got there. Crikey! If only I had a movie camera. Been thinking a long time of getting one."

"You pacified them?"

"Pacified 'em!" Lawton broke into a guffaw. "Strike me green, they was all pacified enough. Round about eight we heard the roarin' and screamin'. Boss came over from the house, but we told him to let 'em alone. He wanted to pacify 'em, as you call it. Arnold said they'd quieten down by the time we wanted to sleep, and we were arguing about it when Meena came tearing up to say if something wasn't done there'd be killings for sure.

"So we went along. Would have toted our guns, but Wootton wouldn't have it. Said we didn't want shot abos lying around. Like I told you, there was plenty of abos lying around, but they wasn't shot. You'd have laughed when we got the camp fire blazing for light. Kids screaming; lubras yelling; abos shouting dirt and abos crawling round looking for waddies and things they'd dropped.

"There was old Canute rollin' about, and when I asked him what he thought he was doing in his dungeon he tells me

that a Kurdaitcha knocked him down. Feller called Jimmy Wall Eye thought he'd start something and made a lash at Arnold. You should have seen it. It was a beaut. Arnold prodded him on his good eye, and that fixed him."

"But what was it all about?" asked the unsmiling Bony, and Harry Lawton laughed again and said no one knew or would tell. He went on:

"Next morning, the boss sent Arnold to the camp with the truck. Sent me with him. Said we had to gather up all the wounded and take 'em in to Doc Crouch to patch up. But there ain't no wounded, no abos at all. They'd all cleared out except Sarah and Meena. They're back on the job cookin' and what not. Hell! I'll have to get that camera. How Rex is goin' to get his ear back on I can't see."

Lawton stowed his lunch-cloth into a saddle-bag, and the quart pot he strapped to the saddle, then, standing loosely beside Bony and rolling a cigarette, he said:

"Reckon I'll be pushing off. Which way you makin'? Along to Yorky's Lake camp?"

"Yes. How far from here?"

" 'Bout six miles. Bit of horse-feed about the place, but crook in a dust-storm. You doing any good mooching about?"

"Not much," admitted Bony.

"D'you know what I reckon, Inspector? I reckon Yorky ditched the kid in a sandhill, and got for his life over to the railway and jumped a train for the Alice. Easy done, y'know. Me and a mate jumped the rattler out of Loaders and put in a week up there on a bender, then jumped her back again to Loaders. Well, be seein' you."

Harry Lawton didn't mount that horse. He rose up and into the saddle. He did not dismount to open the gate and close it when passing into Mount Eden country; he did that chore from the saddle. Then he waved and cantered into the mirage, which made him look like an ant on a grasshopper. And, automatically, Bony gathered his lunch equipment.

The fracas at the aborigines' camp disturbed him because

he was sure the cause did not lie in his signals, but in that absence of Charlie and Meena for which they had not given adequate account. That Wootton had sent a truck to take the injured to Loaders Springs indicated the seriousness of the fighting.

Meanwhile there was yet one more of Yorky's camps to inspect, and if this provided no clue to the mystery of his whereabouts, the possibility of his having escaped from this vast Lake Eyre Basin was a strong probability. Again riding along the Mount Eden side of the boundary fence, he went back over the visit of Harry Lawton, and his own impressions.

There are many Harry Lawtons in the bush country proper, even in these days when Australian youth heads for safe government jobs. The spirit of adventure burns brightly in the Lawtons and they are free of the herd instinct.

Debonair youth! The spurs, the wide felt hat, the open shirt, the belt holding the array of small pouches, including a holstered revolver, the delight in the long stock-whip having a bright green silk cracker to produce loud reports, ranging from slow rifle fire to the rat-tat-tat of a machine-gun, all told the story of zestful youth.

Harry Lawton could have started the uproar at the aborigines' camp, where were several maidens verging on womanhood. From what Pierce had said, Harry Lawton would accept cheerfully many defeats if balanced by a few triumphs. But the odds were in favour of the cause lying in Charlie and Meena and the suspected association with Inspector Bonaparte.

The first wind gust reached Bony about two o'clock. The sun was then distinctly yellow atop a canopy of light grey haze. Instead of the willi-willies, growing clouds of red dust rolled over the land, and on coming to the 'coast' dunes Bony found all the crests smoking fitfully, as though the storm was stoking fires below. The fence began to switch-back over ranges of sand, so that on coming to the summit of a range he saw down on the flat a dilapidated hut built of

corrugated iron, a windmill over a well, and a rickety horse yard.

Having hobbled the horses to wander over to the drinking trough and seek a meal from the deceptively unedible herbage, Bony entered the hut of some ten feet by ten in area. Here again were the iron oil drums in which were rations of flour, tea, sugar, matches and tobacco, tinned meat and fish. Here again were oddments of ropes. On a bench-table was a hurricane lamp, and in a corner opposite the open fire-place a tin of kerosene. All the ordinary possessions of an ordinary bushman, save that this bushman named Yorky suffered no losses from wandering aborigines.

The strengthening wind had already made the hut's iron sheets give tongue, but the dim interior was entirely free of the tormenting flies, and gave instant relief from the compelling omniscience of limitless space. Bony brought his gear inside and dumped it on the single bunk, and made a fire for a brew of tea; for no sensible man will drink unboiled water if he can ignite a flame and has tea in his kit, and so reduce the danger of stomach trouble.

Presently, sitting on a case at the bench-table, and sipping scalding hot tea, he smoked cigarettes and worked at his ledger, trying to balance effort with results.

Was Yorky holed up inside or outside this station boundary fence? Facts could not be ignored. Inside the boundary of Mount Eden were camps at a water supply, and containing food stores. Outside was nothing but waterless aridity, save in the deep holes in the bed of the Neales River, and that was fifty miles away, and in country where even the aborigines on walkabout starved. The answer was certainly not to be found by riding haphazardly hither and yon.

A less patient man would have despaired at Bony's accountancy.

CHAPTER 14

THE FUGITIVE'S STORY

THE BOUNDARY fence at this end, like that north of the homestead, terminated far out into the mud of the lake, and beyond the efficient barrier a line of old posts told of past years when the mud had been harder and the fence needed additional extension.

Bony sat on the shore-dune and looked at Lake Eyre. He was unable to recall anything more depressing than this vast plain of dark mud fading into the opaque vacuum of neither earth nor sky. This late afternoon there was nothing of the glamorous magic created by the mirage, nothing to break the flat monotony which brought him abruptly to question his sanity for sitting there and looking at it. Even the dunes were more interesting. They, at least, were actively shedding their headgear of sand and building elsewhere.

What at first he thought was a crow only gradually commanded full attention. The object was a long way out over the mud, and moved in a brownish haze. It wasn't hopping like a bird, or walking like one, and minutes later it took size and shape to reveal itself as a dog.

Obviously it was a wild dog, but what it was doing there was not obvious.

Salt! Was that the answer? It might be, because there was no evidence of salt in Bony's range. That it was a dingo was practically certain, and wild animals will often travel extraordinary distances and to extraordinary places for salt. Still intrigued, Bony realised suddenly that the sun had gone down, and he was conscious of the rising wind removing sand from under him, so that he was sitting deeper and deeper into the dune. The dog, the lake, the world could go hang this evil evening which night would blessedly banish, and he tramped down the dune to the flat where was the hut.

There wasn't much of a wood supply, so he gathered sticks and dead roots as he progressed, and among the debris he picked up was a piece of board. The load he dumped beside the hearth, then made sure the lamp was full, and lit the wick. His fire was out and he built another, and then he strapped the bells to the necks of the horses, and shortened their hobble chains. These final chores done, he was returning to the hut when the wind brought to him a man's sobbing cry.

On the crest of landward dune stood an aborigine. He was naked save for shorts. He carried no weapon. Standing there, his legs to the knees were almost obliterated by the flying sand-mist. Then he collapsed and plunged head-first down the steep slope, his body riding in an avalanche of sand.

He was trying to stand when Bony reached him.

"Why the hurry, Charlie? What's the matter?"

There was caked blood on the left side of Charlie's head, and splotched over his right shoulder. His eyes were glazed with fatigue, and now his legs were useless. Exerting tremendous effort, he managed to emit sound like the word 'hut'. Wrapping one of Charlie's arms about his neck, Bony half dragged and carried him to the hut, where he dumped him on the bunk, and stood in the doorway expecting to see enemies cresting the sand ridge over which Charlie had come.

No one, nothing, appeared. The wind brought the tinkle of the horse bells telling that they were feeding undisturbed. Behind him the rasping of the aborigine's breathing was gradually diminishing, and he slammed the door and wedged it with the piece of case board. Then he fed Charlie water, a tablespoon of it, at long intervals.

For an aborigine to be so knocked out indicated how stern the chase had been, how relentless the pursuers. The pounding chest slowly ceased its labouring, and then came a succession of long sighs, and finally Charlie tried to sit up, and was pushed down.

"So the abos are after you," said Bony.

"Yair. Wild fellers. Ole Canute brought 'em. Smoked for 'em. They nearly got me, and I'd already had enough in a brawl in our own camp."

"Calm down, Charlie," Bony urged. "All safe here with me. I'll get the billy going, and we'll eat, and then we'll talk. Head ache?"

"Like hell."

"They try to spear you?"

"Tossed a couple at me."

"They *must* be annoyed." Bony slung the billycan on the hook over the fire, then dug into a saddle-bag for aspirin, and cartridges for the automatic. Fortunately, the iron hut wouldn't burn, and the iron was in fairly good condition. There was the point that the aborigines' spears could be driven through the iron, but this he doubted as he knew of no precedent. Giving Charlie two tablets and a small amount of water, he said:

"Met Harry Lawton today. He told me there had been a fight in the camp night before last. Is that where your head was injured?"

"Crack on the head in that fight. Shoulder gashed by a spear when it whanged past me."

"Close as all that, eh? Must be serious. These wild fellers, where did they come from?"

"Other side of the Neales. They must have travelled fast to of got down here in the time. First thing I know of 'em, I'm having a drink at the bore where you met Harry. Four of 'em. I cleared out fast."

"You were still on my tracks?"

"Yair."

"How come you were in the camp when the fight took place? You were not on my tracks then."

Charlie sat up despite Bony's motion to lie still. His scalp was opened and would need stitching, and sight of the wound recalled Bony to having seen somewhere in the hut a packing needle and twine. The shoulder wound looked less

ugly, but had bled much, and the final tumble down the dune, having added sand to perspiration, completed a picture of sufficient grotesqueness to make a man laugh—or shudder. Charlie rolled a cigarette, and Bony lit it for him, and waited for the reply to his last question.

"Your bloody smokes started it," mumbled Charlie, "I was keeping well back, like you said, when I seen 'em going up, and 'cos they was in line I couldn't read 'em, but I knew they was sent for Canute. They sort of stonkered me." The whites of Charlie's eyes betrayed the inherent fear of the inexplicable, and explained his following actions. "So I sit down and wait to see Canute's smokes, and when none came, I worked it out I ought to go back to the camp and find out what to do."

Now the eyes gleamed, and the nostrils flared.

"I got back when Canute and Murtee and the Old Men were having a palaver, and the first thing Murtee says to me is about the tracks we left at the bore camp the night before. That Canute, he's a cunnin' old bastard. He got to know about Meena tracking me, and he sent young Wantee off tracking her. And Wantee told him all about us camping with you.

"They had Meena hobbled to a tree with a bit of old rope, and Murtee tells me they goin' to knock her on one knee to make out it's an accident, instead of smashing both knees 'cos Pierce would be a wake up. And while they're tellin' me, I seen a tomahawk biting into a tree, and I grabbed it out and ran to Meena, and she seen me coming and put her leg over the tree root, so's I could chop the rope off her with one hit."

Charlie was re-living the scene. The nerves of his face were jumping, making his eyes roll, and his mouth was wide and grinning. His arms illustrated the description of what followed.

"There's Murtee yellin' to the mob to get me, and all I got's a tomahawk. They don't like that, and knows I'd of sunk it anywhere I could. I'm ready for 'em, and then the next thing happened was Sarah. That Sarah! Seems they'd

tied her up to a tree too, and Meena got her loose." Charlie laughed. His voice rose to excited shouting. "Sarah, she's got a tree all to herself, and she wops it against Murtee's head like she's Ma Kettle, and Murtee don't argue. Then the mob is on to me. Rex is lookin' for it, and I'm decidin' where I'll bury the tomahawk in him, when Meena gets between and goes to blind him with her fingernails. Anyway, I gets in a smack with the flat of the blade, rememberin' just in time that Rex and me is mates. And out goes Rex.

"There's old Canute yelling what to do, and the mob's getting close to him, and me in the middle. I can hear that dirty black bastard tellin' 'em not to kill us, and then I gets a wallop on me head and I'm out. Next thing I see is Sarah standing on Canute's belly. Then she jumps up and down on it, and Canute don't do any more yelling. I see Rex up on his feet and he's bashin' young Whistler who's tearing out Meena's hair, and after that what come in front went down, and I had a waddy instead of the tomahawk, and I don't know how. Anyway, they're going down as they comes up, and suddenly there's not so many, and it's getting dark after a couple of 'em sort of rolls over the fire.

"After a bit the truck come with the boss and Arnold and the others. We're all stonkered by now, but that fool Jimmy Wall Eye makes a swipe at Arnold and Arnold woodens him. That finishes the deal, and after finding there's no one dead, but a lot of 'em still sleeping, they go off back to the homestead, takin' Sarah and Meena with 'em.

"Next mornin' we all clear out. You know how it is, Inspector. All the lubras get the young gum leaves and mash 'em with their teeth, so's they have a mouthful of pap, and they push the stuff into cuts and wounds and plaster Lake mud over the lot. Canute, or someone, tells 'em to leave me alone. I can go to hell, and think I'd better go bush while things cool down. Think best I can do is to go back to trackin' you, and I'm doin' this when I seen Canute's smokes and the smokes what the wild blacks sent up. Canute called for a corroboree, but the next thing was them wild fellers

coming at me at the bore. They'll be around somewhere now."

"A good fight, eh?" dryly commented Bony, and Charlie grinned.

"You're tellin' me. That Sarah! Heavy as a ridin' hack. And both feet up in the air and down on Canute's belly."

"And she used a tree as a waddy?" Bony chuckled.

"Musta pulled it out of the ground, a dead stump ten feet long," shouted Charlie. "That Sarah!"

"And Meena really enjoyed it?" pressed the delighted Bony.

"I'll say. That Meena! That Meena!" Charlie rocked with ecstasy of the memory. "You should of . . ."

The hut wall received a terrific blow and cut short the story. In the ensuing silence both men froze against the backdrop of the wind, and at a distance a guttural halting voice shouted:

"You come out, you Charlie feller. Big-feller policeman, you stop there. You all right."

Bony aimed his pistol in the direction of the voice and sent a bullet through the iron. There were no more shouted instructions. Even the wild blacks would know better than to attack openly a representative of the white man's law. Could they lay hands on Charlie, he would disappear and never be found.

They dined off Yorky's tinned herrings in tomato sauce, and drank much tea heavily laced with sugar, and then Bony suggested treating Charlie's wounds.

"They're all right," laughed Charlie as though it were a joke. "They'll keep."

"Don't agree," snapped Bony. "You must have the scalp stitched up. Can't go on looking like that. Make Meena sick."

"That Meena! You reckon so?"

"I certainly do. I've got some salve. Let's see if Yorky has any antiseptic."

They poked about, and Charlie came up with a can of tar.

"Here yar. Heat her up and it'll do. Sew me up like a camel. Okee?"

"You'd get me into jail for cruelty to dumb animals. No. Best thing is kerosene. I've a hold-all in this bag with some strong thread."

The wound was ugly to behold. Bony persuaded Charlie to sit on a case with his face in his hands to protect his eyes, his elbows on his knees. The parted scalp was lacerated along the edges, glued to the skull with sand, and at least four inches long. Water inside the hut was now limited to a couple of pints, and it was a long time until day broke, when, Bony was confident, he could go to the well.

Fortunately for Charlie, the hold-all contained a couple of darning needles, and, having threaded these, Bony dropped them and the thread into a tin containing kerosene. To distract the patient's attention, he mentioned having seen the dingo out on the mud.

"Funny thing about them dingoes," Charlie said, not flinching as Bony sponged the opened wound with kerosene. "Reckon they go right across the lake to the other side. I seen a bitch with her pups once. They were coming in, the old gal and four beaut pups. Looked gold in the early mornin'. You know, like four baby suns and one big one. I watched 'em. Seen the pups was keeping close to the mother, and d'you know why?"

"Why?" said Bony, fitting a piece of leather into the palm of his hand to drive the needle. 'This is going to hurt me more than it will hurt you,' he thought, but didn't say.

"They was followin' a pad," replied Charlie, and moved not a fraction as the needle pierced the lip of the parted scalp. "Them dingoes know their way across. They follow their own roads across the mud. The pups was keepin' close so's not to muddy their feet. I could see the track they was following. I went down to the dog pad and walked out a bit to meet the dingo and her pups and see what they do. And they just turned round and went out again, still following the pad. How's the sewing?"

"Half way through," encouraged Bony. "How old would you say the pups were?"

" 'Bout five weeks, might be six."

"She couldn't have brought them across the lake from the other side. She must have taken them out from your side for a walk?"

"Don't think. She didn't go out on the pad she was coming in on. No fresh tracks telling it, anyway."

"How far did you go out on the path?"

"Couple of hundred feet. Could have gone a bit more, but I knew I wouldn't catch up with them pups."

"Many such pads?"

"No. That one's half a mile this side of the homestead."

"Interesting," drawled Bony. "Well, the job's done. Here's a rag to wipe your eyes clear. You'll have to get someone to cut the stitches in about a week, if you're not dead from tetanus."

CHAPTER 15

BOARDS AND DINGO ROADS

THE WIND clawed the iron roof and now and then shook even the walls. The two men slept fitfully, Charlie tautened by the proximity of the wild aborigines outside, and Bony beset by recent events, plus the need for sleep in a comfortable bed.

Eventually morning came, to reveal several holes in the roof, and crevices about the door frame and under the eaves.

By standing on a case or the bunk, Bony was able to survey the surrounding scene. The wind continued high but had moved to the south, was noticeably cool, and no longer possessed the power to lift dust and move sand dunes. There was no sign of Charlie's pursuers.

"I'll fetch water," said Bony. "Let me out and wedge the door until I return."

He picked up a petrol tin bucket, thrust cartridges into a pocket and the automatic into another, and removed the wedge. The door swung inward. His hand was moving towards Charlie, in the act of tossing the board to him, when a projecting piece of metal halted the movement.

The board was about two feet long, and seven or eight inches wide. One end was curved to a blunt point, and the original sharp edge along one side had been rasped to smoothness. Across the width and at about one-third from the square end was screwed a wooden cleat, and at equidistance from both ends holes had been bored close to the edge of both sides.

Setting down the bucket, Bony examined the board more closely, and failed to discern its use since it had formed part of a packing-case. "Charlie," he called, " what do you make of this? Part of a camel saddle, or what?"

On looking up at the aborigine, he found him staring at a point above his head, his face registering expression of dawning comprehension. Only for a moment was reaction to the board evident, then it gave place to one of vacuity, and the shutters fell behind the black eyes.

"Dunno, Inspector Bonaparte," replied Charlie, the title and surname slipping into the reply unnecessarily. "Bit of ole wood belonging Yorky, looks like."

"Obviously, as it's Yorky's camp. Seen anything like it before?"

Charlie shook his head, and Bony again picked up the bucket, motioned to the opened door, passed outside and heard the door being wedged again.

It was not a time for cogitation. The barren dunes could sprout black figures and discharge a flight of spears. From behind five or six tough mulga trees could step other black men, each with a spear ready to throw. Without haste, or caution, Bony walked the hundred yards to the windmill over the well, where he released the brake to set the mill

working to raise fresh water. Casually he leaned against one of the iron legs and scanned the wind-swept, arid surroundings about the mill and the hut. Nothing human appeared, to relieve the depressing scene.

He carried the filled bucket to the hut, and when Charlie opened the door the change of wind proved that the wide iron chimney could smoke.

"Are you firing the place?" Bony asked. And Charlie laughed too loudly before explaining that the fire wasn't properly blazing. He had started it with brush, and, as he spoke, it burst into flame.

"No blackfellers outside," Bony told him. "Looks like they cleared out."

"Too right. They don't like fight with big-feller policeman. Could be they tell Canute to do his own dirty work, the black bastard. What'll we do now?"

"Use that basin to wash in, have a shave, push on to the homestead. We'll follow the beach, to reduce chances of ambush. And you'll be staying close to the homestead while I argue it out with Canute."

Charlie was decidedly relieved by Bony's cheerfulness. He tossed the case board into the fire, added more fuel to surround the billy with flame, and within thirty minutes they had eaten breakfast, rolled cigarettes, and Bony had brought in the horses. To add importance to the big-feller policeman for unseen eyes, assuming the wild men were watching, they moved off with Charlie haltered by a length of camel noseline and walking beside Bony's hack as though a prisoner of the Law, white man's ruddy law.

Even Charlie, so close to the primitive, so close to 'nature', failed to sense any nearness of warlike aborigines. As the sun lifted from the horizon, the wind weakened to become a gentle breeze, and the flies kept to the shelter provided by the horses. At noon all the magic of this Earth achieved by the mirage had banished the ugliness of the previous day.

Now and then Charlie chatted, but mostly he walked silently, repeatedly glancing to the rear and even more often

directing his gaze to left-ahead, at the shore line of the dunes. Morning passed. A fire and tea and tinned meat separated the morning from the afternoon, and two hours later they sighted the line of pine trees marking the position of the homestead.

"What about that dog pad you were going to show me, Charlie?" asked Bony, and Charlie chuckled and said it was three miles farther on.

Why had the shutters fallen behind his eyes when asked about that case board? Why the dawn of comprehension which had preceded the shutters? What had that board told this aborigine? That the board had brought his mind to understand what he hadn't understood was amply proved. The trick of shuttering the mind without closing the eyes was ever annoying to the questioner, because it was a more emphatic refusal to answer a question than any words could be.

It was but a few nights back that under Bony's questioning Meena had admitted that she did not know where Yorky and the child were, but when asked if she thought Canute knew, down came the shutters. Charlie had betrayed the same reaction, therefore it seemed that neither knew where Yorky was, but believed that Canute did. The board told Charlie a story, but Charlie dropped the shutters on that story.

The subject was occupying Bony's mind when Charlie, still wearing the loop of light rope about his neck, called his attention to the dingo road. From the elevation of the back of his horse, Bony could see it, a thin winding ribbon slightly darker than the bordering mud, and extending to infinity. Dismounting, he strode to the junction of the pad with the beach, and could see the tracks of dogs going out and coming in. On the cement-hard beach were many marks made by dogs coming off the mud to free their paws of it.

Following concentration, Bony decided that the number of dogs was small, but that the age of the pad was old. The dog traffic had depressed the pad half an inch below the

general surface, and when Bony stepped on to it, he found it decidedly harder than outside it.

"A good place to set a dog trap," he told Charlie, and at this suggestion Charlie laughed, and spuriously joked that the dingoes hadn't harmed any white feller, so why trap him? Bony walked on out, and found that the mud wasn't soft till he had proceeded fifty odd feet. It was certainly a poser, why the dogs went out into Lake Eyre, and the answer couldn't be salt, as salt patches lay quite close to the shore.

Again Bony mounted, and they left the beach and skirted the slope leading to the pines and the homestead gate beyond, which crossed the yards. Bony removed the rope from Charlie and they unsaddled.

"Let the horses go, Charlie, and then take my swag and the bags to the house veranda," Bony instructed. "And remember, you are not to leave the homestead until I give word. I'll speak to Mr Wootton about you staying here and doing odd jobs, and then we'll have a good look at that head and decide whether it will do, or if it's a case for the doctor."

"You fix up with Canute?" asked Charlie, anxiously.

"I'll fix him, Charlie."

He found Wootton on the east veranda, and the cattleman was obviously freed from a load.

"Bonaparte! Glad you got back. We've had trouble here, as young Lawton told you. He said he'd found you at Number 91 Bore yesterday."

"Yes. He was quite excited by the brawl at the camp. Said the abos had cleared out."

"They did, but they came back today. I've kept Meena and her mother here for safety's sake. Got in touch with Pierce, and he treated the affair very casually, I thought. Said the blacks often went to market, and that he never interfered unless to stop a feud, or a killing. When I told him there might well be a killing as a result, he asked where you were, then said to give you a couple of days more before he'd move."

"No one is dead?" mildly asked Bony.

"Don't think so. A lubra came this morning to ask for some pain-killer for Murtee, but I couldn't get anything from her about the rest. I never saw the like of it. They were lying about the camp, some unconscious, many of them bleeding, and all the children in bunches and yelling like mad. And here's Meena. Look at her! Just look at her!"

The girl came forward and placed the tray of afternoon tea on a low table. As she again wore a black dress and white pleated apron, the observer had to go to the top of her head to find anything at odds with this smartly dressed maid. She looked at Bony at first shyly, and then with laughter in her eyes, and Wootton said:

"Show him, Meena."

She bent forward to permit Bony to view the linen pad marking where she had lost a patch of hair by violent extraction, and Bony chuckled, saying:

"Not as bad as Charlie, Meena. Have you seen him yet?"

"That Charlie!" Meena laughed. "Charlie says that ole black bastard sent the wild blacks after him."

"Meena!" expostulated Wootton. "You must not refer to anyone like that. What do you mean, sending the wild abos after Charlie?"

"I will explain that," Bony interposed. "You, Meena, make Charlie take a shower and then look at his scalp and tell me what you and Sarah think should be done for it."

"First pour the tea," ordered Wootton. "Inspector Bonaparte must be tired and thirsty."

This she did, expertly, gravely, and when she had gone the cattleman exploded.

"Don't understand it, damned if I do. Look at her, clean as a new pin. Her clothes are right, excepting those red shoes. Speaks all right, too. Any city woman would give thanks for such a maid. And then what? A half naked Amazon clawing, punching, kicking, screaming and biting."

"And thoroughly enjoying herself."

"Without a doubt. Curious way to enjoy oneself. I saw a man with his ear almost torn off. And Sarah, our cook, brandishing a log of wood as big as a tree. Then there's Charlie. What happened to him?"

"Someone dropped a brick on his head. Opened his scalp. I sewed it up last night. Don't worry about the aborigines, I'll deal with them. By the way, I'm low in tobacco. Can you let me have five or ten pounds in quarter-pound plugs?"

"Of course. But five . . . ten . . ."

"I'd like to borrow your car or a truck to run along to the camp for an hour. After, of course, we have eaten all these delicious scones baked for us!"

CHAPTER 16

BONY BUYS A WOMAN

WANDIRNA, CHIEF of the Orrabunna Nation, alias Canute, ordered a eucalyptus bath. He was feeling unwell, what with the rheumatism and the pounding of Sarah's feet on his stomach, and felt the need for the cure invented by his ancestors long before the original King Canute played the fool with his nobles.

The lubras had brought back from their temporary exile masses of young gum tips, and with these they lined a shallow grave which had been heated by burning wood. Water was sprinkled on the gum leaves and through to the earth, which at once emitted clouds of steam. Finally, when the temperature had cooled slightly and the heated leaves had become sodden, a lubra escorted King Canute and invited him to step down into the grave.

He lay there at full length; a short, fat, white-haired old man, entirely naked save for the ragged beard covering the upper portion of his chest. Steam laden with eucalyptus oils,

strong enough to asphyxiate a steer, rose from the interred, who huffed and grunted and snorted, but stuck it out. The temperature then falling slowly, the victim gave a stifled order, and the lubra placed gum branches over the grave to seal the healing elixir.

Canute, who was now feeling wonderfully soothed, ventured to stretch one leg and then the other, then his arms, and rejoiced that all the nagging pains were no longer tying knots with his muscles. Ah! It was good to be a king. He yelled for the lubras to help him out.

Nothing happened. The lubras were deaf or something. He shouted again. There must be a lubra to remove the top branches and hold in readiness for his hot and rejuvenated body a military overcoat supplied by the Protector of Aborigines. He was not fool enough to stand and meet the chill air of late afternoon.

"Ah!" The branches were being removed, those over his feet first. The outside air told him this. Then, instead of his lubra's voice, he heard another he had remembered.

"Get out, Canute."

With the suppleness of youth, the King arose and stepped from the grave . . . into the military overcoat held ready for him by D.I. Bonaparte. By an arm he was drawn away and urged smartly to the communal camp fire tended by the awed lubras.

"Sit down," was the next order, and the King subsided on to a tree stump, the heat of the fire scorching his shins and face. Gravely, he was presented with a stick of tobacco and told to chew. He obeyed by halving the tobacco stick with his teeth, and wedging one half into a cheek.

"You tell Murtee come here," commanded Bony. "And the Old Men."

Canute moved the lump from one cheek to the other, and shouted orders. Lubras ran from their jobs, then halted like startled rabbits. Children were hushed, save one small baby lying on an old blanket in company with several others. Men appeared, one after another, and squatted

about Canute, and lastly, wearing a mud plaster and looking positively savage, came the Medicine Man. A eucalyptus bath twice as hot might possibly have benefited him, too.

From the truck nearby, Bony brought a packing-case and a papered parcel. The parcel he placed on the ground before the semi-circle of aborigines, the case he put over the parcel, and on the case seated himself. Then with slow deliberation he rolled a cigarette, licked it, lit it, and stared at the black eyes watching him with the cold impassivity of iguanas.

Taking up a stick, he drew a tiny circle on the ground at his feet, as though it had to be perfect. Then to the right of the tiny circle he drew, with exaggerated effort, a much larger circle. Done to his pleasing, he spat once into each circle and watched the spittle sink into the sand.

On his throne stump, King Canute chewed vigorously, his sightless eyes, destroyed by a grass fire, moving slightly as though they could serve the brain behind them. Beside him sat an ancient who looked a thousand years old and probably was not quite ninety. His claw-like hand encircled Canute's wrist. The anthropologists wouldn't believe it, but Bony knew that the Old One was passing what he saw to the mind of the blind man. Thus he had proceeded slowly, and continued so to do.

With his stick Bony indicated the larger circle, saying:

"That is Canute-Wandirna, Head Man of the Orrabunna Nation." There was sudden relaxation of tension. He pointed to the smaller circle. "That is all other blackfellers inside one humpy." His stick passed over the ground as though expunging the circles, returned to the large circle, saying: "That is big-feller policeman, ME. And this small one is Constable Pierce."

There was silence while he stared into every pair of black eyes, and held his gaze for a long minute on the eyes of the old man holding Canute's wrist. What the old man saw in his blue eyes, Bony knew Canute was seeing, too. The lubras were silent and still, bunched just beyond the communal

fire, and the men and children stood also in packed units. Bony said:

"Long time ago, Sarah promised little baby Meena to Canute. Now Canute is old, and he takes eucalyptus bath and likes tobacco better than young lubras. He likes to sit in the sun and hear happy voices of his people about him, and tell them what the spirits of the Alchuringa would have them do. What do you say, Canute?"

"Big-feller policeman speaks true," agreed Canute, adding: "There's blackfeller law and whitefeller law."

"Canute speaks true," agreed Bony. "But whitefeller law more strong than blackfeller law. Still, we palaver now about blackfeller law. Bimeby we palaver about whitefeller law. We talk about Sarah and her Meena she promised to Canute long time ago. Long time ago Meena belong to Canute. All right! Okee! I am sitting on forty plugs of black tobacco, as many as your fingers on both hands make five times. I trade all that tobacco for Meena."

Silence followed this proposition until Murtee said:

"Meena Orrabunna lubra. You are Worcair man. No can do."

"I am whitefeller policeman," countered Bony. "I say for you to go to jail, you go to jail in Loader Springs quick and good. I see you Murtee; I can see you. You tell Canute smoke for wildfeller to come play hell on Mount Eden. You break whitefeller law. I big whitefeller policeman. You, Canute feller, forty plugs of tobacco for your Meena, eh?"

The tendons along the skeleton arm of the aborigine, acting as Canute's eyes, tightened when urging acceptance without argument, and Canute said:

"You sit on tobacco?"

"I sit on forty tobacco plugs."

"I trade okee, all right."

With his stick, Bony now erased the two circles. Then he drew two very large circles slightly overlapping. He called Meena, and the girl emerged from the car parked just

off the track and came to him through the gathered aborigines. She was wearing white shorts, and nothing else save the pad of linen on her head.

She stood inside one of the circles, and into the other circle Bony emptied the plugs of tobacco. The old man urged Canute to rise, and brought him forward to stand chest to chest with Bony where the circles overlapped. Behind Bony was the tobacco; behind Canute stood Meena, Canute's left wrist still grasped by the Counsellor.

Murtee now came forward and gave to Canute a flint, and the King explored Bony's chest with his free hand and nicked the flesh. He passed the flint to Bony, and Bony nicked his chest. Each wetted a fingertip with the other's blood and pressed the finger to the blood on their own chest.

The deal was accomplished. Canute fell on his knees and pawed the tobacco like a miser counting his gold, and Bony caught Meena by a forearm and marched her over to the car, pushed her in, closed the door and returned to the communal fire.

The tobacco had vanished. Everyone, men and women and the older children, were chewing tobacco. Canute was back on his throne. It was some time before King, Grand Vizier and Counsellors regained their pre-business gravity.

"There is another trade," Bony told them. "Blackfeller law for whitefeller law. What for you all go crook when I send up smoke telling Worcair feller I am okee, all right? What for you catch Sarah and Meena? What for you all fight in camp? You tell me, eh?"

Faces like gargoyles. Eyes blank like shuttered shop windows in a riot. Bony slowly rolled a cigarette, actually making what looked like a cigarette.

"I tell you, eh? You tell Charlie track along big-feller policeman. I catch-um Charlie. Then I catch-um Meena. They don't tell me but I know why you tell Charlie to track me, see what I do. You tell Charlie to do all that because you scared I find Yorky and Linda. All right! White-

feller law say you all go to jail. You track white policeman. You try to lame Meena and bash up Charlie. Then you smoke for wildfeller-blackfeller come along to catch up Charlie, kill Charlie, hide his body in sand dune, no white-feller policeman then know where Charlie is. You say Charlie gone long way away. No good to whitefeller policeman. You all go jail okee, all right."

The sun was westering and bars of light gold lay athwart the scene and illumined the faces of Canute and his Counsellors. All were distinctly uneasy, obviously recalling the tales of jail existence told them by Pierce in previous conferences.

"Blackfeller live blackfeller law," observed Murtee, spitting tobacco juice towards Bony.

"You live blackfeller law, eh?" Bony said. "I trade. You all live whitefeller jail pretty quick. You tell me where Yorky is, and you no live whitefeller jail. You all trade, eh?"

Eyes lifted from the ground. Men looked at men, and the lubras frowned, scowled, muttered. Finally all eyes were directed to the blind Chief. Even Murtee waited on his decision. The minutes passed, and tension increased so that when Canute stood and the greatcoat, unbuttoned, opened to reveal his enormous paunch and spindle-stick legs, still there was proof that the aura of authority can crown an aborigine.

"Yorky is whitefeller-blackfeller. Blackfeller not trade."

He sat down on his stump, and instantly Bony said:

"Bimeby blackfeller trade. Bimeby blackfeller trade in whitefeller jail. You forget about Sarah, about that fight. Anything you do to Sarah, you all look out. Anything you do to Charlie, you all look out. You tell wild-blackfeller go back to camp, clear off your country, stay off your country, pretty quick. Palaver finish. Trade finish. Meena my woman. Tobacco your chew. Okee, all right!"

"Okee all right! Meena your woman," agreed Canute cheerfully, obviously happy that the conference was ended.

Bony stepped forward to prove the proven. He stood before the King of the Orrabunna Nation and held out his

hand. The blind man detached his hand from that of the Counsellor and reached forward. They shook hands.

Gravely Bony walked back to the car. Without speaking, he went backward into the seat behind the wheel and drove on towards Loaders Springs. Meena was puzzled, waiting for him to speak. For fifteen minutes Bony drove and then stopped.

He made two cigarettes, one of which he gave to the girl and then he said:

"You belong to me. I bought you with five pounds of tobacco. What Marie, my wife, is going to say doesn't bear thinking about."

"Don't tell her."

"You don't know why I bought you, do you?"

"Of course I do. You bought me because you desire me."

"Don't be silly," Bony said, severely.

"Silly! What's silly about it? A man doesn't buy a lubra unless he wants her."

"Or something else from her, Meena. You are my woman, remember. So you will tell me what I want to know. The other night I asked you a question. I asked you if you knew where Yorky is holing up, and you said you didn't know. Do you know?"

"No, I don't," replied Meena angrily.

"I asked also if Canute knew where Yorky is, and you would not say. I ask you now if Canute knows. Tell me."

Meena tossed the cigarette end beyond the open window, tossed her hair without regard to the pad, and sulked. Bony partially turned and slowly rubbed the palms of his hands together.

"These can hurt more than a waddy," he said. "You are my woman, as I have told you more than once. What you tell me is no longer any business of Canute, so leave your side of the gulf and meet me."

"Gulf! What d'you mean, gulf?"

"Never mind. Answer my questions. First, does Canute know where Yorky is?"

"Yes, he does. So does Murtee."

"Does Charlie know?"

Quickly the girl shook her head.

"But Charlie knows that Canute knows?"

The head nodded.

"What else does Canute know?"

Reluctantly the girl turned to meet his eyes, tears in her own.

"We been trying to find out, Sarah and me. Ole Fren Yorky was always kind to Sarah and me. What for he went and killed Mrs Bell we can't find out. Sarah and me are glad he wasn't caught by Mr Pierce, and if we knew where he was we wouldn't tell you."

"I'd make you tell me," snapped Bony.

"No, you wouldn't. Nor make me blackfeller way, either."

"But what of little Linda Bell? A white child, frightened, perhaps hungry, living like a dingo with Yorky."

"She'll be all right with Yorky. I know. Yorky is my father. There's no white man good like Yorky."

Bony sighed.

"There are times when I am a very poor policeman, Meena. I should take you from this car and beat you, and no one could interfere because you are my woman. It is said that your father, for a reason we don't yet know, murdered an inoffensive woman and abducted her small child, and you are in sympathy with him. You don't believe, do you, that Yorky didn't shoot Mrs Bell?"

"I don't know, Inspector, I don't know," she wailed. "He must have been mad or something. And now you make me want to help you catch him, and have him sent away and killed. Go on, beat me. I want you to beat me. I'm your woman. You bought me."

She twisted farther round to bury her face in her arms, and gently Bony twisted his fingers in her short black hair.

The hell fired by the meeting of two races and ever open to receive him, he knew was open to take her, too.

"Would you like me to tell you why I bought you, Meena?"

Abruptly her face lifted, and she was looking at him with tear-washed and grey-flecked eyes.

"I bought you from Canute for Charlie."

CHAPTER 17

BONY TRADES HIS WOMAN

BONY STOOD before the open french window of his bedroom and regarded the rising slope topped by the pine trees, and the slope was the rock he had not yet cracked although he had chipped it; the inscrutable surface of this land he was unable to delve into, although having scratched it.

Were it not for the possibility that the abducted child was alive, he would have enjoyed to the full the tussle with the aboriginal element behind his investigation into the murder of Mrs Bell, would have accepted the hardness of the rock, the imperviousness of the surface, as a test for his patience. What had appeared a long period of effort was actually less than two weeks, during which he had achieved more than Pierce and his half-hundred men had done in a month.

Now he would hammer and delve in other places.

Donning a gown and slippers, he opened the door and listened for sounds of domestic activity. As anticipated, it was too early for the staff to be at work, and silently he passed along the short passage to the living-room, and crossed to the kitchen.

He was smiling as he primed a kerosene stove with methylated spirits, recalling that he owned a lubra who ought to have been up long since to minister to his thirst, and that, when all was said and established, the Canutes and the Mur-

tees got along very nicely, thank you. The sun about to rise, and the wife still abed! Enough to challenge any aborigine.

He was seated at the kitchen table drinking his third cup of tea and smoking his fifth cigarette, when sounds introduced the cook to her kitchen. Wearing a man's gown she paused a moment to wipe the sleep from her eyes, and then banged the clock on the dresser and ruffled her hair back from her forehead. Still ignoring Bony, she left the kitchen, came back with kindling wood, lit the stove and departed for the outside wash-house.

She reappeared at the same inner door, and this time dressed for the day's toil in a yellow dress, protected by a faded blue apron.

"You are up late," Bony said.

"Sunday morning," Sarah countered.

"There's tea in the pot," he coaxed. "I'll make you a cigarette."

She poured tea, brought it to the table and drew up a chair. He could not but note that her forearms were the size of his legs, and regretted he had not witnessed her performance with the tree. He estimated her weight at fifteen stone, and her age still under fifty. On her face were the cicatrices of her totem, and behind her dark eyes the shutters were already lowered to repel his attacks. She accepted the cigarette and evinced surprise when he proffered a light.

Bony sat at ease and regarded her. She came to the point of looking directly at him, and, expecting him to speak, became anxious when he did not. Dark eyes clashed with blue eyes and the table was a gulf between them. A glimmering of the truth met the mind of the primitive woman. This man was not one of her own kind, but, being a woman, her heart was bound to triumph.

"What for you trade Canute for my Meena?" she asked.

"Didn't she tell you?"

Sarah shook her greying head. She had forgotten the tea. The cigarette burned unnoticed between her stumpy

fingers. He could see the beginning of anguish creep into her eyes, but he withheld speech, and presently she said:

"What for? You are man from whitefeller country. What for you trade for my Meena? Meena's my Meena. Ole Fren Yorky lie with me. Ole Fren Yorky my man. Ole Fren Yorky marry me blackfeller way. To hell with Mission feller."

"Better for Meena to be my woman than belong to old Canute," Bony said. "What for you promise little Meena baby to him?"

"Long time ago Canute say he tell policeman about Yorky and me, I not promise him baby. I promise him baby then he still say tell policeman. Yorky little feller. He fight Canute. Canute no more tell policeman."

"But he stuck to the promised baby?"

"Yair. She grow up and he try for her. We beat him, we always beat him. We try beat you, too."

"You may, but not Meena," he said, smiling to rouse her. "Meena, she marry me, big-feller policeman. She go away with big-feller policeman. You no see Meena no more."

The large black eyes blazed, and the fire was extinguished by the blue ice of his own. She began to emit long-drawn sobs, and down her large face tears fell, reminding him of her daughter. Her voice now wailed:

"What for Ole Fren Yorky shoot Mrs Bell and run away with Linda? What for he do that? What for you come and take my Meena away? What for . . . what for . . . what for . . ."

"How do you know Ole Fren Yorky killed Mrs Bell?" he demanded. "You say Ole Fren Yorky run away and Yorky surely killed Mrs Bell. Other feller p'raps kill Mrs Bell, and kill Linda and Yorky, too."

Hope was born like a star and extinguished like a slush lamp. Sarah's fear and despondency swept back over her.

"They found Yorky's tracks," she fought back.

"Did you see those tracks?"

"No. Bill Harte did, and Arnold, and Constable Pierce."

"They ought to know."

"Yair. Meena and me was put to cooking and housework. The men went tracking Ole Fren Yorky. They find where Ole Fren Yorky went to, and wouldn't say anything. Me and Meena tried to find out."

"Does Charlie know?"

"Don't think."

"Did Charlie see Yorky's tracks behind the meat-house?"

"What for he see them? He was put tracking. They all was that day, soon's the men had their breakfast."

"Now you listen, Sarah," he said slowly. "I tell you something, you promise to keep it secret?"

Slight hesitation, and then surrender. He said:

"Yorky was here last night."

The statement rocked her before freezing her to immobility.

"You come with me," he commanded. "I show you."

She ambled after him through the back door, along the rear of the house, round to the side veranda on to which his bedroom opened. Opposite his room, steps broke the long veranda railing, and at the bottom of the steps were the imprints of a man who walked on the soles of his feet. The woman halted as though meeting a wall in the dark. She bent low, moved to one side and then the other of the three distinct imprints.

On straightening up, her eyes expressed bafflement, and her voice conviction.

"Them's not Yorky's tracks," she said.

"Look again."

She obeyed, shaking her head as again she squinted at the prints from several angles.

"Go fetch Meena. Tell her I want to see her here. Don't tell her about the tracks."

Meena came in shorts and bath towel. As with her mother, Bony hadn't to indicate the tracks. Like her mother, she stooped and squinted at the prints from different angles.

And, like her mother, at first she thought they were Yorky's tracks, and finally decided they were not.

"Yorky here last night?" suggested Bony, and she denied it resolutely. "All right. Fetch Charlie. Bring him but don't tell him why. You understand?"

"Yes. Someone make believe they are Yorky's tracks?"

"Let us hear what Charlie says."

Meena dropped the towel and ran like a moorhen to the quarters.

"What for, Mr Bonaparte, what for someone do this?" demanded Sarah, glints in her eyes. "What for someone make like Yorky came last night?"

"Wait till Charlie's seen them. Even then I mightn't be able to tell you."

They could see Meena dragging the sleepy Charlie by the hand. She acted fairly when she pushed him forward on reaching the veranda, and Charlie continued under the impetus until she saw the tracks. It was comical how those tracks dashed sleep from his eyes.

"Feller like Yorky," he said, summing up. "Walk like Yorky. Don't know that feller."

They waited upon Bony, and Bony was smiling triumphantly.

"We won't say anything about these tracks being crook ones, eh?"

"If you say so," agreed Meena. "But why, who made them?"

"I did. Charlie, could you make them?"

"I'll try."

"Not now. Back to the kitchen, Sarah, and you, Meena. You're both under the ban of silence. I'll explain to Charlie what I think, and he can tell you. Come on, Charlie."

They went up the slope, the aborigine in shorts, Bony in flapping dressing-gown. Bony lit a small fire, as blackfellers for centuries have arranged the kindling wood, and motioned Charlie to squat over it with him. With the supreme patience of his race, the aborigine waited whilst Bony made

two cigarettes, and then it wasn't of strange tracks that Bony spoke.

"Meena tell you I traded Canute for her?"

"Yair. Why the hell you do that? You said you'd work on Canute for me."

"So I did, Charlie. I bought Meena from him. And some time or other I am going to sell her to you."

For the second time this morning hope was born like a star, but this time it wasn't extinguished.

"I paid forty plugs of tobacco for Meena," Bony said.

"I pay you more. I got money on the station books."

"I think Meena is worth five hundred plugs, even a thousand."

"Tough guy, eh?" charged Charlie, heavily frowning.

"Well, suppose I give you Meena, what would you give me?"

"Anything I got."

"True answers to my questions?"

"What you want to know?"

"I'm asking would you give true answers to my questions if I give you Meena?"

Charlie nodded, and slowly a smile spread over his expressive face.

"It's a deal," Bony said, and they shook hands over the tiny fire. "You answer all my questions, I give you Meena. You and Meena go off to the Missioner and be married properly when I say so. Okee?"

"Okee, tough guy."

"I shall be tough, too. Where is the tribe's treasure house?"

"What! No!"

"All right! No Meena for you."

Agony filled the black eyes. Sweat broke in great globules on the prominent forehead.

"I can't tell that," cried Charlie. "You know I can't tell that."

"I know where the treasure house is, but I am testing you

to be sure you give true answers," flagrantly lied Bony, and was given the information that the tribe's cherished churinga stones, the magic pointing bones, and all the other relics which chained this tribe of the Orrabunna Nation to the generations of those who had lived and died before them, were in the keeping of a certain tree in a certain place.

"All right, Charlie. Now I know you speak true. Forget about the treasure house. I am your friend; you are my friend. D'you know what plaster of Paris is?" Charlie shook his head.

"Well, do you know what plasticene is?"

"Yair, we worked with that at the Mission."

"Good! Plaster of Paris is in powder form, and when a little water is mixed with it, it turns to a paste, which dries hard pretty quickly." Bony made a print of his hand on the ground and illustrated the process of taking casts. "That day Mrs Bell was shot, Constable Pierce made a plaster cast of the tracks behind the meat-house. I have that plaster cast and from it made the tracks below the veranda steps. So, Charlie, the tracks I made are exactly the same as those which were behind the meat-house. Get me?"

"Yair. Then Yorky's tracks behind the meat-house weren't left by Yorky?"

"That's true. Someone else made those tracks, Charlie, to be sure that a whitefeller would find them. It just happened that no blackfeller saw them. Do you reckon they were good enough to trick Bill Harte and the others?"

Charlie pondered, gravely serious.

"That Bill Harte good bushman," he said. "Them tracks pretty good, too. I reckon Bill'd fall for 'em."

"And the other whitefellers would, too?"

"Yair, quicker than Bill Harte."

"Now you go down and wait for breakfast. Whisper to Meena that perhaps Yorky didn't shoot Mrs Bell, but is taking the blame for it. Don't tell Meena anything more than that."

CHAPTER 18

DECISION TO DYNAMITE

THE REACTIONS of Charlie and the women to the prints made with Pierce's plaster cast were identical. They were shocked by seeing what they thought were Yorky's tracks, and astounded by the probability that the original prints declared to have been clear behind the meat-house had been made with a pair of Yorky's old working boots.

Yorky, leaving Mount Eden for a spell at the township, would most certainly leave his working clothes and boots in one of the rooms at the quarters. Thus anyone could use the old boots to make the prints, and smooth out his own tracks as he retreated.

The expert tracker, however, does not limit himself to the actual imprints of the feet. He takes into consideration the angle of each foot from the imaginary dead centre line, as well as the distance separating the prints, revealing the length of the stride, and which leg is shorter than the other.

It is possible for a forger to make exact imprints of a man's boots, but he cannot forge the spaces between the placings of a man's feet accurately enough to deceive an aborigine. The aborigine himself could not make a perfect forgery on all counts.

Constable Pierce, wise man, did not make plaster prints of individual tracks, but had made an extensive cast including two left and one right boot-print, and therefore the prints shown to Charlie and the women were exact replicas of those made behind the meat-house.

Why it happened that no aborigine saw the tracks behind the meat-house could be understood. First Harte had found those tracks. He had taken Arnold to see them, and Eric Maundy. Wootton had seen them, too, but Wootton was no tracker. When Pierce arrived, he was told they were

Yorky's tracks, and he saw what he had been led to expect to see. So, the overall acceptance of the forged tracks being genuine, why bother to have them checked by aborigines urgently needed for the task of tracing Yorky and the child?

Nothing squared in this investigation. It was like a semi-deflated bag, which, when punched, bulged somewhere. The only person who could have no motive for forging those prints was Yorky.

Questions: Who forged them and why? Why, if not to create conviction that Yorky had shot Mrs Bell and taken the child? Instead of one murder, there could be three murders? By the aborigines or the whites?

Bony had waited for the sand dune to come to him. He had prodded a sleeping mystery and it had stirred. He had continued this investigation according to the rules laid down in the practice of crime detection. And now he was convinced that his efforts were being frustrated by a force which the rules had not taken into account. This being so, he showered and dressed in a mood which seldom bothered him.

In the living-room he found Wootton making notes at his radio bench, and the cattleman's mind was busy with the news he had received from a station to the north-east of Lake Eyre.

"Water still pouring into the lake down the Diamantina and Warburton, as well as Coopers Creek," he said. "Could be a mighty flood if those rivers continue to run."

"When did water last flow into the lake?" Bony asked.

"Three years back, but the lake hasn't been properly filled for fifty years, I believe." Wootton sat and unfolded a napkin. They chose a cereal from the impeccable Meena. "It would take a hell of a lot of flooding to fill this lake."

"How account for the fact that the shore this side is still moist enough to cover a man's boots with mud, only a short way from the beach?"

"A question I asked a geologist. Pass the sugar, please.

Feller called around shortly after I came. Stayed a week. Interesting ideas. Main point seems that a time long ago Lake Eyre was a sea, with hills and dales and holes and things like under other oceans. Then the sea dried out, sort of, leaving the lake still holding water. When that dried out, all the water left was in the holes and things. Get me?"

"Yes. Thank you, Meena. Bacon and eggs, please. Oh, yes, and coffee."

"Right. The original bottom of the lake is composed of the stuff that forms claypans, like the strip of beach all round. On top of that the wind has blown dust and sand and mullock in which frogs and fish and things have lived and perished, and added their remains. In other words, on the top of the original hard ground there's this thick layer of mud. So what? Meena, I'll have bacon and eggs, too. Well, when the water from the rivers and creeks flows into the lake, it spreads only a little way on the top because most of it seeps down to spread first between the hard bottom and the top mud, as well as having to fill up the deep holes and valleys. So that a heck of a lot of water must flow before the surface of the lake this side shows signs of it, and even then it will appear first under the mud."

"So that in three years, even longer, without rain, the lake doesn't dry hard even close to shore."

"That's about the strength of it, Inspector. Meena! Meena! My coffee."

The girl brought the coffee, and stood behind Bony's chair. She waited for his toast rack to empty, then went to the kitchen for more, making no effort to be so attentive to the cattleman.

"Could I use a horse this morning?" Bony asked. "Mine is too slow. And I don't want a flash one, either. I have work to do. And I need a sugar sack."

"Of course. I'll tell Charlie after breakfast. Meena! More toast. What's the matter with you this morning, Meena? Why all the attention to Inspector Bonaparte, and damn little for me?"

Meena apologised, and departed for more toast. Bony said:

"You have not heard that Meena is now my woman?"

"Meena your woman!" Wootton's green eyes opened wide, and he squared his thick shoulders. "Don't get it."

"Yesterday afternoon I bought her from Canute."

"You did! Didn't know he owned her, although someone did tell me she was promised to Canute when she was a baby. Oh, so that's why you wanted the tobacco. Reckon you got her pretty cheap. What do you think, Meena?"

"Might be too dear, too."

Mr Wootton's eyes passed over her, from head to red shoes and again to her face. From her he looked at Bony, saying:

"Yes, you bought her cheap. May I ask for what reason?"

"Make a profit on my bargain. Meena, please leave us. I am not going to tell secrets, nor will you."

The girl came closer, took up Bony's used plate, smiled at Wootton, and almost ran from the room, delaying the giggle which escaped after she entered the kitchen.

"Secrets!" murmured Wootton.

"Lovers' secrets," Bony said, busy now with a cigarette. "Tell me. I saw that your fences at one time extended farther into the lake than they do now. How long ago was that?"

"Years before I came here. Could have been when the boundary fence was first built. That was in 1923. I do know that. Many of the original posts still standing. Much of the netting had been renewed. But it's still a good fence. You ride along it?"

"Visited Yorky's old camps. Rations at all of them. D'you keep a check on your rations store?"

"Not a strict one. Why?"

"Sarah hand out much to her tribe?"

"Not that I know of. What's on your mind?"

"I'm wondering what Yorky is living on."

"Tucker on homesteads over in New South Wales, even

across in Western Australia by this time. Surely you don't think he's hanging around Lake Eyre, do you?"

"I have no proof either way. I hope to have it this afternoon. But the footprints behind the meat-house and stated to have been made by Yorky, I have now proved to be forgeries."

Wootton was obviously astonished.

"Those tracks were not made by Yorky," Bony went on. "Three aborigines support that opinion."

"But everyone, including Pierce, says they were."

"Did any aborigine see them when they were brought back from the Neales?"

"I don't know. Don't think so. Everything was so rushed. Wait. Pierce had his tracker with him. I did see him looking at the tracks."

"The police tracker isn't a local abo. He might or might not have noted Yorky's tracks in Loaders Springs. Anyway, he would not be as familiar with Yorky's tracks as the locals."

Thoughtfully the cattleman loaded his pipe. He said:

"What does that infer?"

"I'm not sure . . . yet." Bony rose. "Will you have that horse brought in for me?"

"Right away."

Wootton was decidedly disturbed. Having instructed Charlie, he sat at his office desk for an hour without attending to the litter of documents. It being Sunday there was no smoke-oh for the men, but about ten o'clock Meena came to tell him that tea was made. He went with her to the kitchen, then asked:

"What's all this about the Inspector buying you from Canute?"

The girl smiled demurely, and her mother laughed loudly, but the cattleman could see no joke.

"I suppose you know that the Inspector has a wife where he comes from, and sons almost young men?" he pressed.

Both women laughed, and to neither question would

they give answer with words. He was irritated by this evasion, and knew it was futile to be so. He felt that a good deal had happened here on his own territory of which he was ignorant, and that also irritated him. No man likes being a kind of pawn in his own business.

Wootton was again in his office when he heard the thudding of hoofs, guessed that Bony was back, and waited expectantly. A few minutes later Bony entered the office, to put down on the desk the sugar sack he had borrowed. He had taken it away empty; it was now half-filled and tied securely.

Bony asked for sealing wax, and Wootton watched the string knots heavily loaded with wax and sealed with the imprint of a thumb. Then the blue eyes were regarding him seriously.

"The contents of this bag are of value impossible of assessment," Bony said. "Could you make room for it in your safe?"

"I think so," assented Wootton. "What's in it?"

"I don't wish to sound mysterious, but it would be best for you not to know. Maybe I shall ask you to give it back before tonight. I hope so. Under no circumstances hand it to anyone else, excepting Constable Pierce. He may be here later."

Wootton took the bag to his safe, rearranging account books and oddments to make room for it. He was further irritated by the secrecy of Bony's sealing wax.

"Would you like to keep the safe key?" he asked with asperity.

"Thanks, but that wouldn't do." Bony smiled disarmingly.

It was warm inside this room despite the window and door being open. They could hear the low roaring of a willi-willi, and within two seconds a wind rushed on the building as the core of the whirlwind passed behind the men's quarters. The dinner gong, a triangular length of railway iron beaten with an iron bar by the mighty Sarah, broke the tension.

"I have to wash-brush," Bony said, and left the cattleman to follow more leisurely.

Wootton was already in the living-room when Bony entered to use the telephone. A minute later Bony was speaking to Pierce.

"About those footprints, Pierce. Did your tracker see them?"

"Yes. Why?"

"Did he make any comment?"

"No."

"He accepted them as Yorky's, you think?"

"Must have done. He didn't say they were not Yorky's. Why?"

"Well, they aren't Yorky's. The abos here tell me they are not, and they should know."

"But . . . I don't get it, Inspector."

"I don't, yet. The job was done well enough to deceive the men here, and yourself, but they didn't trick the abos. I understand that not one of the local abos saw those tracks at the time. Correct?"

"That's so. We put 'em all on the hunt as soon as possible."

"All right, leave it for now. Another thing. If I don't contact you by six to-night, come out here. I've given myself a difficult assignment. There is a sugar sack deposited in Mr Wootton's safe which must be returned to the owner should anything happen to prevent me contacting you after six."

"Sounds grim. Who's the owner?"

"The contents of the bag will tell you that. Be on hand. I'll ring again at six. I'm in the position of the man who, having tried to push the house down, has decided to blow it up."

CHAPTER 19

EXTRACTING INFORMATION

Canute, King of the remnants of a past civilisation, had the game sewn up. Not for him a crown wobbling on an uneasy head. Not for him financial worries, domestic worries nor the problem of 'keeping up with the Joneses'. Like his ancestors, Canute knew all the secrets of living without heart disease or stomach ulcers.

This afternoon he reclined at ease on an old bag spread in the shade of a wattle, and chewed tobacco. A small boy was shooing away any stray ant, and the chief lubra was baking yabbies caked with mud and buried in hot ashes. It was a beautiful day, in dark shadow; a wonderful existence for a man. It would have remained perfect had not a remembered voice said:

"Take a little palaver with me, Canute."

The King sat up, drew his feet under his thighs, grunted his displeasure. The little boy ran off to the lubras now standing amazed that the big-feller policeman had entered camp without their awareness of his approach.

"We have yabber-yabber, eh?" suggested Bony. "You tell Murtee and that old fellow who is your eyes, and the other old men. Then we all yabber-yabber, eh?"

Canute shouted, and from various deep shadows men stretched and yawned, belched and muttered, momentarily froze on seeing the visitor squatting beside their Chief, and obeyed the order. The visitation was accepted as a tribal affair, and the King was led to his throne and his advisers grouped themselves about him.

The case brought by Bony the previous day was still there, and he seated himself and again, with slow deliberation, fashioned a cigarette, lit it, and stared at each man in turn. There was Canute, heavy from easy living, grey of

hair and beard, still powerful, probably still under seventy. There was his eyes, a very old white-haired and white-bearded man named Beeloo, who was a human lath and crippled, but mentally on top. There was Murtee, the Medicine Man, about forty years old, savage of aspect, still savage in mind, his tongue pierced and his body carved with flints, as befitted the holder of such office. Finally, there were six other men, all older than sixty. Not one had attended a whitefeller school.

"You tellum those wild abos go back to camp?" Bony asked; and Canute nodded, on his face a sullen expression, ill-fitting his normal jovial nature.

"You smoke for them again, and you all be sorry," threatened Bony. "Which feller not go walkabout up to the Neales? Come on now, you tell pretty quick."

"All blackfeller went walkabout that time," declared Canute.

"You cunning feller, eh? Which blackfeller come back quick; come back look-see Mrs Bell lying dead outside kitchen door?"

"No blackfeller do that," replied Murtee.

Bony expelled smoke, gazed at chattering finches in the tree above, deliberately inhaled and again blew smoke in a thin blue line. Ebony idols regarded him with shuttered eyes.

"I look-see find Yorky and Linda. You say big-feller policeman no find Yorky and Linda. I say you know all the time where Yorky and Linda are camped. You say: 'Go to hell.' Now I go crook. Whitefeller law is more strong than blackfeller law. What for you not tell the lubras and the young men where Yorky and Linda are camped? What for you all cunning fellers like this? Mrs Bell wasn't a lubra. Yorky isn't a blackfeller. Linda is a white child. Nothing to do with blackfeller law. You tell, eh?"

No movement. No speech. Graven images in human flesh. Bony persisted.

"One blackfeller stayed in camp that time you go walkabout, or he came back pretty quick. He went to homestead. He saw Mrs Bell dead on ground. He saw the blood mark on her back. It was like this." With a stick Bony drew the mark of interrogation. "He wait here till you all come back from the Neales. He didn't send up smoke about Mrs Bell because he knew Mr Wootton and the men thought all blackfeller off on walkabout. Okee! All right!

"You all come back on trucks, perhaps. I don't know properly. But, when Canute and Murtee come back, that blackfeller who stayed in camp and saw Mrs Bell told about her, and showed Canute the mark on Mrs Bell's back. He held Canute's wrist like he's doing now, and made Canute see that mark. You, Beeloo, was blackfeller who saw Mrs Bell dead. Well, you now tell me about Mrs Bell all dead, eh?"

Not the flicker of an eyelid.

"Okee! All right, you-all! You know big old red-gum, your treasure house? I find treasure house. I find magic churinga stones, and head bands, and magic Kurdaitcha shoes, and the pointing bones. I find all them. What you-all say to that?"

That defrosted them. Murtee leaped to his feet, stumbled when Bony's automatic was directed to his paunch.

"Sit down, Murtee. You-all sit down. Feller that gets up till I say so is pretty quick dead. I am big-feller policeman. Whitefeller law. You try fight whitefeller law you get shot pretty damn quick. You listen.

"You Orrabunna fellers all finish. I took away the treasure, the pointing bones, everything. I lock 'em up. Blackfeller law no good any more."

The loss of their tribe's treasure was devastating. Minus their magic stones, their precious heirlooms of human hair, their ancient dilly-bags, and the all-powerful-with-magic pointing bones, they were divested of family, of tribe, of origin, almost of being. As Bony had said, without

command of their treasure they were as nothing. There sat the whitefeller law. Death looked at each from that pistol, and now all protection from the white and the black laws was withdrawn from them. They were naked, defenceless against their enemies that had been kept at bay by generations of forebears with and by that hoarded treasure.

It was a body blow that Bony hated to deliver, and not for an instant would he have done so, had it not been for Linda Bell. Those shuttered eyes, the stubborn minds, were barriers not to be surmounted by bribes, threats, persuasion, argument, or even physical punishment.

"I have other pointing bones," snarled Murtee. "I kill you. Short time, long time, I kill you."

Bony puffed cigarette smoke, lifted his upper lip in a magnificent sneer.

"Wind, Murtee. Strong-feller wind. Pointing bones I took, more powerful than your other pointing bones. I point the bones back at you. You die slow time, long time. Then you-all die."

Livid fear mastered them, tautened every lip, tensed every muscle.

"We trade, eh?" said Bony softly.

Canute dashed drops of sweat from his forehead. Murtee seemed to shrink into himself. The ancient man shook, but his claw-like hand continued to grasp the Chief's wrist.

"What trade? You say," pleaded Canute, and Murtee shouted. He attempted to stand, but his neighbour hauled him down. It seemed that Murtee's protest strengthened Canute, and the others nodded as though he could see their support.

"You tell about Yorky and Linda, I give back your magic treasure."

"Okee, all right."

"I give back your treasure and Murtee not point the bone at me, or any whitefeller."

"Okee, all right," agreed Canute; and the others, including Murtee, nodded agreement.

"You tell all about Yorky and Linda, and I get treasure from lock-up at homestead, pretty soon, quick, eh?"

"We seal it," Canute said, and Bony drew on the ground between them two interlocking circles. The ceremony of the intermingling of blood followed, then Canute ordered the ancient who was his eyes to speak. His English was so light that a translation is given.

"I am a very old man, but still active about the camp. I could not go so far on walkabout as the Neales River. When the tribe went walkabout, I go bush. My heart is heavy. I am old and lonely. By and by I come back near homestead. I hear Mr Wootton shoot crow, and I say this is strange, because this day Mr Wootton he go to Loaders Springs. I sit down long time. Then I get up and look-see out over lake, and I see Linda and Yorky out there on walkabout.

"I think Mr Wootton gone off to Loaders Springs, and I go on to homestead see if Mrs Bell give me tobacco. I tell her the tribe left me behind, and I am lonely and my heart is heavy.

"When I come to homestead, I don't see Mr Wootton. I don't see any feller. Plenty of crows, though. I go round back of men's quarters. No one there. All the men away. I see something on ground near kitchen door. By and by, I go over and see it is Mrs Bell. She's lying on her stomach. She is dead. I see the blood on her back. Then I run like hell, and all day and the next day I see the mark of blood on her back. Long time I think I go bush. Then I know the tribe is back in camp and I come back, too. I tell Canute about Mrs Bell. I tell about Linda."

"Did you see Mr Wootton's car?"

"No."

"Or the dust of his car on the way to town?"

"No."

"You tell lies, eh? If Yorky and Linda walkabout on lake, whitefeller see their tracks," taunted Bony.

"Yorky wear whitefeller Kurdaitcha shoes. Yorky follow

dingo pad. Yorky not leave clear tracks. Whitefeller don't think to look for Kurdaitcha marks on dingo pad."

"Good! You speak true. What Yorky do out on lake? He go right over other side?"

"Might be he camp along little-feller sand dune."

No matter how he probed this last statement, Bony made no further progress relative to this point. The curtain had been lifted just a little to reveal the purpose of that discarded case board he had found outside Yorky's last camp. The whitefeller's Kurdaitcha shoes were certainly shoes for walking on mud. The 'little-feller' sand dune could be a tiny area of sandy-dry land in the sea of mud, the summit of a mountain in the mud sea, as the Pacific Islands are mountain tops rising above the ocean. The picture was clear enough, but the reality was to be questioned. Bony asked:

"Why didn't you tell all this to Constable Pierce?"

The answer was good and sufficient. Canute said:

"Ole Fren Yorky white-blackfeller."

"Now you, Beeloo, you tellum truth. You say no one at homestead that time you find Mrs Bell dead. Who did you see near the homestead?"

"Yorky and Linda."

"Who else?"

"Saw horseman way up on rise."

"Pine tree rise?"

"Other side of homestead. Long way 'way. Going like hell."

"Who was he?"

"Don't know. Long time. Long . . ."

"Could be a mile," interposed Canute.

"What colour was the horse?"

"Not look. Much dust that day. Just horse and whitefeller."

"When you saw that horseman, where were Yorky and Linda?"

"Way out on the lake, like I told."

They sat on the ground like so many squat idols on one

side of two blurred circles, the circles representing the gulf between ancient and modern Man. There remained much to be explained. For instance, there was the crucial point of contact between Yorky and the aborigines during those periods when Yorky must have collected food.

Who met Yorky with the tucker? Had he to go to the camp for it? What had he told the aborigines of the motive behind the shooting of Mrs Bell? These questions yielded little save the impression that Yorky had given nothing away from which anyone, like Pierce or himself, might gain.

"Okee! All right! We finish trade, eh?"

Canute smiled with infinite relief.

"You come with me to homestead, Murtee. I give back your treasures."

The two men walked the track to the homestead. Neither spoke a word. Bony's mind was occupied with the horseman riding from Mount Eden long after Wootton had left for Loaders Springs. He wasn't Arnold Bray, who was driving a truck that day. He was Bill Harte, or Eric Maundy, or Harry Lawton. If not one of these men . . . It had to be one of them.

Wootton was waiting in the doorway of his office, watching the approach of Murtee and Inspector Bonaparte. He saw Bony nudge the aborigine, frowned with perplexity when they both turned and skirted the house and walked up the rise to the pine trees. They stood there for a few moments during which Murtee indicated with out-flung hand a point on the long rise on the opposite side of the homestead.

Arrived at the office, Bony asked for the sugar sack from the safe. Before parting with it, he stood calmly staring into the dark inscrutable eyes of the Medicine Man.

"You big Medicine Man," he said, adding: "I big-feller policeman. Perhaps you not a cunning feller. Perhaps you just a bloody fool. I find out that Canute see blood mark on Mrs Bell's back. Canute tell me about that blood mark. He tell me with dijeridoo. Perhaps you all bloody fools. Perhaps Yorky didn't kill Mrs Bell."

CHAPTER 20

THE WAGES OF BLUFF

MURTEE STALKED away over the bare track towards the homestead gate and the camp. Bony called to Charlie, and when Charlie reached him, he loudly called for Sarah. The cook emerged and divided her attention between the departing Medicine Man and Bony, who said:

"Come with me."

He took them up to the pine trees and told them to sit beside him. There was silence while he rolled the inevitable cigarette.

"Now will you tell me everything I want to know," he said smoothly. "There will be no more backing and filling. You don't understand, but no matter, that all you aborigines have been bricks in a wall I have battered down. Now I tell you something else.

"Remember those tracks I made at the veranda steps? Same tracks that were found behind the meat-house, and which every whitefeller said were Yorky's. Someone else made those tracks, to make believe Yorky made them. I find out that old Beeloo didn't go walkabout that time. He came to homestead thinking to get tobacco from Mrs Bell after Mr Wootton left for Loaders Springs. He saw Yorky and Linda walkabout on the lake, and he saw a horseman galloping up the rise back there. That horseman could have been the feller who made those crook tracks at the meat-house. He could have killed Mrs Bell."

Sarah's eyes were now blazing black opals. Bony went on:

"That horseman was too far away for Beeloo to see who it was. If the feller on that horse killed Mrs Bell, then why did Yorky clear out with Linda? You tell me, eh?"

"One of them sums the Missioner asked us kids," Charlie grumbled. "If it takes two minutes for a boomerang to

go round in the circle in a north wind . . . Something like that?"

"Yes, Charlie, something like that. Sarah, I'm telling you this because there's a good chance that Yorky didn't kill Mrs Bell. That's a good reason why we must catch up with Yorky. Supposing he didn't kill Mrs Bell. All right, then Yorky took Linda away, and if Linda died after he took her away, then Yorky is going to jail for a long time. That's why you must tell me all you can.

"Now Beeloo saw Yorky and Linda out on the lake, and he says that Yorky must have been wearing whitefeller's Kurdaitcha shoes. Remember, Charlie, I showed you a board out at Yorky's camp, and you wouldn't say what it was. I know now. It was a board for Yorky to walkabout on the mud."

"That's true," admitted Sarah. "Yorky wore them boards when he had to work on the fence where it goes little way into the lake."

"Then he could go out a long long way along a dingo pad wearing those board shoes, couldn't he?"

Sarah nodded, her eyes now like garnets. She shook her head when Bony asked if ever she had gone with Yorky far out. Sensing opposition building to meet further questioning, he asked:

"What's out there? Dry land?" They looked at each other, each waiting for the other to answer. "I'll tell you. There is dry land out there." Their eyes showed relief when Charlie said:

"Bad place out there, all right. Pretty near the middle. Nothing only sand and a bit of scrub. That's what Murtee says. He's been there, but no one else has, or won't tell."

"Anything to eat?"

"Plenty of rabbits. Along one side, so Murtee says, there's a long waterhole with fish in it, and ducks nesting all about."

"A good place for Yorky to hide up with Linda, eh?"

"You sure that Murtee not telling lies?" inserted Sarah. "First time I hear of that ole place."

"You're a lubra," Charlie told her loftily.

"Yair. I'm a lubra. One time I'll choke that Murtee."

"One time Murtee point the bones at you, and you fall down and grab your stomach and die. Murtee is plenty powerful."

"That will do," commanded Bony. "Charlie, would you make me a pair of Kurdaitcha shoes to walkabout for Yorky?"

"Too right. When d'you want 'em?"

"By tonight."

"Okee. Boss let me work in carpenter's shop?"

"He will. That sun's getting low, Sarah. What about dinner?"

They went down the slope to the homestead, where Sarah entered the house to fence with a wildly curious Meena.

Having showered and changed, Bony found Wootton in the living-room.

"That little scheme of mine paid dividends this afternoon," he said, sitting with the cattleman. "Will you be talking to your neighbours after dinner?"

"Probably. Why?"

"Could you arrange with them to listen in to a broadcast at five tomorrow morning?"

"Yes. What's it all about?"

"Who is your oldest neighbour; been living out here the longest?"

"People named Petrie down on the south of the lake, I think."

"I'd like to talk with them tonight. Would you contact them?"

"Easily."

Meena appeared, to set the table, and the cattleman knew something had happened from her excited eyes and energetic movements. He was frowning at the polished tips of his leather slippers when Bony asked if he would loan him a rifle.

"Of course," he replied. "I've a Winchester .44 and a Savage .25."

"The Savage. It would be lighter. Who are your nearest neighbours to the south?"

"The same. The Petries. Their homestead is about a hundred miles from here. Well in financially. Two sons working there, and generally half a dozen white stockmen."

"I don't remember the place," admitted Bony. "Must have passed by on my way up when I skirted the lake. Track, of course?"

"Yes. You go up the long rise to the old homestead where the Murphys once lived. You know, the people from whom I bought Mount Eden. On from there to the bore where young Lawton met you the other day."

"That day Mrs Bell was shot, Arnold Bray was sent to the old homestead for iron?"

"Yes, that's so."

"Does he do much riding?"

"Very little. You're damned mysterious this afternoon, Inspector."

"I'll tell you something. You will recall that I said it was possible for one of you five men to have returned here that morning and murdered Mrs Bell. After you left in your car that day, a man was seen riding hard from the homestead up the rise and heading for the old homestead. I am rather curious to know who he was."

"Is that so?" drawled Mr Wootton. "Then one of three of us five could have ridden back and shot Mrs Bell?"

"Don't take me too literally. That rider could have come from the Petries' station. He could have had nothing to do with shooting Mrs Bell. He might have come on a legitimate visit, found Mrs Bell dead, and rushed away in a panic. I have made certain plans, and you will learn something of them this evening when we talk to the Petries and arrange tomorrow's broadcast. Dinner seems to be served."

Wootton's excusable curiosity was unallayed by Bony during dinner and, immediately afterwards, Bony left the house and sought Charlie, who had returned to the carpenter's shop.

The aborigine had fashioned the mud-shoes and fitted to them leather straps, and Bony now tried them on, finding them most awkward.

"Not that way," Charlie told him. "You slide 'em. Sarah show me; I show you."

"Good! I'll have to get the knack. Remember that dog-pad we saw half a mile from the pines? How many more pads like that nearby?"

"One more—at the hut on the boundary. Two more up by the Neales."

Charlie agreed to keep watch on the pad near the homestead, as from after dark, to inform Bony if any blackfeller went out to warn Yorky. Later, for an hour, he talked with the surrounding neighbours over the transceiver, and, indirectly, gained much useful information about the country, and nothing whatever concerning the centre of Lake Eyre, save that it must be a bog even during the long period of drought. Still later, Wootton became interested in certain preparations. The Savage rifle was checked, ammunition poured into a small calico bag, dry biscuits and tinned meat brought from the store, and an old rucksack Wootton remembered having for several years.

Bony slipped away from the house and sought Charlie, who was faithfully on duty at the appointed dingo pad. The aborigine reported having seen no one on that part of the beach, and Bony sent him home to his bunk, and himself cat-napped the night away until just before dawn.

It was five o'clock when he and Wootton sat before the transceiver, and Bony began his broadcast. He said:

"It is now six weeks since Mrs Bell was shot here at Mount Eden, and her little daughter vanished. You all know of the extensive and the intensive search which followed. You know that it is strongly suspected that the man who killed Mrs Bell and abducted her daughter is a locally known identity named Yorky. From information received, and following the results of my own survey of the country, I have reason to believe that somewhere in the middle of Lake

Eyre is an area of dry land forming an island in a sea of mud, and that the man Yorky escaped to that island, taking the child with him.

"Also from information I have gathered, I think it is feasible for a man to cross the mud to that island by following one of the dingo pads, when wearing mud shoes. By this means I intend to test what are as yet only theories. I intend to try to reach the island by one of the dog pads from near this homestead, starting within an hour.

"I have been informed by the aborigines that these dog pads are not numerous. They are certainly not easily discernible. Assuming that there is a dry area of land somewhere towards the centre of the lake, then we may accept as fact that the dingoes use that place to gain food or rear their pups. Picture that dry area of land as the hub of a wheel, and the dog pads as the spokes of the wheel.

"To reach the hub, I must follow one of the spokes, and, should Yorky observe me approaching, he might well leave for the shore by one of the other spokes. Therefore, you will appreciate my difficulty in apprehending him.

"I ask you to co-operate with me by arranging among yourselves to watch Lake Eyre. In view of the length of the shore-line, it will be difficult for the number of men available to watch all points, so we can only do our best. I do not anticipate contact with the wanted man until late today. I am sure you will realise how delicately this operation must be carried out. Our main objective must be the safe recovery of Linda Bell, if alive. I leave the risks to your imagination.

"Finally. There is to be no shooting unless a life is in grave danger. I want you to understand clearly that I am far from satisfied that the man Yorky actually did kill Mrs Bell. I feel that I can rely on your common sense, and know I may rely on your co-operation. Thank you."

Bony faced about from the transceiver to regard calmly Wootton's outside staff, his inside staff, and the cattlemen, who turned about with him.

"I have something to say before I leave. You have just heard me broadcast that I am not satisfied Yorky killed Mrs Bell. That he and Linda Bell are somewhere out on the lake, I am hoping to prove within hours. Two matters cause me to doubt that Yorky is our man. One is that tracks found behind the meat-house and thought to have been made by Yorky are now proved to be forgeries. Thus they were made by someone wishing to incriminate Yorky. The other reason is that on the morning that Mrs Bell was killed, after you men had left on your duties for that day, after Mr Wootton left for town in his car, a horseman was seen riding away from this homestead."

Sarah had provided early morning tea for the hands, and when all were in the kitchen, Bony telephoned Constable Pierce and spoke for five minutes. Ten minutes after that, he started out for Lake Eyre.

CHAPTER 21

THE SINK OF AUSTRALIA

THE SUN rose above Lake Eyre, and it was like facing car lights ten yards distant. It was no hindrance to Bony, who had to concentrate his attention on the whitefeller Kurdaitcha shoes, fashioned so differently from the soft feathers worn by that fabulous creature. But the sun masked him completely from Wootton, who stood on the white beach, as well as from others standing high among the pines. He found that weight related to the area of the boards attached to his feet was not sufficient to clog the footwear if he proceeded by sliding one foot forward, then the other, and at the beginning of the journey the dingo pad was quite easy to see.

Progress, however, was slow. Muscles unaccustomed

to particular stress began to tire, so that, on glancing back, he was dismayed on estimating that his voyage over The-Sea-That-Was was but a mile begun.

A hot wind was strengthening from the north, and it seemed to enshroud him in isolation completely foreign to that experienced on 'dry land'. One cannot be completely isolated when trees are neighbours, and sand dunes are dwellings, but here was nothing of the comfort of familiar things. Here was menace to spur imagination, to emphasise the hopelessness of help in distress; pictures of himself slowly engulfed by dark and evil mud, or trapped by monstrous things, flashed across his mind.

Grimly he went on when he longed to go back.

The dingo pad was seldom more than twelve inches wide, and often was reduced to four inches. At some places it was quite distinct; at others only a good tracker could follow it. When he was three miles from shore, the pad wound about a great deal, which aroused his interest, because, under normal circumstances, a travelling dog proceeds straighter than does a man. Presently the pad became less twisted, and gave him his first surprise . . . a narrow strip of hard sun-baked mud.

He was glad to remove the boards from his feet and pause for a smoke, and it was something of a shock to realise that his interest in these surroundings had subjugated the purpose of the journey. Where the pad met the dry patch, the dogs had scratched their paws clean of mud.

Having rested, he returned to the pad, noting once again that his board tracks were exceedingly light, and when examining the depressions with his fingertips, he learned that the resilience of the mud would within hours entirely obliterate them. That the pad itself remained clear was due to the number of dogs that had used it since water covered the mud so long ago.

This dry patch of only a few yards wide and a hundred in length was a resting place, as he himself was using it. The marks of claws on the hard surface proved that. It was

perhaps four miles from the shore, now distorted by the mirage creating wide rivers in the declivities, and vast lakes between the slopes of gibber-covered uplands. Vast sheets of 'water' lay about, the mud surface visible only within a radius of half a mile.

Not only dogs, but crows had rested on this 'island' in the mirage. And not only crows had stayed a little while, gone on. Two spent matches told of human visitation. The matches told him nothing but that . . . which was most satisfying.

To leave this patch of hard land was as easy as to arrive, there being only the one pad. Refreshed, Bony fastened the mud shoes and continued along this highway of the dingoes, the mirage receding before him, and ever flowing after him, the immediate surround always the same—flat, uniform of colouring, the top surface lifted to brittle pieces of crisp mud crust. A journey deadly monotonous, were it not for the little mysteries.

Why did the pad turn sharply to the right, continue in that direction for a quarter mile, again turn left, to continue the over-all course to the east? Why did it proceed for three miles more straight than a man-made path, and then zigzag over a full mile? There was nothing which could be seen to account for this.

The day wore on, and he was beginning to wonder what kind of night he would spend if he had to camp on this narrow dog pad, when again the pad angled sharply. It had reached the border of a large area pitted by open holes the size of a florin. The dogs had not crossed it, had skirted it, and he saw why when a green finger emerged from one of the holes, beckoned to him, sank again into the mud. Then while he watched, other green fingers appeared, beckoned, and disappeared.

Curiosity was suddenly submerged by desire to get away from this place of the unknown; the beckoning fingers became the miasma of a nightmare, and the board shoes the leaden feet of it.

An hour later he was thankful to reach another patch of bone-dry mud, to rest and take stock of his progress. The sun said four o'clock. There was no landmark, and how far out in the lake he had come it was not possible to assess.

This hard patch was about an acre in extent, and, having rested his aching muscles, he strolled over it and found evidence of a dingo rest, and again the spent matches. Of human tracks there were none, the ground being too hard to register any.

He decided to spend the night here, although he could not dismiss from his mind those sinister green fingers. He was less concerned by his food supply than by the three pints of water he now carried in the canvas bag.

Since daybreak he had consumed one pint, and, despite the aid of the pebble he had sucked all day, he felt this was the minimum for existence. The aborigines could live for a week and more on half a gallon of water, but not D. I. Bonaparte with his preference for countless cups of tea.

Until the sun went down, it was not possible to see land, and Bony occupied time by testing for water under the mud. He had found a short swathe of tree debris, among which was a four-foot stick, and although he didn't find water even by seepage, he did uncover the mystery of the erratic course of the dingo pad. The true bottom of Lake Eyre was not flat, as the surface of the mud overlay indicated, but rather was similar to the sea bottom, with its valleys and hills and mountains. The dogs followed the summits of ridges, and the two areas of hardened mud merely covered the tops of subterranean hillocks; and that area of mud from which upthrust those extraordinary green fingers must mark a valley or chasm.

The mirage ebbed, to form long silver strips, and these shallows disappeared slowly, to vanish entirely when the huge red fireball tipped the distant uplands. There was the land ten miles away, and there was an object three miles away which certainly was a moving human being.

Seated on the hard mud, his arms clasping his knees, Bony

watched and waited for the being to identify himself. Slowly colour faded from the sky, and the lake revealed all its true starkly drab and loathsome self, from which the sky blenched. As the minutes passed, the figure on the mud appeared to be no nearer, and yet was following the pad by which he had travelled. The dusk deepened, and there was no skyline, no background to gain a silhouette and so learn whether the person was white or black.

When half a mile from Bony, when he could dimly follow movement, the figure stopped, stood for a few seconds, finally sank to the pad. It was obvious that the man did not know of this second resting place, and had decided to park himself before darkness blinded him to the depths of mud either side of him.

For a space, Bony lay on his back looking at the unwinking stars, only those of the first dimension able to penetrate the high level haze. Restless, he sat again, smoked cigarette after cigarette, being careful to shield the flame of matches, and knowing it wasn't his match flares that had determined the follower to walk that pad in the dark.

He heard the impact of mud shoe with shoe one minute before the figure emerged from the darkness to reach the island in the mud and give vent to a sigh of satisfaction. The figure stooped to unstrap the boards, and then its identity was revealed.

Bony chuckled.

"Welcome, wife!" he called. "Welcome!"

He advanced, struck a match, saw the dark eyes meeting his own above the tiny flame. She stood silent, waiting for reprimand, making no movement when he slipped behind her and eased from her back the rope slings holding the laden sugar sack.

"Your eyes are better than mine, Meena, but I am sure your legs ache more than mine do."

"I thought you would be angry," she said, and obeyed when he suggested she sit with him. "Are you?"

"Not at the moment. Why did you come?"

"Yorky has a rifle."
"I have, too."
"Yorky is a dead shot, Inspector."
"You may call me Bony. I am a dead shot, too."
"Yorky might kill Linda. I came to stop him."
"Well, leave it. When did you eat last?"
"Before I left Mount Eden."
"Then you must eat before you explain, and before I become angry, if I do. And, somehow, Meena, I cannot believe I shall ever be angry with you."
The starlight emphasised the vastness of this place in which was no security against natural forces, no protection from unknown powers. The wind came softly, in fitful little gusts, bringing scents unknown to them, and strangely repellent. Presently, Meena said:
"What were those green things coming up out of the mud?"
"Whatever they were, I feared them," admitted Bony.
"Could be Carlinka," the girl said, and when Bony pressed for information, she went on: "Story told by Canute. In the Alchuringa Days three blackfellers out hunting met a giant centipede. The centipede said: 'Don't kill me. I'm Carlinka.' So they didn't kill him. They turned him over on his back and scooped sand over him. They found they couldn't cover him properly because his legs waved about so much, and then a dingo came along and said he'd help, and he did by scratching up the sand till all they could see of Carlinka was the tips of his feet wiggling about."
The reddish light gleamed on her shoulders and naked breasts, her slim arms, and was reflected by her eyes. He knew himself to be old only in pride bidding him to remember not what he was, but who he was. When he spoke his voice was unnecessarily harsh.
"Now tell me why you came."
"It's like I told you, true. Yorky has a rifle. So have you. You're a policeman, like Constable Pierce. You go after Yorky. When Yorky sees you and fires, telling you to go

away, you won't because you're a policeman. You will fire back if Yorky doesn't give up. And he won't. And there's Linda. Sarah kidded Canute to tell about Yorky and Linda camped in the middle of the lake, and Canute told Sarah Yorky could stop all the policemen in the world from getting him. So I came to talk to Yorky. Better to talk than shoot."

"Much better, Meena," agreed Bony. "Who made your Kurdaitcha shoes?"

"That Charlie." Meena looked down and smiled. "Me and Sarah told him. He wouldn't at first, but we made him. Sarah was in a tantrum. We found Charlie hiding in the motor shed, and after a little time he made the mud shoes for me, all right."

"The men, what were they doing when you left?"

"They were all gone. Constable Pierce came and went away with Mr Wootton. Like you said on the radio, they went to catch Yorky coming off the lake. The men rode away before Mr Wootton. The men took their guns, too. I heard Harry tell the others to shoot Yorky on sight."

The quivering voice was an entity fleeing away into the silence, and presently it came again.

"You don't know Yorky, Ins. . . . Bony. Yorky wasn't cruel to anyone. He never treated us aborigines like dirt. He was kind to everyone. He's the kindest whitefeller who ever was, not a dingo to be hunted and shot."

"Are you sure it was Harry Lawton who urged the others to shoot him on sight?" pressed Bony. And when she answered affirmatively, he said: "Take it easy. We have to be on that dog pad at first sight of dawn."

CHAPTER 22

THE CORPSE OF THE PAST

THEY WERE four miles on to the east when the sun blotted from that quarter the endless rusty mud and began hastily to lay the mirage over the putrescence of its own creation. It had been comparatively straight going, proving the dogs followed submerged ridges, when sharply the pad turned left towards the north and away from the glaring sun. Minutes later they saw movement at about half a mile, and stopped.

"What is it?" cried Meena, who was close behind Bony. "I don't like it."

A something rose and subsided erratically, never in the same place, and, without replying, Bony proceeded with his rifle more easily accessible to hand. They could see the lake floor was moving, and ultimately the pad skirted this area of disturbance. Great mud blisters rose and sank without bursting, the light glinting on them as though the skin was stretched taut with pus. There was no evidence indicative of thermal forces agitating this area of several square miles of turbulence.

"Go on, Bony. Don't wait here. I don't like this place," Meena urged.

Far away something rose above the general level which was no blister. It was like a wave running end-forward, then abruptly it turned towards them and drew close in zigzag fashion. It suggested the movement of a great reptile swiftly passing under the mud which rose to curve away from its back. There was certainly no solidity anywhere except that under their feet. The wave thing skirted their end of the area and slowly sank among the recurring blisters.

"What's doing it, Bony?" Meena whispered, but Bony merely shrugged and pressed on. What could he, the big-

feller policeman, say in answer to so simple a question? How to explain something apparently behaving in opposition to natural laws? How to explain those green fingers? Or to bring logic to bear on the rotting corpse of This-Sea-That-Was?

The pad skirted the area for more than a mile, and twice the whale-like back of mud rose and moved with astonishing speed as though the mass were a living thing. Merely a quarter mile from them, a hill of mud rose many feet, to disintegrate as though from internal combustion.

The sky was white, the sun itself tawny, and the wind came to hurry them onward to safety from this blistered menace. A possible explanation, in Bony's opinion, was that this area of deep mud was agitated by water pouring into the north-east section of the lake, thus creating pressure and stress, and were this so, then danger to themselves was to be reckoned with.

He gained another opinion later when skirting a smaller area of liquid mud bearing distinct traces of oil. The wind then was so strong that the surface was ridged with sluggish ripples.

When the sun was searingly hot on their backs, they came to the next dingo rest. Both were physically exhausted and disturbed by the implications of the mud's behaviour, for should the water rise to cover the surface, the dog pad would disappear, and they would be engulfed.

"Two hours ago I urged you to go back. I do so now," Bony said, and all the reaction he produced in the girl was a slow smile and a negative shake of the head.

"Yorky and Linda are somewhere out here," she reminded him. "And I wouldn't go back past those things for anything. You don't seem to mind, though."

"I mind all right, Meena. I'm not liking this at all."

"I know. If there was a wall of fire half a mile on, you'd go straight through it instead of going back. The Missioner told us that pride goeth before a fall. I hope you don't fall."

"We haven't that kind of pride, you no more than I. You

and I are merely animated shells crammed with fears and inhibitions, humility and pride. What white people might name courage is in us instinctive revolt against the abyss for ever opening at our feet. We must not fail. We dare not think of failure. So we must go on, even if we have to travel right across this abominable lake."

They ate slowly. Sips of water immediately issued from them in the form of perspiration, the natural bodily function having ceased since leaving Mount Eden. For a little while they lay with their faces pressed into folded arms to give relief from the glare to eyes sore and heavy.

"You don't really think Yorky shot Mrs Bell?" Meena asked without raising her head.

"No. But don't ask me why he bolted with Linda. I couldn't answer that."

"D'you know who did shoot her?"

"One of two men, possibly. It could be one of five men, but I think it's one of two."

"Which two, Bony?"

"It is now three hours to sundown, Siren. We should press on and hope to reach another dog rest before darkness stops us."

"All set. I'm ready."

She was lacing her mud shoes when he raised himself and blinked against the fierce light. He offered to carry her store of food, but she refused. She stood straight and strong, and the beauty of her body defeated the grime and dust and mud flakes adhering to it. Over her deep-gold face was the smile again, a smile of daring, with a dash of inscrutable woman.

Now and then she watched him pushing on ahead, seemingly making light of the gear he carried and finding no difficulty with the boards, and, as with their maternal forebears, both possessed that rare ability of closing their minds to physical discomfort and concentrating only on the important matter of arriving.

They came to a break in the pad of several yards, and after tentatively testing the surface, managed to cross by hurrying.

Another area was pocked by mounds two feet high, and from the mounds came sucking and gurgling sounds. Bony, having heard and seen the giant earthworms of Gippsland, wondered how enormous must these worms be, if worms did produce the sounds and the surface casts.

Often he expected the water to flow around them, and as often was fooled by the mirage, so complete was this trickery played by Lake Eyre. Four crows came from the east, mocking them as they passed. That morning he had noticed three flying to the east, and as he laboured onward, he speculated about the additional bird.

When the sun went down, the wind was furnace-hot, the sky a flaming fire, and the surface of the lake was a red-gold sea. Far ahead tall masts towered to the sky, and from tip to tip of these masts sped something resembling nothing. Abruptly there appeared an object looking like a crab walking on the edge of its shell.

"That's them," shouted Meena, and Bony turned to say:

"Could be. But how far away?"

The question baffled her. The shadows of the voyagers magically lengthened and were barely the width of a hair. The flame of the sky darkened to crimson, and the mirage turned to green and swiftly from green to steel. Overhead the crimson pall quivered, became ribs of blood veined by black valleys and moving ever to the east before the wind; the mirrored surface of real water to the north enflamed by the setting sun.

They could see the gradual darkening as the sun passed over the rim, and swiftly all the colours under the sky faded into drab brown oblivion. Quite suddenly they saw, barely two hundred yards distant, a low wall of reddish sand, topped with tussock grass. And a man and a child!

"Down," shouted Bony, as he sprawled forward on his chest, wriggled slightly to pull the rifle off his back and bring it to the ready.

Facing the glare of the western sky, the man and child sighted the voyagers moments after they themselves were

seen. Yorky, for it must be he, flung himself down behind the robust tussock grass, but the child continued to stand on a miniature hummock of sand.

The moments were those between the magic hours of day and the shrouding hours of night, when this country is revealed in true perspective, and this evening, stereoscopic clarity. Over the barrel of his rifle, Bony watched the movement behind the grass, and actually witnessed the muzzle of Yorky's Winchester being pushed through the fringe.

A swift glance backward showed him Meena still standing, and he called to her to go down. She shook her head and shrilly shouted to Linda:

"It's me! Meena! Tell Yorky, Linda. Tell Yorky!"

Meena provided a perfect target. Bony, who was better than average, could see the tip of Yorky's rifle and knew precisely where the man's head was in relation to it. The range was only about two hundred yards. The light held. Perspiration ran like rain down his face to wet the stock of his rifle against which his cheek was pressed. If Yorky fired first, Meena or himself would die. If he fired first, curtains for Yorky. Instinct drove him to pull the trigger; training commanded him to wait.

CHAPTER 23

A MIXED RECEPTION

BONY WAITED.

A lesser man might not have hesitated before speeding a bullet into Yorky's brain. He would act on the impulse of survival of the swiftest, and subsequently would be commended for preventing the possible murder of the woman so rashly exposing herself to danger.

Great men are natural gamblers. Bony gambled that

Yorky wouldn't shoot his own daughter; and that Yorky wouldn't shoot him, not yet. He believed that Yorky thought himself behind full cover, and therefore safe from destruction and in command of the situation. And, like all great gamblers, Bony won. Linda shouted:

"Come on, Meena. Tell that man to stay there."

Above his sigh of relief, he heard Meena sliding along the pad, and when the sound stopped and he heard her panting, he said:

"You will have to step over on me. Do it quickly."

"That Yorky!" she exclaimed, almost crying. "That ole fool of a Yorky! I thought you'd shoot first. Why didn't you? Why? He could have killed you easy. I'll fix him."

He felt the board press lightly on the small of his back, its toe-tip dig into his neck as she stepped over, regained her poise and stayed to look back at him.

"I'm all right, Meena," he told her. "Go on and pacify Yorky. Get his rifle if you can, but don't try fighting for it."

Obediently, she went on along the pad, and Bony continued to hold his rifle sights at a point one inch above Yorky's rifle muzzle. That muzzle wavered not at all, informing Bony that it was aimed at him, and not the girl.

Even though concentrating on Yorky, Bony could see Linda dancing in her excitement as Meena slowly neared the sandbank. He heard the child's cries of joy, and the girl's rapid questions and commands to Yorky to point the rifle elsewhere. Then she was on the narrow hard crust dividing sandbank from mud, and the child was in her arms. After a few moments, the child was running to Yorky, and Meena was removing her mud shoes. Obviously, Yorky issued an order, for Linda screamed:

"You man over there! You come here. Yorky won't shoot."

Bony walked to the solid land with taut expectancy. On sliding to land he had an impression of fluffed water beyond the dune, and mud extending into blue-tinged

darkness. Meena and the child came close to him, and nearby a man chuckled mirthlessly, and said:

"Linda! Take the rifle from that feller."

The little girl's brown eyes stared up at Bony as she held out her hands, and Bony smiled.

"Thank you, Linda. I want to take off these silly boards. My word, I shall be glad to be rid of them."

"Bring the rifle to me, Linda," commanded the hidden Yorky, and Meena said sharply:

"Cut it out, Yorky. You're not on the films."

"I'm a desperate man," snarled Yorky, and Meena retorted:

"You will be if I get at you. Point that gun some other place. We haven't come to shoot you. You are all right, Linda darling? That Yorky! Wait till Sarah gets at him."

Yorky stood at the edge of the sandbank, a small, wizened, sun-blackened man in working trousers and shirt so repeatedly washed as to be negative. His greying hair was over-long, and the grey moustache suspended long tails to the tip of his pointed chin. His eyes were light blue, small, and red-rimmed. The Winchester still pointed at Bony.

The culminating surprise of this day was the contrast between the hunted and the hunters. Both Yorky and the little girl were clean and tidy. Yorky had certainly shaved that morning. Bony could not forbear gazing from them to Meena and himself, then back to Linda, and laughing.

"Linda, who looks the dirtiest? Meena or me?"

"You do, lying out there in the mud like that," replied Linda severely. "But we have a private lake, you know. We can have a bath whenever we like, can't we, Yorky?"

"Yes, I suppose so," agreed Yorky, and a further surprise was the faint whine in his voice. "Comin' barging in like this. How'm I to know you didn't come to get me? Anyhow, who are you? Ruddy stranger to me."

"I am a person of little importance," countered Bony. "Linda mentioned a lake, and that indicates water. We have been severely rationed. Where is this lake?"

"Over there," shrilled Linda. "I'll show you. Come on."

Following her pointing finger, they saw the steely sheen of water seemingly close enough to step into, and Bony, with Meena, who was being dragged along by the eager Linda, heard Yorky say:

"Now look-see, Linda. You've been in there all of two hours already. Don't you be going in again, or you'll be getting a cold or something."

There was the water, inviting, alluring, limitless now in the deep dusk. Linda shouted. Meena shouted. Bony shouted. Meena stepped down from the sandbank to the bordering hard ground, stepped into the water and, finding the bottom hard, went farther in, splashing as the water rose to her waist. Bony followed her. Behind them the little girl and the man were silhouetted against the pink sunset sky.

Water in the middle of Lake Eyre! Water in the centre of a near desert at the end of a rainless summer. Clear water, and fresh, and seemingly miles of it lying cool and sweet under the serene stars and the flaming meteors.

When emerging to be met by the impatient Linda, Meena was even more beautiful, but Bony, still wearing shirt and trousers, looked like a near-drowned cat. Pulling off the shirt he wrung it out, thankful that it was cleaned of mud, and after all the surprises of this day came another when Yorky said:

"Better come on up and have a drink 'er tea."

The invitation belied Yorky's hostile attitude. Stepping back, he motioned them up on to the sand-bar, Linda leading the way to a shallow dell where a small fire burned before the dark opening of a grass humpy. Beside the glowing embers stood a billycan, and close by were fruit tins for cups and one filled with sugar.

Linda ran into the grass shelter and came forth with a towel, which she presented to Meena, who quickly dried herself and passed the towel to Bony. Shorts and trousers began to steam in the fire heat, and Linda expertly poured

tea into two tins, and went again to the humpy, this time returning with a dainty cup and saucer.

Juggling the hot tin in his hands, Bony turned his back to the fire to face Yorky, who was sitting on the ground several yards away, and stubborn yet with the Winchester ready for action.

"You answer questions?" demanded Yorky, the whine still in his voice. "You march into my camp without any by-your-leave. You don't say who you are. Why?"

"Sorry," Bony said. "I've become so accustomed to asking questions that I find it tedious to answer them. Now listen to me." Authority had crept into the cold accentless voice. "I am Detective Inspector Napoleon Bonaparte, of Queensland, assigned to locate the whereabouts of Linda Bell, and apprehend a man concerned with a crime of violence. Having found Linda Bell, I have yet to apprehend the slayer of you know who. Now, suppose you answer a question? You tell me why you cleared out from Mount Eden, and brought Linda with you."

Yorky advanced until he was within a yard of Bony, the rifle aimed at Bony's chest. The firelight gleamed in his eyes made small by suspicion.

"Suppose you tell me what you're driving at?"

"I'll answer that one, Yorky, by suggesting that talking of serious things be deferred until Sleepy Head has retired for the night."

"That don't satisfy me," snarled Yorky, and Meena cut in shrilly:

"No, it wouldn't, Yorky. You told Linda all that happened?"

"No, I haven't yet."

"Then shut up and put the rifle down. We're famished. Where's our packs, Linda? There's tinned stuff in one of them for sure."

They disappeared in the direction of the 'beach', and Bony said, proceeding to push fire sticks together:

"I don't believe that you shot Mrs Bell."

"But everyone else must," replied Yorky.

"I don't."

"You don't! D'you know who did?"

"My guess is good. Had you shot her I'd have had the cuffs on you before now. Easy man easy! They are coming back. We'll talk of other matters. Do you know that the floods are pouring into Lake Eyre?"

"They are? Bad?"

Yorky sat in the circle of firelight, placing the rifle at his side. He was still suspicious, and almost furtively began to chip flakes from a plug of tobacco.

"Down the Coopers and the northern rivers."

"You see water on your way?"

"No. But there was the mirage of water in the sky. You must have seen that."

"Didn't think." Yorky fell to watching Meena opening tins. Linda appeared, this time carrying two large dolls, one the image of Ole Fren Yorky, the other that of Meena. She began to croon to them.

"We saw strange things," Bony went on. "That great slough of soft mud is being agitated. Could be caused by water pressure building up underneath it. Did you see it?"

"Didn't travel that way since we come out here first. The mud was quiet enough then. Must be the flood," agreed Yorky. "Have to shift camp first thing after daybreak."

"Where to, Yorky?"

"Where to! Don't know, exceptin' back to the shore." In the ensuing silence the only background sound was Linda's crooning voice.

"There is another way to the shore?" asked Bony.

"Yes, the pad I take to the old hut at the south end of Mount Eden boundary fence. Much shorter. I've been back there twice for tucker."

"You must have been to the homestead at least once, for the dolls?" pressed Bony.

"No. Friend of mine brought 'em from the homestead."

"Friend of yours!" echoed Meena. "What friend?"

"You stop askin' questions," whined Yorky. "Just a friend, that's all."

"Did you meet this friend, or did he leave the dolls in the hut?" pressed Bony.

"Left 'em in the hut."

"And this friend didn't leave word that the water was pouring into Lake Eyre?"

"No. Musta forgot."

"Must have forgotten! He would know that the water would cut you off, that you'd starve to death, or drown trying to reach shore, wouldn't he?"

"Yair, I suppose he would," admitted Yorky. "But . . ."

"And he forgot to leave word. Nice friend, Yorky."

"Damn nice friend," jibed Meena, and Linda said sharply:

"It's rude to swear, Meena."

"Must of forgot," obstinately averred Yorky. "Anyhow, we'll have to move in the morning. Linda, you be off to bed. We got a long way to go tomorrer."

"But you haven't told my nightie story yet," protested Linda. "You always do, Yorky."

"I know, but not tonight. I'm too sleepy tired."

"I'll tell the story," volunteered Meena. "Now you show me the inside of your little house. Come on!"

Linda gathered her dolls under one arm, and picked up the cup and saucer. Politely, she wished goodnight to Bony, threw her arms round Yorky, and said he must go to bed, too. With additional interest Bony studied the nondescript little man who had abducted a child and had cared for her exceedingly well under hazardous conditions. The humpy constructed with tussock grass thatched to a frame of driftwood accepted the little girl and Meena, and after a short silence Yorky said:

"That right you reckon I didn't shoot Mrs Bell?"

"Did you?" countered Bony, and Yorky sighed like a man long and sorely perplexed.

"I was sozzled and all on the boss's whisky. I don't rightly remember, but I must have. Things happened sort of out of

order. You said you got a different idea. What do you think?"

"While not quite certain," Bony tersely replied, "I think your friend did."

CHAPTER 24

THE QUAIL SHOOTERS

WITH DWELLERS in the Outback, it is often the rule to wake by habit when the first sign of coming day appears in the sky. Such a bushman was Yorky, who stirred from his bed of sand and added wood to the still red embers of the camp fire. The resultant flame enabled him to see the empty billycan, and he departed for water. On his return he found Bony cleaning the Savage rifle, and while waiting for the water to boil he watched Bony at work on the high-velocity weapon; and neither spoke nor made a move to halt the progress.

Having tossed a handful of tea into the boiling water, Yorky lifted the billycan with a stick, and cut chips from his plug while waiting for the leaves to settle. Thus the day began completely normal.

Having cleaned his rifle, Bony set it carefully against his pack, and nonchalantly strolled away to wash at Linda's own lake. Meena and the child joined him there, and all returned together. The Savage still reclined against the pack. Yorky hadn't touched it. Smoking his first pipe of the day, Yorky ambled over to the water, and Bony finished dressing, simply by donning an old coat over the now dry shirt.

They were ready to move before sun-up, by which time Bony had surveyed their immediate surroundings and learned that the tussock-covered sand was barely a hundred yards wide, and in varying width extending as far as he

could see to the north and the south. The 'private lake', enclosed by sand, was about an acre in area, and must be maintained by springs.

They left the soft sand for the narrow beach, where Yorky led the party to the south. An hour later, when he halted for a rest, they were still walking the beach, and still the sand-bar was on their one side and the mud on the other. Now well beyond the place of recent occupation the rabbits were fairly numerous, and already two dingoes had been seen.

"How much farther have we of this easy going?" Bony asked.

"About another seven miles," replied Yorky. "Nearly all them seven miles towards the shore, for this sand takes a turn like the elbow of a boomerang. That leaves only about eleven miles of mud. There's water at the end of the sand, but not like Linda's lake. After that no water till we get to the hut. How you going, Linda?"

"All right, Yorky," replied the child, a trifle doubtfully.

"Expect I'll have to carry you a ways. Easier on this hard beach than later on over the mud. Mind you, Linda, sweetheart, you're doing good, but them legs of yours are too short, and them Kurdaitcha shoes aren't much good for the job."

The shoes Charlie had made were slung about the child's neck by the leather thongs. They had been fashioned with the bark of a tree to the shape of a boat, or like an Eastern slipper, having a curved toe-cap. They were too long for Linda unless she was also wearing her normal shoes, and, in fact, were not meant to be worn save in play. The yellow comb of a white cockatoo adorned each shoe immediately behind the raised prow. Along the sides of each shoe Charlie had scored aboriginal pictures, and glued to the raised edges were the herringbone feathers of emus. Toy shoes made for a little girl.

"I shall be glad to be on the mud," observed Bony. "That

friend of yours could have decided to meet us, and could be waiting comfortably behind a clump of tussock grass."

"Who's your friend, Yorky?" demanded Meena. "I'm tired of you not tellin." Looking back at Bony, and noting the slight frown of anxiety, she went on: "You wait. Sarah'll get it out of you. You say you didn't do it. Bony says you didn't do it. Bony says your friend did it. Wait till we get back to Sarah, Yorky. She'll make you talk fast enough."

"That feller didn't do it, I keep tellin' you," exploded Yorky. "He's been pretty decent all through. Only one I could trust, anyhow. And I'm not talking until we're all facing him. Then we'll see. I'm not a one to talk behind a friend's back."

"All right!" exclaimed Bony impatiently, for he had spent an hour the previous night arguing this point. "But we're not taking unnecessary risks. I shall walk well ahead, and if he is waiting for us, I'll try to flush him from cover. You are being extremely foolish, although it isn't vitally essential that I know the name of your friend at this moment. Nor do I need your co-operation.

"Before leaving the homestead, Yorky, I broadcast my intention of hunting you here, and by now the lake is being patrolled by men waiting for us to make shore. I made no secret of our ability to walk the mud by following the dingo pads. And I let it be known that I do not believe you are guilty of murder.

"Broadly, that was the situation when I left the homestead. The guilty person anticipated that you would be cut off by the flood water, then he would always be safe. Now that he knows he isn't safe from the consequences of his crime, it is most likely that he'll attempt to stop us returning. Where better to do that than somewhere along this sandbar? He could drop one of us, and take his chances in a duel with the other man. Better that than inevitable arrest. This pal of yours, does he know of this shorter route to the shore?"

Yorky had been staring at his boots, and now he gazed steadily at Bony.

"You done it purposely, drawing the killer out here?"

"I did," replied Bony. "This rifle is able to out-range any Winchester. I gave him the chance to come here and fight it out because of that, and because I thought I'd have you to back me up. Now that you won't, then I'll go ahead and take the risk of being dropped before I can locate him."

"You said you guessed who done the killing," argued Yorky, eyes small and hard. "Why didn't you arrest him before you started?"

"It's a long road between knowing and proving."

Again Yorky stared at his boots, and Meena watched, silently, Linda cuddled against her, tired and fearful from this, to her, inexplicable conversation. Abruptly, Yorky stood and, without looking at them, said:

"You got it all over me, but I'm stickin' to me guns. I could be ratting on a mate. You and me'll go on ahead of Meena and Linda. We'll take equal chances. You're the Law. But law or no law, anyone starts after Meena and the lass, I shoot and keep on shootin'. We got to get off this flamin' lake, and quick. She's startin' to heave already. I can see it."

Looking over the mud, at first they saw nothing unusual.

"You're referring to that moving ribbon of reflection, are you?" asked Bony.

"Yair, that's it. I've never seen it before, but the abos got a name for it. It's a low sort of swell, and the sun's glinting on it along one slope, like a water wave. Old Canute told me about it. The water keeps on pushing into the mud, and instead of running over the top of the mud, it comes up from under."

Yorky turned to the girls.

"Drop all your traps. Me and the Inspector'll carry 'em. You take the shoes, Inspector. I'll carry the water-bags. Dump the rest. Meena, you tarry awhile. Give us half a mile lead, then come on."

"Okee. Don't worry about us."

"My dolls!" cried Linda. "I won't leave my Meena and Ole Fren Yorky."

"We'll carry them, Linda," soothed Meena.

"Keep to the beach," instructed Bony. "Any firing, crouch down against the sandbank."

The two men spaced themselves and advanced along the bar, their weapons ready for instant action. They could see for miles above the grass and the wind-fashioned hummocks of sand, and less than fifty yards ahead into the grass or over a sand hump. It wasn't dissimilar from stalking quail, but anticipation of action was certainly based on far different conditions.

The good general projects himself into the mind of his opposite number, and Bony tried doing just this. It would be unlikely that the killer of Mrs Bell would delay his first shot one moment after the distance between him and them fell below two hundred yards. The odds were grossly in favour of the ambusher dropping one or other of his adversaries, who were under the compelling urge to get clear of the lake. Just too bad if he manœuvred himself so that they both passed him before he fired.

Fortunately it was a calm morning, and the stiff tussock grass was still. They held a slight advantage given by the eagles and the rabbits, and by four crows which had followed them from the camp. The crows often flew on ahead, but certainly would behave erratically did they see a man prone on the ground beneath. It was easier to watch them than the eagles, two of which were flying high.

An hour passed. Yorky constantly glanced across at Bony, keeping abreast. The sun was rising to the zenith and the heat was powerful. Bony thought of Linda, argued whether to make a halt or not. On looking back, he could see the upper portion of Meena, and the head of the little girl above the edge of the bank. They were keeping distance very well. He called to Yorky:

"Leave one of the water-bags on the beach for the girls."

Yorky nodded and the march proceeded, each man zig-zagging along short legs, each tensed to dive for cover at any instant, Yorky also watching the birds and working widely with Bony when the sandbar widened.

An hour before noon, Bony fancied he could see the extremity of the sand, and he was laying odds in favour of the ambusher waiting there, when just ahead of Yorky a pure golden dingo appeared on the top of a sand hump, saw the men, and loped away, followed by four well-grown pups. Bony sighed his relief.

Having decided that Meena and Linda hadn't halted at the water-bag to eat and leave scraps, the crows came on after the men, passing them, and flying on over the dogs. The end of the bar, now clearly seen, was perhaps half a mile distant, when the four crows arrived there, and swept skyward as though from a ground explosion, and at height swirled like black snowdrops. Their cawing came to the men, and the tale was told.

"That's him sure enough," shouted Yorky, and converged to Bony. "We gonna move on like we done in the blasted war?"

"Yes," agreed Bony. "We can each keep to a beach to gain partial cover. Now for the drill. Although I don't look it, I'm a law officer. Although you don't look it, you're an Australian citizen. Our job is to get that fellow alive, and he isn't going to be of much use to you dead. So, unless you are pushed badly, don't shoot to kill."

"Suits me."

"Back to the beaches," cried Bony almost gaily.

There they gained two feet of sandbank cover, and yet were able to mark each other's progress. The crows were circling over the end of the sandbar, their suspicion prolonged by an object lying prone, and their behaviour brought low the two eagles, soaring in gigantic circles, with seldom a wing flap.

It was then that the enemy knew he was sunk, and his nerve, what there was of it, failed. Two men stalking him

when they should have been walking blithely into his gun-sights. He could both see and hear the damned crows betraying him to the men, one of whom was reputed to be the finest rifle shot in the back country.

Hastily strapping on his boards, he slithered over the dog pad, watched by the fearful dingo bitch and her curious pups. On Bony and Yorky reaching the end of the sandbar, which was fashioned like a crab's claw about a small sheet of gleaming water, the mirage had given him stilts.

The disappointed eagles rose to cooler altitudes. The crows were decidedly annoyed. Bony sat down and produced tobacco and papers.

"That your friend?" he asked.

"How do I know?" replied Yorky. "With your rifle I could drop him. Got better range than mine. That particular bastard means nothing to me."

"To the contrary, he means very much to you," insisted Bony mildly.

"That bloke's still in range. He'd have got one of us, and then if he'd got the other he'd have killed the lass and Meena. Gimme that Savage."

The Winchester was aimed at Bony's chest, and casually Bony set down the Savage on his far side.

"Meena and Linda would see you shoot me," Bony explained. "That wouldn't do, Yorky. Load your pipe instead. I know how you feel on being betrayed by one you trusted. Who is he?"

Yorky shook his head, and the stubborn perversity of his class came out when he said:

"You're a policeman. I can't inform to a cop."

CHAPTER 25

PINNED LIKE A SPECIMEN

HAVING RESTED for almost an hour, chiefly on account of Linda, Bony led the party on to the mud, the pad clearly marked by the impressions of the boards worn by the retreating ambusher. It was then one o'clock, and Bony pointed out the advisability of reaching land before five, after which hour the westering sun would blind them, but not the man who might decide to stage a battle from the cover of a sand dune.

The child was subdued, but walked a full two miles before complaining. Then Yorky demonstrated that little men are often physically stronger than larger men. He passed his rifle to Meena, took Linda astride his shoulders and carried her as though her weight was identical with that of the weapon. The afternoon was exceedingly hot, completely still, and the surrounding mirage dazzled the eyes and limited shooting visibility to eighty yards.

Having insisted on a lead of two hundred yards from Yorky and the girls, Bony constantly peered ahead, worried by the fact that, as time passed, the sun would place him at increasing disadvantage. The crows had refused to follow the party, preferring no doubt to take shade among the foot-high grass, and now to look to the sky for the eagles was torture to sweat-rimmed eyes. Above and about there was nothing but colourless light.

On reaching an area of hard ground, he waited for Yorky and Meena, and eventually they appeared, first as tufted masts, and then walking on stilts, and became normal only when within yards. Yorky was still carrying Linda, and on setting her to ground, he stumbled to his knees and sprawled forward, wiping his sweat-drenched face on a bare forearm.

Meena poured water over the back of his head, and he told

her to stop it, as they had yet five or six miles to reach land. Thereafter they all drank sparingly, and the men smoked little, the terrific heat pressing in from all sides equally with the direct rays of the cosmic sun. Yorky did spare water to saturate the towel which Linda wore for head covering.

"That'll be better, sweetheart," he told her gently. "It isn't far to go now, and when we get to the hut we'll pour buckets-full of water over each other." To Bony he said: "On a bit there's another dog-rest. It's small and only a couple of miles from the shore. It'll be there that bloke will be waiting again. After that there's the shore dunes for him and open spaces for us. Then the fun'll start. It'll be all his way with the sun behind him."

"Maybe not," Bony said. "I'll get along. Give me time. I'll wait on that dog-rest if he isn't there."

Yorky brought his wandering eyes to focus on Bony. They were inflamed, and like agates set in beef.

"You forget you're a copper. Just remember you got a Savage what'll out-range a Winchester, and remember that we got to get off this stinkin' mud before it bogs us. This ain't no time for the ruddy Law and gentlemen policemen."

"Correct, Yorky." Bony smiled grimly. "The water under the mud is the boss from here. I'll be waiting at the next rest."

The man and the woman and the small child watched the mirage shape grotesquely the departing Bonaparte, and Meena said angrily:

"You shouldn't of said that. You got us all in this mess, and he knows what he's doing without you telling him."

"Had to chiack him," retorted Yorky, glaring at his daughter. "Me, I can look after meself. But we got our little Linda sweetheart. Well, up we come and off we go."

. . . . .

The heat was relentless and Bony was dismayed by experiencing a slight attack of giddiness. He thought perhaps he had been moving too fast, and slackened his pace a little

to recover. He did, until minutes later, when he had another attack that almost sent him down.

It was then he saw it, the slow passing of a mud wave. It caught stronger light along its forward face than along its summit and rear, bringing foreboding of disaster. Half an hour later another mud wave tended to upset equilibrium, and then soon after that a wasp buzzed, and he heard the report which sent him chest-down into the mud, and his eye peering across the sights of his rifle.

"You've said it, Yorky. This is no time to be a gentleman," he remarked. "Let me see this murderous swine that I may prove it."

The frustrating light was much worse at mud level. He could not determine where the mud horizon met the scintillating atmosphere. Again the wasp fled by, and again came the report loud and sharp. He aimed at the point of the sound and fired, and the report of his rifle seemed to be blanketed about his own ears. It was worse than being blinded by fog. Irritation gave place to dull anger, and anger banished all veneers, leaving a man no longer a gentlemanly copper.

There arose, in this man of two races, emotion he rarely permitted to surface. It was like a heatless fire deep behind his eyes, and he swore at the blinding sun and the frustrating mirage. Pinned like a moth to a specimen board, he and those behind him were being vitally delayed for the mud to engulf them.

Ah! There was movement of a sort, a shape impossible to identify. Swiftly it grew to monstrous size, swiftly to diminish to vanishing point. The sniper was retreating.

Bony made to leap to his feet, and was brought to reality by the mud-shoes. He wanted to run, but again the boards restrained him. In a semi-crouching attitude, Bony hurried after him, with the nightmare sensation of leaden feet.

He came to the dingo-rest where the sniper had staged his last hold-up, and instead of waiting for the others he pressed on, determined to nail the enemy before he could

gain cover behind the shore dunes. Now how far to the blessed land, the clean, the beautiful land? How much farther over this filthy mud? What had Yorky said? Ah, yes, two miles. A long way, and yet not so long when clean red sand and a hut near water waited.

An hour later he saw the red sand, sand rising in billows as of red spray suddenly suspended, great red cliffs of it, gouged and gullied by the shadow drifts of graphite powder. And he saw, without distortion, a man run from the mud and race up the beach. Without expending time sprawling, Bony halted, sighted and fired. He heard himself shout when the running figure staggered. He heard himself curse when the running figure recovered, to run on between two cliffs of red spray.

He was down on the mud yet again, fighting for control of breathing and nerves. He struggled to sink yet lower into the mud, knowing that his adversary was calmly selecting his cover from behind which he could pin down a regiment. How far was he from the beach? It was impossible to assess distances in this shimmering colourless radiance.

His rifle was ranged to fire point-blank up to 350 yards. He could do nothing now but wait, hoping to see the spurt of flame before hearing that wasp, thus learning the position of the adversary. Vain hope, indeed, when the sun is directly before one, and a bare five hands' width above the summits of low dunes.

He was thinking how to place himself beyond range of the Winchester and still keep the dunes within range of his own rifle, when a sound like a cork being withdrawn came from his left, followed about two seconds later by the report. To turn about and retreat in manner dictated by mud and hampered feet was to ask for a bullet in the back from a man able to see clearly with the sun behind him.

The next bullet hit the mud several yards immediately in front of Bony. He saw the tiny spurt of mud so disturbed, and found consolation in the obvious fact that the marksman could not see where his bullets hit, and so correct his errors,

for the impact raised no dust. The following bullet informed him that the marksman was immediately to his front, and probably behind a low declivity between two humps.

To his complete bewilderment, therefore, he witnessed the appearance of a dark figure at a point at least two hundred feet to the right of this place; and the figure was a man who was waving something white. Then in the shimmering light haze he saw that the man was moving in a crouching manner along the foot of the dunes, and towards the place where the rifleman should be. Bony aimed at this position and fired, and was rewarded by the miniature avalanche of sand marring the face of the dune.

Now there was distinct movement on the top of the ridge between the dunes, and two things happened. A bullet plopped into the mud on Bony's left, and the man at the foot of the dunes began to run, still crouching, towards where the marksman must be. He was stalking the rifleman, and had taken advantage to cover ground when knowing that the marksman was concentrating on his shooting.

Good man! Bony proceeded to assist him further by now and then claiming the rifleman's full attention. The stalker entered a shadow, disappeared. A bullet plopped into the mud eighteen inches in front of Bony's rifle muzzle, and he realised that, fortunately, bullets do not ricochet off mud. Then he saw the white fabric being waved atop a sand ridge much nearer the marksman, and Bony tried to dig a furrow across the ridge.

Minutes passed. The sun sank lower still, even more effectively blinding Bony, who could now see only by shading his eyes. Shortly afterwards even that was useless. Lying there utterly helpless while the sun sank behind the sand ridge were moments suspended for ever. Now the distant land was sharply silhouetted against the light; for the first time the odds were in Bony's favour. The shadows were gone, the light shimmer was banished. He could see clearly the scar of the avalanche made by his bullet on the virgin face of the dune behind which lurked his adversary.

Then he saw a movement directly over his sights, and settled to make this a victory shot, stilling his nerves, freezing his arms and neck muscles while beginning the slow pressure on the trigger. This was it. He could actually see the top of the fellow's head over the smaller blob of rifle muzzle resting on the sharply etched red sand line against the saffron sky. He knew now that the range was well under two hundred yards, and in his hands was a superb weapon. Conditions were ideal. Now to despatch a high-velocity bullet into the brain of the killer!

One fraction of increased pressure on the trigger and the bullet would have been sped, one fraction of a second more would have achieved finality. But the second passed and the pressure was stopped, for just beyond the marksman rose that waving white object. It rose above the ridge, revealing the head and body of the man waving as he mounted the opposite slope. The man lifted his arm, and his hand held a rifle or a waddy. Whichever it was, it was brought downward with severe force.

Then on the summit was an aborigine waving vigorously for Bony to come on.

Reaction almost caused Bony to sob from sheer frustration. He wanted to shout oaths and curses. Having waited all that time, having exposed himself to bullets all about him, having come to the moment of equalisation, to be frustrated by a damned abo!

Standing, he sloughed the mud from his clothes, and congratulated himself that there wasn't a smear on the rifle. Turning about he saw Yorky and Meena still far out, the man continuing to carry the child, and when the storm of unreasoning anger subsided, he placed the rifle on the mud without a qualm and went back to meet them.

"He pinned me to the mud," Bony said. "Just when I was able to let him have it, that blasted aborigine clouted him."

Yorky, standing like Atlas, screwed his face into a peculiar expression, part admiration, part incredulity.

"You pinned him behind that sandhill, too, for a full hour. I'd sooner be talking to Linda than lyin' where you was. Better get going, Inspector. This mud'll turn to soup any minute."

"Let me carry Linda. Edge round me and go first. That aborigine . . . I must admit . . . is our friend for life."

"It's Charlie," Meena said, quietly, and with infinite pride. "He's still waving."

Yorky headed the short procession, swaying drunkenly with fatigue, and followed by Bony with Linda astride his shoulders. The mirage vanished into the miasma of nightmare, and the land of salmon-pink urged them off the rusty-iron Lake Eyre.

"I don't want to see that ole lake again."

"Neither do I, Linda. I like lakes with cool water, like your private lake out there. And when I reach a shower I'll stay under it all night."

"You can't. Mr Wootton wouldn't like you wasting all that water."

"Wouldn't he?"

"No. Mr Wootton is a careful man, my mother says."

He set her down on the hard beach, and thankfully removed his mud shoes. Yorky and Meena were looking up at the laughing Charlie standing on the sand ridge, a white handkerchief about his neck.

Behind the ridge a white man sat with his knees hunched and his face resting on his arms. There was blood on the crown of his head. His rifle lay a dozen feet away, a Winchester.

"Is this the friend you were telling us about, Yorky?" asked Bony, and the little man looked vaguely about before nodding.

CHAPTER 26

BREACHING A WALL

BEFORE THE dominant sun rose again, Bony was writing his report on the veranda at Mount Eden. He was wearing steel-blue silk pyjamas under a sky-blue dressing-gown, and although he had spent a full hour under the shower late the previous night, he had this morning showered again, and carefully tended his straight black hair.

At six a.m., through the french windows came Meena with tea and biscuits, and Bony found it difficult to reorientate this young woman wearing a white apron over a bright green dress, and red shoes clip-clopping on the veranda floor, with that girl in the once-white shorts who had accompanied him across miles of scabrous mud.

"Good morning, Meena! You're looking delightfully fresh this morning. And how is Linda?"

"Like a crane with its head under a wing." Meena smiled her own indescribable smile, which would live for ever in Bony's memory. "Looks like she'll sleep all day, too. What will happen to her?"

"Well, from what Mr Wootton said last night, I believe he intends to adopt Linda."

"Make her his own little daughter! Oh, that'll be beaut. Then she'll be staying here for always?"

"Excepting when she will be away at school in Adelaide, and that will be some time ahead. Is Sarah happy to have Yorky back?"

This time the smile ended in gurgling laughter, and Meena managed to say:

"That Yorky! He was sitting in the kitchen after supper, and Sarah was all talk, talking at him. Suddenly he was fast asleep, and d'you know what? She picked him up like he

was Linda and carried him to her room and put him to bed. And crying all the time, after all she said she'd do to him."

"And did I see you and Charlie holding hands on the truck last night coming back from that hut?"

"I had to let him for a little while. Then old Murtee told him to stop. He said didn't Charlie know I was your woman, that you bought by blackfeller trade with Canute. Went crook, ole Murtee did." The smile began and quickly vanished. "That Murtee's a bigger wowser than the Missioner."

"Now we are gossiping, Meena. Take away this tray and leave me to my writing. And don't forget that you are my woman, not Charlie's."

Gazing into his stern face, so unbalanced by the twinkle in the blue eyes, she said with siren softness:

"I'm not arguing about that, Bony."

Bony lit another cigarette, and discovered that concentration on the report demanded effort. He was busy, however, when Sarah tapped her iron triangle, and a few minutes later the cattleman called him to breakfast.

"Feeling better for a good sleep?" Wootton asked and, on being assured, added: "What's the drill today?"

"After breakfast, I'd like to talk to everyone," replied Bony. "Might we have them all on the side veranda? Then we all go to Loaders Springs for statements to Constable Pierce. I told Pierce we'd be there at eleven."

"We shall have to leave at nine." Mr Wootton looked at Bony appealingly. "About Linda. Think you could help by supporting my application to adopt her? We spoke of it last night, remember, and Pierce was keen when he went off with his prisoner."

"As far as I know there are no near relatives entitled to claim her. However, the authorities would have to be sure that she would be cared for properly. I have no doubt you could give that guarantee, and later today I'll offer a few suggestions which should support you. Thank you, Meena,

I'll have bacon and soft fried eggs. Never again tinned meat. And, Meena, close the door."

. . . . .

Linda had fallen asleep too confused and weary to probe Meena's story of her mother having been bitten by a snake. She woke to find Bony sitting on the edge of the bed and nursing the replica of her mother.

"You are having breakfast in bed, Linda," he said. "Meena is bringing it. Afterwards, we are all going to town to buy a present for Meena. But that's a secret."

"And see my mummy at the doctor's? Is she better?"

"I'm afraid not. It was bad. It was too late and everyone was away at the time."

Bony offered the doll, but what Linda saw in his eyes and face caused her to twist aside the bedclothes and seek warmer comfort in his arms. When Meena came with the breakfast tray the shock had been cushioned, and he left the child being coaxed to eat her breakfast.

Passing to the side veranda, he found Mr Wootton waiting with all his staff bar one, who was within Constable Pierce's lock-up, and, having lit a cigarette, he said:

"It is not customary for an investigating officer to address all his original suspects at a gathering like this, but I decided to do so, chiefly because I've had to contend with grave obstruction built by loyalties.

"Loyalty, as you must know, is often in error, and is certainly not a virtue limited to one nation, one race or colour. About this you will agree as I proceed.

"On the morning that Mrs Bell was murdered, three men rode off to work on horses, one drove a truck for roofing-iron, and Mr Wootton left by car for town. When the men returned, they found Mrs Bell shot dead, and Linda missing. It was a wild windy day, but they found tracks which they were sure were left by Yorky, and, remember, before Mr Wootton returned and told them he had that morning found Yorky at the deserted aborigines' camp.

"Then it was automatically accepted that Yorky was the murderer. Efforts were made to track him, but not until late next day could aborigines be brought back from Neales River, and sent to track Yorky early the following morning. There was only one man in everybody's mind. Yorky. No other person was suspect, and so no other man's tracks would have been of interest.

"On my arrival, I found universal anger that the crime had been committed, but an almost unanimous good opinion of the man who was thought to have committed it. Everyone told me that Yorky was a nice fellow, and that his last bender must have sent him crackers. Opportunity for murder was present, the means were proved, but the motive was hidden.

"What gave me furiously to think was the behaviour of the aborigines. They lost interest in tracking Yorky, gave up before it could be expected of them, in view of the fact that Yorky is a white man and that he had taken away a white child. Yorky was said to be very close to them by long association, and, were this so, then it could be assumed that they knew where he was hiding. Effort to prove this assumption gradually achieved results. I was confronted by two tasks: to find the murderer of Mrs Bell, and to locate Linda Bell.

"I don't claim to be an anthropologist, but I do know that the aborigines in the central districts of Australia have been very much less influenced by the outside world than have the aborigines in the far north by the Melanesians and the Polynesians. These central Australian aborigines are being erroneously referred to as Stone Age men, when in fact they were thinkers and dreamers long before the Stone Age. The anthropological furrow ploughed across the Lake Eyre Basin by Spencer and Gillen at the end of the last century hasn't since been deepened by a fraction of an inch in furthering our knowledge of this, the most ancient race. At risk of being reviled by the alleged experts in this field, I admit that I gained my first lead in my investigation from Chief Canute and his dijeridoo.

"All the aborigines, so I was assured, were away on walkabout at the time Mrs Bell was murdered, and yet blind Canute knew the shape of the bloodstain on the dead woman's back. That the shape had been described to him by Yorky, or by any other white man, could not be seriously considered, because to a white man the shape would be relatively unimportant. Therefore, one aborigine did not go with the tribe on walkabout; one aborigine actually saw the body and the shape of the bloodstain, which he conveyed to Canute.

"I was compelled to employ unorthodox means of finding that particular aborigine. He is called Beeloo, a very old man for whom the walkabout was too much for his strength. Beeloo stayed behind and went a little walkabout alone. Coming to the day Mrs Bell was killed, he knew it was a Thursday, and that every Thursday Mr Wootton went to Loaders Springs. He knew that, save for Linda, Mrs Bell would be alone at the homestead, and he decided to ask her for a plug of tobacco.

"On reaching the homestead by his own devious way, he saw Yorky and Linda out on the lake, and he saw, too, a man riding away on the track taken by Arnold in his truck earlier that day. Unfortunately, distance, plus dust, plus mirage distortion, prevented him from identifying the rider or even the colour of the horse. He looked upon Mrs Bell's body, and then believed that Yorky was involved in the murder, and, finally, he knew where Yorky was heading to gain sanctuary.

"This adventure of Beeloo's was ultimately reported fully to Canute, and still I haven't yet answered the question of why Canute pulled his young men off hunting for Yorky. Yorky isn't a blackfeller, but Yorky was sealed into Canute's tribe and was married to Sarah by aboriginal rites. So Yorky, despite his colour, is one of themselves, and consequently entitled to their loyalty. That loyalty would remain even if Yorky had killed Mrs Bell.

"I was like a man bushed until I tested the prints said to

have been left by Yorky and proved them to be forgeries. By whom? Not by Yorky, but by another who had planned to inculpate Yorky. That man must be he who was seen riding away. He was one of the three stockmen who had ridden from the homestead before Mr Wootton left, or someone from the station to the south of Mount Eden.

"At the time Yorky came back from town, I reasoned that he might know of the northern rivers in flood and yet be unaware of the seriousness of the flooding. I reasoned that the horseman seen by Beeloo would know where Yorky was going, would know about the flood-water sweeping into Lake Eyre, and be well aware of the probability of Yorky and the child being isolated on a sandbank in the centre, and therefore doomed. Lastly, I gambled that if he knew that I was to bring Yorky and Linda back from the lake, he himself would be endangered, and would make a move to stop us, and so disclose himself.

"I made that early broadcast so that that man would know my intention to seek out Yorky. The murderer had built an edifice to safeguard himself, and he knew it would crash to dust once I contacted Yorky.

"What he didn't know is that, had he remained inactive, he might have got away with murder for lack of sufficient evidence to put him into the dock."

CHAPTER 27

A PRESENT FOR CHARLIE

"WOULD YOU care to tell your story, Yorky, or shall I?" Bony asked.

The little man was sitting on the floor, with his back against the house wall, and beside him sat the enormous Sarah. Finding himself the object of general attention,

Yorky swiftly looked down at his legs and was shaking his head when Sarah replied for him.

"You been tellin' stories goodo, Inspector Bonaparte. You tell 'em better'n my ole fren Yorky."

"Very well, Sarah. Yorky says that when Mr Wootton left him that morning at the camp, he started off for the homestead, but that shot of whisky given by the boss made him a little sleepy. So, before reaching the homestead gate, he slept for a period he cannot estimate, in the shade of a tree.

"Still jittery, he staggered on to the homestead, where he remembers seeing a saddled horse tethered to the yard gate, took little notice of it, and proceeded direct to the open door of the kitchen.

"There he heard voices within, voices raised in angry argument. A man was accusing Mrs Bell of encouraging him, and Mrs Bell was loudly denying anything of the kind. Not wishing to intrude or to be discovered listening, Yorky dropped his heavy swag and leaned his Winchester rifle against it, intending to find Linda and talk with her for a little while. He says that when passing the office on the way to the playhouse, he noticed the key in the closed door, and remembered that Mr Wootton sometimes kept a bottle in the office. To use his own words, he was feeling 'bloody terrible'.

"I think that in Yorky's condition I might have succumbed to the same temptation. Anyway, Yorky entered the office and he found a bottle, a full bottle of whisky. He intended to take just one hearty nip and replace the bottle exactly where it was, but the nip was so hearty that the tide ebbed by one-third before he realised that a tiddler's mouthful was actually a whale's.

"He was sitting in the boss's chair, and talking to an imaginary companion, when he heard the shot. At first he thought it was the boss shooting crows. Then he remembered that Mr Wootton had gone to town. He decided he had better leave the office, and found difficulty in recalling

exactly where the bottle had stood before the tide went out.

"Eventually he left the office and carefully closed the door, and I believe him when he says he was partially blinded by the sunlight, and that he didn't see Mrs Bell lying on the ground until about to trip over her body. He heard sounds inside the house, which, I've no doubt, was the transceiver being smashed. Befuddled with whisky, still a little blinded by the sunlight, he says he picked up his rifle and swag, and was intending to clear out, when Harry Lawton appeared and said: 'By crikey, Yorky, what the hell did you shoot her for? You must be crackers.'

"Such was Yorky's mental state that he gazed with terror at the weapon in his hands, then at the body. From the confusion of mind emerged one idea. His rifle was his dearest possession; he had cleaned it the morning before Mr Wootton had stopped at the camp, and now, sniffing at the muzzle, he could register the smell of the expended cartridge.

"He said, dully: 'Yair, I must be.'

"Lawton said: 'You killed her all right. I saw you fire. I rode over from the yard to see Mrs Bell about me lunch I'd forgotten to take out, and I saw you. I don't want to be mixed up with it, Yorky. You better clear out and keep going.'

"Yorky panicked. He filled his gunny-bag with rations and cooked food, and said he'd cross the lake to an island he knew of in the middle. Lawton asked how was he going to stay there without food and water, and Yorky told him there were rabbits, and that he could find water.

"It would appear that Lawton was greatly concerned about Yorky, and Yorky told him there were rations in the hut on the south end of the boundary fence. Lawton assured Yorky that he would replenish the food at the hut, that Yorky wasn't to worry. Just stay out on his island. And he had better take the kid with him.

"Yorky says that he argued against taking Linda, and that he was overruled into doing so. He was tormented still by

the effects of a long carousal, partly revived by a small dose of whisky, and more than revived by too much in too short a time. We can imagine his state if we cannot wholly sympathise with him. Always a quick thinker, Lawton found it easy to think for Yorky, telling him that mates have to stick together, that he would do all he could to put off the trackers and the dirty coppers, and so on. 'Yorky's good friend!'

"Lawton knew what Yorky in his condition did not know, that the floods were about to enter the lake. He foresaw that Yorky on his island would wake one morning to find it surrounded by water, and would be marooned there. And, finally, Linda opened two doors for him.

"Having shot Mrs Bell, he knew he would have to destroy Linda, for although the child had not appeared, he could not risk her seeing him cross to his horse and ride away. The shooting of Mrs Bell had been done in mad lustful anger. It was with cold deliberate purpose that Lawton determined that Yorky take Linda with him, for then she would drown with him.

"All this came out in his confession last night to Constable Pierce. He was a young man who ought never to live in conditions of such isolation—not without a woman. When he was stopped from interfering with the lubras, he stood on the brink of an abyss, when he turned his mind to the only woman at Mount Eden. I have no doubt his claim that she encouraged his advances was due to imagination. All the men absent, he returned to conquer by compulsion, and when Mrs Bell ran from him he thought she was running to Linda. About to rush after her, he found the swag with the rifle leaning against it, snatched up the rifle, pumped a cartridge into the breech and fired. Recognising Yorky's swag, he wiped off his own fingerprints, and put the weapon back where it had been, and before finding Yorky, re-entered the house to smash radio and telephone.

"Now to tidy up the plan which almost evolved itself. Yorky said he would have to get his mud-shoes. Lawton urged him to collar Linda from the playhouse while he

went to Yorky's room for the boards. There was more quick thinking now when confronted by the desperate urge to get Yorky away with Linda. Obtaining the mud-shoes, he met Yorky coming from the playhouse, carrying the child, and he hurried them round the back of the office to avoid the body. And, lastly, not knowing that the boss had seen Yorky, and in order to make sure it would be known Yorky was at the homestead, he obtained a pair of Yorky's old boots and made the prints for Bill Harte and others to see.

"Although Yorky could not remember shooting Mrs Bell, he was bullied into thinking he must have done. Lawton knew that his 'frame' would collapse once I found Linda and Yorky. When he knew I was about to do that, he determined to prevent the four of us ever getting off the mud, and on learning from Yorky that the shortest track from his island came in at the boundary hut, he anticipated we would return that way. He had taken rations and the dolls to that hut for Yorky to collect.

"Now, Charlie, you tell."

Charlie's round face rippled into a wide smile.

"Well, Inspector, you told me to fox Harry Lawton and do nothing only if he started shooting somebody. After you went out on the mud I was watching Harry, when Meena jawed me about making her some mud-shoes for her to go after you. That Meena! Time I done them shoes for her, Harry and the rest have cleared out, and I asked the boss where Harry went. The boss said to Yorky's old fence hut down south.

"All the spare horses are gone, too, so I had to walkabout down there, and it's sundown when I came to the camp, and Harry's cookin' a feed for himself. Doin' what you said, just fox him, I has to do a perish that night, and next day late, when Harry mooches over to the lake sand dunes, I gets me chance at tucker in the hut.

"In the afternoon I seen Harry mucking about with case-boards, and I knows what he's up to. But he don't do nothing that night, and the next morning he's gone. I track him

to the lake and see where he's taken to the dingo pad, but I can't see him 'cos the sun's in me eyes."

Charlie burst into prolonged chuckling.

"There's me sitting like a crow on a windmill, and there's Harry out there with a rifle what I haven't got. I can't fox him on the mud, so I goes to the hut to get a feed and a drink. After that, I lie on the dunes waiting for Harry to come back, but he don't, and next day I decides I'd better get back to the homestead and tell the boss all about it, even if I been told not to tell anyone anything about Harry.

"I'm on me way along the beach when I hears shooting out on the lake. So I rushed back. Then I sees Harry well out. The sun's my way, and I can see he's coming to the shore, and fast. He's still got his rifle, so I burrows up and watches him. Then I see the Inspector comin' after him, a long way back. Harry gets to land, whips off his shoes and runs for the sandhills. There's a shot and Harry gets it in his leg. He gets to cover and starts shooting, so I has to creep up behind him, and at the same time tell the Inspector it's me what's doin' the stalkin'."

Once again Charlie broke into chuckling laughter.

"I got him okee all right. Right on the bonk."

. . . . .

When the Mount Eden party left town for the Mission, Constable Pierce went with them. The Mission wore its Sunday atmosphere, for it was after four o'clock, and none of the children were in evidence. The doors of the little church were wide, and at the main entrance waited the Missioner to greet the visitors.

Between him and Bony with Wootton and Pierce was a short conference, then the Missioner entered the church, and Arnold said to Charlie:

"Come on, you. You're for it."

Charlie, who was wearing a white cotton shirt and flannel trousers, might have been going to the guillotine, and after he left there appeared the Missioner's wife, who brought a

colourful garland of flowers which she placed around Meena's neck. Wearing a white silk dress, patterned with red roses, nylon stockings and white shoes, all of which Mr Wootton had that day bought for her, Meena recoiled with startled eyes on receiving this token of distinction.

"What's it all mean?" she asked Bony, who had slipped her arm through his own. "You're married already. You told me."

"By right, Meena, Yorky should be doing this," he said, and Constable Pierce laughed and nudged Yorky. "But as you are my woman, I have the honour of giving you away at your wedding. Everything has been arranged. Mr Wootton is going to build you a cottage at Mount Eden, so that you may keep an eye on him and Linda."

Linda, wearing her favourite pink dress, smiled shyly at her pretty Meena.

The church was filled by the Mission children. Charlie and his best man were waiting, and the Missioner's wife was playing the organ. With Meena on his right arm, and Linda's hand in his left, Bony walked the one and only aisle.

Charlie was stunned; Bony presented him with the golden ring, which he was still admiring when Linda reminded him to put it on Meena's finger.

In the vestry Charlie and his bride signed the register, then Meena turned about to the smiling Bony, her eyes twin black opals, and flung her arms about his neck, kissed him hard, and more than once. The astonishment of the onlookers turned to merriment when Charlie laughed so heartily that he had to regain control to shout:

"That Meena."